CAPRI II

JAHQUEL J.

Copyright © 2024

Published by Jahquel J.
www.Jahquel.com
ALL RIGHTS RESERVED

Any unauthorized reprint or use of the material is prohibited. No part of this book may be reproduced or transmitted in any form or by any means, electronic, or mechanical, including photocopying, recording, or by any information storage without express permission by the publisher. This is an original work of fiction.

Names, characters, places, and incidents are either products of the author's imagination or are used fictitiously and any resemblance to actual persons, living or dead is entirely coincidental.

Contains explicit languages and adult themes.
suitable for ages 16+

Jahquel J's Catalog ✦

Jahquel J. - Author

Brookwood Series
Interconnected Standalone Series
- From Come Over To Come Home
- He's My Next Mistake
- From Replied To Wifey
- Welcome To Brookwood

Lennox Hills Series
Interconnected Standalone Series
- I'm Fine...Thanks
- Yeah... Thanks
- Never Better... Thanks

Mathers Family
- Confessions Of A Hustla's Housekeeper 1-4
- Confessions Of A Hustla's Daughter 1-2 ✱

Davis Family
- Staten Island Love Letter 1-5
- Staten Island Love Affair 1-4✱
- A Brownsville, Harlem & Staten Island Holiday Affair ✱

Vanducci-Cromwell Family
- A Staten Island Love Story 1-3

Harlem King Saga
- In Love With The King Of Harlem 1-5
- In Love With An East Coast Maniac 1-3 ✱
- Rose In Harlem: Harlem King's Princess ✱

BAE Series
- BAE: Before Anyone Else 1-3
- He's Still BAE 1-3✱
- BAE: Holiday ✱

Homies, Lovers & Friends
- Homies, Lovers & Friends 1-5
- Homies, Lovers & Wives ✱

Series:
- Crack Money With Cocaine Dreams 1-2
- Never Wanted To Be Wifey 1-2
- To All The Thugs I Loved That Didn't Love Me Back 1-4
- All The Dope Boys Gon Feel Her 1-2
- Good Girls Love Hustlas 1-3
- I Got Nothing But Love For My Hitta 1-2
- She Ain't Never Met A N*gga Like Me 1-3
- Married To A Brownsville Bully 1-3
- Thugs Need Love 1-3
- What A Wicked Way To Treat The Woman You Love 1-2
- Finessing The Plug 1-2

Standalones:
- My Lover, My Dopeboy
- I Can't Be The One You Love
- I'm Riding With You Forever
- Forever, I'm Ready
- Emotionless
- Blaquehatten
- Ho, Ho, Housewife
- When Can I See You Again?
- What You Know About Love?
- Hearts Won't Break
- Pretty Little Fears
- Save Myself
- Two Occasions
- I Didn't Mean To Fall In Love

✱ Spinoff

www.Jahquel.com | hello@Jahquel.com | @Jahquel_

SYNOPSIS:

My family is being tested. My brother's freedom is in jeopardy, and in my hands. How could I be so happy in my life and scared at the same time. No matter what, I know what needs to be done, and that's to protect my brothers. The one person I never thought I would see was standing a foot away from me. When Tasha was sent out my life, I never thought I would see her again. I never got to handle her the way that I always wanted to, but now it was time to make sure this bitch joined her son – in the dirt. On my unborn child, I was going to make sure that the family came out on top. Emotions are high, things could go very different for us.
However, nobody wins when the family feuds.
Niggas came at my fiancé; they came for mine and now they had to answer to me. Chrome Vipers had been on a war path since Tookie been locked up. Looking to anyone to be their leader until Tookie returned home. Funny shit – Tookie was gonna return home to bodies. You don't try and touch Mrs. Inferno and think I'm not airing shit out behind her.
Game over.

Nothing is ever what it seems. Our family is being tested in the worse way possible. Bonds are broken, while new ones are formed. Mistakes will be made, hearts will be broken, but at the end of the day, we're family and we ride for each other.

I'm about to step into a new role, shedding the Delgato name for the last time, and stepping into my new role as Capri Delgato, the wife of Quameer Inferno, the sister-in-law of Quasim Inferno, head of Inferno Gods, and the daughter-in-law of Mina and Papa Inferno.

When it's all said and done, I will make sure the Delgatos and Inferno always end up on top.

TRANSLATIONS:

Translations:
Wherever the fire is, is my territory - onde quer que esteja o fogo, meu território
Rest in shit, my love - descanse na merda meu amor
Anjo – angel
Mama – mamãe
My nasty girl… take your dick - minha garota desagradável...pegue seu pau

Senti falta de ver aquele sorriso. – I missed seeing that smile.

Mal posso esperar para sentir Big Pa esta noite. - I can't wait to feel Big Pa tonight.

Você é meu coração. Minha vida. Eu vou te amar até meu último suspiro. – You are my heart. My life. I will love you until my last breath.

Big Pa vai usar essa merda. – Big Pa gonna wear that shit out.

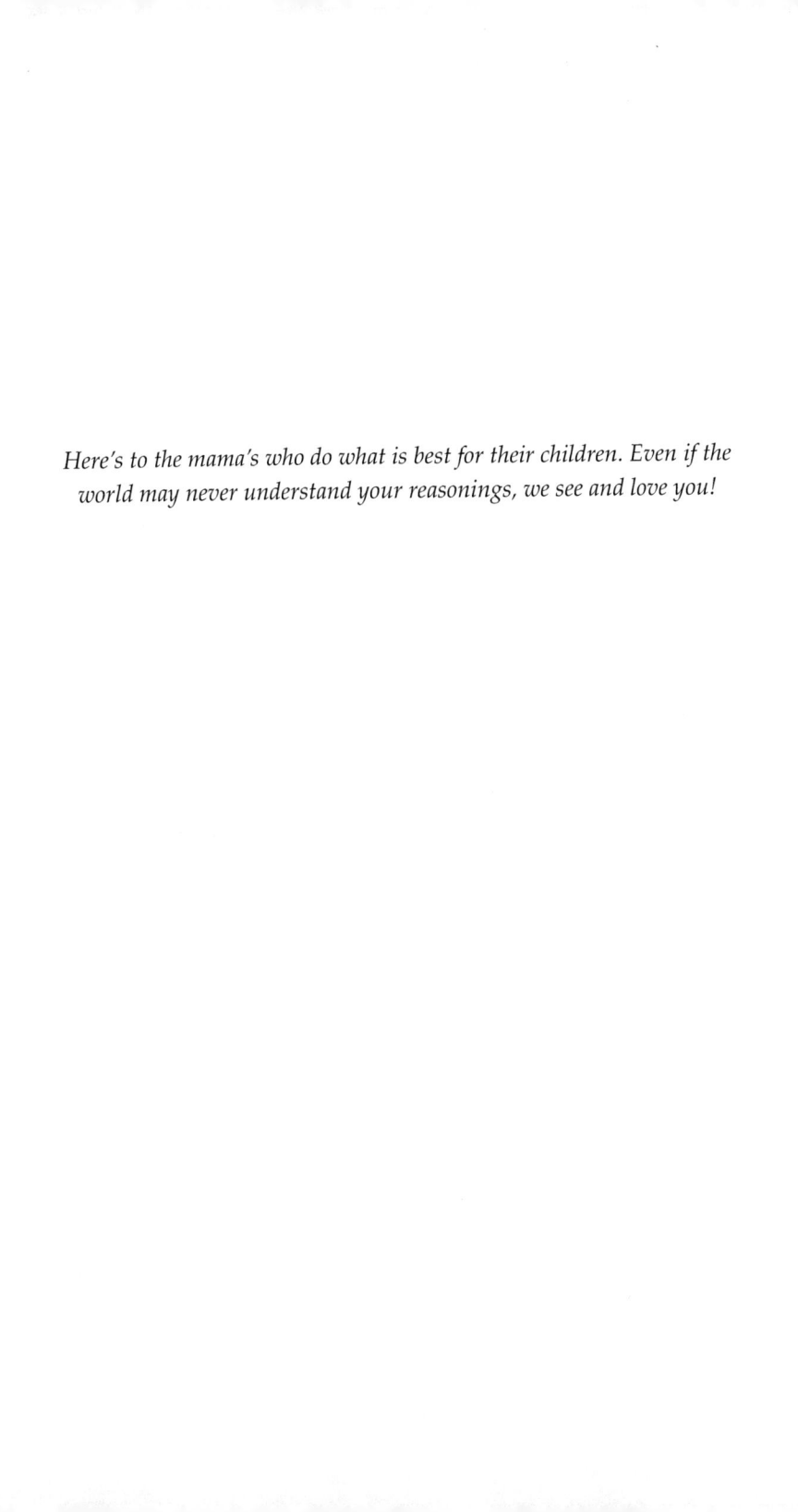

Here's to the mama's who do what is best for their children. Even if the world may never understand your reasonings, we see and love you!

PROLOGUE

TASHA JACKSON

"Jackson, go on through there," the correction officer, who couldn't stand me, ordered.

One minute I was in my cell relaxing after finishing my GED class, and then the next they were telling me that I had a visit. I never got visits, not even from my own family. Once they shipped me away, my mother wrote me off, and my daughter, now a bit older, acted like she didn't know me whenever I tried to call her.

My mother was now her new mother.

Fuck 'em both.

I did what I had to do for our family, making sure my mama's bills were always paid. This was how she decided to repay me. The only reason her ass didn't have to punch a clock after leaving the streets alone was because of me, and now she blamed me for the death of my own son. Timmy was hardheaded and followed behind Trilla thinking he could lead him. I told his ass to stick with the Delgatos, and he decided to go against them which turned our entire life upside down.

I walked into the room and saw two white men in suits sitting at the metal table. One heavy set, and the other of medium build. Part of me was expecting to see them behind the glass while holding a phone in their hands. Pausing, I took both of them in and knew something was different.

What was different?

I had no clue.

All I knew is that something seemed different with these two than the others that have come to visit me in the past. "Sit yo ass down, Jackson," the correction officer continued to bark orders at me, and I sighed.

Once upon a time ago, I would have slapped the shit out of a bitch for coming out their neck sideways. Now, all I could do is sigh and do as I was told. I slid onto the metal stool attached to the table and stared blankly at the men.

"Hey hey, you can relax a bit when it comes to talking to her that way," the tanner of the two said to the correction officer. "Do I need to talk to your superior about this?"

"No, sir... my apologies," the husky voice she used with all of us inmates dropped, and she was a little proper princess now.

"They are inmates, humans. Treat them with respect," he continued, as he cut his eyes at her and then turned into my direction. "Hi, Ms. Jackson."

"Um, hi." I was confused on why this man was being so nice to me. The lawyer that I did have that was working on my appeal acted like it was a headache to show me some kind of kindness. His responses were always short, and he barely had time to explain even the simple shit to me. Possibly because it was a pro bono case, and he wasn't getting paid to be nice and warm like he was with his other clients.

"I know you have a lot of questions on why we're both here," he looked toward the other man beside him. Cow licks, crow feet around his eyes, and permanently stained brown teeth from over consumption of coffee. He seemed stressed.

"Is this about my appeal?" I grew hopeful, praying that it was granted, and I would get out of here.

I sat in my cell day in and day out thinking about what I would do if my appeal was approved. How I wanted to just escape and live my life. I wanted to feel the sand between my toes, a warm bath, and good food. It was the simple things that I never cared about when I was out.

"Yes and no. Your appeal was denied; however, I have friends that have found a way around that." He smiled; his ice blue eyes pierced into my soul as he looked at me.

His gleaming blue eyes, structured square jawline unclenched as he smiled at me. You never realized how much a smile meant when you were constantly giving the stink eye while in prison. His short brown hair was brushed neatly, with a deep part on the side.

From where I sat, he looked pretty in shape, unlike fatso sitting beside him. The crazy thing was that the man beside him seemed to be a bit younger than him. "If it was denied, how did you find a way around it?"

He fixed his suit jacket as he looked at me. "Ms. Jackson, when you have friends like me, you can always work your way around anything."

"Why would you do that for me? I don't even know you."

He did a deep chuckle. One of those rich men chuckles, and from the watch on his wrist, I could tell he had some money. The man smelled rich, and it was a welcomed smell from the usual nasty shit I smelled from these bitches.

"My apologies. I'm Vincent Morgan... your future mayor."

I didn't keep up with anything outside of these walls. What was the use of doing that? I had one kid in the grave, and then two kids that didn't know me. Naheim made sure he kept his word and didn't send me anything about my son. I could walk right by him on the street and wouldn't know it was my own son.

"Nice to meet you.... I've been alive long enough to know that nobody wants anything for free... can we stop beating around the bush with the nice act and tell me why you are really here."

"Cappadonna and Capone Delgato... names ring a bell?"

"Nope." The reason I was in here was because of Capone Delgato.

I would never forget the look that man gave me when I was in the back of that cop car. It still sent shivers down my back when I thought about it.

"Tasha, we know that you were connected with Capone Delgato for some time."

"Now how would I be connected to a man that I never met." As much as I could have snitched on Capone, I wasn't stupid.

This man set me up so bad that I was serving a life sentence. I guess I feared death more than my loss of freedom. Capone had set his entire family up to be unstoppable. It wasn't a coincidence that Capri had been put through law school. Last I heard Cappadonna was home, and that was a different demon that people didn't want to touch.

"Listen, bi... Ms. Jackson," he cleared his throat. "You know the Delgato twins, and if you know what's good for you, you will cooperate as an informant, for your freedom. We know you didn't kill those men... why are you protecting them?"

It was less about protecting them and more about protecting me. "Not protecting them."

He leaned back a bit and smiled at me. "I have pulled some tight strings to get you out of this dump hole... you will come through and make all of this worth it, as my fiancée."

"Huh?"

"I need a woman on my arm, someone to make my image look good and being that I need your people to vote for me and to keep an eye on you, this is how I will do both."

"Out of all the women, you want me to be your fake fiancée. A felon."

He dusted imaginary dust off his suit jacket and gave me the creepiest smirk. "I promised some very important people that I would keep a tight leash on you... you'll be processed out; however, it will still remain that you are in custody... this is where you say thank you."

I was so caught off guard that I didn't know what to say. I've dreamt of the day that I would get out of prison and now it was finally here. Now that the time was here, I didn't know what to say or do. The feeling of regret consumed me because I knew the way I was getting out would end with me in the dirt.

I was tired of running, tired of doing what was best for everyone else. Playing one side for the other. It was time for me to play the game for me. Make sure that I came out on top this time.

Fuck these men.

CHAPTER 1
CAPRI

WITH HOW QUICK I ducked behind Corleon, he was confused, and quickly turned around and ushered me back toward the bathrooms.

Besides looks, that was one of the main things that he and the twins had in common – their height.

Both Capone, Cappadonna, and Daddy towered over me and Mommy with their tall statures. However, Capone and Cappadonna both outgrew Daddy, and it was a running joke when we were younger.

"Yo, you pregnant with my niece or nephew... don't be tossing yourself down like that." He held my shoulder as I tried to steady my breathing.

Corleon looked down at his phone that was pinging like crazy. "She...she's supposed to be serving her life away in prison... how... why... fuck," was all I could make out.

"I can see you uncomfortable as fuck," he paused and looked around. "We out through the back... Aimee, you got that phone?"

Aimee smirked while holding up the iPhone in her hand. "Piece of cake."

Corleon looked at her and paused. "Don't fucking be pick

pocketing me... I know what you do because I do what you do... I'm watching you."

She shrugged as we exited near the bathroom. Corleon called Menace and told him he was leaving early, as we walked back around to the front. Aimee took an Uber from the hotel, while I came with Core. While we waited for valet to bring his car around, I looked around while trying to process everything in my head.

How the fuck did Tasha get out, and why didn't Forty tell us this? He prepared us for everything and didn't tell us about the possibility of Tasha getting out. I knew she had an open appeal, however, I never expected that it would have been approved. The evidence surrounding her case was astronomical. I even went to look through files to see for myself and nobody beat a case like that one unless you had a damn shark for a lawyer.

Last, I remember, she didn't have a shark for a lawyer. Tasha was broke as hell, and didn't have a pot to piss in or a window to throw it out of. The valet whipped around Core's Maserati, and he held the doors open for both me and Aimee before he swaggered around the front of the car.

"How is it possible that he has the walk, Pri?" Aimee whispered just as he got into the car, and then quickly sped away from the venue.

It was crazy how I just found out that this man was my brother, and I felt so comfortable with him. As if he was Capone or Cappadonna. He whipped through the streets of DC while I remained quiet.

"Clue me in, baby sis'... who is shorty and why did you get all tongue tied and dive damn near at my feet when seeing her?"

I took a deep breath as I checked my phone. "She's my ex-best friend and has a baby with my ex-husband."

"A lot of ex shit going on."

At first, I didn't know the logistics on how Tasha had gotten caught up because Capone never clued me in on it. At the time, he was still living in denial about me stepping into he and Capp's world. Now that I was full invested, and had done the research on my own, I needed his ass to give me all the details that they may have been missing. I looked over at Core and explained everything that I had found out from her case files, which were public record.

He cooly nodded his head as he took in everything that I was saying to him. I watched as he switched between lanes, and then made an opposite turn. "Um... this phone is pinging." Aimee held the phone up.

"You tried to disable it?"

She quickly tapped into her mode and did a few things on the screen, and then looked up. "Not working... sounds like it's getting louder."

Core looked in his rearview mirror. "Makes sense why that blacked out navigator has been tailing us since we pulled out from the valet."

I quickly turned and sure enough the black truck was driving slowly. "We cannot do this right now."

"Chill..." Core calmly replied.

"Aim, you—"

"I'm strapped," she replied before I could finish my question.

Core looked in the rearview mirror, biting down on his lip as he hit a sharp left turn onto sixth street. He had done it so fast that the truck had no choice but to continue going straight because they couldn't make the turn in time.

Never letting up, he hit another sharp right onto H street and then gunned it down the street. It was late so traffic was minimal. I watched as he swerved in and out of the cars that were there until we turned down a few more streets.

"You alright?" Core looked over at me, as if I hadn't been in my fair share of shootouts. I loved the fact that he was concerned or cared.

"I'm alright. You think they know it was us who took it? They were following behind us, so they saw who we were."

"They following the phone. My plates are digital and switch every few minutes, so for all they know, I'm one of the pricks from the ball."

He slowed down and dipped down another block and reached his hand to the back. Aimee handed him the phone and he looked through it while slowly cruising. "Shit is useless."

"What you mean?"

"Wrong phone." With a few taps on the screen and within an app, the sound that was coming from the phone stopped. "This is the phone he uses for CH... shit doesn't have anything on it that is useful to you."

"Let me be the judge of that." I snatched the phone, briefly eyeing my brother before going through the phone.

It was a bunch of dates, encrypted messages and money transfers. No small amounts either but sums that were people's salaries for the year. One of the transactions was dated for today. It didn't tell much, and there wasn't shit that I could do with this. It didn't mean it was useless either.

"Would using this fall back on the Caselli's?"

Core stroked his beard, then looked over at me. "Nah. I've built a system to make sure nothing could ever fall back on them. Even if it did, I would make sure nothing ever fell back on them."

"Makes sense."

"They're family, Capri." He made sure I knew how important the Caselli family was to him, and all I could do was respect it.

As much as it stung to hear him refer to another family as his, I couldn't fault him. My family wasn't his family – yet. There was trust and understanding that needed to be established from every part.

"I can respect that. I don't think this would give us anything we would need anyway. What are the transactions for?"

"Pussy," he bluntly stated as he pulled off the block and drove back to the hotel, we were staying in.

Aimee snickered. "Kind of gathered that from all those beautiful women with those dusty old men."

I sat back and tried to process everything that I found out so far. "If you need the phone... keep it. I'm gonna make sure everybody is protected if you want to use that. However, there are other ways to get what you need from him."

"How is that?"

"Your best friend is his daughter... direct access right there. Hell, you can get closer to him than anyone of us."

"Tasha is the only problem," Aimee replied from the back.

Core snapped his fingers. "You right, Grasshopper... you right." Before he could turn onto the next block, he turned and faced Aimee. "She doesn't know you... does she?"

Aimee smirked. "She doesn't."

"Let's wait to talk to Forty before we put anything into play. I need to know what he knows before we do anything." I put a pin in Aimee and Core's little plan they were conjuring up.

When we pulled up in front of the hotel, Meer was sitting next to one of the pillars while smoking a spliff. I could tell from the doorman and valet's face that they were pissed that he was even out here smoking.

From the look on my man's face, he was giving them that *I dare you* face, so they knew not to come crazy at him. Meer had been on edge ever since my birthday party and refused for me to go anywhere without him. He didn't like how they came at me, and he was determined to handle business when it came to me.

He noticed Core's car and trashed his spliff before coming over toward the car. Core opened the door for me and Aimee. "That ball shit over already?"

Meer peered down into my face, and I could see it register in his eyes that I wasn't alright. "Some shit went down," Core explained.

He kissed me on the lips a few times. "You alright, Suga?"

"I'm alright... just confused. We do need to talk."

Meer nodded toward Core. "Good looking on protecting her."

"Already know." He nodded back. "Let me in on what the plan is... I got you. I'm sure Menace would want in, too."

"I'll call you later this week so we can discuss everything

with Capone and Cappadonna," I replied, as Meer held my hand and pulled me toward the entrance of the hotel.

Aimee had gone to her room, and we went to ours. I needed to talk to Meer about everything. He knew about me becoming the ADA, because we had a conversation about it. However, he had no clue that I would be going in under Naheim's last name. Not to mention he needed to know about Tasha being out of prison.

This weekend was the Father's Day brunch at my parent's lake house, and as much as I hated to bring this up then, my brothers needed to know what was going on when it came to Tasha. Soon as I opened the door to our room, I paused and smiled at the rose petals that were tossed on the floor, making a trail further into the room.

"Baby, what is this?" I turned and looked up at him.

He kissed my lips. "I know you have a big part to play in all of this, however, I also know that I need to do my part to make sure you're not stressed."

"Cause I'm stressing your baby out," I laughed.

He held my chin and kissed my lips. "No, because I don't want you stressed out. I would have done this even if you weren't carrying my child. My job as your fiancé and then husband is to protect you and that doesn't just mean in the streets."

I reached up and kissed him on his cheek and he wrapped his arms around me. "Are we really going to get married?"

Every time I looked down at my ring, I couldn't believe that I was going to get married again. I swore after my divorce that I would never get married again, and here I was actually excited about marrying Quameer Inferno.

I never thought our paths would cross again in the way that they had. It was so crazy how God gave us what we needed but made us practice patience. I wanted everything that I was currently experiencing with Meer, however, he had me wait before I was able to have those things. I thanked him for making me practice patience, because Capri a year ago would have fumbled this good man.

"I wanna give you the wedding of your dreams, Sug. I wanna see you walk to me in a dress, share our vows in front of our families... I want all of that shit."

Kissing his neck, I pulled away and looked him in the eyes. "I want those things too. It would mean a lot to me to do it in Barbados. My brothers each got married there and look at their marriages... I just feel like there's a good energy there."

He kissed my teeth mid conversation, and I cut my eyes at him. I don't care how many times he has done it, it was something that I wouldn't get used to because it was weird as hell, like my baby.

"Then you know what needs to happen."

"Telling my family."

He took my hand and led me into the bathroom. "Sug, what you really worried about? You a grown ass woman."

"My mother, Meer. You know how she is, and she's going to judge the hell out of me... she's still on the Naheim train and I'm tired of all our conversations always being brought back to him."

Meer held my chin and looked into my eyes. "Fuck her opinion. I have respect for your moms, but I don't respect how she's pushing a nigga that fucked you over onto you."

"We both fucked each other over."

His jaw flinched as he continued to look me in the eyes. "You told me that the nigga was fucking around on you soon as he was home... you forgot about the condoms in the laundry, Sug? Stop letting her make you feel guilty for fucking with Kincaid. If she wanna guilt you, then she needs to guilt herself too cause where was she when you were spiraling out of control? You forgot the reason we stopped getting drunk on facetime together?"

"Yes."

Meer said he noticed a pattern with me, even over facetime. He said the moment I got in my feelings about something then I would start drinking and want to get drunk. Our weekend happy hours over facetime had stopped the moment he noticed, and I thanked him for that.

I wasn't an alcoholic; however, it was heading there if I didn't stop using alcohol to numb my emotions, and really deal with real problems that I had going on.

"Things have always been so complicated with me and my mother."

He kissed my lips and pulled me behind him into the bathroom, where he had run a bath with bubbles and candles. "I'm all for you fixing things with your mother because everybody needs their mom. You also need to put her in her place when it comes to your life. She don't ever give your brothers any shit about their love lives."

He was right.

My mother worshipped the ground that Alaia and Erin walked on, and I loved that for them. All I wanted was the same kind of treatment when it came to me. I didn't want to feel like I always had to defend myself or my life choices whenever I came around my mother.

"Thank you for this, Meer."

He unzipped my dress and helped me climb into the tub before sitting on the edge while looking at me. Whenever Meer's eyes locked on me, I never had to question how he felt about me, or if his feelings were true. His eyes showed me just how much he cared about me, and how much my heart was safe in his hands. When he spoke, his words weren't just words to me. He meant every word that he said, and his actions had proven it more times than a few.

I've always wanted a man that didn't play about me, and often wondered what it felt like. I knew exactly what it felt like because Quameer had shown me, and he would continue to show me even when he became my husband.

"Tasha is out of prison," I blurted.

My chest continued to hurt knowing that I saw Tasha Jackson tonight. Free and out in the world when she should have been in prison serving life.

Meer started to dissociate, and I snapped my fingers in his face. "Baby, what the fuck?"

"You were drinking while pregnant with my baby, Sug?"

"Quameer, she really is out and free. Aimee and Core were both there when I saw her."

He continued to stare at me like he didn't know if he should believe me or not. "Aimee don't even know her ass. I don't know what your techy ass brother knows, but I know Aimee don't know her."

"She and Core witnessed what I did. Jesse's father is also Morgan." I continued to lay everything out on the table.

He jumped from the edge of the tub and paced the bathroom. "Sug, you sure you weren't drinking tonight?"

"Meer, I'm being fucking serious. Jesse was there with her father, and his fiancée who happens to be Tasha. Core escorted me over there and that's when Aimee bumped right into Tasha. She's not in prison anymore."

"Forty didn't think this was important information to know?"

"I don't think he even knows. He would have told us if he had known... this shit is deeper than we thought."

"Fuck," he muttered as he continued to pace the floor, then stopped to look at me. "That bitch pussy so loose she slipped through the fucking prison bars?"

Leave it to Meer to make me laugh when I was in the middle of panicking. "We need to talk to my brothers and Forty. Baby?"

"Hmm."

"I kind of left this out... I'm going in under ADA Browne."

I expected him to freak out and continue pacing faster. He leaned on the sink and then looked over at me. "I don't like that shit... you're a fucking Inferno, Suga."

"Meer, I know that. It means nothing to me to go under Browne... I'm just doing what needs to be done."

He bit down on his bottom lip. "Just means that name needs to be switched sooner. You're my wife, Sug... I don't like that nigga's name being attached to you, but I know you gotta handle business."

Meer came over and shoved his entire tongue down my throat, slipping into the tub fully clothed. "Meer, what the hell?"

"Sug, I know you have this little soft spot for that nigga but let him pretend that name being attached to you is more, and I can promise his son gonna end up in foster care."

I gulped because the look on his face told me that he meant everything that he was saying. "I hear you."

He looked at me. "Shit is going to get real, Capri... we all are gonna be tested like nothing before. We need to make sure this between us is solid. Nothing or no one could come between us. Don't let nobody trick you out your boots, Sug."

I nodded my head. "I know."

"Love you, Mrs. Inferno."

I kissed his lips as he got comfortable in this tub like his ass wasn't fully clothed. "Love you, Meer."

It was Father's Day weekend, and we were all having brunch at my parents' lake house. I was excited to celebrate all the men in my family. One thing about those Delgato men, they were good fathers and providers.

Instead of just my family, I invited my in-laws to come and stay with me at the lake house. They were my family, too, and I enjoyed being around them. Quinton had brought Gam and Mina, Meer's mother, to the lake house.

I made sure that I set the guest rooms up for them to be comfortable. In the formal living room, I had a huge rocking chair delivered so she could look right out the huge bay window that was in there. Quameer was nervous to bring her up to the lake house, and I wanted him to feel more comfortable with it.

This was going to be my mother-in-law, and I wanted her to become familiar with me. She also deserved to be with the family too. Since it was too much to bring her over to my parent's house, I had a chef prepare dinner over at my house so we could have an Inferno Father's Day dinner.

Brandi had insisted on driving Ryder to the lake house since Father's Day fell on her days. It pissed Meer off because he was prepared to drive and pick her up. I had to remind him that he needed to stop being so bothered by her antics and appreciate that Ryder was going to be spending Father's Day with him.

"Good morning," I greeted Quasim as he sat at the kitchen counter with his coffee.

My nose was super sensitive with this pregnancy, so I smelled the coffee the minute I opened my eyes. He was staring out the window at the lake and nodded as he finished off the rest of his coffee.

"Morning, Pri... this coffee good shit."

"Right? It's from this café near the apartment in Singapore. When the owner found out that I was leaving, he gave me a bunch of bags to bring back with me."

Coffee was the way to my heart. Every morning, I sat and had a cup of coffee. It didn't matter if it was iced or hot, I could always be found with a cup of coffee in the morning. Whenever I ran out of this coffee, I knew I would get on a flight to go get more bags because it was that good.

"You serious about your coffee, huh?"

I noticed he was sitting at the counter with his Bible, and a notebook sitting on top of it. "Very. I'm glad that you're awake... I wanted to give you something while it's just the both of us."

He raised that infamous eyebrow, confused. "Oh yeah, what's that?"

I held my finger up and ran into the office at the front, pulling the top drawer out and grabbing the small box. When I returned into the kitchen, Quasim was at the sink rinsing out his coffee cup.

"Happy Father's Day, Sim." I handed him the box.

He slowly took the box while staring down at me, and then opened the velvet box. When his eyes landed on the gold dog tag necklace with Harley's picture lasered on it, he looked away and then at me. I could see the emotion fill in his emotionless eyes.

I hated to say his eyes were always dead, however, they were. There was never any life in them whenever you looked at him. I guess that was why it was so easy for him to be on go whenever his brother or mine needed him.

"Pri," his voice cracked.

I looked up at him. "Can I hug you, Sim?"

Sim was so guarded and to himself, so I wanted to ask before assuming he wanted to be touched. He held his arms open, and I fell into a hug with him, and he squeezed me tightly. "How did you get this picture of her?"

He still hugged me, as if he didn't want to let go, and he didn't have to until he was ready. "Don't call me weird. When I was at Gam's house, I snapped a picture of her picture in the foyer. I knew Father's Day was coming and I wanted to get you something along with your brother and father, because Sim, you are still a father. It doesn't matter that your baby is in Heaven, you are still her father."

"Damn, Capri," he gently removed himself from me and leaned on the counter, hanging his head. "Wasn't expecting this."

"We're gonna be family, Quasim. I care about you like I care about my own brothers. Harley is a part of you, so she's a part of me just like Peach is. I wanted to give it to you privately because I know how private you are."

I expected him to burst into tears because Capone and Cappadonna probably would have. Instead, he kept that stone facade up, which was fine with me. In time he would feel comfortable enough to let it down.

He abandoned the counter and hugged me once more, kissing the top of my head. "I appreciate you, Pri. This means a lot to me… for real. I need some air though."

"Fair."

He took the jewelry box with him and went out the backdoor to the backyard. I put on a fresh pot of coffee while straightening up the kitchen. The chef would be coming over while we were over a brunch at my parents' house.

I was so damn nervous to tell my family that me and Meer were engaged. Then to add onto that, I was pregnant too. For so long everyone always had an opinion on how I lived my life, and I allowed them to have that opinion. I was now in this space with my life that I wasn't asking how they felt about my life. I didn't care, and I was moving however I wanted and what felt right to me.

Quameer felt right to me.

Peach felt right to me.

I felt a pair of hands wrap around my waist as I watched Sim sitting out by the lake. He was sitting on the dock and all I could see was his back. The soft kisses on my neck made me feel all warm on the inside.

"Good morning, Meer. Did you wake up with a better attitude?"

He softly bit my neck. "Nah. It's still fuck Brandi, and I'm gonna make sure she knows that shit when she comes. Why the fuck would she want to drive her instead of letting me pick her up. Then she claim she need to talk to me."

"About what?" I turned in his arms and looked at him, while he was staring out the window at his brother.

"Shit tough for him today." He ignored my question while looking out at his brother. I could only imagine how hard it was to celebrate Father's Day every year without your child.

Especially seeing your younger brother have that with his own daughter. I could see how it would fuck with you, and keep you secluded like Quasim was.

"Yeah."

Gams shuffled into the kitchen, and I smiled. I loved being around Gams and was so happy that she was here. "First time in a long time that your parents shared the same bed."

"How did she do last night?" I wondered.

Meer's parents didn't live under the same roof, so I worried about them sharing a room. "She did good... he said she woke up during the night, but she was cool."

"Better question is how was he?" Meer kissed me on the cheek as he went to pour coffee into my favorite mug.

Gams heaved a sigh as tears slid down her face. I walked around the counter and hugged her. "I wish things weren't this way for them."

"I wish the same, Gam." Meer slid the coffee cup onto the counter and looked at me and his Gam hugging. "I wish he took more time for him... maybe start dating or something. He's always alone in that house."

"Where do you think your brother gets it from. Quinton would never move on from your mother. She's the love of his life... I know sharing a bed with her has done something to his soul. Having her near him must have felt nice."

"I think it would be nice for you guys to stay up here for the summer too. She loves that front window, and she even came in the kitchen yesterday."

Gams looked up at me and smiled. "She did... didn't she?"

Yesterday while Gams was baking cookies for the brunch, Mina had made her way into the kitchen. She didn't say anything, however, she sat in the kitchen with her hands crossed like they usually were.

Gams kissed her on the head and continued to make cookies. My lake house had been the only house not filled with love, and it felt nice having love inside of my home. I spent so much time here alone that I enjoyed having the company.

I knew Quasim and Quinton wouldn't stay for the summer, but that didn't mean that Gams and Mina couldn't stay. Quameer was back and forth between his house and here, so the nights he didn't come here, it would be nice having company.

"Good morning," Quinton's voice caused us to turn, and he was coming into the kitchen holding Mina's hand.

"Morning... want some coffee?"

Gams went right to her daughter, and kissed her, while

moving her curly hair from her face. "I'll get her ready for the day."

"You sure?" Quinton was hesitant.

"Yes. Sit down and enjoy some coffee. You handled her all night; I can get her ready for the day."

Quinton went to make himself coffee and stopped to look at Quasim who was still sitting by the lake. I sat at the counter and enjoyed my coffee while enjoying the comfortable silence we all fell into.

"Capri is pregnant," Meer announced, ending that comfortable silence that we had all fell into.

Quinton didn't react right away, something I noticed that Quasim did too. His reactions were always delayed. I assumed it was because they were digesting whatever had been told to them. Meer on the other hand showed his reactions right away.

"I'm gonna be a grandfather again... congratulations to us... we're growing. Something I have always prayed for." He came around the counter and hugged me, kissing my forehead.

"Thank you." I smiled.

"Your parents don't know... I would have heard from Des if he knew his baby girl was having a baby."

"I plan on telling them today... wish us luck?"

Quinton chuckled. "Your mama gonna blow her shit. Check it though... this is you and Blaze's life... you don't gotta answer to anybody. When me and Mina was living our lives, we did what we wanted and never gave a fuck what anyone thought."

"Yeah?"

He pinched my cheek. "Yeah. My boys are gonna live their lives for them, and all I ask is for them to include me and they mama in it... I'm not here to control their lives, just enjoy it with them. I've done my job."

"Thanks, Quinton."

"Papa," he hugged me once more, and then went to hug Meer, who was stiff at first and then softened in his father's embrace. "This is what you wanted... becoming a husband and a father again. I don't have to tell you not to fuck it up because you'd end yourself before you ever let her and your little family down."

"Shit makes me feel guilty." He looked out at his brother.

Papa paused and looked at his other son. It was a tough situation to be in while one son was mourning the loss of his little family, the other was building his. No matter how tough the situation was, Papa handled it with grace and understanding.

"Your brother, no matter the pain he's in, is always going to be happy for you. I can promise something good is coming for your brother, he just needs to be open for it. He's not ready right now, but when he is... that shit is gonna be beautiful."

He kissed his son on the side of his head and then went out the back to be with the other one. I abandoned the stool and wrapped my arms around Meer. "Baby, you know I love you."

"Love you, too, Sug," he replied, never taking his eyes off his brother in the back. Squeezing him tighter, he looked down at me. "I promise I'm not gonna fuck this up."

"I promise I won't fuck this up either."

"United front, Sug... no matter what your moms says, this is for us."

I stood on my toes and kissed the side of his face. "United front." He kissed my lips. "Another one." I told him.

He kept giving me kisses until I told him it was enough. "I'm about to go smoke real quick."

"Okay."

I returned back to the stool and finished drinking coffee before going upstairs to shower and get dressed for the day.

"Sug, you don't have to offer to keep my Gams and mother up here for the summer," Meer said as I rushed into the bedroom.

Erin had called to ask me to check if Cee-Cee had left her teddy bear in my closet the other day they were over here. I was trying to help her soothe a screaming baby and here he was starting this mess again. Instead of looking for my niece's teddy bear, I turned to look at him. "Stop with this shit, Meer."

"Fuck you mean?"

"Exactly what I'm saying. Did you not ask me to marry you? Or did you only ask to make Brandi jealous?" He leaned up in the chair and looked at me like I had lost my mind. "I can talk out my ass, too. You asked me to be your wife, which means your parents, Gams, and Quasim are my family, too. Gams is so at peace out here, and I enjoy having her around. If staying up here gives her some peace, she deserves it."

He stared at me from across the room, his eyes low because he had just finished smoking. I stood firm as he crossed the bedroom until he was standing right in front of me. "You got a lot of 'fuckin mouth, huh?"

"You cannot keep wanting the marriage and this baby, then getting scared that you are putting too much onto me. Your family is never too much for me... they are my family too, and like you protect them, I am going to do the same." I shoved him and went into the closet to finish my quest for this damn bear.

As I tossed the clothes I was donating, I felt his hands around me. "Who the fuck you talking to, Suga?" I heard him whisper into my ear, and I shuttered feeling his beard against my ear, and his cool breath caressed my nose. I could smell the weed and the mint, because he always popped a mint whenever he was finished.

"You know exactly who I'm talking to, Quameer." I removed myself from him and looked over near the dresser that Cee-Cee kept playing around when she was in here. Meer pushed me against the dresser and pulled my maxi dress I wore up.

"Bet. Let me see if you got all that mouth after I give you this dick."

My body shook just hearing him say those words to me. I wanted him all the time and thought of sex with Meer on a daily basis. I loved how he always took control, and showed me who wore the pants in our relationship.

I've prayed for a man that took control, and Meer was that man. "I bet I do."

I felt the breeze from his shorts dropping onto the floor and felt him spreading me apart. His dick always fit perfectly inside of me. I whimpered, holding onto the same dresser I was supposed to be looking around for a teddy bear.

His hand was on the back of my neck as he pressed me further down on the dresser and held onto my waist with his other hand. "You gotta be quiet, Sug… none of that fucking screaming… ight?"

"Uh hmm," I bit down on my lip knowing that I had to be quiet because everyone was downstairs.

We were all supposed to walk across the street together, and I only came up here to look for the teddy bear. I assumed Meer was already outside smoking before we made it to my parent's house. He slammed his dick into me and shook the dresser while I murmured like a fool.

His hands released my neck as he held my hips and hammered into me like a jack hammer. The dresser hit the wall in my closet as I held onto the dresser and bit back my moan. I felt him pull out and tease my opening, making me damn near jump up on the dresser and scream out.

"You always so fucking wet for Big Pa, huh? Where all that mouth at, Big Mama? I don't hear that shit now."

My phone in the pocket of my dress started to ring. "I…I'm sorry," I pleaded, as he continued to fuck me so good.

"Answer the phone, Sug… it's rude to ignore calls."

"I…I can't answer like this."

"Answer the fucking phone, Suga," he demanded, and I searched the pocket of my hiked-up dress until I found the phone.

I didn't bother to look at the name before I answered the call. "Hmm, hell… o?" I stammered because Meer wasn't letting up.

"The fuck? Capri, you good?" Capone asked.

Meer slammed me back onto his dick while I squealed. "Hmmm… C…Capone… I gotta ca…" I didn't bother to finish; I just ended the call because I was pretty sure my brother had just heard me fucking over the phone.

"Why you didn't finish your call, Baby?" Meer asked with a hint of sarcasm in his voice.

"Meer... my bro'..." I couldn't finish my words because it felt so good. My face was nearly planted on the top of the dresser while Meer showed me no mercy.

"You lucky I can't be rough as I wanna be, Sug... once you drop this baby... it's on sight," he snarled, as he slapped my ass hard.

"Slap it again, Big Pa," I begged, and he did exactly what I needed, because I came, falling limp against the dresser.

Meer continued, slamming me back onto his dick until he finally came, and then kissed me on the shoulder. "Watch who the fuck you talking to next time, Sug," his cocky ass said as he left the closet while fixing his shorts, while I was still bent over the dresser.

I couldn't even say anything because I hadn't said a damn thing because Big Pa always put it down. It didn't matter if it was a quickie or not, he was gonna make sure that he came out on top, and I loved that for me.

CHAPTER 2
QUAMEER

NO SOONER THAN I started buckling my belt to my shorts, my phone buzzed with Brandi's message.

> Water head: Can you have her let us through the gates?

I didn't bother to reply, I called the front and told them to let her through. Brandi was starting to piss me the fuck off with the shit she was doing. I wanted Peach today. She was the main reason that I could even celebrate this day, so of course I wanted my daughter with me today. Brandi knew that shit which is why she used it to her advantage. There was no reason for her to drive all the way out here – again.

Then she had the nerve to want to hold a conversation while dropping Peach off. I just knew she was about to come at me with some bullshit and I wasn't in the mood for the shit today. It was supposed to be a peaceful day, and nothing about her big-headed ass was peaceful. On Mother's Day, I sent her ass to a spa and hit her with some bread because no matter how I felt about her, she was my daughter's mother.

You see. Very peaceful. Very get the fuck from around me.

Why the fuck couldn't she return the favor by not being

around when I had to get my daughter. Capri came walking out the closet like her legs were broke and I smirked knowing the reason.

"I'm going to shower again, Meer," she tossed over her shoulder, and went into the bathroom while I went downstairs.

I was determined to get outside before Brandi's bladder suddenly became full and she needed to come use the bathroom. Soon as I came out the house, Brandi was pulling into the driveway. She parked next to Suga's motorcycle, and then waited a second before climbing out.

Peach jumped out her mother's car and rushed into my arms. "Happy Daddy's day, Daddy." I kneeled down and kissed her on the cheek.

"Wouldn't be one without you, Peach."

She smiled. "I'm kind of a big deal, huh?"

"The fuc.... the freaking biggest." I looked at the gift bags that she had in her hands and smiled. "What's in the bags?"

Brandi walked over with her arms crossed. "I got Grandpop and Uncle Sim a Father's Day gift, too."

"You too sweet, you know that?"

"I've been told."

"Guess what?"

"Nanny and Gams are inside with Grandpop and Uncle Sim."

Ryder damn near tossed the gift bags as she rushed to the front door. "Nanny is out the house?"

"She is." I smiled, feeling this big ass sense of pride that my Suga made that happen for us. It was her who told Gam the game plan, and my pops who went along with it.

Peach quickly kissed and hugged her mother before running into the house with the bags in her hands. I stood up and looked at Brandi, wondering what the fuck she wanted to talk about. Her arms remained folded and from what I could see, her husband wasn't in the car with her.

Leaning against my truck, I waited for Brandi to get on with whatever she needed to discuss. After fucking, I was hungry as fuck and ready to get across the street and grub. "Quameer, the fact that you didn't discuss getting engaged and involved our daug—" she paused when I held my hand up.

"I'm really trying hard not to violate you. I don't have to run anything that I fucking do by you. If I wanted to marry this fucking truck and have our daughter officiate it, I don't have to say shit to you."

"Then why the fuck are you hiding it?"

I laughed. "If I was hiding it, I damn sure wouldn't have told Peach. Baby can't keep a secret to save her life. There's a difference between secret and private... what we got going on over here ain't got shit to do with you."

"You are doing this because I went and got married," she accused, which further pissed me off. It was bad enough she was wasting my time with this conversation, and now she wanted to start throwing baseless accusations.

"You want me to still want you so bad. Brandi, I don't give a fuck what you do and who you marry. If you cared about your marriage, then I wouldn't have been dicking you down the night before your wedding."

Brandi was stuck and didn't know what to say. "You promised you wouldn't say anything about that."

"I kept my word... now leave me the fuck alone before I pull up on Marty and explain how I had his fiancée in my bed when she should have been putting curlers in her hair or some shit. Stop playing with me, Brandi. My fucking life is my business, and it has nothing to do with you... when it comes to me and my future wife, our shit is ours. What we allow you to know is up to us... now go and celebrate your husband today."

"He's not a father."

"Shit... look like he carrying for six." I shrugged and walked back toward the front door while she remained there stuck.

Brandi always had fucking nerve. The bitch had nothing else, but she made sure she had nerve in her purse. What I did with my life wasn't her business, and she knew this, and yet she continued to ask me questions like I was going to answer them.

I didn't give a fuck about her husband and would tell him how I fucked his wife the night before they were supposed to get married. When Brandi showed up to my door, everything told me to send her away.

My fucking heart was fragile, and I knew allowing her in, knowing she was about to get married the next day was a bad idea. Bad ideas were common when you were in your feelings and deep into a bottle of rum.

After I finished fucking and having her suck all the nut out my body, I sent her on the way, my feelings stopped for her. I realized that Brandi was for whoever. She asked to end things and had been all over talking about this new fiancée. Brandi showed up to my crib knowing where it would end, and cried while I fucked her, telling me how much she loved me.

Shit was fucking me up because the more we fucked, the more the connection and love I had for her started to fade. It was how she was getting fucked by me, while there was an event planner working tirelessly to put the finishing touches on her wedding.

Quasim was kissing Peach while holding the bag she had got him. "You know you my favorite niece, right?"

"I'm your only niece, Uncle Simmy."

He kissed her cheek. "Don't grow up anymore... promise?"

She nuzzled her cheek against his. "I'll talk to God about it, okay?"

"Appreciate it." He kissed her nose, and then put her back onto the floor as she ran into the kitchen to my father and Gams. "Hopefully Pri is having a boy, so she can remain my only niece... Congrats, Blaze," he winked.

I smiled, as I went upstairs to see what was taking Capri so damn long. How the hell were we going to be late, and we were across the street.

We had been at the brunch for an hour, and I was on my second plate of appetizers. All the women were inside setting the table up for the actual meal. "Nobody told you to smoke before coming here... now you bout to eat us out a house and home," Cappadonna's smart ass said.

I bit into the wagyu slider and flipped him the middle finger. "Nigga, you got beef or something... the fuck you keep looking at me." I looked at Capone while polishing off the rest of my slider.

"You know why the fuck I'm looking at you."

I racked my brain for any reason this nigga was staring at me and then broke out into laughter. When Suga answered the phone for his ass, while getting fucked. "Why the fuck you calling anyway?"

Capp looked at both of us confused. "Do I even wanna know?"

"Hell fucking no!" Capone damn near hollered and stood up and walked over toward the pool where the kids were playing.

Capp eyed me down while I continued to fuck up my food. "The fuck he talking about, Meer?"

"I promise you don't wanna know, Capp." I squeezed his shoulder before going into the house.

"Hey Meer... we're about to eat now, so you don't need another plate, unless you want one," Erin took my empty plate from me.

I was no longer focused on the food, but on the look on my baby's face. I could tell something was wrong from the way she was mixing the sangria in the glass pitcher, disassociated. "Nah. I'm good, Erin."

"Hey Quameer," Alaia called from the stove, as she took out the last of the fried chicken. "The chicken is done, so can you please relay the message to my husband."

I bypassed Erin and walked further into the kitchen where all the women were. It was noisy as shit, as they were all talking about a million things at once. Still, somehow the conversation flowed effortlessly.

"Hey Quameer... how are you doing?"

"I'm straight, Ms. Jo... how you doing?"

She smiled as she looked at me making my way to Suga. "I

am doing great... so happy to be celebrating all of you men. I love active Black fathers," Jo went on a rant about black men handling their responsibilities as fathers.

"Come with me real quick, Sug," I whispered into her ear, and pulled her behind me. She allowed me to pull her behind me as Jean watched us closely, not saying anything, but continuing to mix the pasta salad.

We found an empty room, and I closed the door behind us. Capri leaned against the door, and I leaned over her, staring down into her eyes. No sooner than our eyes locked, tears poured from her eyes.

"I can never do anything right when it comes to her. She's upset because Capone told Erin not to invite Naheim to the Father's Day brunch. I had no control over if he was invited or not. Why is she upset with me when I didn't know until we got here."

The shit made my chest hurt when I saw my baby crying. It pissed me off that Jean was putting shit on Capri that wasn't her fault. Why the fuck would Naheim be here if he wasn't family. In a perfect world he would have been around and still able to co-exist like he had done in the past. That shit wasn't healthy, and I didn't give a fuck what anybody said. They went through so much in their marriage that ultimately ended with them getting divorced. Because of her heart, Capri allowed Naheim to still come around, helping him with his child, all because of her heart. Everybody had me fucked up with the way they allowed her to make the decision, and didn't step forward and make it for her. I understood the spot that both Capone and Cappadonna were in, but both of them should have made the decision for Capri. I knew my baby, and she wanted to be there for everybody, even if the shit drained her.

"Aye, you know I don't like when you crying." I used my free hand and wiped the tears from her face. "Sug, I need you to stop taking shit because she's your mom. Not when she got her own fucking secrets... where the fuck she get to judge you for your life. Only you can put that shit in a smash. I can't have you stressing yourself and our baby out... either you say something, or I'm gonna say something."

"Even with my brothers here?"

I screwed my face up. "I'm not scared of your brothers, Sug... I'm not in they back pocket, and they don't control my cash flow. There's respect there always, so I would hope they would understand me standing up for my woman, like they would do the same for their own."

She took a deep breath, and I kissed her on the lips. "I'm looking forward to dinner back at the house."

"Whenever you ready to bounce, you know the letters you need to send me."

She kissed me on the lips, and I opened the door, allowing her to go out first. By the time we joined everyone, the men had come inside and were figuring out their seats. Capp watched as Capri squeezed my hand before going back into the kitchen. I took a seat at the table while the women served the food. Des took the head of the table while Jean sat beside him.

Pops took the other side of the table while Quasim sat beside him. I was in the middle of the table with the empty seat for Capri. She was running all over the kitchen with Erin and Alaia, and I wanted her to sit down.

Once all the food was on the table, everyone sat down, and Des said grace before digging in. I made Capri a plate before my own. "I'm supposed to be making you the plate."

I smirked. "Nah. I need you to eat because you think you're about to live off coffee this whole pregnancy," I whispered into her ear.

"I ate something this morning... cookies."

"Stop playing with me, Suga."

The conversations were flowing around the table, and I wasn't paying attention to any of them. Capri was too busy playing footsie under the table with me. Her ass ain't had enough from earlier, so I was gonna have to double back.

"Only if Capri can figure out what she's going to do... you seem to have it all planned out with you and Big Mike." Jean's voice and hearing Capri's name pulled me from the intense game of footsie my baby was playing with me under this table.

Ryai, Erin's cousin, giggled, her swollen belly jiggling in the process. "I don't have anything put together. If it wasn't for my mother, I would be lost when it comes to this baby."

Big Mike kissed the side of her face and rubbed her stomach. "I cannot wait for the baby to get here... I've been buying everything." Erin jumped in, hoping to switch the conversation.

"Pri, don't you want this with a husband?" Jean sipped her sangria. "How long do you expect to be single?"

In my opinion, somebody needed to cut her ass off because she had been sipping that shit through a straw since she sat down.

"Jean, I know you wear glasses sometimes, but I know damn well you see that she and Quameer are together."

"For how long? Until she decides she doesn't want it anymore and then goes to the next man? Capri runs from everything that scares her, Meer... so make sure you're aware... girl has always been great at running and keeping things from me."

Capri was silent as she messed with the silverware in front of her. "Let me know, Sug."

"Chill out, Ma... you need to drink some water," Cappadonna spoke, removing his mother's cup, and she snatched it back. "I'm your mama, not the other way around."

It wasn't like Jean was slurring or was really drunk. Still, I could tell she had too much to drink from the way she kept making every conversation return back to Capri.

"Oh word?" Capp nodded his head.

"Yes word. Everybody is celebrating her coming home and I'm trying to figure out what the fuck are we celebrating? She took off for a year, and avoided all responsibilities, and then returned home like nothing happened."

"Not true, Ma," Capone added, and Erin held his hand, while trying her best not to get involved. "She needed that time away."

"Time away from a husband she never wanted to try with."

Capri shot out the chair. "Naheim fucked more bitches

than I could count, and you wanted me to stay. I was collecting empty condom wrappers like damn infinity stones, and you wanted me to stick it out. For what? Because a wife doesn't give up on her husband. He didn't give a fuck about my mental health as long as I was still fucking him and his relationship with Nellie was good, then he was straight."

I reached up and rubbed her lower back. "Watch your damn mouth, Capri."

"Fuck that, fuck you, and fuck this!" Capri continued to yell, the vein appearing at the side of her temple. "I went to college, graduated law school at the top of my class, hold this fucking family down and all I'm ever reduced to is Naheim's wife to you. I am much more than his ex-wife. I'm a fucking good woman and I'm tired of you making me feel like I'm not because I chose to divorce him."

"You're a good woman because you parade around with your brother's friends? Quameer is the new obsession and then you'll be done with him...he is a close family friend... our families have been close for years, and your hotness is going to ruin that... this girl has more secrets and nerve than anything," her accent became thicker as she waved Capri off.

I watched my pop take back his drink while watching everything unfold in front of us. "Well, I'm having my baby, and I am engaged to Quameer. This is the exact reason I didn't want to tell any of you."

"*Our* baby," I corrected.

Des smiled and held up his glass to my pops who in return did the same thing. "Bless up, Q."

"Bless up, Des." He took back another drink with Des, as they celebrated the fact that Capri was pregnant.

Erin and Alaia sat there shocked, unsure on what to say or do. "I don't care if you don't agree with my choices. This one I made on my own, and it feels so right. This man has healed me when I was too broken to give a fuck. While all of you were lost in your own world, he saw me spiraling and paid attention. He healed me more than he will ever know," she reached down and held my hand.

Erin started crying while Capone hugged his wife. "I'm so happy for you, Pri... for the both of you."

"Now why in the fuck would you do some mess like that?" Jean pushed her plate away from her.

Capri squeezed my hand. "Why the fuck would you have a child and then fucking hide him from us?"

Des choked on his drink, while Jean looked like she had saw a ghost. "Nah, Ma... go ahead and continue with that mouth," Capp softly patted his mother on the back. "Inquiring minds would like to fucking know... Pops?"

"Capri Shelly Ann Delgato and Cappadonna Leroy Delgato, you both watch your tongue and speak on what you know."

"We wanna know what the fuck is up... that's what we wanna know!" Capone roared, pushing away from the table.

Des sat at the end of the table, stroking his beard, and not saying anything. As his wife stared at him, he looked straight ahead and said nothing.

"Daddy, what is going on?" Capri's voice cracked.

She had stood on business when it came to confronting her mother, and now she was realizing what happened, so the tears started to fall.

"My job as her fiancé and future husband is to protect her... make sure she is good mentally, emotionally and physically. As much as this brunch was appreciated and cool, I'm getting my baby out of here. I think it's best for everyone to cool down and regroup." I looked over at Capone and Cappadonna. "When you done here, come over to her house because we need to talk... As much as you're still caught up on Naheim as your son-in-law, we're not about to keep disregarding her feelings to protect his... not happening on my watch... feel me?"

Cappadonna and Capone both stood up to kiss and hug their baby sister. Capri had tears coming down her face as she kept looking over at her mother, who avoided eye contact with any of her children.

I held her hand as we made our way out the front door and kissed the back of it. "I'm proud of you, Suga."

"Why do I feel like this? I know I needed to stand up for myself, but it doesn't feel good. I told my mother fuck you."

I laughed. "Sometimes it be like that, Baby. I know you and your moms will fix this…and if she doesn't want to fix it, know that you tried."

"Maybe she's right, Meer." She looked up into my eyes with her lips poked out, believing what her mother said.

I stopped in the middle of our walk back to her house. "Long as I know what it is between me and you, it doesn't matter what anybody else thinks. You're going to be my wife, and we're going to have a seed together… ain't no running. You gonna leave me, Suga?"

She smiled. "Never."

"Then fuck what anybody else thinks. This shit starts and ends with us, no outside opinions on what we're doing."

"I love you, Meer Cat."

Wrapping my arms around her and squeezing her ass, I kissed her head. "I love you, Sug… don't ever forget that my track star."

CHAPTER 3
AIMEE

I SAT at the table watching how Jean was so stoic and went on like Capri didn't just drop a bomb on this table and leave. Capone and Cappadonna sat next to their wives while looking at their mother.

"So, we about to act like nothing fucking happened?" Cappadonna roared, pissed that his mother went on eating like nothing happened.

"Watch yourself, Boy," Des finally spoke up, and Cappadonna stood up, pissed that nobody was saying anything.

Capone remained seated messing with his beard. "When Pri wanted to marry Naheim, I was the one that said they should wait… not to push her into marriage right away. She was young and needed to live. You both weren't a fan, but you quickly switched and fell in love with Naheim's orphan prison boy situation." Capp stood by the back door and looked out at the pool while his brother spoke. "You told me that she needed to learn how to be a wife, Ma… you told me that shit. I was the one that pushed her to attend college, and then law school because I don't believe no woman needs to learn to be a wife that young."

"Tread lightly, Boy-Boy," Des warned his second son.

"I have my own shit I have to answer for when it comes to how I dealt with Capri. When the fuck is anybody else gonna take some accountability. Erin told me that you scolded her because of a decision that I made. Naheim shouldn't be here… why the fuck would he be here when he's not her husband."

"Because he is family," Jean countered.

Capone slammed his hands onto the table, causing all of us to jump along with the plates and cups. "More family than your actual daughter? You make him feel more welcomed than her. He works for the family, nothing more! We allowed him to be comfortable when he should have gotten his shit stomped in. Even you, Capp. I don't give a fuck if you raised the nigga behind bars. I don't give a fuck what she did back, my main priority is her… my sister. It breaks my fucking heart knowing the shit she was going through and we all ignored it. Pri good… Pri handles shit, and the shit almost fucking handled her. You put too much pressure on her, Ma. Naheim is her past and you keep bringing him up. The only reason Capri has allowed him to be invited to shit is because of you and her fucking heart, which we all know is big."

"I think it's about time that we start acting like Capri is a very important part of this family. Baby Doll is about to do some shit that could have her behind bars, and I don't think she gets the credit she deserves. Ma, you need to end whatever delusion that Naheim and Capri will get married again. Baby Doll is going to become an Inferno, and Quameer deserves that respect. I told that nigga to hold her down once, and he's been holding her ever fucking since and ain't never let up. We keep this shit up, and she gonna make sure none of us have access to her. She left for a fucking year… I'm not trying to lose Baby Doll again."

"You on her case and hid a brother from us. Capri could have come in here airing shit out and she has always shown you more grace than you do for her," Capone continued. "Both of you hid a sibling from us and never said shit to us about it." Capone was doubling down on business as he confronted his parents. "And yeah, my bad for cussing at you, Ma."

I held Capella's hand as he watched everything go down

between his grandparents and then his uncle and father. "I thought my family had issues."

"Your bum ass family still holds the title, Aim," he whispered back.

I got offended at first, then nodded in agreement. "Yeah. You right."

No matter how angry the twins were with their parents, all they had to do was call and both of them would come running. I couldn't say the same when it came to my own family.

"You don't know what the fuck happened or why we made the decisions that we did." Des took back his drink and stared his son in the eyes. "Until your back is against the fucking wall like ours was, you won't ever know what it feels like to make a decision like the one we ma—"

"I made," Jean whispered.

Cappadonna and Capone's eyes softened as they looked at their mother. "Jean baby, this ain't all on you and I've told you that." Des kissed his wife's shaking hand, as the tears fell down her face onto the dining table. "We knew eventually this would come back and we would have to tell them."

"I think we need to leave and give the family some space," Jo whispered as she and Big Mike helped Ryai up and took the kids back over to Capone's house.

I wasn't moving because I wanted to know the tea just as bad as Capone and Cappadonna. How did we all miss another Delgato that had been out in this world. Well, I knew how I missed it. I never saw Corleon when I did little licks for him. It was always through Landon, and even then, I didn't give a damn what he looked like.

The money I was making to do something I loved was all I was concerned about. I wasn't Rory's mama or Capella's girlfriend, I was Aimee. The chick who had always been obsessed with tech. All I was concerned with was learning more so I could be a force to be reckoned with.

Cappadonna remained by the door as he looked over at his mother. "Why?"

Alaia whispered something to her husband, and then she eventually left with Jo. I knew she was going to check in on Capri. "I had no other choice, Cappadonna. I was a single mother raising two boys alone with no damn money. New to the country while trying to figure it all out without family... not to mention I was young."

Capp looked toward his brother. "Aye, Capo, call Capri back over here."

"Fuck no... I'm not ever calling her phone again. Gorgeous, call Capri for me." Capone was serious as shit as the words left his mouth.

We all looked at him confused. "Any fucking way, how were you a single mother? You and Pops have always been together... as far as I know."

Des looked across the table at Papa, and he nodded his head. "You gotta tell 'em, D."

He refilled his glass and took a minute before he took it back and then spoke. "I got caught up and locked up. Your mother found out she was pregnant when I was trying to fight the case. No money and a bullshit lawyer had me sitting on Riker's Island."

"My whole pregnancy," Jean recalled, still looking straight ahead. It was like she was envisioning everything that had happened in this moment.

As much as she was too much on my girl Capri, my heart went out to her because nobody knew what she went through. "You boys probably don't remember everything. There was a time when your mother would bring you up there to see me while pregnant."

Capp finally took a seat as if all the memories were finally coming back to him. "You wore tan."

Capone looked at his twin, desperately trying to remember the same thing that he did. "Capone used to cry every time it came time to leave, and I told you that you had to be strong for the both of you. Your mother had that baby while I was locked up, and it was fucking hard for her. Raising two boys while working, and then adding another mouth to feed. I sat behind that wall fucked up because I couldn't do shit. I would listen to her on the phone sound exhausted. Capone was always in and out of the hospital for his sickle cell... shit was tough."

"Then they spoke about deportation after you were sentenced," Jean continued on. It was like she wasn't a part of the conversation, just saying random things that all connected with the story Des was telling.

He held her hands and gave them a squeeze. "I couldn't do that to your mother. She was tired, and she could barely feed the both of you, and then adding a new baby. When she brought up putting Corleon," his voice cracked when he said his third son's name. "When she brought up giving him up for adoption, what the fuck was I supposed to say? I was facing deportation... it would have been selfish."

"There was a single woman that always brought her clothes to the laundromat I worked in. She came in every Tuesday. I did her laundry, and I remember seeing blood stains all over her underwear and work pants. I tried hard to get most of the stains out, and showed her the clothes that the blood didn't come out from." Jean paused, tears continuing to fall from her face. "We built a rapport with each other; she knew my situation and I knew hers. I envied her because she was everything I thought I would be when I came to the states. She told me she had miscarried the week before."

"You mother left Corleon with our crack headed neighbor while you both were in school. We couldn't afford daycare, and the vouchers from public assistance didn't do shit."

"I loved my son, but I also knew it wasn't fair to keep him. I barely had time for the two of you and then he came along. I prayed about it for a month before I brought it up to her. She thought it was a joke, until she saw how desperate I was." She paused. "She even offered to give me money and I refused. I would never sell my son... ever. I spoke with your father about it, and he was against it, but knew that there wasn't anything that he could do."

"Too proud of a man," Papa spoke up.

Des looked down. "You had your own wife and children. I couldn't allow you to take from your kid's mouth to feed mine."

"I would have... we would have shared... we're family, D."

Jean sniffled as she squeezed her husband's hands. "I packed up what little things I did have and brought him to work while the boys were at school."

"Neighbor's baby," Cappadonna whispered, as the pieces were connecting. It was so funny how a scent, sound, or conversation could trigger something within our memory to cause us to remember. He had gone the majority of his life never remembering the fact that he had a younger brother, and now it was all coming back to him.

Jean shook her head while crying some more. "Yes. You both used to ask about him and I told you both he was our neighbor's baby. Eventually you both stopped asking about the baby and then started in on your father."

"He's away in the army," Capone said, looking at his father.

I wiped my own tears watching them. "We thought he was coming home and then he was deported. It made me feel better about the decision to give Corleon up because I couldn't do it without your father."

Des had tears come down his eyes as he looked across the table at Papa. "If it wasn't for Quinton, I wouldn't be sitting here. He smuggled me back into this country. Got me the forged documentation so I could still travel back home to visit family. He's the reason that I was able to be the father that I am to you kids. So, when I refer to the Infernos as family, it's because they are."

Papa saluted. "Wasn't shit, D... I'm always gonna ride... you'd do the same."

Des looked at Capone, Cappadonna, and Quasim. "And now our sons ride for each other the same way."

"We're meeting with him."

Jean nearly jumped out her skin. "Seriously? Cappadonna, did you go and find him?"

"He found us," Capri's voice sounded from behind us.

She was leaned in the doorway with Quameer behind her, his head bent down to rest on her shoulder. I could see the love that man had in his eyes for her, and I felt like this was her one. Quameer was meant to be with Capri.

"Does he hate me?"

Capri remained in the doorway. "He doesn't hate us.... Core wants to know why you gave him up. His mother gave him a good life, and when she passed, she told him about us."

"Linda passed?" Jean squealed, holding her hand over her mouth.

"You would know if you didn't stop writing him when he was seventeen. I read the letters and then you stopped."

"A lot was going on at that time. Cappadonna had just been locked up; Capone was on his own for the first time in his life, and then you. I was working so much, and your father was, too. Life was hectic and I thought it was best to bow out peacefully."

"Didn't know that you ever wrote to him." Des looked at his wife.

Jean's voice cracked. "He was my baby. I couldn't just move on like he never existed."

"What changed when it came to Capri? We were still broke," Cappadonna questioned.

"I couldn't do the same thing... my first and only baby girl." She looked at Capri. "Your father was back in the states and money wasn't great, but I would make things stretch for her."

"You should have given me up with the way you act toward me."

"Capri," Des said.

"I'm saying. You were fucking hard on me, and you still are hard on me... nothing I do is right."

"I didn't want you to struggle like I did. Capri, I wanted you to be better than me... better than the decisions that I have made."

"She's accomplished more than some women have. Did that shit with one hand behind her back. You are hard on her, punishing her because she had become something you wanted to become," I blurted.

Everybody turned to look at me. "Baby, this ain't the moment to be adding your shit."

"Nah, Aimee continue." Capp nudged me on.

"You said that Linda was everything that you ever wanted to be when you came to this country. From what I've learned about Core, his mother was a boss ass chick that worked in tech and taught him everything he knows. He didn't grow up poor, and always had more than enough. Capri has degrees, is a lawyer, and she's become more than you can imagine... everything that you wanted for you. So, you unknowingly, or maybe knowingly punish her because of it." I shrugged.

Capp stared and smiled. "Next time somebody call her a ditz, you gotta see me... Aim-shizzle ain't a fucking ditz."

"Who calls me a ditz?"

Capella kissed my temple. "Don't worry about it, Baby." Capri looked at me and mouthed the words thank you.

"Tasha is home, and we need to talk. As much as I want to sit and discuss everything with Core... I think you both owe him this explanation on how he came to be given up." Capri walked past her brothers onto the back porch.

One by one, Capone and Cappadonna followed behind their sister. "Fuck, I love when she's in that mode," Quameer mumbled as he followed behind his future wife.

I went to follow behind them and Capella held my hand. "I'm very much a part of this, too, Honey."

He followed behind me to the backyard where Capri was standing near the fireplace. "I put that bitch away for her entire life." Capone was so sure of the work that he did to make sure she went away forever.

"Capone she's out and she's fucking engaged to Morgan. Jesse is his daughter... I can't make this shit up." She paced back and forth.

"Jesse the friend from college?" Capp questioned.

"Yeah. She always spoke about her father being so inconsistent and not having the best relationship with him. I didn't fucking think he was Vincent Morgan."

"You spoke to Forty?" Capella asked.

"I left him a message. You know Forty always pops back up... I don't think he knew about this. He would have warned us."

"Certain shit is higher up the ladder," Cappadonna replied, deep in his own thoughts. "This on you, Capo."

"Say what the fuck you mean, Capp?"

"I said what the fuck I mean... No loose fucking ends, Capo... no fucking loose ends and you got this bitch out. Do you know how much shit she knows about us? She should have been in the fucking dirt with her damn son! I don't give a fuck if she was pregnant at the time. Naheim would have had to eat that, or he could have joined her ass!" Cappadonna barked.

"Nigga, I fucking did what I thought was fucking best!" Capone stood up, going chest to chest with his brother.

Capp shoved the fuck out his brother, and Capo found his footing and went to throw a punch, and Capella jumped in. "Chill the fuck out... why the fuck you both fighting each other."

Erin ran into the backyard to her husband. "What the fuck is going on? Fighting each other isn't going to solve anything."

"Everything always falls back on Capo... I fucking handled business while you sat behind bars comfortable as fuck."

Capp nodded his head walking away coolly, then double back and went to lunge at his brother, and both Capella and Quasim had to grab him back while Capone was rushing toward him.

Quasim held Capone back, while talking to him. "You don't want to fight this nigga... this your brother. After you both get your licks in, you still gonna be brothers... come walk with me, Capo."

Cappadonna looked like a damn animal with how wild his eyes were. "You take me away from my wife and seeds, I'll never fucking forgive you!" Capp hollered at his back.

Capo smirked as he turned around. "Don't even fucking worry about it... I'm gonna take it on the chin and do the time, Bitch."

"I'm gonna put my foot in his as—"

"Chill out, Cappadonna," Des spoke to his son. "When you both used to get into it as teens... Capo knows what buttons to press just like you know what buttons to press with him."

"I'm gonna push this fist in his fucking face."

"Why the fuck are you trying to fight your brother, Roy?" Alaia came over, standing in front of her husband who was still watching his twin walk away.

Capone and Cappadonna both have said that they would sit up for the other one. I think with all the emotions that had been swirling at brunch, it finally took a toll on Cappadonna that he could be going back behind the wall again, and he snapped. It was easy the first time because he didn't have a wife and children.

"He did the best and did he make some mistakes, yeah. Don't put it all on him because he was putting in work alone... doing it without his right hand. You came home and I admit, you put in work alone, but you had your twin right there with you, too. I'm not saying I agree with his choice to keep Tasha alive, but I know my husband and he does what he thinks is best for this family. He wanted to step back and has been by your side ever since you been home... remember before you came home, it was Capo running this shit – alone," Erin said, and then went to follow behind Quameer and her husband.

"Erin not too much on my man now," Alaia called to Erin.

Erin turned around and laughed. "Joy, please."

Alaia smiled as she continued to calm her husband down. Capella was standing there trying to figure out what the hell had went on.

"Honey, can we go home?"

"Hell fucking yeah." He checked in with his aunt before we walked through the backyards to our own home, away from the craziness that had occurred today.

CHAPTER 4
CAPRI

WHEN JESSE INVITED us girls out to lunch, I considered even going. We hadn't spoken since the ball, and that wasn't unusual for Jesse anyway. She would go weeks, even months without checking in, and then the moment she needed something, she would make useless conversation before sliding in whatever she needed.

I had been so used to how our one-sided friendship work that I didn't expect anything more from Jesse. Being that she was connected to the man that wanted to destroy my family, I put my best foot forward to pretend to be excited for this lunch.

The one person I wasn't looking forward to seeing was Brandi's ass. I could go my entire life without seeing that woman. It was always some smart ass comment she made whenever we saw one another. She already knew about the engagement, so I knew that was going to be the topic of lunch, which isn't what I wanted.

Meer was still asleep when I went to kiss him on the head, and he pulled me into the bed with him, wrapping his arms around me. "How you feeling, Sug?"

"I'm good, Meer... promise."

"You tossed and turned all night and kept saying mommy."

He kissed me softly on my lips, as I rested my head on his pillow.

My mother had been on my mind since we got into that argument at Father's Day brunch. Since then, we hadn't spoken to each other, and neither of us reached out to the other. We were across the street from each other, and we both were so stuck in our ways that we refused to fix it.

"How could she be the one with the attitude after the things she said about me?"

Quameer pulled the blankets over me, even with me being fully dressed and prepared to leave out. "You finally stood up for yourself... shit taste bitter."

"Do you think we will eventually make up?"

"It depends... are you willing to bend for her?"

I scoffed. "I'm always bending to her. Whenever she says things, I ignore them because she's, my mother. It's me that always fixes things between us because I hate when we're fighting... I'm not doing it."

Quameer kissed my cheek. "Everything will work out and I'm gonna make sure of that... ight?"

"Meer, you cannot try and fix everything for me."

He removed himself from the bed and went to pee, as I remained in the bed, not wanting to go to this stupid ass lunch with Jesse and Brandi. The only thing I was looking forward to was seeing both Zoya and Blair.

Quameer came to the door with his toothbrush in his hand. "That's my exact job. I will fix every and anything when it comes to my wife. Get used to that shit, Sug."

"You're taking this husband role to heart, and we haven't even made it down the aisle."

His expression remained serious. "I take being a father and husband serious. Other niggas may play the fuck around, but that shit ain't me. I was shown the example of how a man is supposed to love his wife."

"Your baby mother is going to be at this lunch, Meer," I

groaned as he went to spit in the sink, then returned to the door. "You know she's going to ask about us getting engaged."

"Fuck Brandi... it ain't her business and you need to start telling her that shit, too. Fuck all that being nice and cordial. Brandi ain't gonna learn her place until you put her in that shit. She already know where she stands with me."

"She's Peach's mom... I never want any conflict when it comes to her."

Peach was coming to spend the rest of the summer with us, which was exciting and had me nervous. I've only spent a few days with Peach at most, and we always had fun together. I was Suga, her father's fun friend. Peach was a good kid and never got into trouble, however, I couldn't tell her yes for everything like I usually did.

This wasn't me and Meer as friends anymore. I was going to be her stepmother, so I had to establish my place in her life as someone responsible for her. I was nervous about having her the entire summer because I didn't want to ruin the rapport that we had with each other. She was Peach and I was Suga.

We laughed and had fun together. What happened if she did something, and I had to be the one to talk to her about it? Would she hate me, and not want to come over because I was here? He climbed back into the bed, pinning me down to the bed as he shoved his tongue down my throat. I could taste the toothpaste and mouthwash he had just finished using.

When he broke our kiss, he gave me a few small kisses while biting on my neck. "She's Peach's mother, and I respect that you want to make sure Peach has a peaceful environment between me and her mother. Just because she's Peach's mother doesn't mean she can come at you sideways. I peep the little remarks she makes, so you need to put her ass in her place, and I promise shit won't change when it comes to drop off and pickups with Peach."

"Okay."

"I gotta head into the city so I'm gonna drop you at Blair's crib," he told me, kissing me before getting up to finish getting ready.

While I waited for Quameer, I sat downstairs with Mina. She was rocking in the chair, and I sat down beside her responding to the thread of Jesse's text messages she had sent. I felt her cold soft hand on my forearm and smiled, giving her my hand.

Our fingers laced between each other, as she continued to rock and continue to look out the window. "She doesn't even do that with me. Only does that with my father," Sim took his place in the doorway, watching me and his mother enjoying the view.

Capone and Cappadonna were still not talking and happen to be outside with their daughters at the same time. Capone flipped him the middle finger while Cappadonna tried to abandon Promise's bike and run across his lawn to fuck his twin up.

Both Alaia and Erin were screaming at them while Capone continued to smirk, knowing he was getting under Cappadonna's skin. Since Cappy was always so serious and played little games, it was always easier to get under his skin than it was with Capone.

"Sitting with her brings me a sense of peace."

"Yeah... I feel the same way. Thank you for thinking of this, Pri. It's easy to go on with my life knowing that Gams will handle things. Seeing her here, she's at peace while still caring for my mom."

"Gams deserves a break, too, you know? I want to learn how to care for your mother so we can take the load off her at times."

"Shelly, you ready?"

"Oh, fuck no, Quameer." He wasn't about to run around here calling me by my damn middle name like Cappy and Capone. "I am Suga, Meer... tell me your middle name so I can piss you off."

"Pissy," Quasim snickered.

Quameer cut his eyes at his brother before coming to kiss his mother on her head. "Sim?"

"What up?"

"Fuck ya."

I kissed the back of Mina's hand before putting her hand back on top of the other one. "I'm going to pee, and then we can go."

"Hey Sug," Meer called, as I was headed out the living room.

"Hmm."

"Change those fucking shorts."

I sulked. "Meer, I gotta get these fits off before I start to show."

Meer was being dramatic. I wore a pair of ripped denim jeans that I can admit were a little short, but they were part of the outfit. Since I had to look like I tried, I tossed on a pair of Louboutin thigh high boots and finished the outfit with Meer's bike week oversized shirt that I tied up, so it could be tighter on me.

"You gonna have me get these bullets off if you keep wearing short ass shorts like that, Shelly."

"Ugh." I rolled my eyes and stomped back upstairs to use the bathroom, because I had no plans on changing this outfit. His ass was gonna have to get over it, and I knew he eventually would.

By the time we left from the lake house, Blair was already on her way to the restaurant, so Meer drove me to the restaurant instead of her house. Meer pulled in front of the restaurant and hopped out. Before he let me out his truck, he kissed me on the lips.

"Make sure you eat something too... I saw what you had for breakfast, and you need to start eating. Every time you start stressing you don't wanna eat."

I hated how much he knew me. "I will send you a video of me eating... okay?"

He held my chin and kissed my lips. "I'm gonna have somebody come bring your whip to you."

Quameer Inferno was the definition of if he wanted to, he would. "Meer, you don't need to do that. I'm gonna hang with Blair after. Plus, I know you're not leaving the city unless I'm with you."

He smirked, kissing my top lip. "As long as you fucking know."

As I walked into the restaurant, I spotted the girls right away. Jesse was running her mouth as always, while Zoya and Blair looked like they wanted to be anywhere but there. As I neared the table, they both got excited that they didn't have to sit through lunch with Jesse and Brandi.

"Nice of you to join us… was the traffic that bad coming from your place?" Jesse wouldn't know what the traffic was coming from my house because she had never been there.

I've been to her house more than a few times, and she had never made the time to come to mine. We were supposed to do a movie night at my house before I left for a year, and she never came.

"You were at the lake house, right?" Brandi's nosey ass blurted before I could even respond to her.

Jesse looked at Brandi confused. "You have a lake house?"

Now that I knew who Jesse was connected to, I was moving differently around her. I already never shared much when it came to my life, but now I really needed to keep shit under lock and key.

"You talk too damn much," Blair rolled her eyes at Brandi, while I made my way around the table to sit between her and Zoya.

It killed me how Brandi had a whole child with an Inferno God, and still didn't know how to move. Even if she never agreed with Meer's lifestyle, he still provided for their daughter and his family was her daughter's family. She should have been smarter and knew how to move around Jesse, who was a damn government official.

"Anyway. Now that we are all here… I wanted to give you each these." Jesse handed us all folders while being so giddy. "I wanted to tell you about this at the ball and then you were gone… who was that fine ass man you were with?"

"A friend," I lied, and opened the folder, showing a full itinerary to the Amalfi coast. She had everything lined out, including the private yacht we would be spending three days on. From the day we arrived up until we left, she had everything planned out.

"So, you are trying to do this trip before you get married?" Zoya took the words out of my mouth.

"Zoy, this is my last birthday as a single woman. I have to go out with a bang for this one." She acted like this was something that she had to do.

"You couldn't attend Capri's birthday because you were so busy, but you expect us to go to Italy... her birthday party was in Brooklyn." Blair tossed the folder onto the table, annoyed that Jesse even had the nerve to invite us here and tell us about her birthday.

I wish I could have been surprised, but this was Jesse. She did shit like this all the time, and everyone just went along with it because we knew this as Jesse. "Capri doesn't mind, so why do you care?"

"That's Meer's shirt," Brandi blurted, which made me turn my attention to her. She was studying every move that I made. "It's been his favorite shirt since college... I used to sleep in it."

It was clear Brandi came here to hit below the belt. She wanted to say shit to hurt my feelings, and I could admit it was bothering me that she said she used to sleep in this shirt.

"Well, she's sleeping in it now... probably getting it pulled over her head and bent over, not you," Zoya replied because I was still trying to put my words together.

Blair fell back in her chair laughing. "I know that's right... probably turning her every way possible... whew," she fanned herself, and Zoya looked over at her.

"Sim could do the same thing for you," Zoya winked.

"Goon could, too." Blair snickered, and Zoya waved her off and turned her attention back to me.

"Jesse, I have a lot going on right now, so I can't attend," was all I had managed to say. I hated when a bitch knocked me off my block and I couldn't even think straight.

"Have a few drinks and I can promise you're going to change your mind." She shoved over the mimosas that littered the table.

"I'm good." I waved over the waiter and asked for a menu and leaned over Brandi to grab the menu.

She grabbed my hand, and I snatched it back. "Brandi, don't fucking touch me."

"That's the same ring that Quameer proposed to me with... I gave it back to him though," she shrugged.

I froze when she said this ring was the one he had proposed to her with. Why in the fuck would he ever give me this ring if he knew he proposed to Brandi with it. It was nice that it belonged to his mother, however, it had been worn by another woman.

How the fuck do you respond to something like that? Meer had proposed to her with the same ring that I was wearing right now. When he put this ring on my finger, I had felt so proud. Proud that I was wearing a ring that had history within this family. Knowing that Brandi had it before me made me feel some kind of way. Especially because my man decided not to tell me about it before he proposed to me with it.

> Me: you proposed to Brandi with this ring, Meer? Please don't tell me that.

> Meer Cat: The fuck?

> Me:??

He didn't respond, and I looked over at Brandi's satisfied expression on her face. She had managed to get under my skin, and she loved that.

"Aren't you married? Why do you care about what Meer is doing and what he's not doing?" Blair asked Brandi.

"Thought she should know... Meer wanted to marry me, and even cried over me." She picked in her nails like her admitting that my baby was hurt behind her breaking his heart was cute.

"You really miserable, babe. You may need to go sit on that

lady's couch because holding onto a man that used to want to marry you while you're married is sick."

"Zoya, where is your man? We never see you with a man, yet, you always in all of our business. All you do is work around the clock, get you a man with some money and then you won't have time to be in our shit."

Zoya laughed. "Babes, I am the rich man… don't need to fuck with a man because he got money… I'm the big dawg round here."

Jesse looked up from her phone. "Are we done here? Brandi, why would you even mention that ring is the one that he proposed to you with? Have some decorum… sorry, Capri."

Me, Blair, and Zoya nearly fell out hearing those words come from Jesse. I could tell from the way that Brandi was looking, she was pissed that Jesse had called her ass out for being petty. We all settled down enough to order food.

I don't know why Jesse wanted to have lunch together because the table was divided. She and Brandi were having their own conversation, while me, Blair, and Zoya were in our own conversation.

"I'm stressed out and wish I could just get away again. Miami was a well needed break away from everything." Blair sighed, as she popped an olive into her mouth.

Blair had been going through chemotherapy, running a business, and managed to be there for me whenever I called her when I was away. She wasn't private and would definitely tell me when something was wrong, but she was the kind of friend that didn't like to put a lot on her friends.

She was used to doing things alone, so she never felt like she had to lean on anyone for help. I wanted her to find love so bad. A man that didn't play around when it came to securing her heart.

"What's wrong?"

"My landlord has decided that he wants to sell the building the studio is in, and he's rushing me out. He's been weird since the whole shootout thing happened when they took Alaia."

"Damn. Have you had any luck finding another place?"

Blair slouched down in her chair and shook her head no. "Nope. Every place that I find is either too expensive or too small for me. My clientele has grown so much."

"It's about to grown even more." I leaned closer to both of them. "I'm pregnant."

Blair gasped so loud and hard I thought she swallowed her teeth. "Capri, stopppp!"

Brandi and Jesse turned their attention to us, and realized we weren't going to share with the table and went back to their conversation.

Zoya smiled. "Pri, oh em gee... this is big. When did you find out?"

"Me and Meer found out in Miami."

I watched Blair's expression as her eyes widened. "Girl, we were fucked up in Miami... you need to make a doctor's appointment as soon as possible," she whispered.

"On my ever-growing list of things to do." I groaned, thinking of everything that I had going on and everything that I needed to handle.

Including getting my brothers to speak to each other again. They had never got into it where they tried to rip each other's head off. I knew it was the stress of the unknown, not knowing where things could go.

"Miami was very eventful for both you heifers," Zoya teased.

"It really was," Blair smiled to herself while in her own little world. She had tapped out of our conversation and was now thinking about whatever happened in Miami.

"Girl, what happened when he carried you out the club?" Zoya whispered, eager to know what went down between Blair and Sim.

Blair blushed while rolling her eyes. "Nothing... sheesh, you think I'm giving it up like that?"

"Blair, baby... he picked that man up by his neck and made you decide between if you wanted him to choke that man out or leave with him."

"Don't forget he picked her up and carried her out the club."

"Then walked you back to our suite the next morning and came back an hour later with breakfast for you... I mean, I eat, too, and clearly, he didn't think about anyone else in the suite, but yeah, I would have given him the draws in the damn car on the way back to the hotel." Zoya fanned herself.

I laughed and shook my head at Zoya's dramatics. "Admit it, you have the biggest crush on him."

"Focus... I need to find a new space for the studio or I'm going to be doing it in the damn public park... do you need a permit for that?" She pulled her phone out to google if she needed a permit or not.

"Relax yourself... my family owns a bunch of different commercial properties. I will call our realtor and see what they can put together for me."

"Seriously, Zoya?"

"Yeah. I got you girl."

Blair smiled at both of us. "It feels good having friends with connections." She winked.

"What the fuck is Quamee—" Brandi's words were cut off when we turned our attention to Meer swaggering through the doors of the restaurant with his brother and Goon with him.

"Why the fuck is Gerald two stepping?" Zoya whispered in my ear.

The restaurant we were having lunch in was known for their DJ, strong mimosas, and grass walls that everyone always took pictures with before leaving. The music was going while everyone else in the restaurant was sipping, dancing in their seats, and enjoying the vibes.

From the look on Meer's face, I could tell he didn't come for a good time. He hadn't made it home to shower or change, and still had his sweats on. The only difference in his fit is that he had his IG vest on with a pair of timbs on, unlaced with the tongue hanging just like I liked them. It was something about when a New York nigga stepped with his timbs on.

His locs were still pulled up in the bun I put them in last

night. When his eyes landed on me, he smirked, exposing his gold fangs. He wasn't here to be a friend. I almost wanted to sink into this chair because he was about to put Brandi in her place.

Before we left the lake house, he and Sim walked over to a feuding Capone and Cappadonna to talk. When he made it back to the truck, he told me that they all had something to handle in the city, so Capp and Capone would be coming behind us.

Quasim took the chair from the table next to us, and pulled it next to Blair, who smiled at him. "Hey Simmy Jimmy."

"We still on that, Anjo," he spoke a little Portuguese. Meer told me that he didn't speak it fluently, but he knew some words and understood it.

"What up, Ladies," he looked at Zoya and Blair, then turned his attention to Jesse and Brandi. "And bitches."

"Hello, Quameer?" Jesse rolled her eyes, as she continued eating her food, unfazed by his rudeness toward her.

"Meer, wha...what are you doing here?" Brandi stammered.

Zoya laughed. "He about to air her ass out."

"Ms. Lawyer... my calls been unanswered. You trying to send me away for Jaywalking?"

Zoya pinched Goon. "If you don't pay that ticket, I will pay it for you."

"Now when I get to pinching don't start moaning... ight?"

Zoya had to look away because he had her turned on. I don't care what she said, Goon was wearing her ass down. "Stop sending roses to my office, Gerald... every day is a bit obsessive."

"Not for the one."

I stopped tuning into Zoya and Goon's side conversation and turned my attention back to Meer and Brandi. "You know exactly why the fuck I'm here."

"Actually, I don't. Aren't you supposed to be picking up our daughter from my house?" Brandi got a little bolder, crossing her arms while staring at him.

Quameer dug in his pocket and tossed something at her head, and she squealed, holding her forehead. "I told Suga that she needed to put you in your place, and in due time she will. I'm about to remind you to stop fucking with me."

It was the way he tossed the item like he was playing beer pong, and wanted to make it directly into the cup, which happened to be Brandi's forehead.

Jesse's messy ass picked up whatever the object was and tried to hand it to Brandi. "It's a ring."

"So, you only look slow and not actually slow," he cut his eyes at Jesse, who sat the ring next to Brandi, who was still holding her forehead.

"Quameer, you are going too fucking far... throwing a ring at me is crazy."

"I'm going as far as I need to until you learn your fucking place when it comes to my shit, Brandi. That's the ring I proposed to you with... not the fucking ring on my baby's finger. The only woman that has ever worn that ring is Mrs. Inferno, my fucking moms."

"It looks just like the one you gave me," Brandi countered, standing her ground with what she had told me.

"How? That's a damn princess cut diamond ring," Zoya added.

"What kind of cut you like?" Goon asked her.

Quameer kneeled down in front of the table, so he was eye level with us. "I saved that fucking ring for our daughter. It don't mean shit to me, but I was going to give it to her one day. 'Cause despite how much I hate yo ass now, I know Ryder was conceived in love... sorry, Sug."

"You're fine, Baby."

It would be stupid to feel some kind of way about something that happened before me. Quameer and Brandi had a relationship and there was love there. A love that produced Ryder, so I could never be mad at that.

"You knew that ring looked nothing like the one I gave you and decided to be petty. Imagine being as grown as you are, and playing stupid games like you not married to another man." He paused. "I don't give a fuck how you feel about Capri. She's going to be my wife, which means she's going to be Ryder's stepmother, and the mother to Ryder's sibling. I don't give a fuck what you gotta do, you gonna fucking respect her. I show your husband respect every time I see him, knowing that I busted in your fucking mouth the day before he married yo' ass." He snarled.

"Oh shit!" Blair blurted, as she looked away because we all had secondhand embarrassment for Brandi.

Quasim laughed as he fixed Blair's flipped sleeve on the blouse she wore while she avoided looking in Brandi's direction.

All the color drained from Brandi's face as she looked at Meer, and then at me. I don't know if she was processing the fact that I was pregnant or the fact that Meer had put her on blast about cheating on her husband before they were actually married.

"Damn, Brandi... before your wedding is crazy." Jesse was the first person to say something other than *oh shit* or *oop*.

"Y... you said you wouldn't say anything," she stammered, embarrassed because we knew her secret.

"Yeah, well, I fucking lie—"

RATATA! RATAT!

POW! POW!

Everything happened so fast that I didn't have time to process it. One second, we were sitting at this table learning about Brandi and Meer's little pre-wedding sexcapade, and then I was being shoved down onto the floor with Quasim's body over both me and Blair's body.

"Fuck youuu meannn... while I'm with wifey, too, bet!" I heard Goon's voice boom throughout the restaurant.

From under the table, I could see Meer's eyes staring back at me. If I didn't know any better, they were fucking red. The minute he knew I was straight he kissed his two fingers before he jumped from the floor and all I saw was his boots running to the entrance with Goon having his follow up.

"Sim, please go with him... please," I pleaded with him.

I could feel the heat on his body as he made sure we were all good. Zoya crawled over toward us. "They shot up a fucking restaurant with both Menace Caselli's sister and the Delgato twin's sister," he murmured to himself.

I knew the tone and the low talk because I've seen my brothers do the same thing plenty of times. It was that place they went before there was no rationing with them. Quasim stood to his feet and rushed out the restaurant behind his brother and Goon while all of us ladies remained under the table.

"Blair, are you good?" I knew how sis got whenever shots rang out and I wanted to make sure that she was alright.

"I'm good, Pri... we need to get out of here though."

"I agree. Last thing either of us want is to be here when the cops arrive," Zoya said, as she slowly stood up. "It happened so fast that I didn't get the chance to pull my gun out."

"Me either," I admitted. Quasim got us down onto the floor so quick that I didn't have a chance to grab my purse.

"Everyone please relax... I'm a US Marshall, and I am getting the local law enforcement here now," Jesse made the announcement from under the table.

"Back exit is near the bathrooms... my car is parked on the next block in a lot," Blair said, as we grabbed our shit.

"Where are you going? You need to stay here," Jesse said, grabbing my arm like I was gonna stay to be questioned.

That was like getting in a dolphin tank with a condom. I wasn't about to stick around and have them asking me a million questions that I would never answer.

"I'm getting the fuck out of here, Jesse. You stay here and play cop if you want to."

Brandi nodded her head in agreement. "Me too... I have a daughter that I need to get home to." She shoved her clutch under her arm and followed behind us.

POW! POW! POW!

A series of gunshots rang out again, and we ducked down while moving quicker through the restaurant until we were in the back near the bathrooms.

"You sure we should go out there?" Brandi asked.

"*We?*" Blair voiced.

No matter how I felt about this bitch, she was Peach's mama, and I loved that little girl so much. I would never want anything to happen to her mother, and I knew Meer wouldn't want that to happen, either.

As I was about to reply, my phone rang, and it was Meer's name that came across the screen. "Meer... are you alright?"

"Sug, get the fuck outta there now... come out the back... Goon coming around for you."

"Okay."

"Love you, baby," he said.

"Meer, you gotta baby on the way and Peach... you better be fucking careful." Even though my heart was beating, I knew we handled shit.

It was different when we were holding shit down alongside each other. Once kids and a future were introduced, it made this scarier. I understood what Erin meant every time she made Capone promise to come home to them.

"Got you, Suga."

I pulled my gun out and cocked it back, while Zoya did the same thing. When we came out the back door, Meer's truck had bent the block through the back alley of the restaurant. We all ran and got into the truck.

I usually struggled getting up into this shit, but today I hopped my ass in the front seat while Zoya, Blair, and Brandi got into the back. "You good, wifey?"

Zoya rolled her eyes. "Gerald, please."

On the opposite side of the alley, there were dirt bikes coming down the back, and Goon put the truck in reverse, as he backed out the way he came. "Handle that, Pri."

I leaned out the window and hit one of their wheels, which made his bike fall from underneath him. The other one was so busy looking at the way his homie was on the floor howling that I hit him in the chest, and he went over the handlebars.

No sooner than we whipped out, Meer came down on a dirt bike, hitting a wheelie as he saluted Goon. There was a bunch of

Chrome Vipers following behind him, while Quasim made his way through, putting a gun to one of their heads and pulling the trigger that quick. Sim had the look of death on his face as he did each Chrome Viper in.

"Fuck it," Goon said, and he turned on the block, driving right into the CV's on the bike. Quasim moved out the way and nodded while he pushed forward to where his brother was. I watched as Meer was standing up on the bike, as he was gaining on the car.

RA TATAT!

Goon looked out the rearview mirror as he turned onto Malcolm X Blvd., and both me and Zoya stuck our guns out the window. "I got the shot, Pri."

Zoya held her gun with one hand and let it go, hitting the window of the car following us. "What the fuck, Zoya?" Brandi screamed, which killed me.

"Shut the fuck up, Brandi... damn!" I hollered, as I caught the nigga on the bike behind the car.

Blair was turned in the seat so she could look out the back window. "Zoy, right there... coming through the school play yard." She pointed to one of the niggas on the dirt bike.

Goon had turned onto Macdonough Street. On one side there was a school with a huge concrete play yard for the kids, and then on the other side there were town houses with stoops. The men that were on the stoop had run inside the house the minute we turned onto the block.

Before Zoya could get him, I lit his ass up before having to reload. Goon paused as he watched the mirrors and saw the cars and bikes coming onto the block. "Yo, Pri... get in the driver seat and go... you hear me?"

I finished loading my gun and pushed it into his hands. "Take my gun, too, Goon."

The Gods all took an oath to lay down and die for their gang if need be. He realized that he couldn't get us out of here without hopping out the whip to distract them. He reached down and picked up his second gun.

"Gerald, hell no… you stay in this car."

He hopped out the truck, and I climbed over while Blair climbed into the front seat. "Awe, you care about me, Ms. Lawyer… I'mma see you, and when I do you owe me a date."

One second, he was sweet and tender, then the next this look entered his eyes, and he started letting his shit go at the cars. As I was about to gun it, I saw Capp's bike turn the corner with Capone's car behind him.

Both of them, no matter what, was gonna come through for the other. "Get the fuck outta here, Baby Doll… now." He didn't give a fuck where he aimed, he was letting it go with Capone behind him doing the same. Goon hopped into Capone's whip as he hung out the window wiping out anybody that came down that block.

Meer's truck was so big and intimidating, but I hit that gas and sped the fuck off the block. Goon's plan had worked because nobody was following behind us.

When my phone rang, I damn near broke a nail trying to pick it up because I thought it was Meer. "Go through Manhattan and take the tunnel into Jersey… gonna make sure the cameras have some difficulties," Core said. "Grasshopper… you got it?"

"Trying to get in now," Aimee was on three-way with him.

"Digital plates… need y'all to get some cause wiping out these cameras ain't easy," he snickered, knowing he was bullshitting.

"You could do this in your sleep," Aimee laughed.

"Yeah, you right."

"How…how did you know?"

He laughed. "Big bro' decided to call me on that phone again… the restaurant's security is on one of those cheap ass online security systems, so it was easy to erase everything that happened before and after the shooting… don't even have evidence that you were at lunch."

I was glad that I didn't put the call on speaker because of Brandi's ass in the back. "Perfect."

"In… you're good, Pri."

"Good looks, Grasshopper... let Zoya know her brother is already clued in."

"You already know." I could hear how proud Aimee was, and I was prouder of her than she was.

"Thanks, guys." I ended the call and continued into Manhattan and then into the tunnel.

Zoya put her gun away and relaxed in the back. "What a day to be going through the tunnel... free fucking toll. Why don't I ever get this lucky when I'm taking the tunnel?"

I smirked as I maneuvered through the tunnel because it had Core and Aimee written all over. When we got to end of the tunnel and came out on the Jersey side. Where it usually said stay in lane, it now said *you're leaving The Jungle.*

I pulled up at *Fern* and the minute I pulled up Havoc, another Inferno God, came out. Right behind him Papa came out and had the look of death in his eyes. The same look that his sons wore when those shots rang out.

"Take Brandi home... I got them," he ordered.

Havoc saluted, and helped Brandi out the truck, and walked over toward his truck. "Hey Papa, how are you doing?" Brandi greeted, clearly shaken up and confused.

"Keep that mouth shut or you won't be doing good... this never happened, Brandi."

She slowly nodded her head and allowed Havoc to help her into his truck. Papa kissed both my cheeks and gave me a look over. "You alright? You not hurt, right?"

"I'm alright... everything happened so fast."

"Meer called me and told me to come here... he knew you would be heading here." Papa held the door opened for us, as we walked into the bar.

I was surprised that the early birds that frequented the bar weren't here having their morning pick me up. Papa went behind the bar and got us something to drink, handing me a ginger ale before he leaned on the back bar, and looked at us.

"They tried that shit while you're carrying an Inferno... Blaze isn't going to rest until they're handled."

"Have you heard from him?"

"Not yet. You know how this goes... he'll call when he's somewhere safe away from everything."

Zoya ignored the call from her brother for the third time since we sat at the bar. "You need to answer and let him know that you are safe."

"Oh, he knows already. Not much happens without Menace knowing about it. He's calling to do his usual lecture about me moving smarter than the average, like I knew there would be a shootout during lunch."

I noticed how she picked in her nails. "He's going to be alright."

"What are you talking about, Pri?"

I nudged her. "Goon will be fine."

She laughed while swatting me away. "I am not worried about Gerald. He knows how to handle himself."

Papa's phone rang and he answered while nodding and agreeing to everything that was said over the phone. "Bet... lay low. You know the deal... too hot... yeah. I know you don't like it, but you gotta do what needs to be done... I will."

He ended the call and looked at me. "He's safe and is going to sit up because shit was too hot."

"Then I'll go to him."

Papa offered me a weak smile. "Can't do that, Pri... the guys are going to lay low away from home. Nothing can come back to them."

I didn't like that I couldn't see Quameer after everything that happened. All I wanted to do was see him. "I don't like it."

"We gotta move different now... can't move the same since we know everything that's going on. He gonna be good, and so are you. Blaze told me to make sure that you eat something."

"Leave it to him to turn this around on me." I smiled, already missing my baby, and counting down until I could see him.

Papa turned on the TV over the bar and flipped the channels until he made it to the news. The news reporters and news trucks were all on the scene standing in front of the yellow tape.

"We're in Bed-Stuy at the scene and everything is a bit blurry on what has gone down here at the scene. We're hearing motorcycles and cars came through shooting up the popular social media known brunch spot."

"Shit was fucking wild... niggas came through like ahh, ahh, ahh... one nigga was on the hood of a whip letting his shit go screaming fuck you meannnnn!" one man snatched the microphone and was hype about what he had witnessed.

"Gerald," Zoya snickered.

Blair laughed. "Fuck you meannnn."

"Swear that boy came out the womb saying it." Papa chuckled, as he switched the channel. Vincent Morgan appeared on the television, not wasting a second to look like the good candidate that loved his city.

"The violence in this city has been at an all-time high, and I promise if you elect me in, I will put a stop to that. Including opening up old cases that were closed without proper due diligence. We will make this city safe again and put away the men that are ripping it apart, one by one." I got a chill when he looked into the camera. It was like he was staring directly at me as he said those words.

Papa turned the TV off. "I'm going to bring you back to the lake house, and you girls can come, too. None of you should be alone tonight."

> Me: Love you, Meer.

> Meer Cat: Love you more, Suga... see you soon.

It had been a week since I saw Meer, Sim, or my brothers. Alaia and Erin went on like usual, knowing their role. I should have known mine, but I missed talking to him. I wanted him in bed with me at night, not stashed away somewhere until shit died down.

With how much went down, the city was on a spiral wondering how something like that could have happened without them knowing who was responsible. They wanted whoever was responsible now and weren't going to stop until they had any leads. The guys were tucked away, so we knew they were safe.

> 40: *Location pinned* meet me here. Your brothers are meeting tonight. You need to be here. ... memorize the address cause it's gonna disappear in a few.

I looked at the address and repeated it in my head over and over before I watched it vanish before my eyes. We were sitting in the backyard watching the kids play in the splash pad that Cappadonna had set up for them. Alaia and Erin were both staring at me.

I reacted to the text and put my phone away. "Why are you both staring at me like that?"

"Cause you've been so quiet since the guys went into hiding. Always to yourself, checking your phone since Meer had to get rid of his phone," Alaia was the first to say.

"Just processing everything. I'm about to be a mother... how the fuck are you both so calm not knowing where your husbands is?"

"I knew what I signed on for when I married your brother. My role is his wife and doing whatever I need to protect him. I don't like him not being with me, but I sleep well knowing he's safe and not behind bars."

Erin looked at Alaia. "Alaia is stronger than me because I cry every morning in the shower. It's been a week, and I can't even imagine ever doing this because he was sent away."

"Going to do everything in my power to make sure that never happens."

Alaia looked at me. "What do you know?"

"What do you mean?"

She pursed her lips, exposing her dimples. "You know something. They keep you more in the loop than us."

"Forty texted me and said Core is going to meet the twins tonight and said I should be there."

"Anytime Forty appears, that means he has some news. I'm going," Erin said.

Who was I to tell them that they couldn't come. They were just as involved in this as the twins, and as their wives, they should know what was going on and not be left in the dark.

"Me too."

"My brothers are going to be on my neck about you two coming," I laughed.

"Fuck 'em... they can be mad, but we haven't seen them in a week, and I need to know what the hell is going on," Alaia shrugged.

The back door opened, and my mother came out. "Hey Nana's babies!" she went right to the kids and kissed them all before she came over to sit with us.

Ever since the brunch, my mother avoided me and refused to speak to me. I was so over her silent treatment that there was a part of me that wanted to bend and say sorry. Even though I wasn't sorry about anything, I wanted to get rid of this tension that arrived anytime we were around each other.

That had always been our relationship since I was a teen. I would stand up for myself and she would become upset and shut me out. The silent treatment and the passive aggressive behavior always followed. To avoid us walking around slamming things, I always went and apologized, even though I never felt wrong for my actions.

"Ma, can you watch the kids for us tonight? We have to do something with Capri tonight," Erin asked.

Jo was staying at Ryai and Big Mike's house on countdown for her grandbaby. It had been mostly Erin holding down the house alone when she usually had help. I was impressed with how she was able to handle both her kids, who were both young and still needed her full attention.

She did it like it was no sweat off her back and it was something that I commended her for. I was scared to become a mother, and worried if I would do this shit wrong. It would be added to the long list of things that I couldn't get right.

Like being a wife.

"You don't even have to ask me to watch my grandbabies." She looked over at me. "You can't say hello to your mother, Shelly Ann?"

Whenever she was pissed with me, she always called me by my middle name, and I hated it. "Hi Mommy."

"Hmph."

Alaia and Erin looked between both of us, unsure on what to say. They never knew if they should get involved or mind their business. I honestly liked that they didn't get involved because it would have made it worse. She would accuse me of corrupting her perfect daughter-in-laws.

"You got the same text?" Aimee came outside with Rory on her hip. He was going through a phase where all he wanted was his mother.

"Yeah."

"How is my grandchild? Are you taking care of yourself and eating enough?" my mother questioned.

"I'm eating when I feel like it," I responded honestly.

Anytime some shit was going on eating was the last thing that I ever wanted to do. I knew that I had to eat for this baby, so Gams forced me to eat. "You need to eat more for the baby. I'll make some oxtail for you. I know that's one of your favorites."

I guess this was her olive branch and I should have been grateful that she was even offering. If I had to bet, I knew my father got in her ass for the way she acted with me. Especially in front of everyone.

"Thank you, Mommy."

"And we need to get busy on planning this wedding. Unlike

the other one, you will walk down the aisle and do it right on our beach."

Getting married on our family's beach had been a dream of mine. I wanted to experience all the good luck that both Erin and Alaia had within their marriages. I remember being there for both of them and seeing how the love radiated from them on their special days.

I wanted to experience that on my special day. The love that I had witnessed on those days and continued to experience from my brothers and wives is why I didn't rule love out when everything inside of me was telling me that I should.

"She has so much on her plate that I don't even think she thought about the wedding," Erin jumped in.

"Me and your father are set to fly back to the island soon. I will start the preparations, so you don't have to worry about it."

Alaia looked at me and smirked. "Ma, are you trying to say sorry? You can just say sorry, too."

Mommy pursed her lips and looked at Alaia. "Girl hush. You need to make a doctor's appointment for the baby too. Where are you going to live with the baby?"

"Mommy, let her breathe," Erin laughed while leaning her head on her shoulder. "She just found out like three minutes ago. She and Quameer will work on all of that in due time."

"And your land on the compound?"

"I don't know, Mommy... I'm trying to figure everything out now. I promise soon as me and Meer figure things out, I will let everybody in America know."

"Don't get snippy, Shelly Ann." She stood up and gave each of us a kiss on the cheek before she headed toward the door. "Bring the babies before you leave."

Aimee was able to successfully put Rory on the splash pad with his cousins and aunt, before taking a seat next to me. "Doing this solo parenting has been damn hard."

"Tell me about it," Alaia agreed.

Erin laid back on the couch. "I want my man... and you hoes know how."

I squeezed my legs together knowing how Big Pa was gonna give it up when he finally got me alone. "Ew, I don't want to hear that."

"Says the hoe who was getting her shit cracked and answered the phone. Capone is scarred, Capri... he refuses to call you."

I slid down the couch laughing, and Cee-Cee ran over because she thought something was wrong with me. "I'm...I'm okay, baby," I laughed so hard.

She kissed my nose and then ran back to the water while I continued to laugh. "You and Meer look like you both finished fucking when you came over for the brunch."

"And did." I snickered.

"That's why you knocked up. Went away for a year, and came home and he was ready for you... I'm really happy for you, Pri," Alaia said.

I smiled. "He told me to go away for me and to be prepared for whatever when I came back. Truthfully, I was ready for whatever with him before coming back. Meer refused to cross those lines though."

"He wanted to make sure you were ready. Meer's a good one, Pri." Erin smiled.

"He is. I'm about to go shower, then take a little hour nap before we leave. Alaia drive Capp's truck tonight."

"Okay. We all riding together?"

"I'm riding my bike."

"Gotcha... see you in a little bit."

Soon as I walked into the house, I kissed Mina's forehead and then went into the kitchen with Gams. She was in the kitchen snapping green beans for dinner. My kitchen had been getting used since she and Mina had been with me.

The week away from Meer would have been torture if I didn't have them here with me. I enjoyed sitting with Gams and watching reality TV, or junk like she called it. She loved watching it, but called it junk at the same time.

"Protein smoothie and some cookies for you." She pushed

the plate of cookies toward me, and then went into the fridge for the smoothie.

She shook it up and then put it in front of me. "Thank you, Gams. Are you alright?"

Gams was the center of her family and took care of everyone. She made sure everyone was alright, and her family did pour back into her. Still, at times you could forget to check in with people, and I always wanted to make sure to check in with her.

"I'm doing perfectly fine. Worried about my grandsons, but I am doing alright. How have you been? Notice you haven't been sleeping."

"Hard to sleep without Meer next to me," I admitted.

"Ohh, you got it bad," she snickered. "Don't worry, he has it just as bad as you do... I know he probably driving himself nuts without seeing you."

"You think?"

"I know so. Quinton was the same with my Mina when they first got together. He's still like that with her... can never stay away from her for too long. Never too far, always right there." She offered a weak smile.

Papa and Mina's story was one that I wished I could have witnessed before her diagnosis. Then again, I didn't have to witness it then, because I was able to see it now. Mina knew her husband, and the way she clung to him when he was around showed just how much she loved him, and how much he loved her.

"Yeah."

She pushed the protein drink more toward me. "Drink it. Meer may not be around right now, but I know he would be on you to eat some food."

I took a long sip of the protein drink and bit a cookie. "I'm gonna eat. I promise, Gams. I have something to do tonight so I'm gonna shower and take a little nap." Gams smiled and nodded while continuing to snap the green beans.

CHAPTER 5
CAPRI

I WHIPPED my bike in front of Alaia, as we merged through the toll entering Staten Island. Alaia was right behind me with Erin as she whipped her husband's truck with ease. She had come a long way from her learner's permit.

Aimee held onto me as we whipped through the streets, bypassing the store that Meer took me to get a chopped cheese from. I should have known that nigga wanted me with the way he slammed the chip rack on that man's head for even speaking to me.

Even with the windows up, I could hear the base and music coming from the truck with Alaia and Erin. I could tell they were taking this mommy's night out seriously with the way they were ready to leave before me.

Soon as we made it to the block, I saw a bunch of bikes and cars everywhere. Niggas was everywhere and looking at us when we turned onto Holland Avenue. When I looked the address up, the area was called Arlington. Alaia pulled behind me as we slowly made it down the block. The block was so packed with people enjoying the night and having a good time with drinks and their bikes.

The corner store was the location that Forty had sent me, so I pulled up on the sidewalk and put my feet down on the ground.

Alaia hit a U-turn until she was on the same side of the street and double parked. Cappadonna was standing outside the corner store and looked like he was seeing a ghost when we pulled up.

Capone came out the store smashing down a hero, and paused when he saw his wife hop out the truck. Nigga shoved his sandwich to the nigga next to him and went right to his wife, picking her up and kissing her all over.

"I fucking missed you, Gorgeous!"

"Missed you so much, Winnie... the kids miss you, too." Erin was all over her husband, and I smiled because the love they had made your heart warm.

Since they had gotten together, they hadn't spent much time away from each other. Same with Alaia, who came around the truck and rushed into her husband's arm who squeezed the shit out of her. Cappadonna wasn't affectionate with his wife in public, but seeing how he had his tongue down her throat and hugging her tightly let me know he missed her just as much as she missed him.

"Honey!" Aimee squealed and hopped off the bike, and into my nephew's arms when she saw him coming down the block.

She jumped right into his arms and was kissing him all over his face. "I missed you, too, Aim... missed your scent." Capella kissed her on the lips while holding her as he continued walking closer to the store.

"Where's Meer?" I asked, as I sat my helmet on my bike. Everyone was so into loving on their person that they didn't pay me any attention.

"Up the block at the crib," Quasim came out the store with a bag of chips and leaned on the ice chest. "I see you... you got good on your bike, Pri."

I smiled. "I know a little something now... I'm not of Goddess status now."

"You'll get there... I can bet on that." He nodded.

I turned around to address my brothers and saw Meer walking down the block. His hoodie was over his locs, as he made his way down the block not even clued in that I was here. He looked up, and that's when he saw me.

The way I bolted down the rest of the block to meet him should have been recorded and submitted to the Olympics. As much as I made fun of Aimee for jumping in her man's arms, I leaped on Meer like an actual meercat.

"My fucking Suga... the fuck you doing here, baby?" He kissed me on the lips so many times that I couldn't even respond to him.

Each time I tried to speak, he would pull on my lips and suck on them. Everyone had got their greetings, and all eyes were on us as I giggled while he continued to give me soft pecks as he held me up.

"Forty told me to pull up... I missed you, Meer."

"Baby, you don't even fucking know the half... I was about to fucking dip and take my chances to see you. Yo' hating ass brother hid the fucking keys to the whip." He side-eyed Capone who shrugged.

"Chill the fuck out. If I can be away from my seeds for a week, you can handle not seeing my sister for a week. You both need a fucking break... fucking freaks." Capone pulled Erin closer to him and kissed her lips.

"Big Mama missed you," I whispered into his ear, and he held me tighter, kissing me on my neck while sitting me on the ice freezer outside the store.

"Trust I'm gonna fuck the shit out of you, Suga... I'm gonna handle that." He kissed me while whispering in my ear, sending chills up my back.

Cappadonna looked at us while he had his arms wrapped around Alaia. "I'm taking that blessing back."

"Capp, she carrying my seed and wearing my ring, ain't no going back, nigga."

"You carrying this nigga's seed, Pri?" We all turned our heads, and I spotted Naheim walking beside Goon. They were all coming from one of the houses further up the block that we had passed on the way down.

Meer bit the inside of his cheek as he turned around while remaining in front of me. "Why the fuck you wanna know?"

Naheim ignored Meer and looked directly into my eyes. "Capri, answer me... you didn't keep mine, but you fucking keeping his."

Aimee gasped and slapped her hand over her mouth while Meer looked at me and saw my face. He rubbed his hands together as he made his way over toward Naheim, who stood tall, not backing down. "Blaze," Quasim called.

Before anyone of us could react, he punched Naheim in the face and started beating the shit out of him. Naheim stammered back and got a lick in, but Meer was all over him like white on rice.

"Fuck nigga... that's *my* fucking wife... telling her fucking... business," he said while throwing punches left and right.

Naheim got up and staggered for a bit, and then he tossed a hit, and Quameer slammed his ass on his ass, and then held him in a headlock. "Let me the fuck go."

"Fucking apologize to her... who the fuck raised yo' stupid ass? Let me tell you something, that's mine... my fucking wife and unlike you, I ain't letting up on her... she trusted you with something and you fucking told the whole block, bitch." He continued to squeeze his neck while waiting for him to apologize.

"Nigga, fuck you!"

"Bet." Quameer went to slam his head against Capp's truck, but Capone and Cappadonna jumped in.

Cappadonna had to pull Quameer from Naheim because he was trying to take his fucking head off. "Chill... you stood on business for Baby Doll... don't kill this nigga," Capp laughed.

My chest tightened when he revealed what I had told him. A few months into my travels, I sat down and penned a letter to Naheim. It was my farewell letter, the letter that put that nail in the coffin, ended that last chapter with us, and I needed him to know how I felt. I wanted to get everything out so I could truly move on with my life.

The year I was taking for me wouldn't have made sense if I continued to sit in all my feelings. Journaling and getting my feelings on pages had been a big help for me, so I was sending a letter to Naheim to let him know exactly how I felt without the screaming, glassware breaking, and name calling. I wanted him to know that the time we shared would always be one I held close, but we had to both move on.

Even now, I knew a friendship with Naheim was a bad mistake. How could I have a friendship with someone that would scream out something I told him in confidence? He told everyone in front of this store something that I hadn't told anyone. Only reason he knew was because I felt like he deserved to know.

I was wrong.

Meer's chest was heaving up and down as he looked like a lunatic in the eyes. "Chill out, nigga... you straight. Naheim, remember when you wanted to do that to me?" Kincaid broke out into laughter. "For real... congrats, Pri! Blessings for a safe and healthy pregnancy."

"Fuck you, Kincaid!" Naheim barked, while Capone continued to push him away, so he wouldn't try for round two.

"Meer Cat," I called, and even with all the chaos going on, his eyes found mine and I motioned for him to come to me.

He pulled his pants up as he strolled over toward me. Kissing the side of his face, I held onto him. "Nigga sick as shit... get the fuck off by trying to hurt you... that fuck shit ends now... anybody try to hurt my fucking wife, and I'm fucking killing you!" he hollered over at Naheim who tried to get around Capone.

"Say that shit over here."

Meer went to run back over there, but Kincaid jumped in front of him and pushed him back toward me. "Chill the fuck out, Rocky... Pri, keep his ass over here."

"Thanks, Kincaid," I smiled.

I pulled Meer between my legs and wrapped my legs around

him while pulling his locs up into a bun. "You ready to be a daddy again?"

I needed to say anything to get his ass to calm down because he was watching Naheim like a hawk, and he wanted to go over there and do his ass in again.

"More than ready... spent my week away from you thinking about how many more I'm gonna put in you," he said, halfway in our conversation and tuned into Naheim and the show he was putting on.

"Capp you bullshit, man... you allowed that shit to happen! Taking fucking sides, nigga." Capp looked at him, and Alaia stood in front of her husband knowing how once Capp was on, none of us would be able to calm his ass down.

"Naheim, you need to chill the fuck out. Capri is his baby sister, and if you want my opinion, it's about time that Capri is being protected. You told her fucking business and want us all to be on your side... that's crazy," Erin said and mushed him.

He hung his head, realizing that she was right. "Fuckkkkk!"

"You meannn," Goon snickered.

Capone grabbed Erin's hand and let the nigga get out his frustrations out as he headed up the block punching himself in the head.

"Now go take a nap before I beat yo' ass again!" Meer yelled behind him.

I pulled Meer's head back until he was staring up at me. "Stop it, Baby."

"Fuck him... we got beef though, 'cause you ain't told me that."

I caressed his face. "We will have that conversation."

"Ya'll wild as shit over this way," we all turned our heads to Core leaned against the side of Capp's truck watching everything unfold.

So much had happened that we didn't notice this nigga pop up. "Just because you a secret don't mean you gotta move like one," Capp was the first to speak, as he looked at Core.

"Jesus," Erin gasped while looking at him.

Core resembled both of the twins, but he and Cappy could have been almost identical if he had been born a few years earlier. "What up, Capri?" He nodded.

"Hey Core." At this point, I was very familiar with my new older brother. He was still a mystery to everyone else, but I felt like I had known him for years already.

"Quameer."

"What up?" Meer nodded; his head still rested back on my thighs.

Cappadonna was the first to step forward, while Capone followed behind him. He held his hand out, and Core went to dap him, but Cappadonna pulled him into a hug. "I don't…" he choked on his words.

Corleon tossed his arms around his big brother, and Capp held his head, kissing it while squeezing him tight. "Baby, don't smother him now." Alaia wiped her own tears and giggled.

"It's like looking in pop's eyes… shit got me bugged out." He finally released Corleon who had tears in his own eyes.

"I'm not here on no drama shit… just want to get to know my family and figure out some shit about me."

Even though Corleon was nearly as tall as the twins, he was a few inches shorter than them. Capone grabbed him up and they both stumbled but remained hugging each other. "You been running with Menace; I know you trustworthy, Son-Son."

"Another brother… great," I joked, and they turned toward me.

Meer picked me up and put me back onto the ground, and I walked over toward my brothers, and they pulled me into the middle of them. If you were walking by, you wouldn't have even noticed I was in the middle of them.

"Nobody was fucking with Capri before, but they really not now that she got three brothers running behind her and a crazy ass fiancé," Goon barked, while clapping his hands.

CHAPTER 6
CAPELLA

FORTY WAS ALREADY in the house when we finally made it back up the block. Everyone was still drinking and chilling on the block like usual. Being in this crib for the past week with my father, Capone, Quameer, Quasim, Goon, and Kincaid had been fucking hell.

Between Capone's snores sounding like he was the fucking R train, and Goon and my pops getting up at the ass crack of dawn to work out and pray. Since we couldn't leave the crib, they would run up and down the damn stairs at five in the morning. Imagine them two big ass niggas bolting up and down the damn stairs before the sun was up. If that wasn't enough, my father thought making that prison slop was better. None of us, and I mean none of us ate that shit.

Then you had Quameer's ol lovesick ass sleeping all damn day because he missed Capri. I shared a room with him, and I promise I wasn't going to look at my aunt the same with him calling her Big Mama in his sleep. If I didn't know any better, Kincaid was enjoying the space from Jasmine. His ass seemed too damn happy to be locked down with the rest of us instead of home with his girl and son.

Jasmine was private with her relationship with Kincaid, so I didn't get involved. I had enough shit going on keeping my own relationship afloat, so I didn't give a fuck about anybody else's.

The only normal one, and I use normal loosely, was Quasim. The nigga didn't wake up too early, he kept to himself and read his Bible on his phone in the morning. A few times I saw him looking at a selfie of him and Blair in the back of a car.

I wasn't going to clown him because Sim seemed like he should have been committed. While Quameer was that loud crazy, this nigga was the silent crazy, which was deadly. Naheim was in and out because he was bringing us shit that we needed. I was glad that he didn't have to stay under the same roof with us, because I was sure that Meer would have slit his throat while we were all sleeping.

When I saw my baby running toward me, I thought I had died and went to heaven. I needed to get the fuck away from everybody. When Forty called and told us we could move around, I was the first one out the house and walking around the block just to get some fresh air. This was all new to us, because after we caused mayhem, we went on with our lives like nothing happened.

New levels called for new measures, and I would do anything to make sure we all remained out of prison.

"Glad to see we are all acquainted." Forty smirked. "Nice to meet you in person, Corleon." He nodded.

"Likewise, Fuquan." Core smirked.

"The fuck? All these years and I never knew your name, but this nigga gets to know it?" Capone laughed.

Forty looked at Core and laughed. "I see you've done your research, too."

"Come on, I'm always gonna do that…I've been briefed on what it is that we're doing… so what's the next move?"

"How do we even know we can trust this nigga? I don't care if he look like you two, we need to make sure we not letting another snake in our camp." Kincaid was the first to speak up.

"Do you think it was a coincidence that none of you were ever caught on cameras in Philly? I made it where nothing came back to none of you... I erased that. I've been watching and keeping my eyes on you all... waiting for the moment I could step to my siblings and let them know about me. I'm loyal... you got Menace's number... hit him up."

"Nigga kept my baby straight, so he good in my book," Meer dapped Core, as he held Capri closer to him.

Cappadonna took a seat on the couch next to Forty, while we all found spots to post up in, to get this meeting over.

"Forty, why didn't you tell me about Tasha." Capri stood there with her arms crossed, while eyeing Forty down.

"Above me... didn't find out until your text. Looked into some shit and keep coming up blank. Whatever reason she is out, is some top-secret shit which I admit, makes me nervous. It shows she is still in custody, and we know she's not. The plan will continue as planned, but we will pivot a bit... no plan is ever concrete, so this one is the same. From what I see, she's keeping a low profile. Only around with Morgan when he's campaigning and events."

"She knows too fucking much, Forty... we gotta end her," Capone said.

"Should have fucking did that before," my pops mumbled.

Forty ignored both of them. "Aimee, darling, you got something important to do."

Aimee sat up and clued into what Forty was about to say. "What do you need me to do?"

"Dating Morgan. He likes young... for the lack of a better word, bitches... and although you aren't a bitch, you will play that role."

"Well damn, Forty," I said.

"No disrespect. It's been known that Morgan loves younger bitches... as he calls them." He snapped his fingers. "You have no connections to the Delgatos, you are young and in college... take it from here, Core," Forty directed.

"Grasshopper, Morgan is going to be a guest professor in some politics bullshit class at your college... tapped into your school's website and was able to get it on your schedule. You're gonna make yourself seen… make sure he notices you."

"Okay, and once he does?"

"Yeah… I'm not really feeling y'all trying to pimp my girl out." I wrapped my arms around Aimee, as she laughed.

"Everybody has a part to play in this… I know how you would handle this in the streets, but we doing this different. Aimee will be able to get in on the inside, make this nigga comfortable. Baby Doll will go in and see what the fuck they have. They announced opening that judge's case… we need Capri on the inside to find out what they know. Remove some evidence, shake some shit up. Keep an eye on Rich Parker." He winked at Capri. "She will handle shit and let us know what we're looking at… Tasha and ADA Browne will never cross paths, and we will make sure of this."

"The fuck you mean Tasha?" Naheim finally joined us. His face was all greasy like he went and put a bunch of ointment on the bruises that started to settle in.

"Tasha is out," Capri told him, as we watched all the emotion drain from his face. "She's engaged to Morgan."

Naheim looked like he was about to take a shit on himself. "I need to get NJ somewhere safe… I don't fucking trust her ass not to try and get him."

"Hit Nellie and she can bring him to my crib with Rory. Until all of this is handled, he can be tucked away safely."

"Me and Nellie broke up."

No matter how anybody felt about Naheim, we all loved NJ and never wanted anything to happen to him. Despite being a sucky ass husband, he was a good father, and I understood that love a father had for his son.

"This nigga," Kincaid muttered.

"I will have Jo pick him up and bring him with her to the lake house," Erin said, as she pulled her phone out.

"Good looks. ADA Browne?"

"NJ will be in foster care if you think any deeper into the name… that last name 'bout to be Inferno."

Capri laughed and pulled his beard. "Meer... focus."

Naheim wanted to slide down that wall hollering with how he looked at Capri and Quameer. Meer wasn't letting up on letting him know that this was going to be his wife. "You wish that was you don't you?" Goon started laughing.

"Tasha threw a slight detour in our plan but that doesn't stop shit. The plan is still the same, we just needed to revise it." Forty clapped his hands and stood up, ready to disappear again. "Core go ahead and finish it off."

"Vanducci- Cromwell House is having their annual international race in Monaco this year. Case House does their annual client appreciation masquerade party at the same time, on a private island close by to the races. Morgan and every crooked ass official will be there with bitches that they paid out the ass for. Star Vanducci is headlining the race this year... her first year international. You all will receive digital invites and access into the party. Dress code is black tie."

"Bunch a hood ass niggas in suits," Goon laughed. "Too bad I'm on papers and can't leave the fucking country."

Corleon smirked, stroking his beard. It was fucking eerie how the twins did the same shit, and then my grandfather also did it. "Come on, G... I know people in high places that can get you in and out the country without anybody knowing you gone... we need all hands on deck that weekend."

"This about to be some James Bond type shit." I laughed.

Forty looked at all of us. "This shit isn't for the weak, and we about to go against some heavy hitters. This ain't the streets, these men already have the upper advantage on us. We're sending Baby Doll into the lion's den, expecting her to come out with their heads."

Aimee squeezed my hand and clung onto me, as Capri stood with her arms folded with this look of determination on her face. Her confidence oozed into the room, making me fucking proud.

"Bet I come out with 'em though."

"My fucking Suga."

Every time Meer mentioned Suga or wife, Naheim looked like he wanted to die a little bit on the inside.

"I will have everything in your email by the end of the week, and your start date... we're trying to get you in at the same time as Rich." He kissed the top of her head.

"Morgan is dying, Forty... no more loose fucking ends at the end of this." Capp looked up at Forty.

"Patience... we know the end game already... we're not only worried about Morgan. He has people that is helping him put shit in place, so we can't end them all. Some of them gotta be set up... let me handle that. Oh, and handle that nigga Shmurda, please. Those nasty ass Chrome Vipers riding around our city causing all these fucking problems isn't a good look. We got bigger fish to fry, and they ain't it."

"I agree... he need to be handled. He's something small to a giant," I agreed with him, as he headed toward the door.

"Delgato boys... I'll be in touch," Forty looked at Corleon, Cappadonna, and Capone before heading toward the door. Before he turned the doorknob, he looked at Capri. "Oh, Baby Doll... you gotta kill Jesse."

Capri froze as she locked eyes with Forty. "What?"

Core stepped forward with a folder in his hand. "Italy is the perfect time to do it." Core piggy backed onto what Forty had said, and she looked between both of them confused.

"How...how the hell did you get the folder?"

Core smirked. "I have my ways... this little shit seems nice... sounds perfect to get away... would you agree, Meer?"

"For sure."

"Jesse is dedicated to her career and wears that badge hard. If I thought, we could sway her... I would have tried. She's connected to her father, and although he wasn't shit, she's going to be loyal to him. Not to mention, since the shooting, she's been asking a lot of questions. While upstairs doesn't particularly fuck with me, they might listen to her because of who her father is, and the fact that he has a chance at becoming the fucking mayor... feelings on the dresser, and emotions tucked away in the closet. You need to end her." With that, he left out the door, as we all stared at Capri.

"Baby Dol—"

"I don't want to hear what I don't *have* to do, Cappy."

Capone stepped forward. "Capri, you're pregnant and that shit is selfish for us to put that on you... we got ourselves into this shit, we'll find a way to make sure shit goes in our favor."

Capri turned to face her brothers. "I know what I have to do. If you think I'm going to sit back and allow someone to tear our family apart again... you're fucking wrong. I was too young before, but they got the right one now... Jesse will be handled." She turned and headed out the house, and Meer was right behind her.

"Fuck she's intense... she ready for this, Capo," Pops said, his first words other than *I'll fuck you up* to his twin in weeks.

"We're ready for this," Alaia spoke. "My last name never meant shit to me before, but this one means the world to me... I know I handle home, but I'm doing whatever needs to be done to keep you in our home."

"Same here." Erin and Alaia both dapped each other up and turned to look at their husbands.

Aimee cleared her throat, walking into the middle of the room. It was like I was seeing her for the first time. She wasn't that timid girl I had fell for. Like Capri, her confidence had been boosted. "Capri is doing the impossible, and we gotta have her back. You all have made sure we know how to protect ourselves... now let us protect our men like you all protect us." She looked at all of us. "No matter how this goes down, we gonna come out on top."

As happy as I was to be back up at the lake house and in my bed with my girl, all that damn clacking on her computer keys had me tossing and turning. Every so often she would do a sigh or curse under her breath while doing something.

After the fourth *fuck*, I pulled the covers from my face and was actually gonna fuck her. If she wanted to be up, then she was going to get some dick. When I leaned up on the bed, I snatched the laptop and put it on the side table, while pulling her down onto the bed while she giggled.

"Honey, I need to finish this... Landon has me doing something for him."

All I ever heard was Landon, Landon, Landon from her mouth. First the nigga was helping her get money like I wasn't already providing for her, and now I had to hear about his ass while in our bed. I wasn't a jealous nigga by far, but something didn't sit right whenever Aimee brought him up.

I wanted to believe that Aimee wouldn't do me wrong like that. Everything about the way she moved didn't tell me she was cheating on me, and she was forthcoming with information when it came to him. Still, I guess that jealousy was growing stronger, and I was actually a jealous nigga. Maybe I was turning into my uncle and father.

"You can get back to that after I give you some dick... why you up so early anyway?" I kissed on her neck and tried to pull her shorts down and she grabbed onto my arms.

"Capella, no... I'm... I'm on my period," she blurted and tried to wiggle out of my arms, while I continued to suck on her neck, needing the release bad.

"Period don't stop shit but a sentence, Aim," I continued to kiss on her and pull the shorts down, and she slipped from underneath me.

"Not on my period, Honey." She stood up and fixed her shorts, and I looked at her ass funny.

"Since when you don't want me to slide in you when you're on your period?" Aimee was full of shit with how she was acting.

It wasn't like we fucked on her period often, but the minute we both was in the mood, I put that towel down and got down with my baby. Now she was over there standing like I wasn't the period warrior, and I didn't handle that shit when it was her time of the month.

"I can change my mind, Capella... it's heavy and I'm really not in the mood to deal with it." She walked over toward me and kissed me on the lips.

I stared at her, wishing I could read her mind. "You fucking around on me, Aim?"

She sucked her teeth. "Capella, I am not fucking around on you. Why is that your answer for everything? I told you that me and Landon are just friends, and he wouldn't cross those lines. I've been up with Rory half the night, and then had to do this... I'm fucking tired, Capella! Damn!" she screamed, snatching her laptop up and leaving the room, slamming the door in the process.

Rory had been going through a lot and I understood how stressed she was. He wasn't sleeping at night, and then during the day he would sleep on and off with little ass cat naps. I could see the tiredness in my boy's eyes when I held him.

Little shit that he used to love now freaked him out. The texture of his food sent him down a spiral and all he wanted to eat was pizza. While Promise and Cee-Cee were more outgoing, my boy was shy. He didn't like to do anything without his cousin and aunt, which is why they all went to the same swimming lesson together.

Aimee kept saying he was fine and that we didn't need to worry. Her ass always got defensive whenever I mentioned bringing it up to his pediatrician. She was acting like I was calling her a bad mother or some shit.

"Fuck," I groaned, pulling the pillow over my head before climbing out the bed and following behind her.

She was already down in her office by the time I made it down there. "Capella, I'm not in the mood right now... leave me alone."

"Why the fuck you acting different? If you don't want to set up Morgan, let somebody know and we'll adjust." I assumed she was acting this way before she had to go in and be Morgan's little shit.

Hell, I wasn't even a fan of the plan. Sending my girl into the lion's den with this nigga didn't seem like a good idea in my book. I had to trust that Forty knew what the fuck he was talking about.

"I'm not even worried about that. I will protect this family, Capella… whatever I have to do to make sure my father-in-law and son's grandfather isn't tossed back into prison is fine with me. I can take that… I just need fucking space and a break. I'm tired… I feel like I'm losing myself in motherhood. Rory is just," she broke down sobbing and I rushed behind the desk and held her in my arms.

"Aim you gotta talk to me, Baby," I held her face, kissing her lips as she continued to cry, and allowed me to hold her.

I picked her up and sat in the chair, putting her onto my lap. "Something is wrong, Capella. I know when you mention it, I make a fuss and blow up. I feel like something is wrong with my baby… he changed overnight, and I can't fix it."

I removed her hair from her face. "You don't need to fix shit alone, Aim. He has two parents and a whole family that loves him… you're not alone in this."

She laid her head on my shoulder as she continued to cry. I held her tightly, looking at the picture of Rory on her desk. I would do whatever to take the guilt away from her. Our baby boy was different, and that was alright.

Rory Delgato would always be good, and I could bet on that.

CHAPTER 7
JEAN

"DO you think I can be discharged after I have the baby? Are visitation hours allowed with the baby if I discharge myself?" I asked the nurse as she checked my vitals, while a contraction ripped through my lower half. I was in so much pain and couldn't focus on that because I had twin boys at home with my neighbor.

My crack addicted neighbor. She was the best bet that I had when my water broke, and my contractions came back-to-back. I couldn't call on Des because he was locked up, so I had to handle this on my own. I took the bus and train to Brookdale hospital while in active labor.

A mother's determination and love was so strong that she could get through anything. As I laid in this bed, alone, about to have my third baby, I was scared. Worried about my two boys at home who didn't know what was going on. They both looked so scared when water came from between my legs onto our shag carpet.

Capone nor Cappadonna knew that I was pregnant. I kept telling them that Mommy was fat, and Daddy was away in the army. It would have broken my heart to tell them where their father really was. Luckily, when I brought them to visit, I always played a game, telling them that daddy had to wear those clothes and be in that place because he was training for the army.

We had never planned to have another baby. It was hard enough trying to feed the twins, and then we went ahead and made another one. I didn't believe in abortions and felt like God would continue to punish me if I went and got an abortion. He clearly had given me this baby for a reason, so who was I to kill this creation?

"She's ready to push right now." The nurse started pulling the stirrups out and placing my feet there, while the other one ran to grab the doctor and prep the room.

"Al...already?" I stammered.

"This baby is ready to see this world, Mama." She smiled at me.

I held onto the bar on the bed, closed my eyes and prayed for my family and my husband. "Des, I need you baby."

Des had always been there. Every time I needed him, he was there. A man that had been about his word and been there for me. I never had to question his motives because he was a man of his word.

"Come on, mama... he's right there," the nurse coached while the second one held my hand and gave me a squeeze.

I pushed so hard and then relaxed. The minute I relaxed, the doctor pulled my baby out of me and held him up. I smiled seeing him, while they cleared his airway, and wrapped him up before putting him on my chest.

"A beautiful baby boy... does he have a name?"

"Corleon Alphonso Delgato." I kissed his head as he stared me in the eyes.

"Plum, you're burning the rice," I heard Des's voice and snapped out of my head and turned the fire on the stove down.

He stood by the fridge while staring at me. His look had always been so damn intense, and made you want to tell him all of your deep and dark secrets. It didn't help that he passed that look onto our boys. Imagine a damn toddler staring at you with those eyes, making you want to tell them where you hid their Christmas gifts.

I looked away while looking in the pot to see if I could save any of the rice that I had burned while deep in my thoughts. The rice wasn't the best, so I pushed it away, and checked on the oxtail.

Pulling out the rice to wash and remake another pot, I felt Desmond's arms around me, pulling me away from the pantry and kissing me on the neck. "You need to stop beating yourself up about this, Plum."

He had always called me plum since we were younger. My favorite fruit was a plum, and he swore I tasted just like one. The kids never knew the actual meaning of the nickname, and I was glad that they didn't.

"All of this is my fault."

"How the fuck do you figure, Jean? It takes two to make a baby."

"And one to make a decision that altered that boy's entire life. He probably hates us, Des." I hugged him tighter as he kissed my head.

"I don't think he would have reached out if he hated us. If anything, he's confused about who he is, or where he comes from. Plum, you gave him a chance at the best life... he cannot be upset with us for that."

"Was it really the best life since he wasn't with us? Cappadonna and Capone came out fine. What would have been one more? Then I turned around to have another one and keep her... Des, he hates me."

"Cappadonna and Capone came out to be good men. Don't forget the reason that Cappadonna was sent to prison. For trying to help provide for this family. Our boy lost fifteen years of his life because he wanted to help our family out of our situation. Capone has been running for years to make up for the guilt he feels for getting his twin caught up. Always taking care of himself just enough, but always keeping this family first to give us all of this. Suga Cane was that sign from God that he forgives us for giving Corleon up... a baby girl that is soft but as strong as her brothers."

"I don't know, Des."

"Jean, you love our boys and baby them... you don't give that same thing to Capri. She has always had to do more and prove more to you, and it's never been fair. She's been the perfect child, always putting everyone before herself, and showing up when needed. The girl had ulcers in high school because she worried herself to death with her SAT. You've put too much pressure on her to be perfect because your mother had done the same to you."

"Des, I don't want to talk about it." I tried to walk away, and he pulled me back holding my face, while staring down in my eyes.

"You and your mother have the most strained relationship I have ever witnessed. The boys bought her a house, and she complained because it wasn't in the same part of the island as ours. She's always been hard on you. Plum, you've lived your life trying to prove to her that you've made something of yourself, and Aimee is right... you're punishing Capri because the pressure you put under her didn't make her crack." He lifted my chin. "The pressure she put you under made you crack, and you resent your daughter because you feel like she is stronger than you."

My tears slid down my face as I looked up into my husband's face. I have been too hard on Capri, constantly trying to make her someone better than I turned out to be. I didn't want her to have children young like I did and wanted her to finish school and pursue her dreams. I never got that option because I ended up becoming a mama to two at once. My goals and dreams didn't matter anymore because I had two little eyes looking at me to be their mama.

Capri Shelly Ann Delgato was strong. Even when she was young, she had this confidence about her and knew who she was. It took women years to know who they were, and Capri already knew at ten.

I felt like I could never relate to my daughter, and that was my own insecurity. What could I teach her? She knew more than me and could go out into the world and handle business without a man. I needed Des and had always depended on him. The time apart, I nearly fell apart having to do it on my own.

Capri didn't need a man to be her. A man couldn't do anything that she couldn't do for herself. When she told me she was marrying Naheim, I finally had something that I could share with her. I was a damn good wife, and knew I could teach and show her how to be one, too.

Guilt ate away at me when she confided in me that Naheim was cheating on her. Instead of choosing my daughter and telling her that she needed to leave, I told her she needed to make more time for him, and to stop only focusing on her studies.

I should have told her that she didn't need him, and that if he couldn't be faithful, then he needed to leave. Des had always been a faithful man, and had shown her how a man was supposed to love you. Capri was looking for me to tell her that she needed to choose her, a man that would stand up for her, and wouldn't find love in different women.

My daughter was always so bright and bubbly, always the first to welcome someone with open arms. Over the years, I saw small pieces of her chip away and a different Capri emerge. One that wasn't as secure and confident in who she was, and that was because of her husband.

Naheim had become like a son to me, and I was caught between him and my daughter. My shoulders shook as I thought about how I chose Naheim over my daughter. I blamed her for something that wasn't her fault.

"Have I become my mother, Dessy?" I looked up into his eyes, broken because the realization hurt me that much more.

He softly kissed my lips and held my face. "You don't have to become her. Unlike your mother, she is still the same and won't ever change. You have the space and the chance to change and make this right. Suga Cane is about to become a mother and a wife... to the right man. Don't you want to rejoice in that? Our baby is happy, and I see it. Quameer loves the hell out of our little girl."

"He does."

I watched him at the brunch. When he came inside, all it took was one look before he went and grabbed her and brought her into the next room. He was prepared to love and defend her whenever he needed to, and didn't care what anyone thought.

"Our kids are in charge of who they choose to love and marry, not us. We allowed the boys to find their loves and marry them without getting involved. Capri deserves the same thing. As much as it hurts to have my baby girl lose that Delgato name again, I'm damn proud and happy that she'll be wearing the Inferno name. I have a feeling that she's going to heal the Infernos, Plum."

I hugged my husband tighter as we stood in the middle of our kitchen. The life we have lived had been so much. We had been through so much and had always had each other. Life could be beating my ass down and as long as Des was there, none of that mattered. I wanted each of my children to experience the same thing.

Soon as I saw Quameer's new truck pull into the driveway and watched him hop out and then helped Capri out the front seat, I knew she was home. I called over to her house and Gams had told me that they had stayed in the city.

Instead of rushing right over, I waited a few hours because I wanted to give her the space before going right on over. Maybe she wanted to decompress and get some rest and didn't want to see me. After the way I treated her on Father's Day, I couldn't blame her for wanting to be away from me.

Instead of apologizing and making it right, I went over and basically bullied her into letting me plan her wedding and cook her favorite food. How could I be that way to my own daughter and not see anything wrong with it?

When Capone hollered at me and got so worked up, I knew that I needed to change how I moved when it came to my daughter. Des bringing up my mother caused me to dig deep and see how I was repeating the cycle.

Repeating the cycle of my mother by loving my boys too much and not loving my daughter enough. Before my brother passed away, to my mother he couldn't do any wrong. Anything he did that was wrong, she never saw it or called him out for it. When it came to me, everything that I did was wrong. I had to be better, stronger, smarter than my brother.

All I did was continue the cycle when God blessed me with my own little girl. No matter how much I told myself that I would be different with her, I naturally took on my mother when it came to bringing her up.

"I think I'm going to head on over there with you." Des came into the kitchen as I was packing up the last of the food that I had made for Capri.

"Okay... I haven't seen Mina in years, Des. I'm nervous," I admitted.

Mina Inferno was a bad ass when she was in her prime. A wild heart, carefree, badass with a thick curly mane. I remember watching it blow in the wind whenever she rode on the back of Quinton's bike.

Quasim was only a few years younger than the twins, but when she had him, she was back up and at it like she hadn't pushed a kid out. Meanwhile, I had taken on an old lady approach and made these kids my world. She was so lively and always laughing and enjoying life with everyone.

I remember when she threw Des a welcome home party, and we spent the entire night watching our boys and drinking. She had always been so proud of her little family, always kissing and loving on her boys.

In a room full of others, Mina could always find Quinton, and he could always find her. Their love and devotion to each other was something that I loved.

"You don't need to be nervous. Act normal and show love like you always have. Stop getting in your head about it, Plum."

I smiled as I put the rest of the food into the bags, and Des scooped them up and grabbed my hand. On the walk over, Erin had come out the house with Cee-Cee on her hip.

"Miss I made a poo and can only do it in her bathroom had to go." She smiled. "Hey Ma... hey Pops." She kissed us both, and

Cee-Cee nearly tossed herself out of her mother's arms to her grandfather.

"Hey Pop-Pop's baby." He kissed her cheek, and she wrapped her arms around him.

"You do have a favorite," Erin called him out.

I couldn't help but to laugh because it was true. Cee-Cee had a special place in Des's heart. She loved her grandfather. "Is everyone over there?"

"Gams cooked a big feast, and everyone chilling in the back or in the pool... we all need to be together." She put her arm around me as we walked.

"Erin, have I been that awful to her?"

Both my daughter-in-law's worshipped the ground I walked on, and neither of them had mentioned the fight that me and Capri had. They also never chose a side and allowed us to deal with our own mess.

"You have. I don't get involved because I remember how mother and daughter fights used to be," she sighed. "I also know that she needs you just as much as me and Alaia, Ma."

Erin let us in, and I spotted Gams in the kitchen putting cookies on a plate. "Be careful, Capone... those will have you sitting on your ass."

"Gams, you giving my baby boy some edibles?"

She looked up and toward the door and smiled. "Jean Delgato... aren't you a sight for sore eyes. Come on over here, look at you, still looking good."

I smiled as I went over and hugged her. "It's been a while, Gams."

"Too long. A shame it took your boy to come home, and my dumplin' and your girl to get together to merge this family back together."

"I feel awful, Gams. Mina needed me, and I wasn't there."

She touched my face and looked up at me because Gams was so short. "Nonsense, Jean. Everyone had real life happening for them. You will not beat yourself up about not being there when you had your own life to live. Mina has been good and will always be good with me as her mother, and Quinton as her husband."

I hugged Gams and she gave me one of those tight squeezes. "Thank you, Gams."

"Don't need to thank me. I need you to fix things with that girl out there... not tonight because we're all enjoying each other's company but find time to make it right with her. Capri is responsible for Mina even being here. She made that happen because she knows how much she means to Meer. You did right with her, Jean. Don't hold the reins too tight or she will break away, and she won't come back."

I nodded as I looked into her soft eyes. "I hear you."

"Gams... I need a regular cookie... Sug feeling all left out because she can't have one," Meer came in from the back and paused when he saw us.

"Hey Quameer," I smiled.

"I don't know, Mrs. Jean... you had static with me the last time I was in your kitchen." His smirk let me know he was messing with me.

"And I am sorry for that. I should have never got you involved in me and Capri's mess," I apologized.

He came over toward where me and Gams was. "You don't need to worry about her anymore. I told her brothers, her father, and now I'm telling you that I got her. Capri is in good hands."

"Crazy hands, but good... what the fuck is that?" Capone jumped back away from the counter.

"I told you, Capone... I told you that having a another one wasn't good." Gams ran over there and grabbed his arm.

With how short she was and how tall Capone was, it was absolutely comical how she was guiding him toward the back yard. "You see that, too?"

"Is he going to be alright?"

"He gotta ride it out for a bit.... It will settle down." Meer laughed.

The backdoor opened and Des came back into the kitchen. It wasn't him that my eyes were on, it was the man behind him.

The man that resembled both of my twins and the man that was walking in front of him.

"I have someone that wants to meet you, Jean," Des said, as he looked back at Corleon, who had this nervous smile on his face.

I held Quameer's hand and squeezed it, scared to move from where we stood. "This is something that you have to do, and something that he needs from you... this should be done between you three."

He walked me over toward Des, placing my hand into my husband's and then going to scoop the cookies from the other pile, before squeezing Corleon's shoulder and leaving out the door.

"Hi Cor...Hi Corleon," I stumbled over my words as I looked up into his eyes. The same eyes he shared with his father.

"Hey Jean," he smiled, looking just like Capone with that damn smile that could get him his way. I'm sure he got his way a lot when he was younger. From the letters I shared with his adoptive mother, I knew he got his way.

"Can...Can I hug you?"

He smiled again and held his arms out and I rushed into his arms, as I held onto him so tightly. Thinking of the day that I bundled him up and took him with me to work, knowing that he wouldn't be returning home with me.

I remember kissing him so much while my tears fell onto his face, as he slept peacefully. I wished he understood the impossible place that I was in when I had to give him up. Everything was so uncertain with Desmond's case, and we were heading toward eviction with our apartment because I couldn't pay the rent on my own. Capone was always in and out of the hospital, and one more visit to the hospital and I would be looking for another job. Everything was so fucked up.

I laid my head on him as I sobbed, remembering when she hugged me, and took him out the laundromat. The day I had to give Corleon up was the one of the hardest days in my life. The second was watching that judge hand my baby boy fifteen years, and seeing him give me that look, scared that he had let me down.

When I gave him that nod of the head, he straightened up and allowed them to take him to the back where he would be away from us for the next fifteen years. Both those days were etched in my brain and as long as I lived, I would never forget about it.

"I'm so sorry, Corleon... I'm so sorry, Pootie," I called him the nickname that I had called him the moment he came out.

"Pootie? How did you know that was the nickname my mother called me?"

I removed myself from him and wiped my face. "She promised me that she would continue to call you that."

Linda was a good woman, and seeing the man before me told me that she held onto every word she promised me. "When I asked her why she called me that, she said someone very special gave me that nickname, and I would always be their Pootie."

I broke down and Des went to console me, but Corleon stepped in and hugged me. "I'm so sorry about your mom. I'm sorry about all of this... I didn't mean to ruin your life and leave you confused about who you are."

He chuckled. "The reason I found you isn't to force you to apologize. I'm not angry and I know who I am... never been confused on who I am. I'm Corleon Alphonso D. Bruster."

"D?" Des asked.

"On all my documents, D has always been on them. It wasn't until I was able to look into my records and see the original documents to see she never took Delgato out my name, just added her name. I don't know why, and wish I could ask—"

"She knew you would need us one day, and wanted to make sure you knew where you came from," Des replied.

"Why did you stop writing me?"

"I stopped around the time that Cappadonna had gotten locked up... so much was happening in our family that I kind of lost myself for a minute and thought it would have been best to just fall back."

The door opened and Cappadonna and Capri came holding hands. "Capo is tweaking and chasing dolphins with Erin, but we're here. Corleon, you're a part of this family, and while we all question the decision to keep you away, I know they wouldn't have done it without good reason. Jean and Desmond Delgato have always done what was best for their children."

I reached for Capri and wrapped my arms around her as she cried into my shoulder. "I'm so sorry, Princess... I should have been on your side and protected you. I am so sorry," I whispered into her ear as I hugged her tightly. "I haven't been the perfect mother, and I have hid in my glasshouse and tossed plenty of stones your way... I am sorry and I want to be better for you."

"All I want, Mommy. That is literally all I want." She continued to sob.

Des looked at both of his boys, while one was in the back jumping into the pool to save his son from imaginary dolphins and kissed both of them on the cheek and hugged them both.

"Those deeper conversations will happen. Right now, we will enjoy each other as a family," he told them, and Corleon nodded.

He looked over at me and held his arm out for me and Capri, and we both hugged him. "Never had a pops before."

"Oh, this nigga watches bowling for fun," Capp snorted, and Des shoved his son.

The backdoor busted opened and Capone, soaking wet, with CJ in his arms came walking through the kitchen. "Nah, Gorgeous, if you wanna swim with the dolphins, then go ahead... my boy not doing that shit... you preach about it being dangerous and then you got our boy swimming in the pool with them."

"How many cookies did he eat?" I blurted.

"Ma, I had six, but that's not the point... the point is that I'm about to grab my shit and hand—"

Capp stepped in and took CJ, who was tickled by his father tripping, and ran back to get in the pool with Ryder. While Cappadonna calmed his brother and everyone returned back outside, I slid down the hall where Mina was rocking in her chair.

Her curly hair was still as wild as it used to be on the back of her husband's bike. She was caught up on something, never taking her eyes from out the window. As I slowly sat in the empty chair beside her, I saw her watching her husband.

He was getting out his truck and on the phone. "Papa," she whispered, as she held her own hands. Desmond had joined him outside and they were talking about something together, while we sat watching them.

"We're going to be grandparents again, Mina... your baby boy and my baby girl are having a baby."

She took my hand, and we held hands as we rocked, watching our husbands like we used to do back in the day. Life hadn't been kind to either of us, still, we were grateful for those small bits of peace that we had, like in this moment.

CHAPTER 8
QUAMEER

THE FIRST RULE of the game was not to do some wild crazy shit that made you identifiable. I couldn't help the burns on my face, however, I made sure to keep my head down when handling business. If you happened to see them, it was usually the last thing you saw before I snuffed your lights out.

In the midst of worrying about my baby being chased while she was on her bike, these niggas decided to double back and shoot up the restaurant she was in. Had I not went to prove a point to Brandi's big-headed ass, my baby would have been left defenseless. Capri could always protect herself, and I knew she could get the job done. Not with the way those niggas rode through the block, she wouldn't have been able to handle the shit on her own.

While sending one of those CV's niggas on his way to the upper room, I peeped one of the Chrome Vipers ride by with his blond braids flowing in the wind. I was familiar with the niggas in Chrome Vipers. I used to be best friends with the head of CV, before he became CV, and I became IG. Either way, I was someone who observed, so I learned a thing or two about those nasty ass Chrome Pussies.

Daquan Miller had long blond braids. He was also Tookie's

little brother. I used to spank this nigga on his PlayStation when he was younger. What made his ass go ahead and bleach his hair blond was beyond me, and honestly wasn't my problem or fucking business. All I knew is that it was his bullets that hit the window where Capri and everyone was still on the phone. Luckily, Capri had already moved from the table by the time I was able to call her.

Not to mention, it was his ass that had went after my baby the day of her birthday party. He kept trying to trip her out while on the bridge.

I taught my baby always to move in and out, never stay in one lane for too long, so she was able to avoid that. Had she not, the bike would have come out from under her, and she would have been fucked up.

When I looked to the left of him, I peeped his girlfriend on her bike. Just like Inferno Gods had women, so did those nasty ass Chrome pussies. I don't even know what the fuck they were called, but I knew when I saw his bitch, I damn near bit the inside of my cheek off thinking about that get back. How did I know that was his girlfriend?

The purple wig she wore had pieces sticking out as she zoomed past me. All it took was for me to look up Daquan's ass and his social media came up. Nigga in pictures holding guns and pictures with bricks in it.

If he wanted to go to prison, all he had to do was go step in the fucking cell. In one of his pictures there was a shorty with the same tired ass purple wig. What the fuck made her even want to do a purple wig in the first place?

Not only did he come for me and my baby the first time, but he also decided to go ahead and spin the block, so now it was time for me to spin the block. Only difference is I never had to spin it twice, because I was gonna make sure I got the job done on the first spin.

Social media was the downfall of every nigga that felt he had something to prove. The niggas I ran with didn't do the social media shit. Shit, my social media page didn't even have a fucking picture. Suga knew it was me because she claimed I was a stalker.

I needed to make one to keep up with her on her travels. She only posted in her stories because they deleted after twenty-four hours. Other than that, her social media pages were boring with regular selfie pictures.

She didn't have anything recent on her pages either. Daquan was different. The nigga posted whenever he wanted, and even posted a picture of him on his bike on the BQE, the same day as Suga's birthday party.

When it came to my family, I didn't have any sense and wasn't about to rationalize with shit. Shit didn't have two sides for me, it only had one and that was me handling who had the fucking balls to come for mine.

Suga was mine.

You fucked with her, and I was the nigga that was coming for you. I parked my bike in the back of the club.

I hopped off my bike and waited for Goon and Yasin to join me. "You ready for this shit... coming to their territory is big, Meer."

"They came for my wife... all bets are off."

The Maybach pulled up behind our bikes, and the window rolled down. I walked over toward the window, and Core was in the back with his laptop in his lap. "Soon as you in, I'm gonna disable the cameras inside, and the street cameras for the next five blocks."

"Good looks." I dapped him through the window.

If this was going to be my brother-in-law, I needed to know if this nigga was going to slide. When I hit him up, he was down for whatever I needed and had met us out here. The sound of a motorcycle caused us all to look, and I peeped my brother ride up.

"The fuck you doing here."

"They came at an Inferno... shit personal," he climbed off his bike, and played the back, allowing me to run the show.

The pecking order was always Sim first, and I played my role as second. Tonight, he knew that this was personal, and I had to handle this shit. We headed into the club through the kitchen while they made those nasty ass buffalo wings.

Club was packed and everybody was turning the fuck up. Even though this was CV territory, I didn't give a fuck, as we walked past some who were too busy worried about pussy than keeping their head on a swivel. I scanned the club and spotted Daquan dancing on the couch.

A sinister smirk came across my face as I made my way through the crowd to his section. This hole in the wall club didn't have any bouncers protecting the VIP areas, and with the amount of coke and pills on the table, even if there was, they wouldn't fucking know it. When I saw a fucking crack pipe, I knew we were dealing with some crackheads now.

"Fuck you meannnn... this my shit." Goon entered the section after me and started getting sturdy.

Daquan was still getting crazy to the song and turning up while his girl was taking pictures of a pill dissolving on her tongue. The junkies were too into their own world to know that we had come into the section.

"Who th—"

One of those CV pussies flipped over the couch the minute Quasim's fist connected with his mouth. He looked at his fist and then smirked to himself.

I slid onto the couch next to shorty, and her friend was all smirking and make pouty lips at me. Bitch looked like she was having a seizure or something with the way she kept winking at me. Shorty turned and froze when she saw me smiling at her.

"What up, Bonnie? I see crack head Clyde over there turned the fuck up."

She didn't know what to say or do. Her eyes went from me to her man, who was still in his own world as he continued to turn up to the demons in his head. Quasim took a seat on the back of the couch while waiting for homie to open his eyes and notice that we were here.

"W...what are you doing here? This is CV's territory."

I put my finger to her mouth, smearing the tacky ass pink lipstick on her lips. "Onde quer que esteja o fogo, meu território." I smiled widely, exposing my gold fangs.

"I... I don't understand."

"You will." I stroked the side of her face as the tears fell down her face. "Descanse na merda meu amor," I whispered in her ear before holding her neck and waiting until I heard the snap.

Her friend screamed bloody murder as she scurried back on the couch. I looked over at Quasim as he cracked his neck with a smirk on his face. Giving him the nod, he already knew what to do. Daquan must have been off that good shit because when Quasim grabbed him, he squealed like a bitch. As if he didn't know we had been here the entire time.

Quasim pulled his switch blade that our father had given him when he was a teen, and then said something to homie before getting his neck and his switch blade acquainted. He tossed him back onto the couch, using Daquan's shirt to wipe his blade clean, then slid his finger across his nose, and spit on him.

Shorty thought she was free and was about to walk out this bitch free. I peeped a few of the Gods locking down the doors, while the others used the gasoline and hit all the main exits. Just as quick as we slid in this bitch, we were on our way out.

"Burn this bitch down," I told one of the younger Gods, on the way out, and he nodded his head while continuing his job. "They wanted to bring the heat to our city... Let Blaze show 'em the fucking heat."

If sliding through their block didn't send the message, then this was going to show them that I could come onto they shit and do what the fuck I wanted. Soon as Core saw us come out, he saluted and had his driver start to pull away.

"You clear until you make it onto the highway."

"Good shit." I followed behind him until we all eventually dipped around his whip and got ghost, heading back to the highway to head to *our* city.

Behind Capri Inferno, I was a fucking lunatic.

When I made it back to the lake house, I quietly crept through the house because everybody was sleep. As we all rode together, we broke off in our directions. Quasim went home while Goon went back to the city with Yasin.

The lights were off when I opened the door, and Capri had her back turned sleeping. I tried to be quiet as I dipped around the room to grab shit to take a shower. "I'm not sleeping, Meer."

"Damn, I woke you up?"

She turned over and waved her kindle in her hand. "I was reading until I knew you came in… I told myself a little bit, and then couldn't stop."

As I stripped out my clothes, I realized she had gotten caught up in reading again. "What you reading now, Sug? Every time you get into a book, you ignore my ass."

Her eyes didn't leave the kindle until she realized she was ignoring me again. "Huh?"

"Book, Sug?"

She smiled. "Private Location with a Wealthy Kingpin by Theresa Reese."

"So good got you ignoring your man, huh?"

Her ass was back reading and looked up just as I was about to snatch her kindle. "Sorry baby… where are you coming from?"

"To make somebody stand on that disrespect they showed my wife." I smirked.

Capri turned her kindle off and looked at me. "Meer, what are we going to do when the baby is here? Making the doctor appointment today made everything real."

"The test we took in Miami didn't make it real for you?" I laughed and sat on the edge of the bed.

Even though she was up reading, I knew her enough to know that she was in her head. That question seemed random, but it wasn't to Suga. She had thought about a million times before she blurted it out to me.

She crawled across the bed and into my lap. "It was real, I don't know, having to make the appointment made it ten times more real, then I started worrying about everything that we have going on. Are we going to live between two homes? I just don't want Peach to feel like she has to maneuver between three different homes."

"We're going to live under the same roof. I'm not going to knock you up, ask you to marry me, and not live under the same roof as you."

"My family keeps asking what I'm doing with the land on our family's compound." She messed with my hands before looking into my eyes.

"Do you want to live on your family's compound, Sug?"

She nodded her head yes. "I want our baby to grow up close to their cousins… you know? I know it's not ideal for yo—"

"Let me handle it… ight?"

"Okay." She kissed me on the cheek, as I held her closer to me, kissing her neck. I noticed how quiet she was and grabbed her face.

"What's on your mind?"

"I should have told you about the abortion, Meer." She stared up into my eyes, guilt written all over her face.

I could tell she felt guilty the minute our eyes locked after Naheim had told her business. For a minute, I was in my feelings because I thought we told each other everything. Then, I had to step into her shoes, and she hid it because she was ashamed of her decision. Scared what I would have thought about her if I knew the truth.

"Not should… you *could* have told me. I've always been me, Sug… I wouldn't have judged you for your decision. Do you regret doing it?"

"At first, I used to regret it because I felt like God would punish me for being selfish. I couldn't take care of a baby, Meer. I wasn't ready then, and I didn't want one like that," she whispered, tears falling down her face.

"Look at me." I held her chin while staring directly into her eyes. "Don't ever apologize for doing what was best for you. If he wanna be mad, fuck him. You did what you had to do in that time in your life. God spun the block and blessed you with another one, and I know you gonna be the best fucking mom."

"You think?"

"Hell yeah. I know you're going to be the best mother. You wanna know something else?"

"Hmm?"

"You're gonna be the best wife, too... gonna have me out there bragging on my wife. I don't care if you done it before, you never done it with me."

She gave me a small smile. "You really think we're gonna get this right?"

"Baby, the best marriages always start with beating your ex-husband up... it can only go up from there."

Capri laughed so loud and then snorted. "Meer, the way he be staring when you kiss me... I feel bad a little bit."

I shrugged. "Fuck that nigga. I'm gonna love you in front of those that fumbled you. I want them to know that this glow you wearing is because of your man. I put that there, and I'm gonna keep it there. You're being loved and fucked right. Stop worrying about what the fuck egg head thinks."

"I don't know about getting fucked right... since you haven't touched me since you been back."

I laughed because shit had been so hectic that I hadn't been able to put it down. With the wet dreams I kept having when I was away from her for that week, I'm surprised I didn't bring her upstairs when we were holding that meeting with Forty.

She had just been told she had to kill one of her friends, so it didn't seem like the moment to be ready to give her dick once we made it back to my house. I also knew she needed that release, where she didn't have to think about anything except all this dick going in and out of her.

My thumb stroked her chin as I looked at her. "All I'm hearing is that you missed me getting all up in them guts... is that right? I told you Sug, you tell me when you want your dick." I grabbed her hand and put it right on rock-hard dick.

The minute she climbed her fine ass over here, I wanted her. She ain't never had to ask if I wanted her because my dick would always tell her. "I need some so bad, Pa," she whispered in my ear, as she straddled me.

I pulled the thin ass night gown she wore off, exposing her breast and kissed them. She moaned as she tossed her head back, and I bit her nipples. "Tell me how hard you want them bit, Mama."

"Harder, Pa," she moaned, digging her nails into my shoulders as she held her head back, and I flipped her over on her back, pulling my dick out my boxers and sliding right inside of her.

I kissed on her neck as I slid in and out of her slowly. "Remember you gotta be quiet... no screaming, Mama... you promise?" I whispered into her ear as I eased in and out of her.

"Uh hmmm," she slowly nodded her head while continuing to dig her nails into me. "I missed you... I missed feeling you," she continued.

"I know, Mama... I can tell the way you taking it so good... shit... my pretty mama... you feel that in you?"

"Yes... I feel it." She kissed my lips as I went deeper, and I covered her mouth with mine to muffle her, as I held her shoulder and pumped in and out of her. Capri had tears coming down her face with how good this felt.

"You taking it, Mama... this what you wanted right, bonita... Pa giving you what you wanted, right?"

"You always give me what I want." She bit down on my shoulder, while trying to contain her scream.

"Shit... you not playing fair," I smirked as I pecked her lips when I felt her squeezing her muscles, making it hard to keep this nut at bay. "Finish for me, Suga."

Slowly, I stroked her while sucking on her tongue and staring into her eyes. When she looked into my eyes, I saw how much she loved me and trusted me. If I was worried before, in this moment, as we stared into each other's eyes as I gave her dick, I knew my baby was mine. She bit my lip, and I licked her teeth while spitting in her mouth.

Capri opened her mouth wider, as the spit fell down the side of her mouth. Just the sight of her, had me ready to release.

"Minha garota desagradável...pegue seu pau," I whispered in her ear while I plunged deeper into her.

I shoved my tongue back down her throat, while applying pressure around her neck, as we both came at the same time. I rested my forehead against hers, while catching my breath.

"I love you, Meer."

"You don't even know how much I love you, Sug."

She wrapped her legs around me tighter. "What are we gonna do when my stomach gets bigger?"

We both broke out into laughter. "You gonna toot that as up... back shots for the win, Sug." I kissed her lips, as we both fell into a comfortable and safe silence.

When I say safe, she wasn't second guessing anything or allowing her mind to take her to a different place. The soft snores coming from her told me that her mind was quiet, and she felt safe, secure, and protected.

I don't give a fuck who came before me, nobody was fucking coming after me.

CHAPTER 9
QUAMEER

WHEN CAPPADONNA CALLED me early this morning, I should have ignored the call and turned over and continued sleeping with my baby. I don't know what he wanted, but he had about three other muthafuckas he could have called, and my name ended up on his call screen.

Yawning, I climbed into the Ford Explorer that he had obnoxiously decided to beep at three in the fucking morning. My neighbors were probably calling the damn police at this moment. We didn't do that loud shit around here. It was the reason I liked my block, most of these bitches were well into their seventies and went to bed at five in the afternoon.

"Was any of that shit necessary, Capp?"

He shoved a coffee into my hands. "Alaia made us coffee."

It was then that I realized that this nigga had a full NYPD police uniform on. Before even questioning why he was dressed like twelve, I looked at the coffee cup he shoved into my hands. "You had your wife making coffee at this time of morning?"

"Hell nah... she wanted to make it. Plus, she can never sleep when I'm not in the bed.... You wouldn't get the shit... husband and wife shit."

"Capp, chill the fuck out." He spoke quickly, like his ass had a hit of that good shit. Nigga was moving like he had six cups of damn coffee.

He pulled out my driveway and continued to wherever the fuck we were going. "How my sister? She getting enough sleep?"

"You pulled me out of bed to fucking talk about Capri?"

He shook his head. "Nah. We got to handle business, but I figured I would check in since you wanted to knock her up and shit."

"We're straight...you know she's in good hands, right?"

Capp looked at me before returning his gaze back to the street. "Wouldn't have given you my blessing if I didn't think she wouldn't be. Beating up Nah was nasty work." He snickered.

"Nigga needed the shit... why the fuck he yelling her business out like that?" I was still mad every time I thought about it.

"He needs to let go. Since he and Nellie not together, he thought that he had a second chance since Baby Doll was back home. I know the next time he come left, I'm gonna slam his ass *right* on his neck."

He headed through the tunnel into the city. I didn't know where we were going, and with how tired I was, I didn't give a damn where we were going. I took a sip of the coffee, and I saw why this nigga was wired.

"You may not eat pork, but you gonna have fucking diabetes with this coffee... shit sweet as shit? Did she dump the whole bag in here?"

"Good though, right?"

"Hell yeah." I took another sip.

He dug in the back and pulled a duffle bag from the back, and nearly hit me in the head as he pulled it to the front, tossing it in my lap. "Put that on."

"I get to dress up as twelve, too." I became way too excited for whatever we were about to do. This nigga had an unmarked cop car and was dressed in full NYPD gear. I didn't need to ask how he got his hands on any of this shit because it was Cappadonna.

Capp slugged the rest of his coffee and then tossed it back into the cup holder. "We got some shit that needs to be handled tonight."

"And you couldn't call your twin or any of the niggas we run with? You had to drag me out of bed with this sweet ass coffee."

"Chill out on my baby's coffee making skills. And I figured this is a bonding experience for my future brother-in-law... test you out."

"Bullshit. You already know I handle my business. My baby always safe."

"What's your end game with Baby Doll, Meer? No need to beat around the bush and pretend about shit... what's your plan with her?"

"Marry her, Capp... the fuck? The end game is her wearing my ring and last name, having my babies... I want her to be the one that I end this life with... so the end game is us."

Capp held his fist out and I dapped him. "She deserves that more than anything. Somebody that is gonna give her the world and burn it down for her if it comes to that."

I nodded my head in agreement while I pulled a baggie of weed out and started to roll me a spliff. If he had me out here this early, I needed something to mellow me out. As we drove through Manhattan, I rolled up enjoying how still the city was at this hour. There were people still out doing their thing, but there wasn't the loudness the city usually had.

We were able to throughout each block until we made it the Brooklyn bridge. As if she knew she was on my mind, her name came up on my phone. I answered, putting her on speaker phone while still trying to get this spliff nice and thin like I enjoyed them.

"I don't like you left and didn't tell me you were leaving, Meer," she yawned into the phone. She was sleeping so well that I didn't want to bother her.

"My bad, Suga... I put the security on the house, so you and Peach are good."

We were staying at my crib because we were trying to give Peach a good summer. It was Suga's idea to take her to some museums in the city and give her the true New York summer. We planned to head back to the lake because Capone was going to have CJ this weekend, and he and Peach had become obsessed with each other.

I finished that spliff and went on rolling the next one for the ride back home. "Hmm, I need Big Pa," she moaned in the phone.

"What the fuck? Cappadonna!" I hollered, as I watched the weed scatter all over my damn pants and the front of the car.

This nigga was floating it across the bridge and had opened his car door and was trying to jump out. "I will jump the fuck out this fucking car. Baby Doll, I'm in the fucking car!" he barked.

"Oh my God, Quameer!" Capri screeched.

I laughed. "Sug, you gotta chill. You 'bout to have your brother drive us off this bridge... but don't worry I'm gonna take ca—"

"Qua fucking Meer, don't make me take this bitch over... don't even finish that sentence," Capp threatened.

"I'm going to go... Meer, next time tell me when I'm on speaker... first Capone and now Cappadonna."

"They know how you got that baby in yo—"

Cappadonna snatched my phone and ended the call. "Is that why Capone don't wanna call her? What the fuck you did to him?"

He didn't even want me to answer him, as he continued off the bridge. We were silent for a minute while I laughed to myself because the shit was so funny how they acted realizing their sister was actually grown. Now, I didn't expect for Suga to call me and tell me she was ready for more.

It only showed them that she was grown, and she may have

been their baby sister, but she was about to be my wife, and she was grown.

"Since we on the subject... give a price."

"What fucking subject was we on, Meer?" he snarled, as he avoided even looking at me. "Keep yo' shit to yourselves."

"This is all I asked for when I asked for your blessing. I'm gonna handle my business with Capri, in more ways than one."

"I promise I will shove you in the glove compartment... I promise I will do the shit, Quameer," he threatened. "What subject are we on... speak yo' mind and switch this subject quick."

"I want to buy Capri's land on the compound."

"The fuck I look like making you pay for the land when you're about to become family?" Capp looked real deal offended that I even asked.

"Capp, I'm a man and you more than anything know what I mean. I provide for my family, and I can't have you or Capone paying for my wife anymore... that's my job. I appreciate you both having it this far, but I got it now... feel me?" I wiped the weed residue from my lap. "Suga said she wants to live on the compound, and I want to buy her land and build on it for our family."

We pulled down a quiet tree-lined street a few blocks from the Barclay center. He doubled parked in front of a townhouse and looked over at me. "You deadass, huh?"

"So fucking deadass. You asked me to hold her down, and I took that shit seriously. I'm comfortable, and I can take care of Capri."

"That year really did something for the both of you."

"Let me see what I was missing in my life. It taught me discipline and showed me that I was ready for her. Capp, the way she loves me and my daughter... that shit makes me feel like the luckiest nigga on the planet. I don't even like to see her crying for one of her sappy romance movies. I wanna be damn near perfect for her."

"Can't be perfect, Pissy." I ignored the pissy because he was about to give me some wisdom that I needed to hear.

Had it not been for that, I probably would have thrown a damn fit because these niggas kept calling me pissy, including my own fucking blood brother.

"You can always aspire to be."

"She doesn't need perfect, Meer. She needs who you been… I'm not a perfect husband and me and my wife have our moments. I lose my temper at times, and she knows how to push my damn buttons. I know I get on her nerves, so we do this ten-minute shit that she saw on social media. For ten minutes she vents her frustrations or whatever is going on. I listen to her, and hear her… I mean really hear her. Alaia is the love of my life, and I plan to be with her forever, and in order to do that, I don't need to be perfect, I just need to be her Roy."

"I hear you."

He got out the car and then looked at me. "Put the uniform on."

"Where, nigga? Ain't no fucking dressing room."

"Get the fuck out and put that shit on… I'll be back." I still didn't know what the fuck we were doing, but I had enough trust not to ask this looney ass nigga.

While he went across the street, I had got out and quickly changed into the uniform and tossed the duffle bag in the back. When this nigga crossed the street with a White woman and little girl, I was really fucking confused.

"I cannot believe this small case has gone this far," the woman complained as he helped her in the back of the car.

"Ma'am, I didn't think it would go this far either. My job is to make sure you and your daughter are taken somewhere safe, so your husband can get to you."

I didn't know what the fuck we were doing, but I got into character quick. "And I can't use my phone to call him? I left it back in the house."

"We're going to bring you right to him," I replied, and she

settled back with her daughter, scared about whatever the fuck Capp had told her.

"Thank God you got to us in time... I don't know what I would have done if they came into our home while my husband was gone."

"Good thing you never have to worry about that. Brothers in blue take care of our own." I held back my laugh, as Capp gave me that *really, nigga* look.

"Sammie always says that. Says he never found brotherhood until he joined the force." She went on yapping about her pussy ass husband.

We drove through Brooklyn, and I settled back in my seat while reading the text messages from Suga, yelling at me for talking like that on speaker. As if I knew she was about to get freaky over the phone.

I wish I could pretend to even be a little surprised when this nigga hit a switch and lights came on. How the fuck did he get an unmarked cop truck to begin with. I learned a long time ago not to question the shit that Capp did, or how far he would go for his family.

"Do I even wanna know?"

"Having a best friend with connections pays sometimes," he whispered as he pulled behind a black Honda and hopped out the truck. "Sit tight, Cheryl."

I remained in the truck and watched him tap the back taillight before making his way to the driver's side.

Finishing my coffee, I got out and joined him, standing on the passenger side. It was empty and the man was talking to Capp like he was a loyal brother in blue. Not even knowing he was talking to a certified nutcase.

"Yeah, man, I must have not been paying attention... let me off with a warning. I'm just getting off work and I'm tired as shit... my daughter is sick, and my wife has been having to do the nights alone while I've been working."

"I remember those nights... don't you, Officer Pissyton."

I bit the inside of my cheek as I looked at this nigga over the car. "Yeah. Sure do... I also remember how we got in that situation, too. Was too much fun and screaming."

Capp damn near wanted to come across the top of the car as I smirked to myself. "Yeah... I can't wait until they are behind me."

"Hey, step out the car for a second... you know how they're always on our ass to make sure shit is done by the book."

He was confused at first, and then got out the car while Capp kept it casual. "We're not about to write you a ticket... nobody is hurt, and everyone is sleep." I continued to ease him over, while he leaned on the back of the car.

Capp put his arm around him and laughed. "But I do wanna show you something that's funny." He turned him around, and the man had a clear eye view of the woman and girl in the back seat of the car.

"Wha...what the fuck is going on?" he started to panic, and Capp put some pressure on the back of his neck.

"You sat there and watched as that man beat on my son. So, now I had to show you what it feels like for someone to touch your family and feel helpless. I went in your house, took a piss, and picked your wife and daughter up all while you were serving for the boys in blue."

I understood why cops always rested their hands in the front of their vest. Shit was comfortable as I stood there with my legs shoulder length apart, watching this man go through every emotion possible.

"Th...I had to take my partner's side... I couldn't sit there and go against them. You don't know what they would have done if I went against him."

"You about to see what the fuck I'm gonna do to your daughter and wife... I'm different, Sammie. I love children, but I love my child fucking more... wanna see how crazy I can get."

"I mean, man, he already out here dressed as a cop, got your family in the back of the whip, and can do whatever to you while your wife and daughter watch... I wouldn't play if I was you."

"Wh...what do you want me to do?"

"Withdraw that statement and tell them that you lied for your partner."

"What?"

Capp looked at the pepper spray. "Or I can spray this in your eyes, put you in the trunk and take you to a scrap yard that will crush this car if I shoot them a little cash. Ever been crushed alive, Sammie?"

The man was trembling so bad that we had to turn him away from his family, because his wife was starting to look nervous. "You'll get your wife back the minute you go back to work and do what needs to be done... you can fuck with anybody else, but when it comes to Capp's kids, I'm gonna raise hell about mine. Especially when it's some bullshit charged. Go back to work do what needs to be done and you can have your wife and daughter."

"J...just like that?"

"Uh huh. I usually like to tie up loose ends, but I feel like you're smart enough not to fuck with me. Then again, I got your passports and socials, so you can't escape me, Bitch."

"Wifey a little nervous. Go ahead and turn and make sure she all good," I told him, and he turned around with a smile on his face.

"Go handle that, Sammie." Capp got close to his ear. "Or I will make sure that you speak about your family in past tense."

He was so damn scared that he ran to the car, and quickly made a U-turn back to his job to withdraw that statement. "Certified."

"For my wife and seeds, there is no limits to what I will do. Let's take them to that diner and wait for his ass to call me."

"And his partner?"

"You'll see." Capp smirked, as he headed back to the cop car with a smile on his face like he hadn't told his man he would kill his family.

CHAPTER 10
TASHA

THIS WAS the first time that I was seeing Morgan in a week. Ever since the ball, I had seen him on and off, but then he went completely ghost on me. He still made sure his handler came by the condo he had me living in, to check in on me. Morgan had been so busy floating on the high of this campaign and loving the fact that the violence was happening because then he had something to promise to these poor people.

If they were smart, then they would have seen that he was as connected in the drug world as the Delgato twins. Morgan had his hands in so much shit when it came to the streets that he should have been getting indicted on some charges. All the fancy suits, watches, and that expensive condo that overlooked Central Park couldn't be bought on the salary of a district attorney in Baltimore. New York City was one of the most expensive cities in the country, and he was floating around here with a full security detail, and all the bells and whistles, while nobody spoke on it.

The same reason I was even out was the reason nobody spoke on it. Morgan had his hand up someone's ass far, and they were pulling a lot of strings for him. I don't know what he promised them, but he was on a high with the success of all his campaigning.

According to him, I was supposed to be his fake little fiancée, and the only place I had been was to the ball. The accommodations he had me in were nice, and an upgrade from the cell I had spent time in.

I was nervous.

In the past, I didn't give a fuck what I had got myself into as long as the money was good. This man moved federal mountains to get me out of prison, so the debt I would owe him could very well kill me.

He finished up his conversation and then put his phone down, finally paying me some attention. We were at some fancy restaurant having an overpriced lunch that came with a side salad that cost $40 and only had three pieces of lettuce and a drop of dressing.

"Sorry about that. It was Jesse calling to check in on me." He gave me that tight lipped smile that I learned to hate in this short amount of time. "Enjoying your salad?"

Jesse was Morgan's older daughter. Apparently, he fucked around with some Cuban chick, and that was how Jesse came to be. He has a younger daughter by his ex-wife, and from the vibe I picked up on, he only dealt with Jesse outside of his actual family. Even though he was divorced, he didn't bring Jesse around that side of the family.

I felt bad for the girl because it was clear she wanted to desperately please her father, and although Morgan pretended to be interested, he didn't give a damn about that girl, or how much she wanted to make him proud. The only reason she was invited to the ball was because that shit was a front for a big ass freak nasty convention for all the old freaks that wanted to play while their wives were away.

You couldn't tell Jesse that with the way she was snapping pictures and acting like she was the first lady or something. The girl couldn't even tell the world who her father was, and she was settling for that. I guess when your mama was a side chick, you learned to play that role, even if it was to your father.

"How is Jessie doing? It was great meeting her." I bit back how much I hated this man. It was crazy how I hated him more than I did Capone, and the reason I was even in prison was because of that lunatic.

"She claims she might have some information about that shooting with the Chrome Vipers, and those pesky fucking Inferno Gods... told her that I would let Rich handle that since he is their handler." He cut into his raw ass steak and popped the piece into his mouth.

The fact that Jesse didn't even know her father was involved with Chrome Vipers was crazy. I'm sure Morgan wasn't clued into every little thing that they did, but he was making his money with them.

"Hmm."

He pointed his fork at me as he annoyingly chewed and stared at me. "With Rich Parker in my back pocket, I have no worries. I just need to meet this new ADA that they brought in... How much will it take her to forget she has morals and do what needs to be done."

"And she would risk her career for money?"

Morgan laughed loudly as he looked at his phone. "Everyone has a price, Tasha... even you. Freedom was your price, right?"

I didn't ask for his ass to come rescue me to put me back into some more shit. "Not everyone has a price."

He cut another bloody ass piece of steak and looked at me. "Hmm... maybe. Let's hope ADA Capri Browne doesn't."

My face remained neutral because he was like a fucking shark and would sniff the blood. When he said Capri's name, I damn near panicked. I stepped on my own foot, so I didn't react when I heard her name. This is why I didn't want to be involved because the damn Delgatos were like damn bed bugs. Once they got on you, it was nearly impossible to get rid of them.

"Can I have more wine?" I asked the waitress when she came to refill our water glasses. She smiled and went to grab the bottle.

"So, we both can agree that you know Capone Delgato."

"I've heard of him, Vincent." I used his first name, because I was tired of him trying to get me involved in this wicked ass web that he had spun.

This was dangerous, even for me. Morgan was going down a road that I wasn't sure he was going to survive to speak about.

"Listen, Bitch. The only reason you're out is to help us with information. We know he is behind Judge McLaren's murder... we can't prove it, but I know he is."

"If you cannot prove it, then how do you know that he is?"

He looked around him and did a few smiles before his eyes locked with mine. "My colleagues don't know that McLaren's son was a damn kingpin, but I know he was, and I also know that he and Capone Delgato had issues with each other. You worked around that man, so I know you know what went on. I know you cooked for him and know that you know more than you're letting on. Tasha, I advise you start chatting before you end up back in prison."

If he knew that Judge McLaren was my late son's grandmother, he would really think he hit the jackpot. "Are you going to hold prison over my head this entire time? If so, you can put me right back in there. Morgan, you don't want to enter this fight with them... I can promise you that."

I don't know why I felt like I had to protect Capri. It was weird because her brother was the reason that I was in prison, and she was probably somewhere playing house with my son and Naheim.

Something about Morgan told me that I didn't need to get on the wrong side of this, and I needed to protect me. What was keeping Morgan from doing me just as dirty. There were no limits to what he would do.

His phone rang, and he quickly picked it up and spoke for a bit before his security came over. "Heading there now. Don't worry about it... it's great publicity to be there and pretend to care about those hood hooligans... get a fucking job and you wouldn't need public assistance." He snarled, disgusted. "I know, I know. Were you able to get us a private jet for Monaco?

I'm not flying there commercial. Well, have someone fucking donate the money for it."

I was sure it was his campaign manager, who happened to keep him everywhere that was good for his image. "Everything all good?"

He squinted his eyes at me. "You are lucky I have this to handle or else I would slap that smirk off your face... I can see why he set you up on all those bodies... just useless." He stood up, grabbing his suit jacket from the chair and leaving with one of his security details behind him.

I continued to enjoy my lunch that was paid for before they brought the car around and brought me back to my condo. I was tired of being around Morgan, and I had just gone a week without seeing him.

Even with me not being seen much, Morgan made sure he had a whole list on how I should dress in public. Heels, two-piece skirt suits, and a bunch of damn pearls. I felt like I was going to a damn funeral every time I put them on.

I dialed my mother's number, and grabbed a bottle of wine from the fridge. Being a fake fiancée meant I got the good shit, and not the toilet hooch those bitches were cyphering out the toilet in prison.

"Tasha, what in the hell do you want? I'm at work and can't talk long," she answered the phone with such an attitude.

I remember when I used to call, she used to be ready to chat, knowing she would end the conversation by telling me what she needed. How times had changed when the money dried up. My mother used to run with the best of them. She was the one who taught me to cook work because she had learned from the best. Now, she was retired from that life and swore she found the lord.

"If you're busy I won't keep you long... just wanted to talk to her."

"She's in damn school... call your other damn baby. Bother those folks all day. I don't have time to sit on the phone!" she hollered and ended the call.

Tossing my phone on the counter, I sauntered across the

carpet and down the hall to my bedroom. I never had a problem with being lonely back then, mainly because it was by choice. I had a large picking of men that I could choose from, so once I got money and dick, I chose to be alone. This time, it was by force, and I craved finding someone to scratch that itch. I was so desperate that if Morgan offered, I would fuck his ass.

I unzipped the dress I wore today as I pushed into my bedroom and screamed. "Ahhh!"

Cappadonna Delgato was on my bed with a deadly smirk on his face, and if that wasn't enough, a lookalike came out the adjourning bathroom. I was so confused that I stood there frozen like a deer in headlights.

I was scared no doubt, but why was I so turned on. He was sitting on the edge of the bed with a white tank top, leather vest, and then had his feet kicked up with a pair of wheat construction timbs on.

I would have continued on drooling over him had my eyes not landed on the gun with the silencer on it. Then the lookalike looked just as good as he leaned on the wall, looking at me like I was worthless.

The nigga didn't even have to tell me he wasn't pleased with me, just his look alone told me that I disgusted him. "Wh...what do you want?"

That was all I could say because what did they want? I was so damn scared I was considering darting back down the hallway and out the front door.

"Run and I'll chop yo fucking legs off, Bitch," he spoke lowly, as he sat the gun down on the night table, next to my Bible.

Cappadonna Delgato was that nigga and seeing him in the flesh reminded me just how much that nigga he was. I would jump on his ass and fuck him if I knew he wouldn't put me in a head lock and toss me out the window.

"Fuck she staring at you like that? Ya'll got history."

Cappadonna looked at him like he had called him the foulest shit in history. "Fuck no... I'm stingy with my dick... not too many can say they rode this fucking ride."

Even before he went to prison, he was stingy. You couldn't just whisper sweet nothings in this nigga's ear, and he would want to fuck. He was like trying to crack a vault to get some dick. His wedding band told me that somebody was riding that ride.

"Sit down." The lookalike kicked over the round ottoman that had my night clothes on it. I slowly took the chair and sat down and waited for my death.

We all had to go sometime. It wasn't like anybody gave a fuck about me in this lifetime. Maybe I would see Trilla and could swing on his big ass for all this shit he caused. It was because of him, and some of my actions, that caused me to end up here.

Life was good before he got into Timmy's head and tried to convince him that his ass could fucking become Capone in the streets. As his mother, I did what I had to do to protect him. After lying and getting his ass out of dodge, this nigga decides to come back and think he was gonna be the man.

I knew that voice on the other end of the line was Jaiden. Although I loved my son to death, Erin had always been right. Jaiden was too good for Timmy, and he would have ran him down the wrong path. While Jaiden was out in the world in college, my son was stinking in the ground.

"How the fuck are you out?" Cappadonna held his hand up, stopping me before I spoke. "It's in your best interest to answer honestly and not play games with me... I'm not my twin, sweetheart. Capone has his ways, and I have mine and they involve leaving muthafuckas stinking."

I gulped. "Vincent Morgan got me out of prison."

"I'm guessing because he wants me?"

I shook my head. "He wants Capone."

Cappadonna sat up. "This nigga is like a fucking leech that won't fucking die... what does he know Ho-esha?"

I was taken back by the sudden nickname but decided not to say anything about it. It wasn't like I was in a position to make demands or demand respect. "He knows about the judge.

Mostly because he has connections in the streets. Chrome Vipers and Rich Parker run with him deep."

"You want me to believe you never said anything?"

"I'm not stupid enough to believe that Morgan will protect me or gives a fuck about what happens to me once he gets what he wants from me. I'm playing the game... staying out as long as I need to until he forces me back in prison."

"Why not just tell them about Capone?" Lookalike asked.

I turned toward him. "Cause I'm not stupid. Your sister is the new assistant district attorney. If you can pull some shit like that, there's no limits to the shit that you will do to me if I open my mouth. I know street code. Morgan will become the mayor and forget all about me."

"What up, Tasha?" I jumped when another fine ass man with a bald head came into the bedroom.

He was so quiet.

Stealth.

Had he always been in here?

"Um, hello?"

"You don't need to know who I am; you just need to know that I'm here so he doesn't kill you. He thinks his twin should have sealed the deal with you."

"I can admit it would have saved the headache." I jumped off the stool and nearly into the lookalike's arms when Capone came behind him.

"Fuck no... fuck no.... I didn't say anything. I swear... Cappadonna will tell you." The fear in my eyes was evident as I clung onto the lookalike who kept trying to push me away, but I was trying to climb into his skin to get away from that man across from me.

"What up, Stanka Butt?" Capone grinned, showing his grills.

Usually, this was a dream and the perfect set up for a why choose situation with all these fine men in this small bedroom with just me. I loved a challenge, but now I was scared and didn't know what to do.

"Cappadonna isn't going to like what I'm about to say, and I don't either, but I've learned in this work you have to bargain."

"F, what the fuck you gonna say?"

"You help us take down Morgan, and I can promise your release."

Cappadonna kicked the nightstand over, causing me to jump closer to the lookalike. "You're not in the fucking position to be making deals and killing fucking witnesses. She is out on whatever deal that Morgan has spun. What the fuck do you think will happen if she ends up dead? Huh? I don't want to make this deal, but in my world, you make deals you don't want to get shit done."

"Kinda like that WNBA player and the angel of death switch the government did." Lookalike shrugged. "My question is how do we know we can trust that she won't backdoor us?"

He seemed calm, mixed with a little bit of crazy if he needed to be. I was staring at him trying to figure out where he fit into this. Who was he? And why did he resemble the twins?

"When she hears this deal, she would be a fool to backdoor us."

I looked from each man and took a large breath. "I'm listening."

"Morgan is gonna squeeze you for information and then put you back behind bars if he doesn't set someone up to murder you. It goes either way with him, so you never know. You help us, we help you. Play your role while we set him up. Evidence will appear on someone's desk that shows you never had anything to do with those bodies in your case."

"So, I wouldn't have to spend the rest of my life in prison?"

"Not if you play your cards right and do as I say."

"What's stopping you from killing me after I do whatever you need?" I eyed the man suspiciously.

"My word. If I give you my word, you can take that bitch to the bank. Do what needs to be done, and you're free to live your life."

I looked behind him at the twins who looked like they didn't agree with me living. "And them?"

"If you handle business then you don't need to worry about them... what do you say?" he held out his hand, and I walked forward and put my hand into his, and he pulled me close to him. "Oh, and Tasha... I'm a different demon. You cross me and I'll nail your fucking tongue to the cross while your head is somewhere in the Atlantic." His voice was low, and his eyes appeared black. "You don't know Capri... if you shall cross paths with her while with Morgan, she's a stranger and you just met her. Capri knows her role."

I gulped, knowing what I had to do. Going against the Delgatos for Morgan would have been stupid, and I would have been discarded.

The outcome from both seemed like I would be discarded either way. Except, with one, I had the chance to have a second life outside of prison. With Morgan, I could be sent back to prison, or like the man said, killed.

"Deal."

CHAPTER 11
CAPRI

IT WASN'T OFTEN that I was on social media, and whenever I did go on, it was always to be nosey and scroll. I had slept in today, and Meer told me he was going to get his hair retwisted. As I laid in his bed, seeing what everyone had going on, I rolled my eyes at Jesse finally posting videos from the bachelorette trip from hell.

If I hadn't attended myself, I would have assumed that she and her girls had the time of their lives. I was thinking about what I had to do when it came to Jesse. Did I ever think that I would have to take my friend out? How would I even do it? I had taken a life before, but nothing like this. Those people didn't mean anything to me when I put shots in their chest.

Jesse was someone that I knew and had memories with. No matter how bitter those memories were, we had them, so killing her wasn't a piece of cake. Then again, she had the power to ruin my family, and I couldn't allow that to happen.

Forty wasn't wrong. Her career had always been important to her. It made sense why she was always so disappointed when her father couldn't make an event, or didn't show he cared. Jesse was a marshal for her father's approval, so she would do anything to help him win this election and give him any information she knew.

It was the reason I kept ignoring her text messages to meet up to talk about what happened. Something told me that she wanted to get more information, especially since Core had wiped every piece of video evidence that existed for that day. I knew I couldn't avoid her forever, and eventually I had to text and let her know that I was going to come for her birthday. Knowing it was going to be her last birthday.

I scrolled right on past her bullshit, and landed on a random reel from someone that I wasn't even following.

She was recording a video of her retwisting a man's hair, and that wasn't the problem. Girl, get your coins and promote your work. It became a problem when the caption on the video was

POV: When your man begs you for a retwist.

The biggest problem was the damn man that was in her chair was my fucking fiancé. Meer was in his phone in deep concentration while she was doing weird kissy faces and shaking her ass behind his head.

I snatched the damn blankets from my body and rose out this bed like the little bitch from the exorcist. While I was tossing on his favorite sweatpants and T-shirt, I slid my feet into my sneakers and grabbed my purse.

I could get to Brandon's barbershop with my eyes closed. Money was good, so he went and expanded to the space next door for the chick that did hair. He had a few women that did hair now out that space.

Before he cut his locs, Capella used to go to the one who was doing Meer's hair. Capone had been going to Brandon for years. Naturally when Cappy was released, he started going. Not to mention, all the Gods got their hair cut there, too.

I didn't bother to call Meer because I was gonna pop up and handle it myself. I didn't need him putting her in place because bitches always thought it was cute when a man called himself putting them in their place. She needed to hear from me, his future wife. I wasn't even a jealous person, yet, I had sat back and allowed bitches to play in my face for too long.

Meer wasn't Naheim, and I trusted that he would never do me wrong like that. He was part of the reason that I was a healed woman today. I'm sure he didn't even know the bitch was recording or the fact that she was doing all of that behind his head.

Meer wasn't someone that was always on his phone. Whenever he was fully engrossed on his phone, it was because he was making money. He was probably buying stock or responding to emails, which is why he wasn't paying her ass any attention.

I should have been inducted into the world record book with the way I flew across the bridges, and into Brooklyn. As I turned onto the block, mostly all the Gods were on the block chilling. I was surprised when I saw Cappy posted up talking to Capella. It was sad that auntie's baby was about to see his aunt crash out, but I was here to do what I came to do.

Soon as they recognized my car, and I double parked next to my brother's truck, I hopped out and rounded the truck. "Baby Doll, what you doing out here?" He kissed the top of my head and did his usual look over. "My niece or nephew good?"

"Yeah." I was short with him as I headed toward the salon suite.

Cappy leaned off the car and watched me with concern, unsure what was going on with me. There were different rooms, but the room on the far left had that tacky ass logo on the door. The same logo she had plastered all over her page.

I opened the door and Meer's eyes rose from his phone and met mine. "You good, Suga?" he was immediately concerned, with half his hair twisted.

Sis' smiled and tried to pretend like she had been in this bitch working the entire time. "Meer, you were begging this bitch to do your hair?"

"The fuck? Shelly, what the fuck are you talking about?" I was so pissed that I couldn't even acknowledge the fact that this nigga used my middle name.

Her face dropped when the words had left my mouth. "Tika here seems to think that you're her man, and you were begging her to do your hair."

Meer went to say something, and I balled his lips up while standing inches from this bitch. "It was just for content... Meer know how we rock with each other."

Meer was still trying to say something, and I squeezed his lips tighter. "I've met more than a few of you bitches that try to disguise your disrespect as a fucking joke, or in your case, content." I opened my purse and pulled out my gun while staring at her. "This one is mine... don't fucking use him in yo' fucking content. Matter fact," I shoved my gun back into my purse and leaned over the chair and bopped her right in the mouth.

"Bitch, I'm not the one... you insecure so you trying to come in here and tell me what to do with my sal—"

Her words were cut short when I threw a punch that landed right in her bubble lips. As I tried to leap on her ass, I felt Meer's hand wrap around my waist and pull me away.

The door opened and I saw Cappy and Capella standing there while shorty was holding her leaking mouth. "Make content with this one again...I fucking dare you to make content with him again." I pretended to be cool, so Meer let me go. No sooner than he let me go, I tried to run back over there, and he grabbed me, pulling me out the salon. "You bitches gonna get enough of fucking with me... you posted the right one!" I screamed, while Meer carried me out the salon.

He had this smirk on his face as I started pacing in front of Cappy's truck. "You be talking shit about me, but you out here crashing out over yo' man."

"Quameer, you not getting your hair done by that bitch." I pointed in his face, and he took my finger and put it in his mouth.

"Yo, Baby Doll, you gotta fucking chill," Cappy laughed.

Kiki, one of the Inferno Goddesses came out the salon. "I told her doing that shit was gonna get her ass beat... you good, Pri?"

I folded my arms and watched how everybody was now watching. "Stop playing with Lady Inferno, Meer!" Yasin laughed.

"I ain't even know that bitch was doing that shit," Meer waved him off, and pulled me closer to him, and I mushed him. "Big Pa got you out here wilding out, huh?"

I stared up at him. "I'm not playing about you, Quameer... find somebody new, and don't play with me."

"Yo, Kiki, you got me?" He looked to Kiki, who was talking with Yasin.

"Yeah, give me like ten minutes... I got you."

He kissed me on the lips, and then the forehead. "You gonna wait for me?"

"I'm going back to your house... I don't feel good."

Soon as I mentioned that I wasn't feeling well, he immediately became concerned. "What's wrong?"

"I feel nauseous, which is crazy because I hadn't felt that since Miami... I'm going to get back in bed."

"Let me drive you home then."

"Meer, I can go home... I am going to be alright," I promised him.

He whistled and nodded his head. "IG's gonna make sure you get home then... call me when you make it to our house."

"Your house," I smirked, and he pulled me back.

"Our house... stop playing with me." He bit my bottom lip and pulled it. "Love you, Mrs. Crash Out."

"Whatever... long as that bitch knows." I walked back to my truck, and Cappy held the door open for me.

Soon as I pulled away, one God was on my right, left, back, and two on my front as I pulled off the block. Meer kissed his two fingers as he watched me pull away. In the past, I allowed bitches to play games and take my man.

That man was a good one, and I wasn't playing games when it came to him. If a bitch wanted to suck on the barrel of this gun, she could, because like Meer said, it was all gas no sense when it came to him and our family.

Quameer did laundry like every other man in the world. Just throwing all his clothes in one pile and washing it. He had to run some errands, and I should have been getting ready because he told me once he came back, we would be heading to my doctor's appointment. Instead, I was in-between his room and Peach's room gathering up all the dirty laundry to wash.

I had finished washing the sheets and blanket for his bed and was tossing Peach's clothes in the dryer while putting Meer's motorcycle clothes in the washer. I had always washed my own clothes, even when I could have hired someone to do it for me.

My mother worked at a laundromat for most of my life, and I was taught early how to wash and fold clothes like a professional. As I flipped Meer's pockets, a holographic wrapper fell out of his pockets and I paused, holding onto the washer while closing my eyes. The last time something fell out of a man's pocket, it was a piece to a condom wrapper.

Slowly, I picked up the paper and held it in my hand before looking down at it. When I flipped it over, I smiled. It was a sticker from Peach's sticker book, and it said best daddy on it.

"Relax Capri, he's not your past... Meer is not him," I whispered to myself as I took a few deep breaths and saved the sticker on the shelf on top of the washer.

Laundry always had brought me peace, I enjoyed washing and drying clothes. For the longest time, it left me traumatized by the shit I used to find in Naheim's pockets. I was finally finding peace in it again, and I needed to remind myself that Quameer would never do anything like that to me. I trusted him.

"You know damn well I'm not." I jumped out of my skin when I noticed Meer leaning on the door to the laundry room.

"Why...why the hell would you do that? I didn't hear the chime of the door."

"I silenced it because I knew yo' ass wasn't ready and wanted to catch you in the act so you couldn't have some wild excuse... we're gonna be late, Sug."

"Just wanted to do the laundry before we went out. Meer, you need to start separating your whites from colors… this shirt is expensive and now it has a red tint to it," I held up the shirt that I tried to revive and failed.

He stared at me; his eyes low so I knew he had finished smoking before coming inside. He refused to smoke near me, even though our favorite thing to do was smoke while sitting and looking out at the lake.

"You know that, right?" he spoke lowly as he continued to stare at me. "I need you to know that, Capri."

I always winced whenever he called me by my actual name. Suga had become my name when it came to him. Meer referred to me as Suga, and it didn't matter who he was talking to. I was *his* Suga and had been that before I even told him that I would marry him.

"Meer, I know that. I just saw it fall and it reminded me of that time, and I slightly panicked. Had nothing to do with you."

He walked further into the laundry room and stared down at me. "You don't never have to worry about no shit like that when it comes to me. I'm not out there looking at nobody. Only shit you gonna see fall out my pockets is wrappers from Peach's snacks."

I reached up and held his face. "I'm sorry, Meer."

He kissed me on the lips and tried to pull back and I continued kissing him, slipping my tongue into his mouth. "Don't apologize for your trauma. I just need you to know that your heart is safe in my hands."

I smiled as he snuck kisses all over my face. "Meer, stop… that tickles," I swatted him when he stuck his tongue into my ear.

"You know what else is safe in my hands?"

"What else?" I kissed him again.

"That pussy, Mrs. Inferno." He bit my earlobe, and I tried to leave the laundry room because I knew where this was heading.

"We're gonna be late… remember, you came in here about to fuss at me about it," I reminded him, and he pulled me back.

"Nah… you wanna be prancing around the crib with my shirt and…" he paused as he lifted his shirt up. "No panties on."

"Meer, we're gonna be so late," I moaned.

"Let me taste you, Sug… I need a reminder why I call you Suga." He licked his lips while sucking on my neck.

Before I could protest, this man picked me up and put me on the washing machine as it was in the middle of the spin cycle. He opened my legs and then went in like he had been starving all day.

Between his tongue, and him sucking me dry, and the vibration from the washing machine, I couldn't keep my eyes straight. They kept crossing as I held his head in place. "Meer… omg… right there!" I screamed out.

My moans put a battery in his back because this nigga's tongue matched the vibration of the damn washing machine. "Bring it here… don't run… let me finish my meal, Sug."

His words sent a ripple up my back, as I looked down at him. Our eyes locked as he smirked, exposing that he had his fangs in his mouth. He bit down on my lips before slurping every liquid that was coming out of me.

"Taste so good…. Why you so sweet, Suga?" he said between each slurp, while staring into my eyes.

His stare was enough to send tingles below my legs, as he put my legs over his shoulders. He paused, kissing my feet before diving right back in, while shoving his finger inside of me. I rotated my hips on his finger, while throwing my head back and enjoying the feeling he was creating.

My legs started to shake as I held the side of the washing machine and squealed. "Baby… I'm… I'm…" Meer kept his head locked between my legs as he lifted my bottom half and kissed my lips before his tongue moved down to my ass.

I felt the pressure building from the bottom as he flicked his tongue over my asshole while humming. I didn't know what to do or what to hold because it felt like I was about to unleash a fucking waterfall from between my legs.

He spit on my pussy, as he slurped me up and kissed my lips

softly. I released myself and collapsed on the washing machine as he softly kissed the inside of my legs while staring up at me. "Sweetest thing I've ever tasted."

I laid there weak and whimpered, he kissed my second pair of lips once more before he made it to my neck and kissed me. "Got pussy juice all in my grills, amor."

"Means you taste me even when I'm not with you." I held onto his neck, and kissed his lips, tasting my own juices. "We really need to get ready, Meer."

He picked me up and carried me to the room so I could get ready for this appointment that I was nervous for. Meer always knew when I was nervous and knew how to take me out my head. He finally stopped kissing on me long enough for us to get ready to head to our doctor's appointment.

Meer held my hand as we waited in the exam room. I had answered a dozen questions about my past history or any past histories. I told them about my abortion, even though it hurt to admit it out loud. The woman never judged me, so I felt comfortable, and Meer held and kissed my hand while I answered questions.

After they did the physical exam, took blood, and urine. Now, we were sitting and waiting for the doctor to do the sonogram and give us any information we wanted to know.

"Still nervous?" Meer kissed my hand.

I smiled. "Hard to be nervous when you're right here."

"I want you to come to Chicago for Peach's birthday."

Meer had told me about their plans for Peach's birthday, and how she wanted both of her parents there on her birthday trip. I loved that they got along enough to make that happen for her. She deserved to have the things she wanted, and I didn't have any insecurities when it came to Meer and Brandi being around each other.

It was clear that Brandi got on his damn nerves, and he would never do something to ruin what we had. If anything, I was more worried for Brandi than them hooking up while on

Peach's birthday trip. That man didn't give her room to breathe once she said some stupid shit out her mouth.

"This trip was for you, Brandi, and Peach to be together... I don't want to bombard the trip."

"I told Brandi to bring her husband. If she doesn't bring him, then that's her problem... Peach wants you there."

I looked at him shocked. "You talked to her about it?"

"She asked me if it was okay if you came and I told her that I would ask you... I know you about to start work and can't take too much time away."

"I can't come for the entire week, but I can come on the weekend because I don't work on the weekend. I'll fly out and be there for Peach."

He pointed to his cheek and I kissed it, and was about to kiss his lips when the door opened and the doctor came in.

A short Black woman with a pixie cut and the straightest white teeth I had ever seen came in. I could tell she was getting money by the Van Cleef bracelets and the YSL sling back pumps that she wore. There was something about a Black woman doing her big one in her career.

It was the reason I wanted to be a lawyer. I wanted to make a difference, so I could represent people that looked like me. You felt more comfortable when you had someone that looked like you whenever you needed a doctor, nurse, or lawyer.

That wasn't to say that other races weren't good at their professions. I've have doctors that brushed me off because they felt I was being extra. I've witnessed doctors discharge my brother because they felt he was addicted to pain medicine in the middle of a sickle cell crisis. So, when it came to a Black woman, or doctor in charge, I wanted them to care for me.

"How are you doing, Mrs. Delgato? I'm Dr. Bia," she introduced herself as she washed her hands. "Husband, boyfriend, or friend?"

"Husband," Meer answered, and I looked at him because one thing that man loved to do was toss around that husband and wife card like we were married already.

"Well, nice to meet you, Mr. Del—"

"Inferno, and her last name Inferno, but clearly this pregnancy already got her forgetting shit," he replied calmly.

"Quameer!" I pinched him.

Dr. Bia laughed, happy that she didn't have square patients, because clearly Meer wasn't about to act like he had any sense, and he didn't care where we were. "It be like that sometimes," she continued to laugh as she instructed me to lay back.

She hit the lights and started clicking around the sonogram machine, while moving the wand around my stomach, while looking around. I watched the little screen while holding my breath and allowing her to do what she needed to do. Meer stood up and was clued in on the screen while kissing my forehead.

I never thought I would have ever gotten here. Being so in love and feeling that love by a man while carrying his child. I thought God was going to punish me and I would be an auntie forever, never a mother.

"There we go," she smiled. "Going from the date of your last period, and from what I'm seeing... you're around ten weeks."

"Look at my boy... sorry, boy... Daddy be turning yo' mama every which way," Meer said with a serious expression while I hid my face. Meer swore we were having a boy.

"Have some decorum, Robert."

He smirked and looked down at me. "Oh, you was talking to Gam's messy ass, huh?"

Dr. Bia put the little doppler on my stomach and moved it around, and our baby's heartbeat filled the room.

A knock at the door caused me to lean up. The door opened, and I saw Erin peek her head in. "Um, I know your appointment was tod—"

"Gorgeous, get in the damn room. I wanna see, too," Capone said, and then my mother walked in behind him, and came over next to Meer.

"You didn't think we would not be here... this is your first baby, Princess." My mother hadn't called me princess in so long that it felt nice to hear her start calling me it again.

The door opened again, and Cappadonna and Alaia walked in with my father behind them. "Sorry... we're really excited about this baby."

Dr. Bia laughed. "We love an excited family." She went back and put the doppler on my stomach, as we all listened to the heartbeat of the baby.

My mom reached up and wiped Meer's tears as they fell from his eyes as we listened to our creation.

"Damn, Pri... you're about to become a mother." Capone sniffled while holding onto his wife.

We heard a sniffle, and all turned to see my father standing there wiping his face. "To baby Inferno... God, continue to bless my Suga Cane as she carries and brings this baby into the world."

CHAPTER 12
AIMEE

ONLY CORLEON and Forty would have me sitting in a class during the summer. The class that Morgan was a guest professor in was part of the political science summer course. The added security search to get into the damn lecture was crazy.

It wasn't like I brought my gun on campus with me, so I was good. I slipped into a seat in the back and watched as he spoke. So sure of himself that he probably said bless you to himself after he sneezed. He floated across the stage and spoke with ease about whatever this course was about.

All the thirstiest students were in the front row drooling over this man. I couldn't help but to see a target when I looked at him. He was someone trying to take down my family, and I couldn't allow that to happen. They were all depending on me, so I had to play my role and do what was expected of me.

Core: this class is boring as fuck.

Me: How do you know?

Core: listening from your laptop.

I shook my head, not surprised because this man was a

genius. Someone that I aspired to be. While everyone wanted to be housewives and mothers, I wanted to have a company like Corleon. He was everywhere and nowhere at the same time.

His knowledge was so informative, and I absorbed everything that he said to me. How he taught me how to trust my gut and not doubt myself was something that I needed at times.

> Core: good luck, Grasshopper... throw that charm on and smile.

I discreetly stuck my middle finger in the camera thinking I was being slick. When "O' Let's Do" it by Waka Flocka blared loudly from my laptop, I slammed it down cursing Core in my head.

"Sorry. My computer has a virus." I smiled, putting my hair behind my ear, praying I looked flirty.

The students that were dick sucking gave me the stank eye, and I rolled my eyes. "Perfect ending," Morgan smiled at me.

"Are you taking questions after class?" Susie cunt licker asked, hoping she would have five minutes alone with him.

"I actually have to get across the city for a new community center that is opening. Thank you so much for allowing me to blabber your ears off."

"You're welcome," I called from the back, forcing myself to make myself stand out. Morgan smirked and clicked the pen he was holding in his hand.

He was intrigued.

Forty said he liked young bitches, and it was apparent that he liked young Black bitches because the bitch in the front hadn't piqued his interest in the whole time she was up there. He couldn't stop making eye contact with me as I packed up my tote bag and prepared to exit.

"I didn't get your name," he called to me, as I headed out the door.

"You didn't ask anyone's name." I paused. "Aimee."

He came up a few steps until I could smell his Tom Ford cologne.

Tobacco Vanille.

I knew that scent because it was one of my favorite scents that Capella wore. In my opinion, only big steppas wore that scent. It was clear that Morgan just knew he was a big steppa with the way he was grinning at me.

"Vincent Morgan."

"Our next mayor." I fed into his ego, even though it tasted like poison. "Well, it was nice to meet you, Mr. Morgan."

I turned slowly and started walking toward the exit while counting in my head.

Four...

Three...

Two...

"Are you looking for an internship or anything?"

I smiled inwardly and turned to face him. "I have been looking into some... no one is looking for one."

"Well, you're in luck, Aimee. I'm actually looking for an intern, and I like how bold you are. I need that energy around me." He walked back to the desk and went into his briefcase and came back to me with a card. "Give me a call on my personal number, and we can talk further about this... I have a good feeling about you."

I held the card in my hand and smiled. "Thanks, Mr. Morgan."

"Vincent."

I looked at the card and then back at him. "Vincent... thanks."

As I rushed out of class and back to my truck, I dug into my bag to grab my ringing phone. I looked at the caller ID and answered while continuing to my truck.

"Hello?"

"Hey Aimee, this is Dina at the woman's health clinic. I was just calling to follow up on how you're doing after your procedure?"

"I'm... I'm doing alright."

"Aimee, it is common for you to feel guilt or sadness after an abortion. If you need to talk to anyone, we have a counselor here that you can speak with."

"I am fine... thanks," I quickly ended the call and jogged down the steps to where I was parked, pushing the conversation out of my head.

Soon as I rounded the corner, I stopped in my tracks when I saw Khalil leaned on my truck. When he noticed me, he smirked. "Hey baby mama."

CHAPTER 13
CAPRI

"I DON'T LIKE this shit, Sug," Meer said as he held my face and kissed my lips, before letting me go.

"I'm gonna be careful, and handle what needs to be done… I got Aimee with me," I told him, and he looked at Aimee on the back of my bike.

"We got her, Meer… she'll be good and protected." Kiki, one of the Inferno Goddesses said, since they were all riding out.

Capone and Corleon had got the drop on where the Chrome Vipers were hiding. Shmurda was smart enough not to lay low with them. They watched them for a week, and realized it was the car they used to transport Shmurda in.

Core added a tracker in the back, and a listening device inside the car. You could imagine how much shit these niggas talked about, including when they were getting Shmurda out the city and back in Baltimore.

It was either now or never to get this nigga. He was smart with where he laid low, he was never at the same spot, and the niggas who transported him moved a bit smart, too. Not smarter than us, but smart for them Viper niggas.

All Gods were on deck to lock down the highway so we could make sure this nigga was signed, sealed and delivered to hell.

Quasim walked over with Cappadonna. "I put Kincaid and Goon on you, Pri. The minute that shit feels unsafe for you... give 'em the signal and they got you both." He looked at both me and Aimee.

"You sure you wanna do this?" Aimee asked.

"I wish you'd all stop asking me like I'm not capable of doing this... he's responsible for shooting up the restaurant I was in... I can handle myself."

Meer continued to look at me while reading my eyes. "She got it," he confirmed.

He checked my protective gear and then handed me my gloves. "Love you, Meer."

"Love you more, Sug." I watched as he walked over toward his bike with his gloves hanging out his back pocket.

His walk was my favorite thing about him. He never had to say shit, the walk let you know he was pressure.

"All eyes on you, Baby Doll," Capp said and kissed both me and Aimee on the head before walking back over toward his bike. "Hold her down, Aimee."

"Got you, Pops."

Capone and Corleon were riding together, while Naheim was in the next car with Capella. I put my helmet on while watching my man, who had all eyes on me.

None of us had our regular bikes because we didn't want any visible markings. We had to move smarter, so we all wore black, without a stitch of our skin showing. Kincaid saluted as he rolled out first, and I followed behind him. There was an Inferno Goddess on each side of me with Goon behind me.

"Lady Inferno, just let us know if shit too heavy... we'll handle it," Kiki said and flipped her visor down to her helmet and sped forward.

"Yo, Capri... you really Lady Inferno," I heard Aimee's muffled voice through her helmet. "Ready to go kill shit."

"We out," I said and saluted Meer, and sped off the block with Goon behind me.

To get to the bridge, they had to come through Staten Island, so the Vanducci-Cromwell's had already been put onto game and had every exit through Staten Island covered. There was no way they were getting off and avoiding the pressure we had for them.

The timing was perfect as we watched them on the overpass heading off the Verrazano bridge straight onto the Staten Island expressway. Everyone knew how short the Staten Island expressway was, so we had to get them before they made it to the next bridge.

Core said he wanted us to stay away from the bridges because of the cameras and stay on the highway where he could control those from the car.

"Remember we gotta fall back if they get to that bridge," Goon reminded us.

"They rolling fucking deep," I looked at them all riding beside the G wagon that was transporting that nigga Shmurda.

"Pri, we handled worse... don't get soft on me now," Kincaid smirked and held his hand out, and I dapped him up.

I saw Quameer and Quasim riding side by side with all the Gods behind them, and that was our cue to get on with them. I revved my engine, and we bolted down the side of the highway until we came onto an entrance. My gun was on the holster on my leg so I could easily pull it while driving this bike.

Cappadonna rode his bike next to Capone's car until they both split and went into different lanes. I came into the middle of their lane and looked at Capp who saluted, and then at Capone and Corleon who both nodded at me, as I pressed forward.

It took a minute for us to fall in the lane, and make sure no cars were in the middle of what was about to go down. All it took was for one Chrome Viper to look back, and he signaled to let them know they had company.

As we pushed past the Slosson and Todt Hill exit, I merged into the HOV lane ahead of everybody. Aimee pulled on my left sleeve letting me know somebody was on the left. Before I could merge in front of them, she pulled her shit and bullets flew.

I continued going ahead of everybody, making sure they

wouldn't get on that damn bridge. As I rode the middle lane, the Inferno Goddesses all closed in around me as we made it down the expressway with ease.

I saw Star's car at one of the exits, and she nodded her head as I rode around her car to go back in the opposite direction. They had closed traffic down, so nobody was getting in or out on this side of the expressway.

As we headed back in the opposite direction, all the ladies all got on the side of me, locking it down. I saw Kincaid with his bike up on one wheel, as he was letting his shit go with one hand and keeping his bike up with the other.

Meer had skidded across two lanes, and popped another CV in the chest, sending his bike crashing out on the shoulder. They were all protecting the G Wagon, and before any of them could get to it, they needed to get the fucking fleas that seemed to be everywhere.

Core had his laptop on his lap with his gun out the window while Capone was hitting the back of their bikes, sending their bikes out of control. Quasim came around, and the G wagon nearly made him stall out, and he fell back, as he went around to the other side of the car. Meer peeped and had his brother's follow up.

Goon rode in front of me and let off a few shots as he skidded across a few lanes. I wanted the nigga in the truck. As they came closer and closer, Aimee and me both went low, she maneuvering to my left and me to the right as I sent a shot straight through the window, cruising right through the passenger's head.

I swerved over toward the HOV lane again, so I could turn back in the right. Aimee hit my right sleeve, and I shot the slimy ass nigga that tried to come at us, while she got the one behind him. We cleared the car with Capella and Naheim, and they both got the ones that were coming on us.

The minute it got heavy, Goon and Kincaid along with the goddesses locked in on me and handled whoever came at us.

Soon as it was handled, I had the clear pathway to the truck. I pointed and Goon nodded and bolted down behind it.

Meer's bike merged next to me, and he looked at me. Even though we couldn't see each other's eyes, I already knew he wanted me to follow him, and I did the minute he took off. He signaled for me to get the other side while Goon took the back, and Quasim had the front.

Cappy rode next to me and made the gun motion for Aimee to take the shot. "Me? I'm gonna fuck this up," I could hear her muffled panic.

He patted his heart twice and then put two fingers to his temple and saluted. "Aim, take the fucking shot!" I yelled because we were getting closer to the cut off.

We were on the weak spot because I had taken out the nigga in the passenger side. While Shmurda and the driver were concerned with Meer and Goon, we had to take the shot and end all of this. I sped up some, so she aligned with the back window.

"Slide on that nigga, Aim!" I heard Capella yell as he sped by with three CV's on his ass. Before it could be a problem, the Gods handled them.

I could feel her hesitation, and then she leaned on my back to get as low as she could and held my waist. I saw the gun aim at the window, and watched her gloved finger wrap around the trigger and she squeezed it until she couldn't anymore. The glass shattered, falling onto us, as she continued to air it out.

Quameer looked at us through the window and signaled with two fingers for me to go forward while he held his gun up and ended the driver, sending the truck barreling across all the lanes, hitting the divider and flipping over.

"Core can't keep directing the police calls... we gotta dip," Capone said as he got closer to me. "Next exit... you and Aimee."

Nodding, I saluted to my baby, and then sped through the mess of bikes and bodies, as the Goddesses surrounded me, and Kincaid hit a wheelie to get in front, while Goon had the back of me.

I held my Hermes work bag, and my purse as I smiled while walking into the district attorney office. Security was a breeze, as I scanned my new badge, and went through the metal detectors.

I wore a sleeveless two-piece black suit, and a pair of strappy heels. It was summer, and hot as hell, and I couldn't fathom putting on a full ass suit today. Just in case I had to go to court, I had a tweed blazer that I could just toss on.

> Big Pa: Good luck today, Suga... you fucking pressure and know it. You Mrs. Inferno, so I know you fucking fire.

I smiled as I stepped onto the crowded elevator and looked at my message. Meer didn't understand how much his support meant to me. He wasn't intimidated by me and supported and understood what I had to do. If anything, I think it turned him on that I was a lawyer.

That was because he was college educated himself, so he understood and could code switch. Quameer could hold an intelligent conversation like the rest of them. It was clear he was smart from the way that he invested and made a way for his family legally.

Our family.

"Ms. Browne, how are you doing? I am Skyler, your assistant... can I get you any coffee or anything?"

"Um... sure?" I didn't know I was even supposed to have an assistant, so I was caught off guard when this pretty pecan complexion girl with wild curly hair and glasses approached me.

She smiled. "I can see what Aimee was talking about... you scream bad bitch."

My head snapped in her direction when she mentioned Aimee. "How do you kn—"

"We're all playing on the same team, Mrs. Inferno," she winked, and then went to grab coffee.

Forty did tell me some things were put into place that I wouldn't know about, and it was for my own protection. I guess Skyler was one of those people that was put in place. If she knew Aimee, that meant that she was involved in hacking of the sorts.

I continued down the hallway, looking for the room with my name on it. Did ADA's even get their own offices? As I was nearing the end of the hall, a man came out the room and snapped his finger.

"Capri Browne?"

"Is it that obvious?" I smiled nervously.

He laughed. "Yes. You're down the wrong hall... we're back over that way. I'm Brian Classen, deputy chief ADA. It's nice to have you on the team... you come highly recommended from the governor. Quite impressive," he complimented as we walked back down the hall, and down a second one.

I don't know what strings Forty pulled to get a recommendation from the governor, but I was gonna roll with it. "Thank you."

"I'm sure you met your very eager assistant. She's new as well, so you both will be showing each other the way." He let out a hearty chuckle at his lame ass joke.

I cleared my throat. "Yes. I have met her."

He snapped his fingers – again. "Oh, the big boss is in early today... let me get you two acquainted."

Before I could even object, he knocked on the door quickly and turned the knob. The man had his back turned as he was shaking off his suit jacket, and that was when I saw the tattoo.

When he turned around fully, I recognized him as the man from the plane when I first returned home. He helped me with my suitcase, and I noticed a small tattoo peeking on his wrist.

He gave me that same charming smile he had given me on the plane. "Hello, Ms. Browne, it's finally good to meet you... Rich Parker," he winked, as he came around the desk and shook my hand.

Not even knowing he was shaking the hand of a future

Inferno. The district attorney's office didn't know they had two sworn enemies working together. A Chrome Viper, and an Inferno.

CHAPTER 14
CAPRI

I WANTED to turn and look into the imaginary camera that was clearly punking me. The man that insisted on helping me on the plane months ago, was standing in this office, and he was not only the district attorney, but he was also Rich Parker. The man that I was supposed to fuck over in the worst way possible.

His hand lingered a little longer than I would have liked, but I quickly pulled my hand back and offered him a smile. "Nice to meet you, Mr. Parker. It's a pleasure to be working alongside you."

Even though I should have been nervous about meeting this man, a man that was known to run with Chrome Vipers, I wasn't scared or nervous. I almost wanted to slide my fingers under my nose and spit in his face.

"Brian, you can leave me and Ms. Browne to get acquainted. I actually need to brief her on a few cases we have."

"Sure thing, Mr. Parker. Again, it was nice meeting you again, Capri." I rolled my eyes hearing him refer to Rich as Mr. Parker, then calling me by my name.

"Ms. Browne," Rich sternly corrected him.

Brian's pale face turned red as he fidgeted with the door. "Sorry… Ms. Browne," he quickly corrected himself before getting the hell out of the room.

Rich sat on the edge of his desk and looked at the door. "He's salty because he wasn't considered for your position. I like when it's a bunch of us in the higher positions... we fucking work ten times harder than men like him." He bit the inside of his cheek, clearly pissed that Brian had the nerve to be upset.

I looked around his office, which still had boxes scattered all over. "We always have had to work harder and always will... even our children and their children," I sighed.

As much as we were enemies, and he didn't know it yet, what he said was the truth and had always been the case for Black people. In law school, me and Zoya had to work ten times harder than our white friends with trust funds and homes in the Hamptons. I don't know how many times we had to correct a professor or file a complaint because the same treatment or grace wasn't extended to us, two out of the six black students in the classes.

We belonged in these spaces, and kids deserved to see people that looked like them on the right side of the law. I wanted to be an example to my nieces and nephews, show them that they could do whatever they wanted.

"So true." He stood up from the end of the desk and walked back around, taking a seat. "I actually have a meeting to get to across town, but I wanted to meet and check in with you... funny that we've met previously."

"It's very funny... thanks again with the help that I didn't need."

He laughed. "You was acting like I was trying to take you on a date or some shit." It was funny how we learned to code switch. The tone and words he used with Brian dropped the minute he closed the door behind him.

"I'm just independent and like to do things for myself... the help wasn't needed but appreciated. What business did you have in Singapore?" I remained standing while he got more comfortable in his extra ass office chair.

I bet his corny ass called it his throne when nobody was

around. "I was on vacation in Thailand with my girlfriend. My layover happened to be in Singapore."

"You always travel back in a full suit?"

Rich couldn't help but to laugh. "When I had to get off the flight and head straight to work. I had got a call ahead of the release of the scandal with the governor. Guess, I shouldn't say too much since you seem to be very close with the governor, I don't know if I can speak freely."

I switched my bag from one hand to the other. "We're on the same team, no? You can speak freely around me. We're both on the right side of the law, right?"

> Erinwiththecooper: Dinner tonight at our house... love you.

I smiled as I briefly looked at the message and then returned my attention back to Rich, who happened to be in his phone at the same time. "Listen, since you're starting on a Friday, I want you to take the weekend, and Monday off because Tuesday starts a busy week for the both of us. Vincent Morgan also wants to have lunch with us next week, too."

"The one running for mayor?" I pretended not to know the man that was trying to put my brothers away.

"Yeah, him. We'll all be working together very closely, so he wants to make sure we're all acquainted."

I snorted. "You sound like you know for a fact that he's going to win."

He stood up, grabbing his suit jacket he had taken off moments before. "We all know how this goes... only the strongest win. With all eyes on the police for that Staten Island massacre... we need to get the right mayor in here that is going to clean this mess up."

His expression went from nonchalant to pissed with the mention of his precious Chrome Vipers getting fucked over. "Yeah, I heard about that... any new breaking news on it?"

He shook his head. "Not as of lately... like they were fucking ghosts or something. All we have is a morgue filled with bodies, and no answers." I could tell the more Rich spoke about it, the more it pissed him off. "Anyway, I have a meeting, so Brian will give you the state issued laptop and show you the ropes."

"We'll find those bastards," I bit back my laugh as I looked across the room at him. "Thanks again." I watched as he quickly headed toward the door like he needed to be somewhere quick.

He hesitated before turning the doorknob and looked at me. "I think we're going to make the perfect team, Ms. Browne."

"I think so too, Mr. Parker. Enjoy the rest of your day."

"Appreciate that."

Brian was loitering outside of the office when I came out and offered to give me a tour of the office. He took me around and introduced me to everyone while talking my ear off. My phone kept buzzing, so I knew I had a few text messages to address.

By the time he had shown me around and brought me to my office, I was mentally exhausted from fake smiling and laughing at his corny jokes. Soon as the door closed behind him, I plopped down in my office chair and took a deep breath before pulling my phone out.

> Zoy: Bitchhh! Take your phone off DND. I've been trying to reach you all week. Heading into court, call you later.

I had my phone on do not disturb all week because I just needed the space to be in my head. All week I prepared myself for work, knowing I would be splitting my time between Meer's house and the lake house on the weekend.

The nerves nearly crippled me and made me want to just sit in silence. I knew I drove Meer crazy because he wanted to get inside my head. He always prided himself on being able to tap into my head and getting me to open up to him.

Between our first doctor's appointment and hearing my baby's heartbeat, then having to spin on those Chrome Vipers, there was so much going on that I needed to just take a breath. With all that I had going on, the last thing I wanted was to stress this baby out. I've always envisioned a stress-free pregnancy and that wasn't what I was going to get.

The knock at the door pulled me from my thoughts. Skyler peeked her head in my office before I motioned for her to fully come in. She had my work laptop in her arms as she sat it down on my desk.

"You're good to bring this one home if you would like. I swept it clear for any software that could be on it… I would recommend using it for only work, nothing personal."

"Thanks, Skyler."

I didn't know much about Skyler, other than what she told me, which is that she was Aimee's friend. "No problem… now, I hate to be this person on your first day, but you need to go ahead and be nicer and not so defensive with him."

"How did you… never mind."

She smiled and lowered her voice. "His office is bugged. I need to get my hands on that laptop, so you need to be nicer, so he feels more comfortable. I'm working on being friendly with his assistant, so I need you to do your part too."

"More nice, less defensive. It's not easy to do when you know what he and Morgan have planned for my family."

Skyler tucked her foot underneath her and looked at me. "I don't know if you know or not, but your brother saved my life."

"Which one?"

"Mr. Capp," she replied seriously. "He could have taken my life the day he ran into the trap that I was in. Instead, he spared my life and gave me a lecture to get my shit together and stop allowing bum niggas to touch me."

I smiled. "Sounds like Cappy."

"So, the last thing I want is for him to be sent to prison… he's a good man. A little twisted, but he has a good heart."

Cappy had the best heart, so I knew exactly what she meant. He always wanted what was best for everyone and to protect everyone. Cappadonna would protect this family with his last breath. Even with him and Capone getting into an argument, he would still do that time if it meant protecting our family.

"How am I supposed to be fake when I meet Morgan? I don't like that man and haven't even met him?"

"If you knew the evils that man has done and plans to do... you'd learn to be fake right away." She tapped my desk and headed out the office, as I leaned back in the chair.

I spent the day learning the ropes from Brian, even taking my lunch with him. It wasn't by choice, he suggested that we get lunch together, and then put on this pathetic ass look which made me feel bad, so we went down to a salad bar down the block from the office. While I ate my salad, and tried to make casual conversation, Brian was more interested in who I knew, and how I knew the governor. Rich was right about him being pissed that position went to me instead of him.

When he tried to chuckle about how it was impossible for someone as new as me to land an ADA position, that was when I faked a phone call and told him I would see him back at the office. Brian had the potential to be a problem, so I was keeping my distance, but also keeping my eye on him.

If push came to shove, I would make sure that his ass was swimming somewhere in the Hudson, because he couldn't fuck this up for us because his ego was bruised. His ego being bruised was going to make me call my fiancé to handle his ass.

The minute the workday was over, I rushed out of there like the devil was chasing me. Rich never came back into the office, and I could already tell what his schedule would look like. He wasn't going to be around much, and knowing what I knew, he was more than likely running behind Morgan trying to figure out how his people got fucked up on that highway.

After chatting with Skyler for a few, I hopped into my car and peeled my ass out of the city back to my lake house. All I wanted to do was eat and sleep on the back porch while spending time with my family. Now that things weren't so tense between us all, I didn't mind being together and spending time with everyone without feeling stressed.

Soon as I was granted access into the lake community, "Pretty Wings" by Maxwell played on the radio, and I got a lump in my throat that refused to go away. My eyes became misty and before I knew it, I was sobbing while riding down my street. Each time I tried to stop, more tears came, and I couldn't stop them.

CJ and Peach were riding bikes in the street while Meer and Capone were watching them and talking. Soon as Peach and CJ saw me pull into the driveway, they ditched their bikes and ran over toward my car.

My tints were dark, so I was trying to stop crying, but the more the song played the tears wouldn't stop coming. This song made me think of Meer, and how much I loved him. I didn't care that this was technically a breakup song. This song meant more than that to me and Meer. It was the song that showed me that he allowed me to go, he had no problem letting me go because he was confident that I would come back to him.

And I did.

"Auntie, you gonna let us in or what?" CJ knocked on the window, and I wiped my face and opened the door.

Soon as they both saw me, they looked concerned as I plastered a fake smile on my face. I stepped out the car and hugged both of them. "Hey Babes... having fun?" I sniffled.

Meer stopped mid conversation when he saw me and jogged across the street. "Peach and CJ... go ride your bikes."

"Daddy, she's cry—"

"And don't I always take care of you when you cry?" Peach nodded her head. "Then trust that I'm going to do the same with Suga... alright?"

With full confidence that her father was going to help me, she ran off with Capone Jr. and went to finish riding bikes in the streets.

"I'm alright, I promise," I wiped my face, as he pulled me into him.

"The fuck happened, Suga... who did something.. that nigga

did someth…hold that thought." He went to toward the house, more than likely to grab his gun.

"Pretty Wings, Meer." I called behind him and he stopped, turning around to look at me to make sure I wasn't bullshitting him. "That song came on and I was crying because of that damn song… I can't help but to think of us whenever I hear that song now. It's our sad-happy love song." I broke down crying more, and now Capone was concerned.

"Yo, Meer… my sister good?"

"Nigga, you did this three times already… you already know what it is," he laughed, and Capone nodded his head in agreement.

With Erin's last pregnancy, she gave my brother so much hell. She was mad with him one day, then she wanted to be in his skin the next, so he more than anything understood these crazy hormones that were going through my body.

"I was fine all day and then out of nowhere, that song plays and I'm an emotional wreck." I held onto him, wrapping my arms around him while he kissed me on the lips.

"I cry to that song, too, Sug… I think about you soon as that song starts. Is it crazy if we get married to that shit?"

I giggled through my tears. "People would look at us like we're crazy."

"Half the people in the world don't know it's a breakup song… only your weird ass." He laughed and kissed me again. "We move to the beat of our own shit."

He gave me one more kiss and a tight hug, one that only Meer could give me, before going into my car and grabbing my work bag and purse. "You was supposed to help me clean this fucking garage, Bitch!" Capone hollered from across the street.

"Wifey home… gotta take care of her. I'll be back over once I make sure she eat and is comfortable."

Capone hesitated. "Fuckkkk!"

Meer broke out laughing because Capone had a flashback and wasn't good anymore. "Chill out… we won't call you this time."

"I'm gonna bust yo' ass, Quameer."

I shook my head and went into the house while those two continued to toss threats across the street. Gams was in the living room watching a movie with Mina. Mina was laying on the couch, with her head in Gam's lap, while she softly brushed her curls while engrossed in the movie they were watching.

"Hey Suga Pie," she smiled.

Meer had everyone calling me Suga, and I had to admit I loved it. It made me feel this sense of warmth and comfort that I only got when my father called me Suga cane. I walked over toward the couch, and she placed a kiss on my cheek while I gently rubbed Mina's curls.

"I hope you're taking it easy and you're not overworking yourself," Gams said, as she continued to brush Mina's hair, while giving me that look Meer always spoke about.

I settled on the opposite side of the couch. "It was only my first day, so there wasn't much to stress or overwork myself over... I'm just tired and a little hungry."

She smiled at me. "I know this isn't easy and even though I don't know the logistics, I know you're going to make this sacrifice for your brothers. Even though you know they wouldn't want you to. I don't have to worry because I know my Dumplin' is going to take care of you."

Just as soon as she mentioned him, he came into the house and placed my bags on the kitchen counter. "Sug, I'm gonna make you something to eat and you're going to finish it."

"Meer, you are not my daddy."

Where Meer was standing, Gams couldn't see him because her back was facing him. "Oh, I'm not." He used the chair and was acting like he was giving me back shots. "I'm not Big..." he smirked as I covered my face with the pillow.

"Big what, Dumplin'?" Gams was lost on what we were talking about, which made it ten times worse.

"Big Pimpin', Gams... you know I'm that nigga," he cleaned it up while flicking his tongue between both his fingers while looking directly at me.

I rolled my eyes while laughing because this man of mine kept me on my toes. "Gams, you know your grandson hid in the trunk of my car."

"What you and Erin and Alaia be saying.... *And did!*"

I howled at his impression of us as he rounded around the counter and went to make me something to eat. "He gets that from Quinton. One time, Mina cut your father off when they were dating. She went on a date with another handsome man in our neighborhood. Quinton climbed through that man's bedroom window and beat his ass because he went on a date with Mina. That man refused to look at Mina whenever he saw her out." Gams was hysterically laughing right along with me.

I wiped the tears out my eyes while laughing. "So, you telling me that the Inferno boys ain't wrapped right?"

"They get it from they daddy... Dumplin', why were you in her truck, and how long were you in there?"

Quameer smirked, no shame in his game as he came into the living room with a plate of food. Gams had rice and beans with baked chicken. "Thank you, Baby."

He dropped a kiss on my head, as he sat on the edge of the couch next to me. "I wasn't in there that long."

"Well, how long isn't that long, Quameer?" I wanted to know, as I bit into a piece of chicken. Only Gams could make chicken that just melted in your mouth.

"I watched you go into that hole in the wall ass bar, and then popped your locks and got in the back." He shrugged like it wasn't nothing.

"What the hell? Me and Jesse were in there for a little while... Meer, you were in there when we drove to the chicken spot?"

"Hell yeah... and I was back there weighing my options on if I was going to climb over the seat and choke that nigga out."

With the way me and Gams were laughing, I couldn't breathe and held the plate out to avoid dropping it. "Dumplin', she got you down bad for her. Remind me of your mama and daddy... your father didn't have any logic when it came to your mother. No sense at all."

"All gas no sense…. where you think I got that saying from?"

Gams shook her head, however, she stared at her grandson with so much pride. "Is Sim the same way?"

Meer snorted. "You saw what the hell he did in Miami? How you even asking that question." He was right.

Sim was always so quiet, and even while he was crashing out, he was still poised, quiet, and lethal. "You right."

Gams snapped her fingers. "Suga Pie, I think I figured out why Mina took to you so quickly."

"Why?" both me and Meer answered at the same time.

"You look just like your mother when she was younger. She thought you were your mother." Gams smiled. "Jean was over here earlier, and they sat out back. Mina held her hand the entire time, like she did with you the first time you met her."

My father always told me that I reminded him of my mother when she was younger. It was funny how I resembled her, and our relationship had always been strained. I prayed that this new path we found ourselves on would lead to us healing and being better to each other.

Meer slid down on the couch behind me, pulling me back on him. "That makes sense. When your mother not tripping and hiding shit, she does have a good spirit to her."

"Yeah." I smiled while watching Mina sleep peacefully on her mother's lap. Gams and Mina taught me just how strong a mother's love is for her child.

Gams had put her life on the back burner to help Mina and Quinton raise their boys. Then Mina's health took a turn, and she was now her daughter's caretaker. To us, Gams was just a caretaker of her daughter. To Gams, she was taking care of her baby, and it didn't matter that she was a grown woman with children of her own and grandchildren.

We chopped it up with Gams for a bit before I headed upstairs to shower and change into some comfortable clothes. Meer sat on the sink while I showered staring at me like he was in awe. I had never had a man stare at me the way that he did.

Whenever Meer looked at me, I felt like he saw something

that not even I saw. I smiled at him as I wrapped the towel around me. "We never decided on when we're getting married, Sug."

"You can run, Meer... run now or forever hold your peace," I teased as I started washing my face.

He smirked. "Could never run away from you... shit would kill me. You know you the love of my life, right?"

"Meer, you—"

He pressed his finger against my lips. "Don't say it because you heard me say it, Suga. It doesn't need to be said right now. Long as you know that you're the love of my life, that's all that matters."

"Okay." I kissed his fingers and went back to washing my face. "I think we should go to the courthouse or something. With everything that is going on, we don't need to plan some elaborate wedding."

"Do you want an elaborate wedding?"

"Not elaborate, but I always imagined having that wedding... you know. Walking down the aisle and having that moment. Like how my sisters had their moment. I want to experience that one day, but it doesn't need to be now." I yawned, as I blotted my face with my facial cloths.

Meer pulled me between his legs and kissed my forehead. "You tired, Sug."

"So tired." I let out another yawn.

He kissed me again. "Take a nap and then I got a surprise for you when you wake up."

"Now I'm not gonna wanna sleep," I pouted.

He kissed both my cheeks and forehead before my lips. "You need to get some sleep... my son needs sleep."

"Meer, we don't even know what we having."

"I know you carrying my boy... thinking of Chevy as his name."

I laughed and put on my moisturizer before slipping on my favorite pajama pants and shirt. Meer helped me climb into bed and covered me up. "Where you going?"

"To help your brother with the garage... Erin on his ass about getting it done because all Cee-Cee's old toys are taking up too much room."

"Okay... see you when I wake up."

He kissed me a bunch of times all over my face before he turned when the door opened. "Suga, can I nap with you? CJ's mom is picking him up."

"Go and change out your outside clothes and then you can come nap with me," I told her, and she quickly ran out the room.

"Love you, Baby... text me if you need me."

"Okay. Love you, too."

Peach went and washed up before changing her clothes. She ran into the room, climbing into the bed, and hugging me before snuggling up under me. Before I knew it, her little snores were the white noise I needed to fall asleep myself.

CHAPTER 15
QUAMEER

WHEN I WENT BACK across the street, Suga and Peach were both still knocked out. Peach with her leg kicked over Suga. I kissed them both before going back over to Erin and Capone's house. Tonight, they had the grill going and everybody was over there chilling.

"She must have had a hard day for her to be still asleep… it's after seven," Jean said, as she sipped her favorite beer imported from Barbados.

Capone had it imported just for her and Des. I was sitting on the single chair with my feet kicked over the arm, since Capone had us playing fucking junk removers for three hours. I was tired as shit and all we had managed to do was one side of that fucking garage.

"Think the pregnancy is finally catching up with her." Erin crossed her legs and popped the top off her beer and settled on the couch.

Cappadonna sat in the opposite chair of mine. "I don't like her doing this shit… she's pregnant and need to be sitting down somewhere."

"You know Capri though. Do you think she's gonna sit still knowing that she can help?" Erin replied.

"Sis', I don't give a fuck what she do... she's carrying a baby. I refuse to be the reason she's stressed the fuck out."

"The minute I feel like this shit taking a toll on her, I'll pull the plug myself. Right now, she told me that's she's good. The minute that she's not... done deal."

Capp held his hand out and dapped me up. "Give me the word and we'll take it over, and figure shit out."

"Now you know that would stress her out more than actually being a part of everything." Alaia handed her husband a mixed drink of what I assumed was of their favorite; sprite and cranberry juice. "We need to trust that she has a mouth and will let us know when she's overwhelmed. Especially, now that she will have a husband... I'm sure Meer can and will handle it."

"Handle it before it even becomes a problem."

"What are we doing about this wedding?" Jean asked.

Sim handed me a beer. "She says she wants to go to the courthouse because of everything going on. I know she wants a real wedding, and I want to give her that."

"On our family's beach," Jean insisted.

Suga said she wanted to get married on her family's beach and I wanted to make that happen for her. "I need all hands on deck to put something together... she deserves her special day."

"You both do," Blair came out the house with a plate of food. With the amount of food on the plate, she could have just carried the shit in her hands.

She sat on the opposite couch from Sim, who kept looking her over. "Blair, you could have a little bit more food...we not rationing or no shit like that," I joked.

"Chemo makes me not have an appetite, so I have to force myself to eat." Compared to the Blair in college, and the Blair from last year, she was much skinner and frail even. No matter what she had going on, she was still a trooper and never complained.

Quasim looked over at her. "You had chemo today?"

"Yesterday... I feel so weak, and I don't have an appetite at all, but I know I need food to keep the little strength that I do have."

He stood up. "I'm gonna make a plate and you can eat off mine, so you don't feel like you're wasting food."

Blair smiled up at him. "Okay… add extra ribs."

Sim smirked. "Got you."

As he walked back into the house, Blair watched him the entire time. "Kiss him already, Blair."

"Shut up, Quameer… you are so annoying," she giggled.

"I'm even more annoying as a brother-in-law."

Erin laughed. "You and Capri being sisters-in-law would be so cute."

Blair waved us both off. "Can we focus on Capri… I can help with whatever you need."

Alaia and Erin both sat up ready to do whatever for their sister-in-law. I watched how they were with Capri and the amount of love they had for her. The shit was beautiful to witness, especially after the friendships my baby had in the past.

"We can lie and tell her that we're doing a bachelorette party and go to Barbados… then you and everyone show up and we surprise her with the wedding."

"Surprise weddings seem to be the theme with you kids." Des chuckled, polishing off the rest of his beer.

"My wedding wasn't a surprise… I knew I was getting married," Alaia protested. "I just didn't know it was gonna be that exact day."

"Surprise," Des teased her.

I leaned forward and looked at everyone. "She deserves this shit. I listened to her today tell me she didn't need to do anything big because we had a lot going on. Capri is used to pushing her wants and needs to the back for the people she cares about. I want to give her the wedding that she deserves because she's fucking worthy… my bad, Mama Jean."

"I agree with you. The girls will get her there, and since Mom and Pops are going there anyway, they can get everything together." Capone said.

"I need you to come through on what we spoke about," I told Cappadonna and Capone, and they both agreed, knowing what we spoke about.

"You can hack into the airports and shit, but can't tell time," Capp said, as Core came into the backyard with a bottle of wine. "Nobody told you to have a lake house way out here... I got the third degree from security before he let me through."

Jean had sat her beer down and quickly turned to face her other son. "Corleon, I didn't know you were coming here." She quickly abandoned her spot and went to hug him.

"Capone and Cappadonna invited me to come stay for the weekend."

"I made the guest suite up for you. We're excited to have you for the weekend," Alaia smiled, as she sipped the drink she had made for her husband.

"What's up, Des?" Core reached out and dapped his father, while Jean continued to cling onto him like a baby spider monkey.

"Ain't shit but the sky."

"I feel you." He didn't know how to respond to the Delgatos special greeting. I can't even front, the first time Cappadonna said it to me, I was confused on how to respond to his ass.

"You respond smooth ass nigga," Capone said.

Core smiled. "Noted for the next time. How's everyone doing... I brought some wine. The good shit, too."

Erin grabbed the wine from him and looked at the bottle. "Oh, you got money," she teased before going into the house to put it on ice.

Core settled on the couch while Jean went back to her seat. "How has everything been with you?" she was eager to know her third son and wanted to make up for lost time.

"I spent the day in my office working all day. Figured I needed to be around some people for the weekend or I'll be in the house working."

"Around family... you are around family," Jean replied.

"Ma, chill out... he knows that. You gotta give him space to breathe," Cappadonna checked his mother because she was too damn eager. All nervous and unsure how to act with her son she had put up for adoption.

I mean, I understood. How the fuck were you supposed to act around a child you gave up when he was a baby? She was nervous and didn't know how she fit into his life. Core was already established, and other than Menace and his siblings, he didn't really have any family. She had to let the relationship come together naturally. It couldn't be something that was forced.

Erin wiped away tears that started to fall before she started to talk. "Capri more than anyone deserves her happily ever after. I've wiped her tears and watched as she lost faith in ever being happy again. Meer, I see how you love our girl and don't play around about her. I love that for the both of you, because I know Pri, and I know that woman loves hard when she's in love... even when it comes to Ryder. It would be our honor to make sure both of you have the day of your dreams. Give us the cards and we'll make sure everything is done."

Quasim came back with a plate full of food and handed Blair a spoon before sitting right beside her. She picked through the food, and ate a little bit while Sim ate around whatever she was eating.

"Sorry... the ribs are so good," Blair apologized with her hand over her mouth as she chewed.

I knew that look that Sim had in his eyes, and even though he would deny it, he was falling for Blair. It was that look that had a sparkle and a hint of possession in it. The same look I had when I looked at my baby.

Blair didn't realize just how much of a crash out this nigga was and would be behind her. The minute Sim allowed himself to love without feeling guilty, the shit would be beautiful.

"She does deserve that. I'll give you anything you need to give my baby the wedding of her dreams. Even do the bachelorette party... We'll wait a few days so you girls can have your time together."

"I'll ask her schedule and then we can go from there." Blair continued to fuck up the ribs from Sim's plate. She was all leaned over on him while picking in his plate, and he held it and didn't mind.

"I'm taking Peach away for her birthday to Chicago… so let me know what you need, and I can book whatever at the same time I'm doing Peach's stuff."

Alaia smiled. "You're such a good father… are you excited for another one?"

It had always been just me and Peach for a long time. We had our own routine and a way that we did our thing. For the first time, I was bringing someone into our fold and things would change. My kid was dope, and I knew she would be able to adjust to all the changes happening in our life. Still, there was this small piece of me that was scared that she wouldn't handle it well. Maybe she would want things to go back to it being just the two of us.

"Meer, you good?" Capone questioned.

I leaned forward. "Not gonna front like I'm not scared to tell Peach… how did CJ take it when Erin had Cee-Cee?" I asked Capone, because he was in the same situation as me.

He was co-parenting with someone that he thought he would spend forever with. Shit, I didn't know if he ever thought he would spend forever with his baby mama, but there was a time when I thought I would have spent forever with Brandi.

"I know how you feel. CJ was good with accepting his little sister and excited about it. I think it was mostly because he was comfortable with Gorgeous. She built that bond with him before we even found out that she was pregnant."

"Baby Doll is so good with her, so I don't see her being upset she's getting a new sibling. Ryder smart as hell… little crumb snatcher scammed me out of fifty dollars for lemonade from my own fridge."

"I see a girl boss. She saw we had the supply and started her business." Alaia laughed.

"Then recruited my nephew to turn against me." Capp

laughed. "Seriously, you both did good with them. They're smart as shit, and know they are loved. Let her know when you and Baby Doll are ready. In the meantime, fuck you."

"The fuck did I do?"

"Now my wife is about to be up at night on her laptop planning this wedding with this one. Now I gotta hear *I know that's right* along with *and did* all night with these two on the phone."

Capone snapped his fingers. "You right... I be trying to..." He didn't finish his sentence when his mother looked in his direction. "Pray with Erin and she gonna be too busy planning your wedding."

> Suga: We're up.

I hopped up out the chair. "My baby up from her nap... I'm about to make her a plate and I'm out."

"Eww, not you leaving us because your baby is up from her nap," Erin laughed, as she finished the rest of her beer. "Then freeloading off our food to feed your girl."

"You forgot you got free fucking labor in that junky ass garage? Yo' man didn't even offer me anything to drink." I snapped my fingers while she fell out laughing. "Yo' ass didn't even offer me anything to drink when I carried that big ass box of wigs in the house for you."

"I forgot about those."

"Erin?"

"Yeah?"

"Fuck ya," I said and flipped her off at the same time she flipped me off, as I headed into the house to make some plates for my girls.

"Tomorrow, we finishing the garage!" Capone yelled behind me, and I flipped his ass off too and went in the house.

When I entered the room, Capri was sitting in the middle of the bed while Peach was behind her doing her hair. They were both so lost in something on the TV before they realized that I was even standing there with food.

"Hey Daddy... We're watching Grown Ups," Peach proudly said, as she roughly parted Capri's hair. She winced but wouldn't dare tell her that she was being too rough.

"I know they had something smart to say with the amount of plates that you got, Meer." She laughed while I sat them on the nightstand.

"Baby, I worked for this food. The way your brother had my ass in that hot ass garage slaving... his ass better not say nothing." I leaned over the bed and kissed both my girls. "Aye... where my kiss?" I pointed to my cheek.

Peach had always kissed my burns since she was old enough to understand. When Capri started doing it, that shit meant that much more. It was both of them accepting that I had flaws, and still, I was perfect to them.

Growing up with burns on my face, it was something that I had been insecure about, so I grew my hair out and then eventually ended up with locs. I was able to wear my hair down and cover them.

In Miami, it was Capri that suggested that I wear my hair up more because she liked it. Once she told me she liked it, I started wearing my hair in a bun, and I only wanted her to put it in one. Every time she rubbed my face or kissed it, she was telling me that she accepted me and everything I came with.

"My surprise?" She remembered and I realized that I wasn't ready to tell her just yet.

"Not yet, Sug... I wanna wait a little bit before telling you."

Both Capri and Peach kissed my cheek and then went back to their movie. Before coming upstairs, I had grabbed some forks and spoons and drinks for them. "Daddy, can we eat?"

"I ate already... all this for you both. I'm about to shower and then check in with Gams." I went into the bathroom while they both went savage on the food.

My girls were my heart, and I would do whatever that was needed to protect the both of them.

"You do realize your girlfriend's dorm room is across the hall, and not this one, right?" Capri held the door opened, wearing a tiny ass shirt and an equally tiny pair of shorts on. Her hair reminded me of a lion's main all crinkly and curly, but that was because she had braids a few days prior and had just taken them out.

"I know where the fuck her room is, but she always over here and you always over there." I pushed my way into the dorm room, and she scoffed, going to sit back up on her high ass bed. "It's homecoming... why you not out at all the parties?"

She held up a textbook. "My mother has been on me about my grades, so I need to catch up. All the parties are taking a toll on my studies and I'm not about to get another lecture from my mom."

"Strict parents?"

"Even worst... a Caribbean mother," she snorted and slammed her book opened. I watched as her eyes scanned the words in the textbook before she looked over in my direction. "Quameer, what exactly do you want?"

I could sit in her company all damn day because it was peaceful. Capri just had this energy that you wanted to be around all the time. She didn't take herself too seriously and was fucking sarcastic as hell with the shit she said. Anytime we were around each other, I enjoyed being near her.

Brandi was always on my ass about being too friendly or nice to her. It was crazy how they hung out when Brandi couldn't stand her. "Where's Brandi?"

"I'm sorry... I didn't know I was your girl's keeper."

I laughed to myself. "She broke up with me."

"Hmm, explains why she left the dorms with those shorts with her ass cheeks out... sis' about to catch her a brand-new fish." She looked at me and realized that I didn't laugh. "Quameer, you really like her, huh?"

"Like," I chuckled. "More like love her stupid ass... I don't know why I do at times because I feel like she's playing games with me."

"Why don't you ask her... communication is very important in a relationship. If you feel like she's playing games, ask her. You're far from shy so that's not the problem."

"Then what do you suppose the problem is?"

"You're scared."

"Fuck out of here... I've spoken to her ass about shit already."

Capri closed her textbook and was now interested in my troubled ass love life that I had with Brandi. When she called me earlier and I was chilling with my brother, she got pissed. Hung up the phone and sent a string of text messages talking about I'm choosing to be part of that life.

The shit pissed me off because she acted like I couldn't spend time with my brother. Quasim was head of the Inferno Gods, that would never change. What the fuck did she want me to do about it? Cut him off because she wanted me to be someone that I would never be.

"This is why I don't involve myself in relationships. They're too complicated and I would rather just be friends... like my little pen pal."

"Who the fuck still has a pen pal?"

"Me. You need to have a conversation with Brandi... squatting in my room isn't going to fix the issue. She's single out there on homecoming weekend... get where I'm going with this?" She hopped down from her bed, and I watched as she went into the mini fridge and pulled out a bottle of tequila.

"What happened to studying and a strict Caribbean mother?" I laughed.

"Just because I'm stuck in my dorm this weekend doesn't mean I have to be bored." She filled her pink Cabo shot glass and took a shot back and refilled it again, taking another one. "Now, I suggest you go ahead and find your girl... 'cause according to Jesse, they weren't coming back all weekend. Both had overnight bags with them."

"Is that right?"

"Yep." She clicked on the small flat screen tv mounted near the door. "Hey, can I ask you something?" her expression turned serious.

"Yeah."

"Do you know what ever happened to Blair. One day she was there and then the next she dropped out and changed her number. I know you're close with Tookie, and they are together."

"I don't fuck with that nigga no more, so I don't know about him and Blair. If she's smart, she would leave his ass alone."

"Why?"

"None of your business, nosey." She handed me another shot glass and filled it and cheers me before taking back her fourth shot. "What you doing after you graduate?"

"Law school."

"Not taking some time in-between?"

"As if my mother would even allow that... I'm trying to get her these degrees quick and fast. What about you? You've graduated a while ago, what are you doing?"

"Figuring out life and shit... I don't have it all planned out like you." I smirked, and she smiled at me while pulling her phone out.

"Wanna play truth or truth? You have to tell the truth no matter what you choose or take a shot." She sat Indian style in the middle of her bed, and stared at me, hoping I would want to play this game with her.

"Fuck it... I don't got shit else to do." I shook off the jacket that I had worn, and leaned back in the computer chair.

"Take the bottle because we know you not about to tell the truth." She pointed to the bottle, and I remained seated.

"You need to take that shit... you not about to tell the truth."

Capri waved me off and pulled her hair up into a bun. "Alright... want to go first?"

I got more comfortable in the small ass chair and looked at her. "Is it true that you single because you gay?"

Capri laughed and stuck her middle finger up. "You don't have to say is it true... just ask your questions." She pulled a bag of chips from behind her pillow. "And no, I'm not gay... the guys on campus suck and I learned my lesson with them."

"What lesson was that?"

"That they suck and not worth my time. I'm here to get my degree, not make love connections," she answered honestly. "Why are you with Brandi?"

"I love her."

"Love isn't always enough, though."

I leaned forward. "Sometimes it is though... you don't believe love is enough in a relationship?"

She pondered on the question for a minute. "I think with the right person love can be enough. However, love doesn't pay the bills."

"I pay her bills though."

"Well, shit... maybe it is enough."

I felt like she wanted to tell me something, and I wasn't ready to hear it so I didn't press her on it. "You was fucking with that football player?"

She laughed. "He was something to mess with. We went on a few dates and then I decided that I wasn't in the mood to have beef with every chick on campus that wants him. He's not even worth it... the nigga dumb for real."

I broke out in laughter. "Word?"

"Yes. I had to calculate our tip for dinner because he was struggling with it." She rolled her eyes, pissed that she had to even talk about it. "Do you have a crush on me, Meer?"

I stood up and walked over toward the bottle of tequila and poured me a shot, taking it back. "Why you asking questions like that?"

"Because you're always watching me when you're around. It bothers your girlfriend... you know that, right?"

"I don't be wat—" she pointed to the bottle of tequila, and I took another shot because I was lying my ass off. Anytime I happened to be around, and Capri was, too, I watched her ass like a hawk.

Everything about her intrigued me. It was this confidence that she had in her walk, like she knew she was that bitch and dared anyone to say something about it. Aside from being beautiful and confident, she was kind too, which was rare. Usually, you found a beautiful woman that was sure of herself and was also a dick head too. That wasn't the case when it came to Capri. She treated everyone with respect and that was something I admired about her.

"You peeped that, huh?"

"She vents to Jesse, and then Jesse talks to me. I'm tired of her always feeling like I'm trying to take you... I don't want you."

"Oh word?"

"Yes."

I settled back in the chair and pulled my spliff from behind my ear. "Mind?"

"Come sit on my bed and blow out the window. The RA is a bitch when she wanna be. Sometimes she doesn't care and then other times she does." She moved over some, and I leaned against her high ass bed and sparked up. "You smoke?"

"Not often. I've smoked before though."

"Want some?"

"I'm good." She was leaned back on the bed with her phone. As I pulled on my spliff, my eyes wandered on her legs as she had them crossed while on her phone.

How she wasn't snatched up was a mystery to me. If I was single, which technically I was, I would have snatched her fine smart ass up. Capri was the kind of woman you dated for the long term. She was who you married and had kids with.

"Do you think you and Brandi are gonna fix things?" she asked, as she moved closer toward the edge, leaning against me.

"Probably. Depends on the fuck shit she does while she's single." I sat here smoking this spliff knowing shit wasn't kosher with whatever Brandi was about to get into. She had blocked me, and Jesse's punk ass kept sending my calls to voicemail.

"Blow the smoke in my face."

"Can do you one better." I gently took her chin, while she opened her mouth and blew smoke into her mouth while she inhaled it.

I should have released her chin and went back to smoking out the window, but I didn't and kissed her lips. Capri's eyes shot opened as she looked at me. She surprised me when she kissed me back before pulling away from me.

"Is your pussy wet for me, Capri?"

"No."

I laughed. "Sounds like somebody need to take a shot 'cause she ain't being truthful."

I finished the rest of my spliff as she sat there stuck. The aftermath of the shots she took and getting smoke blown into her mouth. "It might be a little. I know better though."

"What you know?"

"That you and Brandi will get back together... I would be stupid to do something with you. She's Jesse's best friend."

"Only Jesse's best friend?"

"Yeah. Why?"

"Let me sniff it then."

"Quameer, I know that trick."

"I promise." A lazy smirk came across my face as I watched her contemplate if she should do it. We both had a few drinks, and I was high as shit before even coming here, so I was feeling more than nice.

Since she scooted to the edge of her bed, I stood between her legs and looked at her. Capri blushed and looked away before I brought her face back toward mine. "What are we even doing?"

"You so fucking beautiful, you know that?"

"I've been told a time or two."

Before we could think of some filler words for the way we were feeling or what we were even doing, I kissed her lips softly as her arms found their way around my neck. I sucked on her bottom lip as she feasted on my tongue, moaning in my mouth.

"Let me taste you, Capri," I whispered as I pulled her bottom lip.

"Quameer, if we do this it can't happen again," she stared me in the eyes, forcing me to make this promise I didn't want to make.

Instead of replying, I continued to kiss her as I pinned her down onto the bed. Her legs wrapped around me as I kissed her neck and made my way down her body. The shorts she wore, I pulled them off her, as she watched me. I could tell from her face that she was feeling all the shots she took.

Her pussy was staring at me. Just as pretty as her. My mouth watered looking at it, before I kissed it softly. Capri released soft moans as I kissed her pretty pussy. She squirmed as I grabbed hold of her legs and sniffed it, like I had wanted to do since I came into this room.

Shit, since the first time I saw her. I just knew her scent was going to drive me crazy, and as I sniffed her pussy, it was driving me crazy. The shit was giving me a better high than the spliff I had just smoked. I swirled my tongue around, and lifted her legs up.

Capri's legs opened wider, as my tongue dove wider. She held my head as she maneuvered her hips, moaning and tossing her head back.

"You so fucking sweet, Capri... you know that?" I asked her, sucking on her bottom lips while holding her legs opened.

As she shoved her pussy further in my face, the deeper I sucked. Her panting became louder, as she tried to scoot back, but I had already had my tongue deep inside of her while she let out soft whimpers.

"Quameer..." she panted.

"Meer," I corrected.

"Meer," she moaned out, while pulling on my locs. "I'm about to... cum," she pulled the pillow over her face and screamed out, as I lapped up her juices while looking up at her.

I released her legs, and she laid limp with her legs hanging off the edge of the bed. "You didn't disappoint... shit sweet like suga."

"Sugar?"

"Nah... suga." I laughed, while licking my lips while still tasting her on my tongue.

Once she got her thoughts together and recovered, she sat up on the bed. "We can't do this again, Quameer... I don't do things like this."

"I'm single... you forgot?"

She smiled. "Not for long. You'll be back with her again, and I'll be a memory of one night we shared together."

I watched as she pulled her shorts on and tried to fix herself. Her phone rang and she grabbed it, looking at the number. "Boyfriend?"

"No... it's my pen pal."

With the way she held that phone, I knew a prison call when I saw one. "See you later, Capri."

She picked up the phone and tried to whisper while accepting the charges. "Later, Meer... remember, our secret. Don't get soft and go confessing."

"Yeah... ight." I laughed as I headed out the door, knowing I wanted to taste her again. If it was meant for me to taste Capri again, I knew the man upstairs would put it into play and we would have our moment again.

CHAPTER 16
AIMEE

"KHALIL... WHAT ARE YOU DOING HERE?"

"I can't come and see my baby mama... I wanna meet my son." He continued to lean on my truck like it belonged to him.

I remained a few feet away from him, unsure of what his reason for being here was. Why did he track me down to have a stupid conversation that wasn't true? Rory wasn't Khalil's son, and the DNA test, plus the fact that he resembled his grandfather proved that.

I wouldn't lie to Capella about something like that, and I had never told Khalil he wasn't the father. He was locked up, so I didn't feel the need to keep him updated on what I had going on. In my opinion, he had to be more focused on protecting his booty, so me telling that my baby wasn't his was the least of his worries. As he stood in front of me, a free man, I was regretting not telling his ass that my son was no kin to his ass.

"You are not my son's father, Khalil. I think you knew that before even tracking me down... now what do you want?"

"Forgot you chose up. Got with a Delgato I'm hearing. Your cousin Rowland put me up on game." Rowland was becoming a thorn in my damn side with his big ass mouth. His ass was worse than a damn bitch gossiping with her damn friends.

Why was he so concerned with what I had going on anyway?

"That's funny because Rowland doesn't even know my business, so what was he putting you up on? I don't have time to play the guessing game with you."

Khalil watched my every move. "He even got you moving differently."

"Bye, Khalil," I waved him off and walked toward my car and he grabbed me up.

I yelped, because my gun was inside of my car, and I was defenseless in this moment. "You know that money I left with you, bitch. I need my twenty stacks, so cough em up... matter fact, since I know you got it now, I want fifty just because I know you spent my shit."

I had spent his money.

When me and Capella first started messing around, I knew he had money. I didn't care, and didn't want to look like I was using him for his money, because Capella's money was the furthest thing from my mind. I loved how he treated me as a woman and wasn't anything like Khalil.

So, when I needed money and Ace started acting funny with the money, I used Khalil's money and didn't think anything of it because that nigga was in prison.

"Khalil, I can give you the money I used, but fifty thousand." He snatched me closer to him, so close that our noses were rubbing against each other.

"Stop playing games with me Aimee like you don't know what I'm really like. You want me to tell your new man how you were selling pussy for me? You rewrote your life but left a few chapters out... maybe I should tell him what the fuck you were really doing when you were my girl."

My entire body shivered when I thought about the conversation with Khalil outside my school a week ago. How could I be on a high from making Morgan fall right into my trap, then be slapped on the ground so quickly? I had been so sick since Khalil had reappeared that I couldn't eat or sleep because I was worried about him telling Capella about my life before I met him.

The old life that I had buried in the back of my head, and pretended didn't exist. It was easier to pretend that none of that ever happened to me. Kind of like I had pushed what Ace did to me in the back of my head and was able to have him in my life.

When I first got to New York, Ace didn't agree with me moving all the way to New York for school. He felt there was a bunch of schools that I could have applied to that were closer to home. Ace loved to tell the story that he funded my life, which was true only after I had been in New York for a while, and the guilt of what he did to me started to eat at him.

It was up to me to make my own way since Ace wanted to prove a point. He thought I would return home a failure and I was determined to have my own life, without asking him for anything. He and my mother had no faith in me, and I wanted to prove them wrong. I could make it without them, and didn't need them.

When I met Khalil, he had money, and he did small things for me. I went from spending every night on my aunt's couch to sleeping in fancy hotels or staying at his condo. Whenever I needed something, he never had a problem going in his pocket to give it to me. Khalil had some flaws with him, and I overlooked them because I needed him.

The minute Khalil told me to move in with him, I jumped at the chance to move out of my aunt's house. Any money I did get was going to paying rent when I was sleeping on the couch. I was so damn excited to be away from her and doing something on my own without my brother or mother helping me.

I should have known nobody wanted something for nothing. It was the reason that I never wanted anything from Capella, because I knew how men like him were. Especially after dealing with Khalil.

It started as him wanting us to have a threesome with his home girl. Back then, I was drinking and doing the most, acting out because it was the first time I had freedom away from home. I was down, for the sake of not looking lame. In the middle of the threesome, Khalil removed himself and his homeboy joined us, and I wasn't comfortable, but I didn't want to ruin the vibes.

From that threesome, Khalil had me fucking his 'friends' and disguising it as we were having fun. I realized what he was doing and was too scared to put a stop to it, because I needed the roof over my head. Khalil liked shiny new things, or in my case, new women. Once I got tired, he started acting funny and making me stay out of the condo.

I remember one night he had me sleep in the lobby because he was with another chick. Man, when I thought about all the shit I put up with because I wanted someone to fuck with me so bad, I got embarrassed for myself. At the same time, me and Khalil were going through our shit, I met Capella, and he was so nice to me. I was hesitant because I knew how niggas were, and how they would build you up one second, and drop yo ass right on the ground without warning.

Capella was persistent and different. He made me feel safe, and it was something I had never experienced in my life. With Ace moving into the city, I didn't need Khalil anymore because my brother started tossing money because he felt guilty for not helping me when he should have.

Khalil broke up with me and I wasn't as heartbroken as I thought I would have been because I was so caught up with Capella. Even while we were broken up, he came to my house and handed me some money to hold for him. Despite our relationship being so damn toxic, he knew he could trust me, and I would make sure his money was safe.

Not too long after, his ass had gotten locked up and I had found out that I was pregnant. I had always known that Khalil wasn't my baby daddy because we weren't even fucking like that. Me and Capella was getting it on whenever we could. When Khalil called me talking about, he wanted me to hold him down, I laughed because that nigga didn't give a fuck about me when he broke up and kicked my ass out.

The money he left with me got used because I needed things, and I didn't think he was getting out anytime soon. Now, he wasn't only out, but his ass wanted more money than he left with me.

I tucked the money in-between my school bag as I put the car in park, remaining inside. To keep up with the appearance, I was still taking that stupid ass class and trying hard not to fall asleep. It gave me the chance to head to the bank and withdraw fifty-thousand dollars without Capella being nosey.

It made me sick to even lie to him, but I didn't want him to know that side of me. Hell, I never wanted him to know about what Ace did to me. These were scars that I never wanted anyone to know about. He already looked at me like he felt bad for me, so knowing that I used to fuck for money while being with my ex would further nail me to the coffin.

"Yerrrr," Khalil's childish ass answered.

I don't even know what the hell I ever saw in his ass. Why was I so caught up in him, so caught up that he had tricked me into fucking for money. Money that I never had the chance to touch because he claimed it was what he used to take care of us.

"Come the fuck outside and get this money," I huffed into the phone, and ended the call, leaning back in my seat.

I thought the damn banker was going to call Capella to ask for an approval. When he looked over the account and realized I was on the account, he got the money counter and counted out fifty thousand dollars and had someone escort me to my truck.

Now I was on New Lots avenue across the street from a damn Family Dollar waiting for this nigga to come get this money. I was so disappointed in myself for even being caught up like this when it came to him. Everything inside of me told me that I should have been honest with Capella. Then there was that side of me that felt like I could get rid of Khalil before he even became a problem. He wanted the money, and I got it for him, so it shouldn't have been a problem.

I jumped when he knocked on the passenger window. Rolling the window down, I looked at him as he smirked, making me regret ever messing with his Chris Brown looking ass. There was a time I thought his ass was fine as ever, and it was crazy that he wanted me. Now, I was disgusted looking at his ass. All the chicks used to always call him Chris, thinking he looked like the singer. Now, as I was staring at him, he was fine, I wouldn't take that from him, but he wasn't Chris Brown.

"Open the door... you think I'm about to count this money on the fucking street?"

Groaning, I popped the lock, and he hopped into my truck. If Capella knew he was in my truck, the one he bought for me, he would have flipped this whole truck over with us in it. The more I was with him, the more I saw how much he was like his father.

He was composed when he needed to be, but the other side of him came out without any warning. Soon as he thought I was fucking with Landon; I could see the crazy swirling in his damn eyes.

"Can you hurry the hell up." I snatched my school bag onto my lap, and handed him the stacks of money.

Instead of counting the money right away, he admired the car with a smile on his face. "You really weaseled your ass into something better... told you to use that pussy to get what you want."

I rolled my eyes as he snatched the money band off the stack and got right to counting. "Do you really need to sit here and count this money?"

He continued licking his thumb as he continued to count the money unbothered. The tints on my truck were dark, so he didn't have to worry about anybody running up on him. Once he made it through the first stack, he gave up and collected all the money in his lap, looking at it like an evil fucking leprechaun that had a pot of gold.

"You love that nigga?"

"Why are you worried about if I love him or not, Khalil?"

He looked in the back at Rory's car seat. "Yeah, you love that nigga. Got him raising my seed as his own."

"My son is not your damn son, so quit saying that. Me and you weren't even rocking with each other like that, and I had a DNA test done. He's not stupid."

"He know you smart enough to go ahead and get false results, Aimee? Bet he don't know that shit."

"I didn't do that."

He stared at me for a minute and then laughed. "You'll do anything to make sure you're taken care of. Remember how you got me to take care of you before I realized you were using me. Once I made you start paying your way, then you wanted to dip."

It was clear that Khalil had been taking dick to the face while in prison because his memory was screwed. "Did you forget that you kicked me out and then broke up with me?"

He shoved the money into the Hello Kitty bookbag that he carried with him. I don't know who he swindled to live with them, but it wasn't my business and all I wanted was for him to get out of my car so I could peel ass and call my man back.

"Good looking, Aimee... I'll see you next month."

"The fuck? I'm not giving you more money. That is more than what I took from you, Khalil."

He paused as he climbed out of my truck. "Why the fuck would I let you off the hook when you rolling in dough? Consider this payback for all the times I took care of you... later, Aimee." He chuckled and slammed the door.

Tears rolled down my face while a pain pinged in my chest as I thought of the shit that I was now in. Capella called once again, and I answered this time while pulling away from the block. The thought of running over Khalil as he crossed the street crossed my mind.

"Hey Honey," I tried to disguise my voice because he always knew when something wasn't right with me. Capella had always been good with that. While I grew up with nobody giving a fuck about how I felt, he was always tuned in with my feelings and wanted to make me feel better.

"Why you sound like that, Aim?"

I sighed. "Long day. I'm heading back to the lake house now... everything good with you?"

"Long day like what?"

I should have known a vague ass answer like that wouldn't have sufficed with him. He needed to know everything down to my temperature when he thought something was wrong with me.

"Just tired from having to drive into the city, and then driving back home. This stupid summer class I have to take was boring. I'm mentally drained and just wanna come home and be with you. How was your day with Rory?"

"Good... we went swimming over at my pop's house and he was cool about it. I just put him down for a nap and about to order something for dinner. What you in the mood for?"

"Anything you order is good with me." I smiled, always feeling better when I spoke to him. Capella had a way of making me feel like everything would be alright. Even when our world was upside down, he still carried himself in a way that I trusted everything would be alright when I was with him.

"Sound like you need a big ass bowl of pho from your favorite spot in town."

I did a little dance in my seat because pho was my favorite food in the world. "Sounds like you know your girl very well."

"I know a little something about her... drive safe and I'll see you when you get here... I love you, Aim."

"Love you more than you know, Capella." More tears slid down my face as I held onto the steering wheel, feeling guilty for what I had just done.

How could I be so happy and sad at the same time? Sad because I betrayed him in a way that I didn't think he would ever forgive me, but happy because I loved this man and everything he had done for me.

I had an abortion behind his back and didn't tell him that I was even pregnant. The thought of having another baby made me sick. Rory was so much and having a second one meant that I would lose myself in pregnancy and motherhood again.

While I was pregnant with Rory and even after he was born, my life was all about him. Everything in my life revolved around my son, and I didn't hate it, but it took away from me. I forgot who I was, and what I loved and wanted to do with my life.

I was just starting to feel like the old me, and then I found out that I was pregnant. When Naheim yelled out about Capri's abortion, I nearly died because what were the fucking odds? Capella loved our son, and he didn't mind having more. We had the money to take care of any babies we decided to have, so the money wasn't the problem.

It was selfish to get an abortion when I could afford the child and had a man that was a great father. I felt like Capella wouldn't have understood if I told him that I wanted to have an abortion. He would have tried to talk me out of it because he wanted a shot at a little girl. That man wanted a little girl so bad.

The guilt was eating away at me when he wanted to have sex, and I couldn't because I had just went through with the procedure earlier that week. I was so scared of losing my man, and I never wanted to lose him. There was this part of me that felt like he wouldn't ever forgive me. This was something that would cause him to end things with us, and I never wanted that to happen.

By the time I made it to our lake house, I pulled in and saw Cappadonna and Alaia walking over toward our house with Promise on her little push bike. That little girl wanted someone to push her all over the world in that bike, and Cappadonna didn't mind doing it. Whatever Promise wanted; he would go to the end of the world to give her.

Any of us really.

We were all spoiled in that way when it came to Cappadonna. He was the head of our family, and always made sure we were protected and taken care of. Which is why it was a no brainer when it came to protecting him.

This was my way to pay him back for all he had done for me. When he could have killed me and been done with me, he welcomed me into his home and family.

"What's going on, Aimee-Aim," he pulled me into a hug and kissed me on the forehead when I stepped out my truck.

I wrapped my arms around him as best as I could and squeezed him. "Hey Pops... Tired and had a long day." I walked over and hugged Alaia, who removed my hair from my face and smiled at me.

"You look like you have a lot on your mind. Everything alright with you, Aimee?" Alaia was also always in tune with everyone. She could spot with something was off with someone without even looking at them for long.

"No, I'm good... tired." I bent down and placed a kiss on Promise's cheek as she kicked her feet for her father to continue on with pushing her. "You guys are coming inside?"

"No, we saw you pull up and came to say hey. We're on our family walk." Alaia continued to rub my shoulder, as Capp examined me.

It was like this man could read minds with how he watched you. "Enjoy your walk. I'm about to shower and probably go to bed."

Capp kissed me on the forehead once more. "You know you can tell me anything, right?"

"I know." I offered a weak smile, feeling guilty for not telling him the bullshit that I had found myself in.

"Me too, Aimee. Call me and we can have a girl talk... you're not alone in this. We're family, alright?" Alaia hugged me, and I held onto her for a few seconds longer.

Even with Alaia only being a little bit older than me, she felt like she was years wiser than me. How she was able to fall into motherhood and being a wife effortlessly always amazed me. How was she able to do that and not suffer like I had been since Rory had been born?

With help, I still felt like I was fighting for my life to become a good mother and girlfriend. How was I supposed to be a wife, too? Alaia and Capp went back on their walk while I went into the house. Capella was on the couch watching some bowling tournament that I just knew he got from his grandfather. Des was the only man on this planet that watched bowling.

"You bet your grandfather some money, didn't you?" I

placed my school bag on the counter and stood there with my hand on my hip.

Capella pulled his eyes away from the TV, causing me to lick my lips. This man didn't realize just how fine he was. Or maybe he did, which is why he always got his way with me because I couldn't resist his full oiled beard, thick pink lips, and then those eyes.

His light brown eyes always did something to me. They could be kind when he wanted to be, and then they could be evil when it was time to handle business.

"Old man always shit talking so I had to put my money where my mouth is... come here, baby." He motioned for me, and I came over toward him.

Capella pulled me onto his lap and kissed me on the neck, and I held him tightly. "How was your day... aside from being with Rory all day."

"Anytime I'm with my son is a good day. We did our Daddy and Rory thing, and had a good day. He need a sibling because the way he clings onto Promise isn't good."

My heart knocked against my chest when he mentioned another sibling. "Why isn't it good? She's his aunt and they're going to grow up together."

"Promise is independent and doesn't need Rory. What happens when they start school? It's no telling if she's gonna be in his class."

"We can always make sure that she is."

He kissed my cheek and laughed. "Seriously, Aim. I love that he and Promise are close, but I don't want him to cling to her all the time. Today she hit him because he kept trying to get to her while they were swimming. Sis' wants her space, too, and with her about to get not one, but two more baby brothers, I don't want her to feel overwhelmed."

"And you think the solution is for us to have another baby so he can cling to that one? It would be a while before he's able to play with them anyway."

Capella shifted me on his lap. "You acting like you don't

wanna have kids by me or something, Aim. I'm a bad father or some shit? I been there since you told me you were pregnant, even knowing there was a possibility that I wasn't the father. Fuck you acting like I'm some scrub ass nigga trying to trap you with a baby."

"I never said that, Capella. I'm just saying that I'm not ready for another baby yet. We still don't know what is wrong with our son and you trying to have another one. We're not your father or Alaia. They can have all these kids because Alaia is super mom. I'm not there, and don't think I can ever be."

He removed me from his lap and stood up. "I'm not trying to be my fucking father. That man is him, and his house is his... I'm trying to be me... Capella Delgato. I wanna know if there is a possibility that we will have more children."

> Skyler: I'm outside, girly.

I looked at the text message that Skyler had sent and forgot that she was coming over today. She wanted to talk about the class and how it went with Morgan. Plus, I just needed some girl talk with someone that *wasn't* related to Capella.

The doorbell chimed and Capella abandoned his post by the couch to get the door. I took a deep breath and was about to pull this fucking weave out. "What up, Skyler?"

"Hey Capella... how are you doing?" Skyler walked further into our house.

I didn't like how he was looking at Skyler. "Let me ask you something, Skyler... I'm a scrub nigga?"

Skyler looked at him confused. "Huh?"

"Capella, can you be so for real right now."

"I'm dead ass serious. I must be a fucking bum or something because you act like it's like pulling teeth for you to fuck with me, Aim. The fuck I did to you for you to act like that?"

"I want no parts in whatever is going on. Where's your bathroom?" Skyler asked.

"Down the hallway, girl." I tossed myself back onto the couch and ran my hand down my face because he was being so dramatic.

"I'm about to head out so you can have girl's night. Seems like dinner tonight and maybe some pussy is out the question."

"I forgot that I invited her over tonight, Honey."

"Yeah. You be forgetting a lot of shit." He walked over toward me and gave me an funky kiss on the cheek, and I tried to pull him back to kiss me again, and he removed himself from me.

"Capella, I know one thing, you better not be out there trying to get into some other pussy!" I hollered.

"We'll see where the night takes me. Might need to see what the fuck out there since you wanna be roommates." He slammed the door behind him, causing me to jump and Rory to start screaming at the top of his lungs.

"Fucking asshole," I muttered while preparing myself to soothe my baby boy, in hopes that he settled back down so I could have some wine on the back porch with Skyler.

CHAPTER 17
CAPELLA

AIMEE HAD me in my feelings so hard that I made the two-hour drive to the city so quick that I didn't realize how fast I had been driving until I saw the sign letting me know I was near New York City.

Everybody was all boo'd up with their women, so I drove to the city solo. I hadn't even gotten the chance to let Aimee know that Zoya called me, and they dropped both me and Goon's case. She said something about the other officer recanted his statement, and the other officer had resigned and was now missing, so they wouldn't proceed with the case any longer. Zoya had took over with my case the minute that Capri became ADA. I wasn't stupid and knew my father had something to do with the recanted statement and missing officer.

I pulled up at Fern and parked on the sidewalk next to the bar. It wasn't early, but then again it wasn't late, so it was a decent crowd out tonight. You could always count on Fern to be packed out with IG's. As I walked in, I chopped it up with a few of them before making my way into the bar. Soon as I stepped into the bar, I spotted Quasim sitting at the bar in the corner.

He was on his phone and nursing a drink. "What up, Sim?" I sat down, and he looked up from his phone.

"What up, Chubs? The fuck you doing in the city?" He put his phone down and signaled to Shante to bring another drink.

"Aimee pissed me off so bad that I drove all the way here, didn't realize it until I was damn near halfway here."

He chuckled. "Women be like that at times... the fuck she piss you off about?"

Shante slid the drink over toward me. "Hey Capella... I haven't seen you in here in a minute. How is Aimee and the baby?"

"What up, Shante," I took in her cute ass, and she laughed while going back to tending to the bar.

"Don't do that shit, C." Quasim shook his head.

"What you mean?"

"Looking elsewhere because your shorty pissed you off. If it's that easy to slide with someone else, then you been thinking about the shit all along. Aimee pissed you off, then you need to figure that shit out and talk to her. She's the mother of your seed... make that shit right."

"Shit, Quasim, you sounding like my pops or something. I was only greeting her... I wasn't even thinking about that," I lied, knowing what I had told Aimee before I had left.

It was less about sex and more about the fact that I felt like my baby was slipping out my hands. Shit was different with her and I couldn't pinpoint when the change happened. At first, I thought it was her being overtired when it came to Rory, which was understandable, so I stepped up more. Made it where she didn't have to worry about anything when it came to our son because it was done.

Lately, she was to herself and so irritable that I didn't know what the fuck was up. I told her too many times that if the Morgan shit made her uncomfortable then we would find another way. Each time she would suck her teeth and insist that she knew how to handle herself, and I needed to stop treating her like she was a baby.

"Why the fuck you beefing with Aimee, anyway?"

I sighed and took back my drink, waving for another one.

"She been different lately and I can't figure her ass out. One minute she was all over me and shit was sweet, then she got distant. I thought it was that nigga at her school, but I know Aim... she not like that."

"Then why you out here trying to do her wrong, Chubs. That shit ain't like you at all, and your pops would be disappointed if he knew what you were out here trying to get into."

"Shit is wild childish of me."

"Very childish. You wanna marry Aimee, right?"

"Yeah. She's the love of my life... why the fuck shit gotta be so hard though?" I rested my head on the bar while Quasim snickered.

"Anything worth having is fucking hard. There's a slight struggle, nothing too much, but that's when you know that shit is meant to be."

"Like you and Blair."

He smiled. "Nah."

"You like that girl and you over here telling me to be honest and communicate, but you can't even do the same... bullshit, Sim."

"She a woman... all fucking woman." He licked his lips thinking about her, but refused to go after what he wanted, which was clearly her.

"I'll never figure you out."

He snickered. "I'm not for you to figure out... not trying to fuck you."

I laughed. "Bro', why didn't no one tell me that relationships are fucking hard? Shit is like a damn quiz or something, always on edge never knowing when the damn teacher gonna pull a pop quiz out the bag."

Quasim snorted. "Women aren't as complex as you're making them. They want a nigga that ain't gonna have them looking goofy, like you were about to do. Good dick, reassurance, a provider, and a nigga that would air it out for them... all they want really. Not that fucking hard." Shante brought him over another drink. "The right woman will make it a little hard at first, but that's how you know she's the one. A little challenge ain't shit for a real nigga, especially when she's worth it."

Aimee was worth the challenge we were going through and I felt like a sucka for even trying to give Shante some attention because me and Aim were beefing. "You right."

"You lost when you give another chick something to have over your woman. Never have her looking stupid to these other bitches. Your uncle and pops are the example. Erin and Alaia could walk around with their heads held high because they would never put them in that position. Capri couldn't always do that shit, but Meer got it where she knows no other bitch could tell her shit about her nigga. Aimee deserves the same shit, not you crashing out like a bozo because she going through some internal shit. Girl lost her moms and brother… grief isn't something you can turn off, even if you wanted to. Shit follows you and comes in flows. You could be having a good time then you remember you got people in the ground that you'll never hug or see again." He sipped his drink.

Quasim wasn't one for many words and always sat back and observed, rather than talk. It was meant for me to come to Fern tonight, and run into him because I needed the shit he had said to me.

"That happens to you?"

"All the fucking time. Be thinking about moving on with my life, then think about my babies in the ground and can't do the shit."

I couldn't even imagine going through what this man had gone through in his life. Losing your girl and daughter right behind it would send my ass down a spiral. I probably would have been a damn crackhead sleeping on the street somewhere if I had to go through something as devastating as that.

Quasim didn't take it on the chin, and we never saw how he dealt with it. Aside from his brother, even then I don't even think Meer witnessed what his brother went through. "Sim, you gotta move on eventually. They would want you to move on, and not sit here feeling guilty."

"This less about me, Nigga. More about you fixing whatever shit you got going on and don't ever try some sucka shit cause you in your feelings. Be her strength, not the nigga responsible for her weakness." I followed his eyes, and Blair had walked into the bar and was looking around.

He stood up, squeezing my shoulder. "I see you."

"Chill out, we're friends… don't make it weird, Baby Capp," he smirked, as he abandoned me at the bar and went over toward her.

Quasim mushed one nigga that was trying to get Blair's attention before she hugged him and then playfully shoved him. I think this was the first time I saw a genuine fucking smile on this nigga's face.

The way he looked at her, I could tell she made him happy which probably scared the shit out of him. They both had a difficult journey, so them coming together would heal each other. I continued to nurse my drink while they went to a quiet corner in the bar and was having a conversation.

I went into my wallet and tipped Shante, while gathering the energy to drive all the way back to the lake house. Who the fuck told me to drive all the way out here because I was fucking pissed with Aimee's ass?

"Don't even worry about it… Quasim took care of you." She smiled and leaned on the bar right in front of me. "You know if you were single, I would have taken the bait."

Shante was a fire little chocolate honey. She was beautiful and I always found it sexy when a chick knew she was. That confident shit made my dick hard.

"How do you know that I'm not… assuming always fucks us over, Shante," I pinched her cheek and she blushed.

"Whatever, Chubs… get home safe…" she snatched the money I had in my hand. "And thank you for the tip."

"No problem… later, Shante." I smirked, as I headed outside, and got into my truck. Quasim was right, I needed to straighten up because that shit wasn't a good look.

Aimee wouldn't do no sucker shit like that to me, so I

needed to do the same and hold it down for our relationship, and not flirt with the first chick since getting into an argument with her.

It was a little after eleven at night when I pulled up in my driveway and sat there for a minute. All the lights were off, and Skyler's car was gone so I knew Aimee had gone to bed. As I climbed out my truck, I leaned against it and listened to the silence. When I first started staying up here, the silence used to bug me out. The block was so quiet you could hear a pebble drop.

"Capella, come 'ere," I heard my father's voice loud and clear.

I couldn't see him, so I walked toward his house and noticed him sitting on the porch while rocking Promise, who was sleeping peacefully. He kissed her forehead gently while nodding toward the empty chair.

I slumped down in the chair and he looked over at me. "Heard you out there being corny as fuck."

"The fuck that supposed to mean?"

"Sim called me and told me he was keeping an eye on you."

I sucked my teeth because this was the part about having a father so well connected you couldn't do shit. "I'm a grown ass man, Pops... I don't need you to babysit me."

"I don't fucking babysit you," he calmly stated. "Can't help if you out there trying to be corny because you not man enough to deal with whatever you and Aimee going through."

"Who said we going through something? Sim told you that?"

"Sim didn't need to tell me shit... I got fucking eyes. I can tell when shit is wrong between the both of you. Going out to get into some new pussy damn sure not the solution to the problem."

"Why you got Promise out here late?"

"Me and Alaia got into it because Promise been on one. She's cutting new teeth, and been fussy all night, and Alaia lost her shit."

I looked at him skeptical. "Stop fronting... Alaia is always so calm."

He chuckled. "My wife isn't always calm and she loses her shit often, and I give her that. Hell, I lose my shit too. Tonight we both happened to lose our shit because we couldn't soothe her. Had her second guessing if we were ready to add two more into our lives, which pissed me off."

"I can imagine... babies about to be here soon."

He nodded his head. "So, you can imagine how I blew up on her for saying some stupid shit like that."

"The both of you haven't got into since she tried to open the gates for son-son." I snapped my fingers trying to remember that nigga's name.

"Capella, we argue. My wife is fucking spicy, and she likes a good argument. We don't air our shit out, and I never allow her to go to bed with that shit on her mind... I fix it every single time. We're not perfect and marriage hasn't been a struggle, but it has had its struggles. My wife is younger than me, so some shit we're not going to always agree on. Like tonight, I didn't agree with what she said, and when I finish out here with you, I'm going to put my baby girl down and then go and fix shit with her mother."

"Why the fuck does it always feel like we're good one minute and then the next some weird shit happens."

"I don't know. I do know, when I get into it with my wife, I don't go look for some new pussy to get into. Grow the fuck up, Capella, since you wanna be a grown man. Communicate and figure the shit out."

"I already heard this lecture from Quasim... Pops, I'm not trying to hear this again." I groaned, and leaned forward, putting my head in my hands.

"Yeah, well, when your girlfriend calls Alaia fucking crying because you said you were about to fuck something, I got a problem with that."

"I was fucking with her."

"Grow the fuck up, Capella. Why the fuck you want to have that on her mind? You her man, the provider, that's the shit you always trying to get me to understand, right? As the provider of your home, why would you want your woman to ever doubt you... use your fucking brain."

"I hear you."

"Yeah... you better hear that shit. Don't go losing your woman because you can't open your mouth and speak."

The front door opened, and Alaia stuck her head out. "I can take her now."

"Joy, come 'ere."

She left from the doorway and went over toward her husband, who put his arm around her waist. "I love you... you know that right?"

She smiled. "Roy, you accused me of doing crack... now you love me?"

"Talking all that mess about me growing up." I snickered.

Pops looked at me. "She was talking like we could give our fucking babies up. Like we didn't spend a shit ton of money and got a surrogate with a belly full of our babies... you damn right I was gonna ask if she was doing crack."

"You didn't accuse... you told me to show you where I'm hiding my crack pipe."

I damn near broke a tooth with how hard I laughed as I fell back in the chair laughing so hard that I gave myself a headache. "And we know you not on that shit... don't second guess our children ever, Joy. Stress happens and emotions fly high, but second guessing our blessings is a no."

She kissed her husband on the head, and carefully took Promise. "I understand that now. I'm sorry, Roy."

"Yeah, you gonna show me just how sorry you are." He watched her walk away, while licking his lips and I hopped out my chair.

"Yeah, I'm about to bounce 'cause what the fuck?"

"Fix that shit, Boy... stop being a fucking child and puff that chest out. After you leave, I'm about to go apologize and kiss her feet because I'm wrong, too."

"Later, Pops." I dapped him, and he pulled me to him and kissed my head.

"Love you, Capella."

"Love you, too." I headed back across the street and went in through the garage.

Aimee surprised me sitting at the counter on her laptop with Rory in her lap. She had headphones on and kissed our son's head as she continued working on her computer. It wasn't until I made myself visible that she noticed I had come in.

Even with it being dark, she had a few candles lit and soft music playing, which was probably for Rory. I watched as she removed the headphones from her ears and looked at me.

"Hey."

"How was he?"

"I had some last-minute summer assignments, so I sat him with me until he fell asleep." She looked over at me, nervous, unsure if I had succeeded on what I told her what I would do.

"I didn't fuck no bitches, Aim."

She kissed the top of Rory's head and returned back to her computer. "That was hurtful. I would never say something like that to you. I don't care how frustrated or upset I am... I wouldn't do that to you."

I walked closer to her and removed her hand from the computer. "I know and I'm a pussy for even doing some sucka shit like that to you. I'm sorry, Baby."

She avoided looking at me, and I moved her face toward me. Tears fell down her cheeks, and I could tell she was doing her best not to break out in tears while holding our son. "Shit is stressful for everyone, Capella. I get you wanna fuck all day and I can't give that to you right now... I'm sorry."

"Why the fuck you making it seem like all I wanna do is fuck? I wanna hold my girl, spend time with her and not feel like I'm forcing you to chill with a nigga, Aim. I want you to let me in, Aimee... talk to me because I know some shit is wrong with you."

She pushed away from the counter and carried our son. "I mean, you could just go find some pussy to fuck... remember you said that? You want me to let you in, but you say some immature shit like that. Capella, let me figure my own shit out, alright?"

I watched as she headed upstairs with Rory, leaving me standing in the kitchen. How could shit go so sour this quick? I admit, it was my fault because I was childish as shit for saying what I had said to her.

Closing her laptop, I went to slide it inside of her school tote, and the damn bag slid off the stool. Picking up all her schoolwork, I paused when I saw a bank slip. I wasn't the kind of nigga that went through his girl's shit, because I trusted Aimee.

I almost ignored it until I saw she had taken fifty bands out of our shared account. The account that I kept stacked for her and Rory in case of an emergency. If I wasn't here one day, I always wanted to make sure she and my son were taken care of.

Rory started crying, so I slipped the withdrawal slip into my wallet and headed upstairs to help her with him. Tonight wasn't the night to get into it over this bank slip, but I knew I was gonna ask her as soon as shit simmered down.

CHAPTER 18
TASHA

THIS LUNCH with Capri had been on the calendar that I had to follow for the past week, and I was nervous. This used to be my best friend, and I had a baby with her husband. Or ex-husband, since the last time I spoke to Naheim, he had told me she divorced him. It was the same time he told me I would never see my damn baby again.

As painful as it was to have both my son and daughter away from me, I knew it was for the best. When I was out there, I didn't pay much attention to my daughter. My son was a different story. I had held him for ten minutes after giving birth and he was whisked away to his father, and I hadn't seen him since. Naheim didn't send me any pictures or updates, so as far as I knew my son could have been dead.

As I walked around Morgan's condo, overlooking a piece of Central Park, it was clear this man was into very illegal shit. There wasn't any way possible an old detective and district attorney could afford something like this.

This was the first time I had come to his condo because he had me stashed at one of his investment properties across the city. All I spent my day doing was sitting in the condo and going for a walk when I was permitted. I didn't understand why he pulled me out of one cell to sit me in another.

Even though I wasn't complaining because the accommodations were much better. I walked on eggshells because I had dreams of Capone coming out the closet in my room and finishing the job. That bald man told me that I had his word that Capone or Cappadonna wouldn't touch me as long as I did what he needed me to do.

The thought of being free without Morgan's help kept me awake at night. I couldn't wait to get away from this man and actually have a life. Since being in prison, I had grown closer to God, and was faithfully in my Bible, hoping for some form of miracle. Never did I think that the Delgatos would be that miracle.

"Yes, send them right on up... thank you," Morgan spoke into the phone and then sat it on the side table. "Sell this shit, Tasha. We need her to be on our side... anybody can be bought... don't forget that."

He had no clue that he had a Delgato about to come up in his shit, and I was sick thinking about it. I hadn't had to face Capri, and now I was moments from having her in my face and having to play nice.

I didn't know if she knew I was working against Morgan or not. As I heard the chime of the door, I took a deep breath, and prepared myself to put on the most beautiful act he had ever saw. He wanted me to sell my role as fiancée, then I was going to sell the shit while working for the other side. It wasn't lost on me that I could be double crossed and end up the one in the shit hole. I didn't have time to sit and weigh out my options.

Like Morgan was looking out for himself, I was doing the same thing. I didn't know the end game that Morgan had for me. At least I had been promised by the Delgatos to be free, and not have to depend on Morgan.

"No work talk... we need to feel her out today," he told me, and I nodded my head and prepared to see Capri Delgato for the first time in a long time. "Cozy up to her, too. We need her to feel welcomed so we can get her on our side in all of this."

"I hear you, Vincent." I took a deep breath as the housekeeper announced their arrival and brought them into the living room.

He looked at me once more and fixed the top of my dress. "Call me Vinnie or something... make it seem like we in love, Tasha, damn." He fixed himself and practice his smile before Rich and Capri walked into the room. "Damn, she's fucking beautiful... I thought she would be some plain jane," Morgan muttered under his breath before walking forward, plastering a fake ass smile on his face and extended his hand out.

Morgan had a thing for Black or Spanish women. Yet, he married a White woman and cheated on her with Black or mixed women. Capri was just his type, and from the look in his eyes, I could tell he wanted her.

Once Capri walked into the room, everything stopped for a moment. She was so confident as she walked further into the room, the sound of heels clacking filling the room. "Mr. Morgan, it is a pleasure to finally meet you. Thank you for inviting us to lunch today." She extended her hand and placed it inside of Morgan's hand.

Her fragrance lingered around the room, and her confidence choked all of us. I stood behind Morgan taking in her wide leg olive dress pants, cream short sleeve cardigan blouse, and her black So Kate Louboutin's that was peeking out from under the pants she wore. In one hand, she had her Gucci purse, and a pair of matching sunglasses in her other hand. I could only assume she had just taken them off before coming inside.

She laughed and flipped her freshly pressed hair over her shoulder, while her makeup was perfection. I had spent an hour pulling out this boring black dress with stockings, and this bitch came in here and shut it down.

"Ms. Browne, the pleasure is all mine... I hope the ride over with this old slouch was a pleasant one."

Capri smiled, exposing that one dimple and flipped her hair. "I didn't even notice he was in the car with me... that phone is always glued to his hand."

Rich smirked at her, obviously smitten with her beauty as

well. I can see why Ella used to be jealous of her. I never saw a reason to be jealous of Capri, because she was so thin, and young. The girl wasn't anything to be jealous of. Capri had always been beautiful, but niggas wasn't looking for beauty. They wanted a fat ass and a bitch that was gonna suck the skin off their dick and fuck them dry. There was no denying the flare that Capri had back then though. She wasn't even aware of it. As she stood in front of me, I could tell that she had found that flare and now it possessed her like it did her brothers.

I expected her to be nervous when her eyes finally landed on me, and instead she smiled. That's when Morgan jumped in. "This is my beautiful fiancée, Tasha... Honey, this is the new ADA of Manhattan, Capri Browne."

I plastered on a smile equally as fake as Morgan. "How are you, Ms. Browne, it's nice to have you in our home for lunch... I'm not much of a cook, so Vinnie had our chef prepare something."

Capri gave me a light chuckle. "No? You look like you could dominate in the kitchen and cook the mess out of some food... it looks like your thing." She let out a little chuckle.

I bit back my words because she was being funny, with the whole kitchen comment since I used to cook work for her brother. "I try whenever I get into the kitchen."

"She needs to cook some more. Maybe after the wedding." Morgan kissed my temple while pulling me closer to him. "Hun, show her around the condo, while me and Rich finish up some work so we can enjoy our lunch."

"Sure."

He kissed me on the lips and gave me a light tap on the ass, sending me on my way. Rich and Morgan went to his office down the hall while I stood there unsure on what to say. What the hell was I supposed to say to her.

"Being completely honest, I don't even know where anything is in here," I started down the opposite hallway near the library.

"At least you learned to be honest," Capri replied, her heels loudly clacking behind me on the marble floors.

We made it toward the small library that Morgan liked to read in. The only reason I knew he liked to spend time in here was because he screamed at me when I called him and let him know I needed groceries one night.

"This is where he spends most of his time... seems like his peace away from the hell he causes," I pulled back the pocket doors and we both stepped into the small room.

The room was filled with bookshelves with leather first edition books. He had a couch and a few other armchairs facing the windows. Capri walked around the room, looking at pictures of his daughter who wasn't Jesse.

"Why didn't you say anything when you saw me?" Capri asked, placing the school picture of Morgan's daughter down, turning toward me.

I was shocked that her brothers hadn't told her that I was now working with them for my freedom. "What good would that do for what you're trying to do?"

"What am I trying to do, Tasha?" Her tone was icy, and it sent damn chills down my spine as I watched her stand across the room with her arms crossed. "Let me tell you this... you try to fuck this up and I can promise I will slit your throat and watch you choke on your own blood before tossing you next to your rotten ass bastard in the ground."

I gulped while trying to find my words. "Y...your brothers know," I whispered.

Capri looked at me confused. "Know?"

"I spoke with them... I know the plan... well, some of it. I'm not actually engaged to Morgan... it's all fake."

She didn't relax her shoulders like I expected her to. "Hun, where are you?" I heard Morgan's voice and quickly left the room.

CHAPTER 19
CAPRI

TASHA QUICKLY EXITED out the library while I pulled one of the little devices that Core had given me and planted it behind some first edition Wizard Of Oz books. Why the fuck did he have these books? Morgan didn't look like the type that even read, so why the fuck did he even have these books all up and through this bitch?

Right before Tasha popped her head back in here, I quickly positioned the second device right in the corner next to the picture of his daughter. Judging from the amount of dust on the picture frame, his housekeeping barely touched anything in this library.

I joined Tasha, Rich, and Morgan in the dining room where everything was set up for lunch. How the fuck does a man like Morgan afford a damn condo with a dining room overlooking Central Park?

If that wasn't an indication that he was in something slimy, then I don't know what was. Was nobody looking into this nigga? There was no way a former detective was affording something like this. I knew his money was coming from running with dealers, and now the Chrome Vipers. I was certain he and Rich were making some money together.

"This is beautiful, Vincent. Thank you again for inviting us for lunch. This sure beats the salad bar from down the street from the office right, Rich?"

Rich laughed. "It really does. Don't think I could have survived a Cesar salad with brown lettuce today."

I took a seat beside Rich, and across from Tasha and Morgan. As I looked at the woman responsible for the ending of my marriage. I never thought I would ever have to look at this buck tooth bitch again in my life, and now I had to sit across from her and pretend like I didn't know her.

The chef came out and put our food in front of us and explained whatever bland concoction he had put together in that state-of-the-art kitchen. I looked at the roasted duck on the smeared mashed potatoes and a drop of gravy.

As a pregnant woman who hadn't had anything to eat since this morning. I was pissed that he invited us to serve some damn baby piece of duck and a spoon of mashed potatoes. Morgan was pleasantly surprised with the way he cut into his duck and took a bite.

"How is your food, Hun?" Morgan looked at Tasha, who looked just as repulsed as I did about this meal we were having.

"Very flavorful, Love... reminds me of the dish we had on our first vacation." She tossed him a smile and took a bite of the duck.

As I watched them, I could tell from both of their energy that they weren't really together. Tasha didn't even have to tell me because it was obvious as I stared at them. Morgan didn't want to be next to her ass. He seemed like he was pissed that she was even at this table with us. The Tasha I knew would have never worn that ugly ass dress, or wore her hair in that tired ass french roll.

Her pink wig must have been in the closet waiting for her to pull it out and slap it onto her head. Morgan looked up and smiled at me while I was taking them both in. I guess it clicked in his head that he needed to be more convincing with Tasha, so he kissed her cheek, and I smiled at them before continuing to eat my food.

The duck could have used more seasoning, and the mash potatoes were damn near like liquid. I tried to pretend that this was the best thing that I had tasted since baked mac and cheese, which is something I wished I had right now.

"So, how did the two of you meet?" I asked, wondering if they had sat down and worked out their lie on their relationship.

Morgan chuckled like this was his favorite story to tell. "We met at a bar in Chicago a year ago. I was there for business, and she was there to shop for a friend's birthday. I saw her mouthing off with the bartender, and knew I couldn't leave without getting to know her name." He took Tasha's hand and kissed the back of it.

"God, I love when you tell this story. I went to Chicago to shop for my best friend's birthday gift and met the love of my life." Tasha stared lovingly into Morgan's eyes, and for a minute I felt like this bitch missed her calling as an actress.

She should have been one instead of being the trap's pass around. "That is so sweet... I'm sure the wedding will be beautiful. Have you started planning yet?"

"With me running for mayor, and Tasha moving to New York, we've put the wedding plans on the back burner until everything is settled."

"Makes a lot of sense. Being the future wife of the mayor is a huge thing." I smiled as I took a sip of my water.

Rich reached over and poured wine into my glass. "I got that wine when I was in Italy last year... the best of the best."

"Italy is beautiful... which part did you visit?"

"Florence. My daughter took Italian last year, so I surprised her with a trip there during the summer... she absolutely loved it."

"Wow, that's amazing. I've never been but pray to get some time to visit soon," I lied, knowing I had been to Italy, and had plans to go with his older daughter that he seemed to not acknowledge. The pictures around his condo were all of his younger daughter, none with Jesse. It was like she didn't exist in his world, but in her world, he was all that mattered.

It must have been sad to have a father that never paid you any attention, and didn't make you the center of his world. As a daddy's girl, I was the center of my father's entire world. It always made me feel bad for Jesse.

Morgan sipped his wine. "You should make some time to visit. Life is short and you need to make time for memories and live the one life you get. I tell my daughter this all the time and she calls me old."

"Our careers are stressful with little to no time for ourselves. It can also be heavy, too. You have to take that time away and pour back into yourself," Rich stressed, finishing the last of his wine.

"Very true. Taking care of yourself is very important," Tasha piggy backed off what Rich had said, and I was bored with this conversation.

When the fuck did this turn into a wellness lunch? With the way Rich was never in the damn office, he took more than the allowed time every damn day.

"Capri, are you married with any children?" He continued to sip and savor his wine, before sitting it back down while his eyes took me in. "Maybe a dog?"

I chewed this tough ass damn bird, covering my mouth to choke it down before speaking. "I don't have any children or a husband. I would rather claw my eyes out than have a dog... I like to come home to quiet, not walking an animal."

Morgan clapped as he laughed. "I get it. My daughter's dog just passed away a few months ago and the first few years were hell walking and training him."

"Whew, I can only imagine. I'm pretty much to myself and enjoyed being alone." I continued to play the lonely single woman who made her career her entire life role. "It's always me and my laptop at the end of the day. Maybe one day I'll be lucky to find love like you three." I nudged Rich, since he apparently had a girlfriend.

"When you least expect love, it will come to you," Tasha smiled, holding Morgan's hand, as I tried hard not to roll my eyes into the back of my head.

Morgan continued to eat this nasty ass food like it was the best thing ever. "So, work is your entire life?"

"I'm committed to my career; I try to have a life outside of it." Morgan invited me here to see if he could trust me. This entire lunch was so he and Rich could feel me out. I wasn't a fool, and knew I needed to play into whatever they wanted.

"Which is good. When I become mayor, we're going to be working very closely together. I like to keep a good relationship with everyone I work closely with. You and Rich are the dream team... the best team I've seen in a long time. We're going to do amazing things for this city."

"Well, we both appreciate that." I smiled and looked over at Rich, who was looking down at his phone again.

He looked over at me. "My apologies was confirming something... Vincent, you know we're excited to work alongside you. We just need to get these people out there voting so you can turn this city around."

"I agree. When our own is murdered and no questions are asked, I think it's time for someone to get involved."

I knew he was talking about the judge that Capone had murdered, who happened to be Trilla's mother. "Yes. It's time for someone to take control and lead this city into the right direction." Tasha rubbed Morgan's back.

He gave her a tight smile. "One more thing about work, and then we can forget the rest and finish enjoying this beautiful lunch." Morgan looked right at me. "I want you to be my special guest to the mayor's special society gala."

Fuck.

Aimee was supposed to get in close with him to be invited to that gala, not me. "I'll check and get back to you on that."

"Capri, are you turning down the invitation of the summer?"

Tasha smiled at me. "I would go, but I'll be out of town at a friend's wedding."

If I could have pulled my gun and shot this bitch, I would have. "You're right... I would love to attend the gala with you."

"Perfect. I have a feeling that we'll be spending a lot of time together. You and Tasha seem to get along so well."

Before I could respond, he and Rich's phone both went off and they looked at each other. "Honey love, I have to run and handle something very important with Rich. I'm so sorry, Capri, that our lunch was interrupted." He turned his attention to Rich. "Caselli says it's ready."

My ears perked up at the mention of Menace's name, which meant that Morgan's new phone was ready. Core had fitted it with tracking and extra shit that he wouldn't know about. Soon after we took his phone at the ball, he had reached out for a brand-new phone.

"No worries. Thank you again for inviting me to lunch." I smiled, relieved that this lunch was over, and I could leave.

Rich stood up and put his hand on my shoulder. "You can take the car back to the office. I more than likely will be out of the office for the rest of the day."

He said it as if that was something new. That nigga was never in the office and was always gone. "Sounds good."

I stood up to shake Morgan's hand, and he pulled me into a hug. This man sniffed my neck and at first, I thought I was imagining it until I saw Tasha's face and knew I wasn't. Rich had his head down in his phone per usual. Morgan finally released me and then looked over at Rich, signaling for him to follow behind him.

Soon as they left, I gathered my things to leave because I wasn't sitting here with this bitch for the rest of the afternoon. Tasha had sat back down and poured the rest of the wine into her glass.

"I'm sorry, Capri. I never got the chance to apologize for the way that I treated you," she said, barely above a whisper.

This couldn't have been happening to me today. First, I had

to sit through this lunch and pretend and now Tasha wanted to talk about the past with me. What did she expect would happen? We would sit and braid each other's hair while talking about all the wrong she and Ella had done to me. I wasn't in the place to ever forgive either of them, and I was fine with that. Ella was my nephew's mother, and I still didn't fool with her ass.

Even when we lived in the same neighborhood before she moved away, whenever I saw CJ, it was always love. That didn't mean I had to be her friend or associate with her. What she had done to me had hurt me to my core and took a while for me to get over. Now that she wasn't even a thought in my head, I didn't give a fuck about forgiving her or making good with her.

Tasha was different because not only did she fuck my brother, but she had also been with my husband, too. Then, she had the nerve to get pregnant and flaunt the shit in my face. After I beat her ass pregnant, that had been enough for me.

"There's a lot of things that you could do before playing in my face with a fake ass apology. You weren't sorry when you did the shit, so be a big girl and stand on that shit. We're never going to rekindle a friendship, and I damn sure don't care what happens to you after all of this. Long as you keep that fucking mouth shut, I won't have to shove my gun in it." I patted my tote and walked out the dining room. "Chow, Bitch."

My first question was for my brothers and Forty and why they didn't tell me that they had spoken to Tasha. It was clear she was setting Morgan up right along with us, but why wouldn't they fucking tell me that, and leave me in the fucking dark.

> Me: We need to meet.... Now.

I sent out a mass text to all of them, and then continued downstairs to the car that was waiting for me.

"What's up, fuck niggas?" I stomped into the warehouse that my brothers had in East New York, slamming my tote bag onto the table and pulling my sunglasses off while they all looked at me. Meer licked his lips while slowly rising out his seat to come over toward me, then he saw my face, and sat back down in his chair.

"The fuck, Baby Doll?" Cappadonna was the first one to speak, because the rest of them was shocked that not only did I demand this meeting, but I also called them all fuck niggas, including my baby daddy.

"Why in the fuck didn't you tell me that you cut Tasha into this fucking shit? I looked like a fool walking into lunch with Morgan and she's there, playing it off like we don't know each other," I raised my voice.

Core was on his laptop, leaned back and messing with his beard like the fourth creep. Both the twins and my father messed with their beards when they were thinking about something. Now, we had an extra one messing in his beard while trying to think of an answer to the question that I had.

"Would you have rather her greet you like she knew you?" Core asked.

Forty turned in his chair and looked at me. "How you doing, Baby Doll? How was work? Was it fucking stressful?"

"You know what is stressful, Baldy? Not knowing what the fuck is up your sleeve, and all of you keeping things from me." Cappadonna and Meer snickered at my rebuttal.

"Did she blow you up in front of Morgan?"

"No, she acted like the perfect fiancée, and pretended she didn't know me."

Cappadonna leaned forward. "Then why the hell are you mad that we didn't tell you?"

"Because why are we working with her? She's the fucking enemy and needs to go down right along with Morgan!" I yelled, becoming frustrated that they didn't understand where I was coming from.

"Suga, calm the fuck down with my baby in your stomach...

I'll pull the fucking plug on this shit now," Meer's voice boomed through the warehouse, and I simmered down.

What surprised me was how Capone and Cappadonna didn't interject. They both leaned back and allowed Meer to handle me, which was weird for me. They always had something to say about anything that I was doing, even when I was married.

Naheim sat back and watched the both of us, and said nothing. I knew he wasn't going to say nothing because he and Meer still had tension from the fight they had.

"Baby Doll, I'm not a big fan of this plan either. According to Baldy, you have to make deals with people you don't want to. We wouldn't have to work with her if she was dead, but that's not our situation." Cappadonna cut his eyes at Capone.

"There's history there and we understand that Pri," Capone said, and if looks could kill, he would have been shot down.

"Don't even bring that shit up," Naheim said, looking away from me. He refused to even look in my direction.

"I don't give a fuck about Naheim and Tasha. We're divorced, and the baby is here, and has been here. Stop using my personal shit because that's not even why I'm upset. This has to do with all the games the bitch played... or did you forget the reason you set her up in the first place?"

"Quick question, you hid those bugs in his shit?" Corleon asked.

"Yes. Tasha showed me his private library and I put them there *without* her knowing since we don't even know if we could trust that bitch," I replied, turning my attention back to Capone, Cappadonna, and Forty. "It would have been nice for you to give me a warning."

Forty stood up. "Everything is on a need-to-know basis, Capri. If I thought you needed to know right now, I would have let you know. I knew that Tasha knew her role, and you knew yours."

"I'm walking into that damn building everyday knowing what the fuck I have to do. So, fuck me being on a need-to-know basis. I need to know everything when my freedom is on the line too. I should have known about Tasha the minute you brokered the fucking deal with the hoe… if this is how you all are going to move, I can remove myself now." I slammed my hand on the table, and then eased up when Meer gave me that look. "Sorry, Meer Cat."

He settled back in his seat. "She's right, Forty," Cappadonna spoke.

"Moving forward I will make sure you know even the smallest information. I apologize and will do better the next time."

"This only works if we're all on the same page. I felt stupid not knowing that you made that deal with her. Then I had to sit and listen to the bitch try and apologize to me."

Capone laughed. "The bitch found a conscience in prison?"

"Apparently so. Since we're on this new path of not keeping anything from each other, I've already met Rich Parker."

Meer leaned up. "You tell me about heartburn or the fact that you used to eat boogers when you were in elementary school, and you failed to mention that you met Rich Parker."

Forty turned his attention to Meer. "What do you know about him?"

"I know that he's Tookie's older cousin, and the nigga responsible for facilitating that hit on Cherie."

"I thought Sim got that nigga?" Cappadonna asked.

"He got the nigga that was responsible for pulling the trigger, not the one who put the command in his ear. By then, the founders from both sides stepped in and squashed shit because it was pressure from both sides to end the war."

Forty sat back down and listened to what Meer had to say. "Rich Parker had something to do with that… you sure?"

"I'm fucking positive that he had something to do with that shit. One of the reasons I stopped fucking with Tookie."

"And the others?" Capone questioned.

"He used to beat the shit out of Blair. I don't speak on shit that's not my business because it's not fair to her, but the night he broke her fucking nose, and I had to take her to the emergency room because this nigga was too drunk to get up, I stopped fucking with him. Everybody thinks because he moved to Philly, and we both chose a side is the reason. Nah... that nigga got hand problems, and I regret never breaking his fucking jaw when I had the chance."

Goon pulled the chair out beside him for me, and I took a seat. "She never told me."

"Sug, who wants to be reminded of their past? Especially when she was still fucking with the nigga. She went back to him, and I washed my hands with it because I'm not captain save-a-hoe."

Everyone was quiet as we took everything Meer had said in. It was a good thing that Quasim wasn't here, because it would further piss him off. I knew something was off when it came to Blair and Tookie's relationship. He was always so controlling, and she always played it off like she loved her man to be like that.

Meer was possessive when it came to me, and I understood that. However, there was a difference between protective possession, and a nigga that was just abusive possessive, and that was what Tookie was.

"We know for sure that she's not fucking with him?" Forty eyed me down.

"Blair hasn't spoken to Tookie since the day we got her in Philly. That, I know for a fact," I was confident that she wasn't messing with Tookie again.

The hate she had for that man was strong, and she would never cross me and my family. Blair was as loyal as they came, and I had complete trust that she wouldn't go against the grain.

"Rich isn't to be underestimated, Forty. I'm trusting this plan to send my wife to work aside him. Don't get it twisted, he's a Chrome Viper in a suit with perfect English... not to be underestimated." Meer leaned forward and looked at Forty. "Not only should she know every piece of the plan, I need to know so I can protect mine."

"I hear you, Quameer... Capri is the priority."

Cappadonna looked across the table at me. "How did you meet him before?"

"He was on the same flight as me when I came home... helped me with my luggage. We never shared names or anything like that, but I thanked him and went on my way."

"Did he remember you?" Meer asked.

I flipped my hair. "Everybody remembers me."

"Don't fucking piss me off, Shelly-Ann."

I rolled my eyes. "We laughed about it and shared why we were traveling. He didn't make a big deal out of it, and neither did I."

"Less being funny and more working." Meer pointed at me.

I ignored Quameer and looked at Forty. "If certain things don't cross your table, why do you think they will cross mine? I'm working on cases that have nothing to do with Capone and that damn judge."

"You're not there for those cases. I need you to get closer to Rich, because being close to him gets you invited to private lunches at Morgan's home... feel me? You need to be his right hand, the one he feels like he can trust."

"Morgan invited me to that mayor gala as his special guest."

"Grasshopper was supposed to get invited to go with him." Corleon looked up from his computer.

"Aimee was never going to get invited to that. As much as Morgan likes em young, he wouldn't be seen in public with one hanging on his arm. Tasha is only on his arm because she's his supposed fiancée."

"Which means I have to go with him to this damn gala?" I rolled my eyes, not wanting to be around this man for more than a second. "He wants to fuck me."

Meer slammed his hand on the table. "And you think she bout to go to whatever freak fest with him?"

"Trust that we gonna make sure she's good... Morgan won't ever be alone with her," Forty tried to assure him.

"How the fuck can we make sure of that? Matter fact, I'm

going." Meer was serious, as his jaw tightened, and he looked at Forty.

"You are the brother to the head of the Inferno Gods... you think that's a good idea? Capri is like a little sister to me, I'm gonna make sure she's protected."

"I'll be there with Menace," Corleon added.

"Already got it where Goon will be security for Morgan that night as well. Trust that we know what the fuck we're doing."

"Great."

"Morgan has done a lot of fuck shit during his time as detective and district attorney. I'm hearing he has a lot to do with the scandal going on with the governor. The job isn't to just end him, it's to make sure when we end him, we have so much evidence on him that we bury both him and Rich at the same time."

"Like how he worked with Trilla and got me knocked."

Both me and Capone's head snapped toward our big brother. "The fuck you talking about, Capp?"

"That nigga was working with Trilla. I found it out, and had plans to deal with Trilla my own way, but you handled business for me."

We always knew that Morgan had something to do with Cappadonna going to prison. I never thought the reason he went to prison had anything to do with Trilla. "Can't front like I didn't suspect it."

"You knew shit wasn't right with Trilla, which is why you rose to the occasion and showed him that you can handle shit with or without me. We lean on each other because it's always been us against the world, Capo."

"But what people get fucked up is that you lean on each other, but you don't need each other to handle shit," Forty added.

All eyes were on me. "You know this world better than you think that you do. Monaco is the end game... although Morgan is who we want, we want the others to fall right beside him. The governor is a very good friend of mine, and the reason that I was able to slide you in... he's not responsible for the shit he's being accused of. Morgan needs someone for his smear campaign, and Governor Johnson is the perfect person to use."

"Child porn is kind of fucking wild… how we know that he's not responsible for the shit?" Capone questioned.

It didn't matter that he had known Forty for years, he wanted to make sure we were on the right side of things. "Because if you were accused, I would know the shit wasn't true," Capp spoke.

"He's my fucking brother," Forty announced.

I choked on the water that Meer slid over toward me. "Your brother is the fucking governor… way to fill someone in."

"How do you think I was able to know so much and pull strings? The shit with Tasha slipped by both of us, and that was because by then Morgan already knew he couldn't trust Devon."

"Let me guess… he tried to get the governor in on his plans, and failed?" I questioned.

Meer checked his phone and got up from his seat, coming over near me to kiss my cheek. "I gotta go and handle something… see you back at the house, Sug." He saluted everyone. "Goon, make sure my baby get home."

"You already know."

I turned in my chair and watched as my man walked toward the exit, with that sexy ass bop he had in his walk. Drool accumulated in my mouth when I watched Meer. Goon snapping his fingers in my face pulled me from my thoughts. "That's why I'm not helping you get with Zoya."

"Lady Inferno, focus… you gonna help me. You know Zoya need a nigga like me." He laughed, as he pushed the water bottle I had pushed away from me.

It was when I took a good look at the bottle, I smiled to myself. This man got me a red stainless steel water bottle with Lady Inferno on the front of it. The Lady Inferno was so discreet that you had to really look close to see it. He knew that I couldn't bring this to work with me. Plus, he was always on me to drink more water because he knew I would sip coffee throughout the day and then complain of a headache.

"Like I keep telling you… this shit is bigger than

Cappadonna. He was able to lock Capp and other Black men down with the abuse of his power. This state finally has a Black governor who actually gives a fuck about the people, and he wanna take him out like this. This my brother... I'm not willing to see him or yours go out like that."

I stood up and walked over to Forty, who was so damn mad he couldn't sit anymore. As I neared him, I held my hand out. "Then we gonna bring him down."

Forty pulled me into a hug and kissed the top of my head. "My girl."

CHAPTER 20
MORGAN

WHEN I SAW Ms. Browne walk into my living room, my tongue wanted to roll out my mouth and onto the carpet because she was that beautiful. I expected some overworked tired woman with bad skin, and even worse sense of fashion to come strolling in behind Rich. Never did I expect for a stunning woman like Capri Browne to come into my home and steal my damn heart.

I wanted to toss Tasha back into prison and make this one my fiancée because she was exactly what I had wanted. My infatuation and addiction to Black and Spanish women had always been a damn weakness of mine.

All a Black woman had to do was speak to me and I was putty in her hands. I wanted Capri to slap the shit out of me and humiliate me, because that was a kink for me. Seeing a Black woman in power, in control turned me on more than anything in the world. For years, I would return home to my wife and hate to even share a room with her because she didn't turn me on like I wanted. It was always boring missionary positions with her ass, and then she had the nerve to be a pillow princess.

Denise had never gotten on her knees and choked on my dick since we met. It was like the minute that ring was slipped onto her finger, she stopped being what I needed her to be – nasty.

Naturally, I had to find another way to get my rocks off, and it damn sure wasn't with my wife. That was the reason she was my ex-wife now.

When I met Benita, she was so beautiful that I couldn't help myself. She was a known dealer's girl at the time, and we were breaking bread together. I was just an officer at the time, and working my way to detective. He sent her out to hand me the money one night and it was something that he shouldn't have ever done.

One look at her and hearing her slight accent had me ready to arrest her and bring her right back to my house, even with being married. Benita knew she was beautiful, too, because every man who worked under her man wanted her.

He didn't send her out every time, but he sent her out enough times where I was able to build some rapport with her. She would laugh at my jokes and blush whenever I complimented her. I wasn't a fool, and I knew Benita was a kept woman. Her man kept her taken care of, so she would be stupid to leave her guaranteed money to get with a crooked cop that was married. At the time, me and Denise hadn't even spoke on having children because I was too busy trying to climb the pole and get where I needed to be.

Benita's man eventually got caught up and murdered in front of her. She disappeared for a while, and then she came back around and that's when I knew it was time for me to make my mark. I was making decent money as a cop, and even more while turning my head at the shit that was going down on the blocks.

I didn't give a fuck that these fools were killing each other. All I cared about is that the money continued to grease my palms to keep my mouth shut and to look the other way. If they wanted to sell poison to their own people, who the fuck was I to step in and try to force them to do better? All I wanted was the money, because I had a new wife who wanted to take on the role of stay-at-home wife because her mother and grandmother had done the same thing.

I was raised in a strict Catholic Irish household with a fucking racist for a father. If you didn't have Irish blood, then you were no good to him. It didn't help that we lived in Woodlawn Heights in the Bronx, a predominantly American Irish community. He would come home from work, crack open a beer, eat dinner, and then he was down at the pub a few blocks down with his buddies. He would come home, sleep for a few hours and then wake up to do it all over again.

So, when it came to finding a woman I would marry, I had no choice but to marry the sweet Irish girl that lived a few houses from us. The same girl whose parents always came over for coffee and dessert a few times a week just to shoot the breeze.

Don't get me wrong, Denise was beautiful. She just wasn't what I wanted. I married her because it was expected of me to marry a sweet Irish girl who could give me children and make our house a home.

With Benita, I was someone else. I wasn't the cop that retired home to lamb chops and mint jelly already waiting for me. I was Vinnie, the one she would swallow whole while we were driving. Her Cuban spit fire ass had me turned on every time I saw her. The way her thighs rubbed together, and her hips looked like parenthesis. Only God could have come down and handcrafted her himself.

The sex between us was crazy. I loved when she used to slap the shit out of my face, scratching me with her nails in the process. The shit used to have me ready for her twenty-four seven. With the way we fucked like rabbits, it was no surprise when she told me she was pregnant. I knew I couldn't go home and tell Denise that I had a baby on the way.

Not when it was a struggle for us to get pregnant. Back then, it wasn't something you spoke about. Shit, a lot of shit that went on under your roof wasn't something that you spoke about. The house could be falling down around us, but you never shared your marital business with anyone. How did I look going home and telling her that I got my mistress pregnant, and she was keeping it.

I tried everything to get Benita to get rid of the baby and she refused. She claimed she wanted her baby and if I didn't want to be involved then I could go. I was stuck because I was in love with Benita, but I wasn't ready to be a father to a half-bred bastard. I couldn't bring that baby around my parents and pretend like I hadn't cheated on my wife and had a baby outside our marriage.

Me and Benita continued to be together until Jesse turned three. That's when we broke up because she was tired of me promising to leave Denise, which wasn't true. As a Catholic, there was no divorce. You got married and stayed miserable until one of you decided to kick the bucket, like my mother and father.

They stayed married until she passed away a few years ago, and now my father just sat in his favorite chair and drank himself to death, only pulling it together for his grandchildren and family events. The only thing that kept him going was that his grandsons – my nephews, all followed in my footsteps and became cops. Since my mother passed, I wasn't as close to my family like I used to be.

Jesse grew up well, she didn't have to worry about fighting for food. I made sure Benita always had the money needed to raise our daughter, and I popped in and out of her life. I admit, I wasn't around as much as I should have been. Jesse was always so eager to please me and make me proud. She was always the top of her class, a part of every damn school club imaginable, and class president.

I can admit I didn't show up for Jesse like a father should have. Once I stopped fucking her mother, I wasn't interested in fatherhood. I was determined to become a detective and support my wife. We had my wife's parents and then mine on us for why we didn't have a child together. Life was stressful back then.

Jesse did it without having me there, and I was proud of her. If only she stopped trying to force feed her accomplishments down my throat. She had this vision of us all being this perfect family. She wanted to meet her younger sister, Fiona, and I wasn't ready for that. The divorce was already hard on her and I wasn't trying to rub more salt into her wound with introducing an older sister.

I wasn't stupid though. Jesse was a US Marshal, and it would have been stupid to do away with her. It was best to keep her close to me in case I needed her for something. Right now, she was stuck on me walking her down the aisle at her upcoming wedding, and I was throwing every excuse I had at her.

Benita had aged like wine, and I knew I would find myself fucking the shit out of her at the end of the night. It was best for me to make an excuse and not attend. It's not like it would be the first time I missed an important event in her life.

"Mr. Morgan, I have your coffee and the breakfast sandwich you requested. They stop making breakfast at ten a.m., and I convinced him to make the sandwich for the future mayor," Aimee winked at me, as she sat down my coffee and breakfast sandwich.

"Thank you, Aimee. That gift of gab will be able to take you far." I sipped the coffee that she had made perfectly.

As she walked across my office with the plaid tennis skirt, white tennis shoes, and a cropped white T-shirt, I licked my lips. Her chocolate thighs made me swish the hot coffee around in my mouth.

It was something about blond on Black women that made my penis wet. She had her hair pulled up in a bouncy ponytail while flipping on the flat screen TV. The news came on and Governor Johnson was holding a press conference.

"I have no plans on stepping down because I am innocent. I have the best cyber teams working on this to find who is responsible for planting such sick sh… things on my computer. I have a staff around me at all times, and each and every one of them have and will continue to be interviewed. I am allowing the authorities to do their job and helping wherever I can."

I just knew when we planted those files on his computer, that he would have gone down. Since he was the governor, I assumed there was a special protocol for how they were handling this. I wanted to see him arrested, doing the perp walk outside of the governor's mansion right into a car.

"Thank you, Governor Johnson. I'll take a few questions." His lawyer took the mic.

"Why isn't he arrested? Any regular person would have been arrested by now," one of the reporters called out.

"We're cooperating with the authorities, and they have proof, and we have proof of those files not belonging to Governor Johnson. It's an ongoing investigation, so we can't reveal much. However, Governor Johnson won't be stepping down and he is going to prove his innocence."

"Is he going to be arrested?" another one asked a damn near identical question, which caused me not to want my breakfast sandwich anymore. Aimee stood with her arms folded watching the press conference.

"As of now, he isn't under arrest. This is an ongoing investigation, so we cannot speak about it. Thank you for understanding." He quickly left the podium, and Aimee clicked the TV off.

When I went to Devon and asked him for his help. I needed him to be on the right side of things. He knew I would win this election, so he didn't need to worry about me not coming through on my end of the deal.

I damn near begged him to reopen the case for Judge McLaren. Now, I didn't give a fuck that her ass was dead, but I cared because I knew it was directed to the Delgatos. I wanted those brothers to suffer, and I didn't give a damn if it was Cappadonna or his fucking brother Capone. Trilla told me that cutting the head, which was Cappadonna, and the body would fall in line. Capone never fell in fucking line.

In fact, he made his own line and grew a second head. The money we used to bring in was gone because Trilla was so busy going to war with this man. The money that I needed to continue to live the way I had been accustomed to living.

The money that I was used to receiving every month was cut down. The city was a fucking war zone, and it was all because of Capone Delgato. The man was a savage, causing all kinds of chaos and then got to live his life, and never have to think twice of the money he caused me to miss out on.

Just when I was recovering and bringing money in with the Chrome Vipers, Cappadonna was released and the hell unleashed again without any warning. That warehouse in Baltimore had them written all over it, and we couldn't pin it on them. We had the addresses to their known traps, and for sure thought we would get them.

They moved smart because those houses weren't worth anything. It was like a ghost town staking those houses out. Even the addicts wouldn't snitch them out because they were that scared of them.

One of my top heads in the DEA office refused to hear anymore. He claimed he wasted so much time checking for houses that had no one in them that he could put the resources elsewhere. It took a hell of a lot of convincing to get Tasha out, with the hopes that she would spill everything, and we could build a case.

It was done so far under the table that not many knew she was out. I made sure I didn't parade her around on TV, and she kept a low profile, which she hated. When you went to search her up, she was still processed in prison. Nobody was checking for her since she had been sentenced. There was no way that she had murdered those men on her own.

What would have been her reason?

Then this slow bitch acted like she didn't want to turn on the very people that landed her in prison in the first place. I had been playing nice with her, and now I knew I needed to turn up the heat. Whenever I was done with Tasha, I didn't give a fuck what happened to her. She could rot for all I cared.

I knew I wanted Ms. Capri Browne to be my fiancée, and wife at the end of all of this, and I was going to make sure that she was. No longer was I going to be afraid of what my father would think of me dating a Black woman.

He was on his way out, anyway, maybe seeing that would give him the nudge that he needed to go on and die already.

"I love the fact that we have a Black governor, and he has tattoos... we're coming up in the world." Aimee's voice brought me back to reality, and she was now standing in front of my desk with her arms folded. "Do you think he did it?"

Wide hips had always been a weakness of mine, and as she stood in front of my desk, I was trying hard to contain myself and not grab them. "You never know with these politicians. They act one way and then do the opposite."

"You're a politician."

"I'm the people, Aimee. I've been like every New Yorker out there working hard for a better life. I'm the son of an Irish immigrant who worked as a patrol officer, working my way up to detective while putting myself through school to become a lawyer. I know what the people need because I've been one of them."

She didn't look convinced. "What do we need?"

"We need a lot, Aimee. This city needs a lot," I purposely looked down at my computer so she got the hint to get the fuck out my face.

She sighed. "Anyway, I need your laptop to give to IT... they're adding new software ever since the governor's computer was apparently hacked."

I wasn't new to having interns. Aimee was the sixth intern I had this year, and I didn't expect her to stick around for too much longer. She pretended to care because she thought that's what I wanted to see to keep her job, when in reality I only hired her to fuck me after hours.

I gave her a tight-lipped smile as I handed her the laptop. "You can make sure your friends vote and get the right people in office... thank you for the sandwich," I dismissed her, and she slowly walked out of my office and back to her desk.

Grabbing my phone, I punched a few numbers in before connecting to the line. "Capri Browne, please," I told her assistant once she answered.

CHAPTER 21
QUAMEER

PEACH WAS DOWNSTAIRS EATING a bowl of cereal before we had to leave to head to the private airport. I was meeting Brandi and her husband there so we could head to Chicago for the week. This was what Peach wanted for her birthday, and I was gonna do whatever she wanted because she deserved that. The point of all of this was to give her the world, and all my baby wanted was a trip to Chicago with her parents.

Since it was still early, Suga was still asleep with her mouth wide opened and snoring. She was going to come this weekend, and I was already counting down the days until I saw her. I've never been this attached to a woman like I was with my Suga. I didn't want to leave her, but I knew she was here with Gams and my moms, so she wouldn't be alone.

Pops came over every other day, and her brothers were right across the street. I sucked on her lips before she finally stirred from her sleep, her hair covering half of her face while she yawned.

"Are you leaving already?" she sat up in the bed and held her arms out, and I grabbed her up while she latched her arms around my neck. "I'm gonna miss you guys."

"I'm gonna see you in a few days." I kissed her lips.

When a tear slid down her cheek, I knew I had my baby gone. The crazy part is she had me gone too, cause it was bittersweet for me. I was going to celebrate my Peach but leaving Suga at the same time.

"I know... I'm just being a baby this morning. This is good for Peach, and she deserves to have a good birthday trip with her parents."

I kissed her neck, and she hugged me tighter as she wrapped her legs around me. "She does deserve that. Make sure you feeding yourself and my baby, Suga. Drink a lot of water, and don't work yourself up."

"I have court this morning and its light cases. Then I have lunch with Rich... surprised he even invited me to go." She saw my face and kissed me on the cheek. "Don't be like that, Meer. You know I don't give a damn about him... business, remember?"

"I know this is business... doesn't mean I like the shit. Morgan wanting to fuck you still got me heated."

Suga rested her chin on my shoulder. "I cannot wait until this is all over so we can go hide and live our lives. Every time I second guess something, my baby reminds me that I can do this... I'm their mother."

"*Our* baby... we always rooting for you, Suga... you my wife. I know you can do anything... feel me?"

She got down out my arms and gave me one tight hug before she headed downstairs where Peach was on facetime with her mother. "Did you pack everything, Mommy? You always forget something."

"Ry, I am your mother," Brandi giggled. "And I did forget something... my charger to my face mask I use every night." She ran out the camera to grab it while Peach continued to eat her cereal.

Capri came behind her and kissed her cheeks while Peach giggled, and Capri hugged her from behind. "Gonna miss you so much, Peach. Have the best time with your parents, alright?"

"Thank you, Suga... I'm saving the best things for when you come."

Capri pinched her cheeks. "My girl."

"Good morning, Capri," Brandi greeted when she came back into the camera. Her ass probably never even found what she was going to get. Soon as she heard Capri's voice, she probably hightailed it back to her phone.

"Good morning, Brandi," Capri replied pleasantly.

"How has the pregnancy been? Are you battling morning sicken—" she didn't get to finish her sentence because I snatched Peach's phone and ended the call.

Peach looked at me. "What is Mom talking about? Who is pregnant?"

Ryder wasn't stupid and Brandi knew that when she decided to ask Capri that question. It seemed like an innocent enough question, keeping the peace. Except, Brandi knew that I hadn't spoken to Ryder about it yet.

We wanted to tell her in Chicago, and Capri had even ordered her some custom shirt she wanted to give her. Capri looked at me, unsure on what to say. I could tell she was hurt that Brandi ruined this moment for us. Peach was looking between the both of us confused and unsure on what was going on.

I stood behind Suga and put my arms around her, onto her stomach. "Suga is going to have a baby. You're going to be a big sister." I touched Capri's bloated stomach.

She didn't have a baby bump, but her stomach looked like she was bloated. That didn't stop me from rubbing and kissing on her stomach knowing my baby was in there. I felt like a hooker in church waiting for my daughter to have some kind of reaction.

"Peach, you don't have to tell us how you feel right now. It's okay to take some time to think about it, okay?"

"Promise?"

Capri held her arms out, and Peach jumped down from the

stool and hugged her. "I promise... come and tell us how you feel whenever you're ready."

"Okay. Daddy, I'm going to grab my iPad and say goodbye to Gams." She took off running upstairs.

"Alright, Peach... you good?"

"I'm alright, Daddy." She ran upstairs.

It wasn't until she was upstairs that I realized that I had been holding my breath. "I'm going to break that bitch's neck."

"No, you not, Meer. This is about Ryder, and not the two of you. Did I want her to find out this way... no. However, I'm not going to allow it to ruin her trip." She held my face while staring up at me.

Even though she was trying to be the calm in the storm that was brewing inside of me, I could tell she was hurt with what Brandi had done. Added with the fact that we didn't get the reaction we wanted from Peach, both of our emotions was all over the place.

Capri was more so hurt, but I was fucking angry as shit. Pissed that Brandi would even do some foul shit like that. "I can't keep letting her hurt you, Sug. You want me to keep the peace and all she keep doing is fucking disrespecting what we got... I'm not feeling that."

"I love you, Meer Cat," she tried to distract me from how I was feeling, and it was working for the moment.

"Love you, too, Sug."

"Now, go and finish getting ready." She kissed me once more before going into her office and powering on the computer.

Suga and Gams stood at the door waving to me and Peach as we pulled out the driveway. The drive to the private airport was only an hour away. Brandi should have been on her way since she had a longer drive, but instead she wanted to be messy and reveal the pregnancy to Peach knowing she didn't know.

"Peach, you alright back there?" I looked at her in the mirror, and she looked up from her iPad and smiled.

"I'm alright, Daddy... are you okay?"

"You already know I'm always good whenever I'm with my favorite girl." I winked, and she smiled at me while looking out the window.

"Will I still be your favorite girl when the new baby comes?"

I looked at her briefly before returning my attention to the road. "Are you scared that the baby is going to replace you, Peach?"

"Mommy told me that she didn't have another baby because she didn't want the baby to take all her time away from me."

"When did she tell you that, Peach?"

She sighed. "Last year for Christmas. She told me that having another baby would take all her time from me, and she wanted to spend all her time with me."

I relaxed because I thought I was going to prison today for beating the hell out of Brandi for filling my daughter's head with that shit. I never knew, and I didn't give a fuck, why Brandi didn't have any kids with her damn husband.

Unlike her, I respected her personal business because it wasn't mine. It was fucked up that she couldn't return the favor, because now I had to get into her ass for revealing that to my daughter on purpose.

"That might be true for your mother, Peach. For me, I have all the time and love to give you and any siblings that I may give you in the future. You know what's crazy?"

"What?" she leaned forward interested in what I was saying.

"Suga wanted to do a special thing for you because everyone knows big sisters are important. Me and Capri have never been older siblings, so we wouldn't know. You on the other hand will be like Uncle Simmy… an older sibling."

She gasped. "Really?"

"Of course. Maybe you can teach me and Capri how to take care your new sibling. How do you feel about a new baby, Peach? You can be honest with Daddy and you won't hurt my feelings."

She looked at me with those eyes I loved so much. My kid

was something special, and I loved the hell out of her. "I'm happy, just scared."

"You scared, too? I'm scared about the new baby, too."

Peach's eyes widened as she looked at me. "Daddy, you are scared? You never get scared of anything."

"Peach, I get scared. When I held you for the first time, I was scared. I remember the first weekend your mother brought you to my house to spend the weekend with me. I was so scared and nervous that I wouldn't get it right. Daddy sometimes gets scared because I want to do everything right."

"You do a good job being my daddy."

I smiled. "Thanks, Peach."

As a parent, sometimes you didn't know what the fuck you were doing. It felt like tossing spaghetti on the wall and see which noodle would stick. I always put my best foot forward when it came to being a parent, so hearing her tell me that I was doing a good job was something I needed to hear every once in a while.

"Is Suga mad at me?"

"Why would she be mad at you, Peach?"

Peach looked down at her iPad before returning to look up at me. "Because I didn't act happy with the baby."

I hit the screen in my truck and pressed Suga's name and listened as the sound of the phone ringing filled the truck. "Hey Meer... did you forget something?" I could hear her mouse clicking around in the background.

"Go ahead and tell her what you told me, Peach. In our family what do we do?"

"Discuss our feelings, even if they may hurt someone's feelings," she recited what I had always told her.

I was raising her to be in check with her feelings and to speak her mind always. Her mother was raised in a house where they hid their feelings and didn't discuss them, so when she left home, she did the shit in our relationship. Instead of speaking on some shit, she would do immature ass shit to get my attention instead of just communicating with me.

When I saw Suga doing the same shit, I put an end to it because she knew she could talk to me about anything. In our home, I wanted everyone to get their shit out so we can move on about our life. I wasn't the most open nigga when it came to my life and feelings, but I was always honest once I opened up.

"Are you mad at me because I didn't act happy about the baby?"

There was a silence on the other end of the phone and the clicking of the mouse had stopped. "Ryder, I could never and would never be upset with you about your feelings. I always want you to be honest with me, okay?"

"Okay?"

"Meer, is she smiling because I don't think she is... she sounds sad to me. How could anyone be sad when going to Chicago on a jet." Capri laughed.

Peach smiled. "I'm happy, Suga... I promise."

"Alright, my girl... I love you, so don't think I will ever be upset with you. I care about how you feel... always."

How is it possible that she made me fall deeper in love with her every day? I wished I could kiss her ass right now because from the way Peach was smiling in the back, she had put her mind at ease. She always wondered how she would do as stepmother, and I had no concerns because she was ready.

"Suga?"

"Yes?"

"I'm not sad about the baby... I'm happy to be a big sister," Peach announced.

I didn't need her in front of me to hear the smile in her voice. "Peach, I'm so happy that you are happy. Nothing changes, you are still my bestie. We just have a little bestie on the way now, right?"

"Right!"

"And can I tell you a secret?"

"Daddy's listening." Peach's narc ass called me out like I could close my ears while driving this damn truck.

"It's alright... he can know this secret, too."

"Okay... what's the secret?"

"I'm going to need both you and Daddy's help because I don't know what I'm doing. I've never been a mommy before. They say big sisters know everything and since I only have big brothers, I'm gonna need your help more than ever."

"I promise I will help you, Suga... don't be scared, okay?"

"Whew, thanks, Peach. I was a little nervous and now I feel better... you and Daddy call me before take-off, okay?"

"Okay... bye Suga... love you!" Peach yelled while pulling on her headphones and grabbing her iPad again.

I smirked as I watched her now with more pep in her step. "Love you, Sug."

"Love you more... now I need to get ready for court."

We arrived at the private airport and chilled in the lounge while waiting for Martin and Brandi to arrive. Leave it to your child to have you out here looking like you didn't feed them. Peach had the lady in the lounge bringing her everything she wanted.

I watched as she ate another bowl of cereal like I hadn't made her one before we left out. She sat back enjoying being waited on and I couldn't even be mad with her. This was her world, and I was just the nigga footing the bill for it.

My brother's name came across my screen, and I answered. "Using my niece to guilt me is wicked, Blaze."

"Sim, the fuck you talking about?"

"Ry texted me last night talking about she only has one birthday a year, and I should be there to celebrate with her."

I laughed because my daughter was smooth. "You serious?"

"Hell yeah. Had me up last night looking at flights and booking a fucking hotel because it made me feel bad."

I looked over at Peach accepting muffins now. "Peach, you texted your uncle about your birthday?"

"Yes. He has to come because Capri is coming... I wish Gams could have come, too." She bit into her muffin, and then continued paying attention to her iPad that was propped up on the table.

"How the fuck she grow up so fast, Blaze?"

I shook my head. "I don't know, but I don't like the shit."

"You got a second one on the way, so don't get too sad." He chuckled. "I'll be out there tomorrow morning."

"Should have been using her to get you out the house all this time," I muttered.

"Negative, nigga. For my niece, I'll do whatever... see you tomorrow."

As I ended the call with Quasim, Brandi came into the lounge with her Chanel bag on her arm, and all smiles. Peach abandoned her chair and ran into her mother's arms, while Brandi hugged and kissed on her.

"I missed you so much... are you ready for the best week of your life?"

"Yes!"

"Daddy got some money... a private jet for the princess."

I remained in my seat and imagined slam dunking this damn coffee mug over her big ass head. She finally lifted her gaze and looked over at me. "Where's your man?"

"Martin couldn't make the trip." She pretended to sulk, like this hadn't been the plan all along. As we came closer to the trip, I continued to ask her if her fucking husband was coming, and she told me up until yesterday that he was.

Now we were ready to leave, and she was springing on me that he wasn't going to come. "Starting to really believe that head is really filled with water."

Peach held onto her mother and looked at me. "Daddy, that's not nice to say to Mommy." I bit the inside of my cheek because I never allowed her to see me like this.

My emotions were still raw from the bullshit she pulled earlier with Capri. She ruined her moment to announce her own pregnancy, and thought the shit was fine. I don't care how much Capri told me not to address it, I was going to address it because she wasn't going to keep hurting my baby because her own feelings were hurt.

"Why you in my mouth in the first place, Peach? Adult

conversations, right?" I gave her that look, and she walked her ass right back over to her iPad, not wanting the smoke I had reserved for her mother.

"Quameer, why does it matter that he couldn't come?"

"It matters because I asked and instead of being honest you fucking lied."

Brandi folded her arms. "I have to stay in the suite with you and Peach. Martin never booked our hotel, which is the reason we got into a fight. The hotel is sold out, so I couldn't make another booking."

"You straight... you can stay in the suite, in Ryder's room. There is two twin beds, so you can take one." She smiled, satisfied that her plan had worked. "Just know that I plan to fuck the shit out of my future wife across the suite. So, while you staring up at the ceiling, know I'm slanging dick in the next room." I walked past her to let them know that all parties had arrived, and we were ready to get the fuck on.

Brandi could have chosen to sit in any chair she wanted on this jet. It was only three of us, and a full plethora of seats she could have sat in. Instead, she chose to sit across from me as I worked on my laptop. Peach was so damn excited that she knocked out on the couch after trying every piece of candy that was stocked and supplied for us.

"I didn't mean to ruin the pregnancy thing," Brandi started, clearly wanting to fuck with me. I had paced the men's bathroom for ten minutes before boarding this jet to talk myself down.

I walked from one side of the bathroom to the next convincing myself that just because she had a water head didn't mean she wouldn't drown if I shoved her head in the fucking fish tank in the front of the lounge.

When we boarded, I made sure Peach was good before picking a seat away from her Brandi. Brandi was trying to get on my nerves on purpose and she wanted me to blow up. "Brandi, why do you hate our daughter?"

"Quameer, why would you say that?"

"Cause you keep fucking with me and when I blow up, it's gonna ruin Ryder's trip... so the only conclusion I can come to is that you hate our daughter... you know how it is when I start drawing my own conclusions."

"You sound crazy, Quameer. I'm really sorry for telling Ry. I thought you both had told her already."

She looked down at her phone, and then back at me. "It's me and you... be real with me. You just wanted to hurt Capri."

"Why would I want to hurt her? I don't even think about that girl... please."

I leaned back in my chair and smirked. "Yet, ever since you found out that she was who I was messing with, you've done everything in your power to hurt her. The whole ring situation, and now robbing her of the chance to tell Ryder about her new sibling. Your pussy gets wet by trying to hurt Capri Inferno, huh?"

"Relax, she's not even married to you yet."

"She will be and that's what pisses you off. When you got married, I could have crashed out and showed up at the wedding. I left you the fuck alone to plan the delusion of your dreams. You showed up on my front door and gobbled my dick whole, then kissed your husband the next day. I guess I'm confused on what the fuck you want from me? We haven't been together in years, and you been doing everything to start shit with me. Capri is not about to go back and forth with you 'cause she's happy. Why the fuck would she need to argue you with you when she's getting dick on the regular... you remember how I get down, Brandi. She walking around with a fucking smile on her face every damn day."

She had nothing to say and avoided looking at me.

"Dick breath, I keep giving you grace because you're my baby mother. The next time you do some shit to hurt my baby, I can promise I'm gonna pull up in your driveway, walk in your crib, and let your husband know about our little secret right before I fuck him up under his own roof. Then, I'm gonna get one of the Inferno Goddesses to fuck you up next. Brandi, please don't force me to remind you how I get down. If you do, I can promise I will keep Peach until your black eye heals... now, get the fuck out my face."

She scattered away from me and went to sit on the couch next to Peach, rubbing her curls. I went back to my emails while ignoring her for the rest of the flight. If she knew like I did, she better had stayed the fuck away from me during this trip.

CHAPTER 22
CAPRI

"CAPRI BROWNE," I answered the phone, as I shoved more salad down my throat. The salad bar from down the block wasn't all that great, but they had a corn summer salad that I couldn't stop eating, even if I tried.

"Ms. Browne, I'm glad that I caught you during your lunch... it is your lunch, right?"

I choked down the fork full of salad I had just consumed and sat up. "Hi Mr. Morgan... um, yes... it is my lunch... is there anything that I can help you with."

"Yes. Two things actually. I wanted to personally call and invite you to a leisure trip to Monaco. A few of the higher ups get together and enjoy the races and the country. Rich is also going, and I wanted to invite you."

My stomach dropped because I knew I was going, but not with Morgan. "Um, that sounds great... I just need some tim—"

"Capri, these people are high profile people and can get you where you need to be. I'm sure being an assistant district attorney isn't something that you wanna do forever. You have to play the game with these people. I was an underpaid detective and now look at me. If you're worried about money, don't worry about it because everything is handled. I have a few donations from some people that want to see me in office."

It was very illegal what he was telling me, but I kept my mouth shut. "S..sur—"

"Perfect. I will make sure to add you onto the itinerary. You told me at lunch that your life is all about work... it's time for you to live a little, while climbing up the ladder. I scratch your back, and you scratch mine. Now, that file that I'm sure came across your desk that involves my name... do me a favor and just toss it out. That case is a waste of the court and your time. Just some woman looking for her fifteen minutes."

"Mr. Morg—"

"Vincent, we're friends... right? I don't want to take up too much of your lunch, so we'll talk soon... okay? Alright, have a good day, Ms. Browne," he said, as he ended the call, and I sat there stuck on my words.

> Me: He invited me to Monaco.

> 40: perfect.

Blair's name popping across my screen pulled me from my thoughts, so I answered because I needed anything to think about other than Vincent Morgan. I had court earlier this morning, but now I was back in the office bullshitting because I couldn't wait to be done for the day.

This week moved at a snail's pace, and I found myself counting down the hours until I could be with Peach and Meer in Chicago for the weekend. It was hard getting comfortable without Meer holding me at night. By the time I left here, I was driving back to the lake house to finish packing, and then Meer had got me a car to take me to the airport. Not only was I off this weekend, but the office closed for one entire week every year.

It was different having a man handle everything for you. I didn't have to do anything because he had already handled everything for me. Quameer took that seriously, and I loved that for me. When I was with him, I didn't have to think. As someone who always had their brain on twenty-four seven, it was a special feeling when you got around your person and your mind was quieted, and you didn't have to think because you knew they would handle everything.

"You're going to live a very long time because I was thinking about you this morning in the shower," I greeted while snacking on my cashews that I had become obsessed with.

"From your lips to God's ear because I have been going through it this week," Blair groaned into the phone.

"Why didn't you call me, Blair? I told you now that I am home, I can be there for you in a second."

Blair sighed. "I know you cannot get away from work, but it would be nice to go to your family's house in Barbados. I need to be around some culture and water."

Blair was the kind of friend that never asked for anything. She would never crack her mouth to ask anybody for anything. If she was hinting at going away and needing a vacation, then I was going to make it happen for her.

"What are you doing this weekend?"

"Nothing. Ice cream and cookies while watching movies."

I smiled. "Pack a bag and fly out with me to Chicago. I need to be there for Peach's birthday, but we can fly to Barbados from there... lay out at the beach and rest."

"You more than anyone deserves to get some rest." She giggled in the phone. "Do you think I would be intruding on her trip?"

"Quasim won't mind," I teased, knowing he had flown in earlier in the week because Peach guilted him.

"He's there?"

"Yep... pack your stuff and meet me at the lake house. I'll call Meer and try to figure out the flight situation."

"Pri?"

"Hmm?"

"Honestly, thank you," she replied.

"Blair, I'm already hormonal, please don't make me start crying." I giggled, to avoid crying on the phone with her.

She laughed. "I'm sorry, Prego. Call me when you're enroute to the lake house, and I'll head there, too."

"Got you… see you soon."

I was supposed to go to lunch with Rich today, and never showed at the office. I guess he was taking his vacation earlier than everyone. Other than court, I had nothing to do since I was done for the day.

> Me: I kind of invited Blair to Chicago… what's my flight information so I can book hers.

He didn't reply right away, so I continued looking over this case that Morgan wanted me to toss out.

When he called me the other day, I should have known that he wanted something. I hated his voice, the way he looked, and the bad feeling I got whenever he was around me. The case was an assault case, and apparently the woman was saying that she was sexually assaulted by him when she worked for him.

He tried to convince me that wasn't the case, and that she's mad because he refused to pay her more money. I was smart enough to know that a man in power would always abuse it the wrong way. Morgan had been in power before, and he abused his power when he sent my brother away.

> Meer Cat: I chartered a jet for you, so she can just fly with you.

I couldn't even reply because he was calling me. "Baby, you charted a whole jet for one person."

"Don't be disrespectful. Is my baby not in your stomach?"

I laughed. "You are too much. I could have caught a commercial flight, Meer. It's not a big deal."

"When it comes to you it's always a big deal. The biggest fucking deal, you hear me?"

I blushed. "I hear you, Meer."

"Good. I miss the shit out of you."

Smiling, I turned around to look at the view of another building. "I miss you, too, Meer. What have you guys been doing?"

"Every damn thing. She has dragged us around this city to do everything."

"Is she having the best time though?"

"Yeah. Told me that this is the best birthday, so my aching feet are worth it." He chuckled into the phone. "You been drinking water?"

"Yes. I will make sure to bring my water bottle with me." I giggled, knowing he wanted me to carry that water bottle around with me like another limb.

All week he kept reminding me to drink more water, and even installed a damn app to keep track of how many ounces I drank while he wasn't around.

"Good girl."

Someone clearing their throat forced me to spin back around, and Rich was standing there with takeout bags in his hand. "Hey, let me give you a call later."

"The fuck is this professional ass voice? You talking to me like I don't eat yo pussy," Meer teased, knowing I couldn't respond the way that I wanted.

"Alright…take care." I quickly ended the call and rolled closer to my desk. "Hey, I didn't think you were coming in today." I motioned for him to close the door, and he took a seat in one of the chairs in front of my desk.

My office wasn't massive, and it could be compared to a small closet with windows. The windows made it look larger than it was.

"I wasn't." He sat the bags down on the desk. "Then I remembered that I owed you lunch, and I always keep my word."

My stomach growled right on time as he pulled out containers from Philippe Chow's. It was one of my favorite restaurants in the city. "Please tell me that you got the lobster fried rice."

"Is there any other rice to get from there? The only reason I go there is because of the rice." He sat out the container filled with my favorite rice.

"There is so much to get from there other than the rice... did you try their Bok choy..." I allowed my words to trail off when he pulled it out the bag.

The room was silent as we ate our food. I was so into my food that I didn't feel the need to make conversation. I kept looking at Rich and wondered how he became who he was, knowing where he came from.

How did one work their way to where he was, and allow his past to keep him with one foot in the streets? I understood why I was doing what I was sent to do. It was because I would never allow my brothers to be sent to prison if I could help it.

What was his reason?

What got Rich Parker out of bed every morning to face the world?

"Any plans for our week vacation? I feel like I just got here and I'm already liking the perks of the office."

"A small token of their appreciation for working us around the clock during the year," he spat, spooning some rice into his mouth. "I'm going to DC to visit some friends and family. My godson is turning fourteen, so he requested I take him shopping. We just lost a family member in a fire not too long ago, so he needs this."

He was opening up. I didn't know much about Rich other than what Meer had told me. The fact that he gave me that small piece of information meant that he was becoming comfortable with me.

"I'm sorry. Fourteen is such a weird time. You're not a baby anymore, but everyone still acts like you are. I remember when I was that age."

"Now all these kids want to do is dance on the internet and call you bro'."

I snorted. "I guess that comes with being the friend with no kids. All your friends automatically make you the god parent."

He smiled at me. "How many godchildren do you have running around here?"

I bit into my dumpling and chuckled. "My friends know I cannot keep a goldfish alive, so they wouldn't dare leave a living child in my hands… Thank God."

Rich finished his food and leaned back in his chair with his feet crossed at the ankle. "Morgan called and told me he spoke to you about the case."

"I mean, he didn't really speak to me about it. Just told me to toss the case out because the woman was lying."

"And you don't want to do that?" Rich was trying to read me which I found funny. I was raised by Jean Delgato, so I had become a master at hiding my emotions and feelings.

"Just confused… the girl is saying he sexually assaulted her, and we just push it under the rug."

Rich leaned forward. "When it comes to staying in good with men like Morgan, we never ask questions and just do. I remember that intern, and she was always tossing around how she had a crush on him. Morgan probably didn't pay her off and now she's upset."

I couldn't believe what was coming out of his mouth, but I had to pretend. I kept a neutral face on as I watched him observing me. "Guess I'll toss the case out once we're back from vacation."

My heart sank knowing that this woman had to take one for the team because what was at stake was larger. "Don't worry about it… me and Judge Tanner are locked in. I'll handle it and speak to the *victim* and see how she wants to proceed monetarily." It was the way he said victim, like this woman was making this story up.

Morgan sniffed my neck in the middle of lunch in front of both Rich and Tasha. If he was bold enough to do something like that in the open, I could only imagine what he did behind closed doors.

"Sounds like a plan." I had lost my appetite after having this conversation.

Here I thought I was here to watch Rich, get in close with him to bring down both he and Morgan. When in reality, this was so much bigger than my brothers. This man wanted to become mayor to continue to abuse his power and women. He wanted to be untouchable, and he was damn near there without even becoming mayor.

While Rich was in his phone, I discreetly slid the folder underneath my desk calendar and went back to pretending to enjoy this food. The food was perfectly fine, it was the company that was sour.

Quameer Inferno rolled the red carpet out to bring me to him. I've been on plenty of jets and was never impressed when a man tried to woo me with one. Like how Mason thought it was a flex that he had options when it came to jets.

With Meer, it was different because he wasn't doing it to show off. He knew I had been on a jet before. He wanted me brought to him quick, so he chartered a jet to bring me to him. He didn't want me to have to deal with going through TSA and then a crowded airport while waiting to board, in hopes that the flight didn't get delayed.

He cherished my time and wanted to make everything easier for me. It wasn't about flexing that he could afford to charter a jet, it was about the flex of making his fiancée's life easier. I had my feet kicked up while reading *You Had Me At Hello* by Leondra Lerae. I was on the last chapter when one of the pilots came and gently tapped me, careful not to disturb me.

"We're starting to descend, Mrs. Inferno," he informed me. "Is there anything else the flight attendant can get you? Maybe another water. Mr. Inferno was clear on us making sure you stayed hydrated."

I laughed. "I think I'm aright when it comes to the water.

Thank you again." I squeezed his hand, and he smiled before going back to the front of the jet.

Blair had finally woke up, with her short hair all which way. With the way her hair had fell, it looked like she had a bowl cut. She had been sleep since the moment we took off, which is why I was almost finished with this book. I couldn't blame her because the cashmere throw blankets that were provided felt like a dream.

Had the book not been so good, I probably would have fallen asleep myself. "How is this so normal for you? A man sending you a jet because he doesn't want you to have to deal with the airport is crazy."

"It's not normal for me, but I'm learning not to overthink about it, or convince myself I don't deserve it."

Blair reached across and grabbed my hand. "You absolutely deserve this. Everything that is happening for you, you deserve it."

"I want this for you, too, Blair."

She sighed. "I don't need a jet… just a man that wants to love me and everything that comes with me. Soon as I tell a man that I have cancer, they get weird and start to ghost me. Maybe I'm meant to be alone forever."

"Quasim doesn't ghost you," I reminded her.

She smiled and looked away. "He doesn't ghost me anymore… We met up for drinks a few weeks ago at Fern."

"Wait a second… you ain't never mention that to me. Who invited who? What happened? Did you kiss him? Blair spill everything," I blurted everything out at the same time as I watched her fall back into the chair and laugh.

"He had texted me to ask how chemo was earlier in the week, and I told him it was fine. He asked me if I wanted to have a drink, and I accepted. We had drinks and just had surface level conversation which I could appreciate. I was mostly venting about the studio and how the owner was pissing me off."

"That's a big step compared to how he was ignoring the hell

out of you each time he saw you. I wanna say things changed when he choked that man up for you," I teased her.

Quasim seemed to be coming out of his shell more. He still wasn't the most talkative person in the room. The fact that he reached out to Blair was a huge step, because he avoided her like she was diseased or something.

"Sim is just complicated and needs someone to love him the right way. He's gone so long without love or a woman's touch."

"Wait a minute... you don't think he hasn't had sex since his girlfriend was murdered?"

Blair shrugged. "I don't know. He doesn't strike me as a man that has one night stands or keeps a woman around just to have sex."

I leaned back in my seat. "Yeah, he doesn't seem like the type. Then again, he's very quiet and private so he could have him a little *yeah yeah* that we don't know about."

"He's too tense to be getting pussy." Blair was certain. "A man that tense hasn't had sex in a while... and it probably wasn't something on his mind either."

"Sex isn't everything. I went a year and a few months without it, and I was alright." I shrugged.

There were times when I craved someone to hold me more than sex. I did miss it, but it wasn't the top of my brain like it used to be. Quasim had been through a lot, so sliding into someone probably wasn't a thought for him.

Blair leaned over and lowered her voice as if we were on a packed flight. "With these treatments my sexual desire and libido is zero. I used to enjoy grabbing my rose and having a time with myself, and these days I can't even bring myself to do that. I guess I can say that was part of the problem with ol' boy... he wanted sex, and I wasn't in the mood. That was why I ended up telling him that I was battling breast cancer." She paused. "Anyway, I say all of that to say... whenever I see Quasim, it returns back with vengeance. He doesn't even have to say anything, just the way he looks down at me, smells, and carries himself." She fanned herself and fell back into her seat kicking her feet.

"You gotta crush… you gotta crush," I teased her.

She waved me off. "I don't think anything will come out of it but a friendship, which I can appreciate."

Blair might have been telling herself that to sleep at night, but I could look my future brother-in-law in the face and see that he didn't want to be friends with Blair. He wanted to be her man and was battling with himself on how to do that.

We landed perfectly, despite Blair needing me to hold her hand while she squeezed her eyes shut and recited prayers. We sat back while they headed to where we can exit, and I put away my book and everything so I could get off and go see my baby.

Meer said he was sending a car for us. As excited as I was to see my baby, I was more excited to see Peach and give her the birthday gift I had gotten her.

"How do you feel about having to see Brandi?" Blair pulled me from my thoughts, and I smiled, knowing I felt the opposite.

"Like shit. I don't want to see her or pretend to be nice to her. She ruined my pregnancy announcement on purpose. For the sake of Peach, I'm going to smile and pretend to be nice to her."

"That was such a bitch thing to do, and then to use her daughter to do it… so fucked up." Blair slipped her feet back into her sneakers.

I was so damn excited to get to Meer that I never changed out of my work clothes. All I did was grab my bags and waited for Blair to arrive before I kissed Gams and Mina and was on my way out. I was still in my silk blouse, tailored pants and favorite YSL slingbacks.

"I don't expect anything less when it comes to Brandi. Me and Peach spoke about it and we're good. I do want to have another talk with her without her father, so I know we're really good."

Blair smiled at me. "You were nervous about being a stepmother and you're going to be the best one. Peach is so lucky to have you, Capri."

"Thanks, B."

The pilot told us it would take a little second to open the doors, so me and Blair continued to chat until they were finally ready for us.

We grabbed our things and finally exited the jet. I paused before going down the steps, causing Blair to bump into me. "Girl, you alright..." Her words trailed off when she saw what I had been looking at.

Both railings of the stairs were filled with bright pink and red roses. You couldn't see the metal bar because there were roses wrapped around it going all the way down. I finally peeled my eyes from the roses and my face reacted without any thought.

Meer was standing by the car with roses in his hand. "With the way I was missing you, you didn't think I was gonna wait for you to drive to me?"

I damn near broke a heel with how fast I was coming down those stairs. Running from the steps, I crashed into his arms, knocking a few petals from the bouquet he held. He sat them down on the hood of the car, and I kissed him all over his face, inhaling his spicy peppery cologne that I loved so much.

"Meer Cat!" My cheeks ached because of how hard I was cheesing while he held me and kissed my teeth.

His teeth kisses had become my favorite thing. My purse was on the floor with how fast I dropped it and ran into his arms, wrapping my legs around him as he carried me and loved on me.

"You missed your man, huh?"

I screwed my face up. "Don't even play like you didn't miss me... chartered a whole jet to get me to you."

He squeezed my ass, while holding me up. "You damn fucking right."

"Chill out... it was only a couple days." Quasim laughed, and it was then that I noticed that he was here. He picked my purse up and sat it next to the roses on the hood of the car.

"Hating ass." Meer chuckled.

"Simmy Jimmy... what's going on?" Blair hopped down the rest of the stairs and smiled when she saw him.

He walked over toward her, taking her bag and giving her a hug. "Remember when you told me that you wanted to ride a motorcycle?"

"Yes... in my defense, I was about three drinks in when I started sputtering about my goals." She laughed. "Hey Meer."

"What up, Blair?"

I was still in his arms, and I wasn't getting down no time soon. As I sniffed his neck, kissing it, I wanted to be in this man's skin.

Quasim pointed over toward the motorcycle that was parked next to the truck. Another thing that I didn't notice because I was concerned with my man.

Blair screamed and jumped up and down. "Are you serious? I'm really going to get to ride with you?"

It was rare to see Quasim smile, but he smiled as he looked down at Blair and bit his bottom lip. "Yeah... I heard you were coming so figured I would check one of the things off your list."

Blair swung her arms around him, hugging him tightly while so excited that he was about to take her on a ride. "You've made my entire week... I was just telling Capri I had a rough week."

He held her chin and looked down at her. "Glad that I'm able to put a smile on your face." Sim turned to us. "Meet you at the restaurant."

"We're going to eat?" I got excited because I was hungry. The meal I shared with Rich had long worn off, and I wanted some good food with even better company.

Meer slapped my ass, while putting me down. "You greedy as hell."

"First you complain I'm not eating enough and now I'm greedy." I pulled his card, and he laughed.

"I ain't never complaining about you eating, Suga... I'll feed you until you pop." He snuck a kiss on my cheek, and then held my hand.

Quasim helped Blair onto the bike and was fixing her helmet.

"Hold me tight around the waist. If I'm going too fast, let me know, alright?"

Blair nodded her head while he smiled at her and got on the bike. I watched as he started the bike up, and Blair wrapped her arms around him as best as she could and rested her head on his back.

Sim paused for a second, and I could tell he was trying to figure out how to feel about it. For that brief second, I could see a few pieces of his wall crumbling, and then he was back to business. He saluted his brother, and then sped away with Blair holding onto him tightly.

"He gonna be good," Meer said more to himself as he watched his brother speed away. "You think so?" He looked down at me.

"I do. I also think we need to let Sim come out of his shell on his own. We can't push them both together because they both have had it hard; you know?"

He kissed my lips. "Yeah, I know… I know you need to toss these damn pants away… look at that ass, Suga." Meer spun me around.

I swatted his hands. "I am fully covered up. Can't help that my body is T," I joked with him and ran off toward the car while he chased me.

"That's why you got Morgan's ass ready to risk it all for you."

"He don't know I'm about to marry a lunatic." I kissed him before climbing into the back of the truck and smiling at the roses all over.

It looked like Meer went to the florist and told her to put her entire shop into the back of this navigator. "I love you, Suga. Always want you to know that, ight?"

I held his face and kissed his lips. "Word is bond?"

"Word is bond, son." He kissed me again, before closing the door and walking toward the other side.

> Jesse: I want to have dinner at my house. Think we both need to talk soon. Let me know your availability.

How could everything be so perfect and fucked up at the same time. Me and Jesse hadn't spoken since that brunch, and I was avoiding her because I knew her fate. I knew eventually I would have to see and speak to her and explain what happened.

The thing was that I didn't want to do it because I knew that she would have a million questions that I would never answer. In fact, she would leave the dinner more confused than anything.

Meer took my hand into his as we exited the private airport, and I kissed his hand. I knew what it took to be an Inferno, and the end result was to protect my family.

CHAPTER 23
CAPRI

"SHIT, SUG... DAMN," Meer groaned while holding my head while my head bopped up and down. I held his dick as I ran my tongue down the shaft before swallowing it whole again while he damn near jumped off the bed.

His hands were tangled in my hair as I went to work, squeezing his balls in the process. I could tell from the way he shook slightly that he was about to cum, and I increased my speed, popping his dick out of my mouth to spit on it before devouring it again.

Meer's eyes were so low that it seemed like they were closed, but he was watching my every move. My eyes met his, as I flicked my tongue across the tip while he patted my head with a smirk. "Like this, Pa?" I asked after I popped it out of my mouth and nibbled on the head.

"Just like this... go all the way down. I wanna hear my Suga choke."

His wish was my command as I went all the way down and gagged a bit. Meer was blessed between the legs, and now it made all the sense why Brandi was out here acting out like she didn't have a husband at home.

He moved his hips and pumped in and out of my mouth

while I tightened my grip on him, and he pulled my hair while I stared up at him with tears coming out of my eyes.

"You like sucking Big Pa, huh? You like being nasty, Mrs. Inferno?" He leaned up when I swirled my tongue around his dick while it was still in my mouth.

"I wanna taste you... cum in my mouth, baby, please," I begged, and Meer looked at me for a minute before I went back to work, and made it where he didn't need to think about it because he was about to cum.

"Sug...fuck, shit...damn!" He unleashed his nut, and I took it down like a champ, smearing the tip of his dick on my lips.

"Quameer, breakfast is here and your brother, too!" Brandi loudly yelled outside the door, knocking.

Just like that, our moment together was ruined because her voice alone made Quameer wanna murder something. I wiped my mouth on the blanket, as Meer pulled me up onto him. "I can get her another hotel if you want me to."

"Peach loves sharing a room with her mother. I'm not going to ruin that for her because her mother is petty."

He stared at me. "I can make sure my daughter has the trip of her dreams without disrespecting my future wife's feelings. Peach will understand if her mother needs to get her own room, since Quasim was able to book his own room without any problems."

Blair was sleeping in the den area of the suite we were in. There was a pull-out couch in there, and it converted into an extra bedroom. "Let's have breakfast so we can do everything that Peach has reserved for just me." I kissed his cheek, and tried to climb out of bed, and he pulled me back onto him.

"You heard what I said, Capri. When I said stop being so accommodating, I wasn't only talking about Naheim... in general, even when it comes to Brandi."

I've never had a man consider my feelings. Someone who cared about if I was comfortable or not and didn't care who he made uncomfortable to make me comfortable. Meer would put

Brandi out right this second if I told him that I didn't want her here.

As much as I was tolerating Brandi, I was thinking about the little girl that wanted both her parents here. I could put up with Brandi for the weekend because that meant that Peach would have the best birthday.

"I hear you... now, I have to pee." I climbed over him and he held me in place while on top of him. "Meer, I promise I hear what you're saying."

"I don't give a fuck who I piss off as your husband, Suga. As long as I know my wife is comfortable, I'll be the villain in anybody's story... including your family."

I kissed his lips and smiled. "I know you don't and I think everyone pretty much realized the time you're on."

Meer made it where our business was ours and I didn't have to hear shit from anybody or explain anything. I remember always feeling like everyone had a clear view right into my life, and I never had any privacy. Meer stepped in and put that on a smash, and I knew it was because he was naturally private.

"You be sucking dick-dick, Sug." He smirked, and I punched him and got off the bed. "I'm about to go kill any nigga you did that to, Capri."

"Whatever, Meer... put some clothes on."

"What's they name... never mind, Core will help me figure it out," he continued on while I went to pee.

I quickly washed my face and brushed my teeth before pulling on my pajamas and joining everyone out in the dining room for breakfast. Peach was at the head of the table with matching fuzzy pajamas with her mother.

"You both look so cute." I smiled, as I took a seat beside Meer, who had already fixed my plate.

"Thank you, Suga... I forgot to get you one, too."

I waved her off. "It's so fun to match with your mommy... I used to match with mine when I was your age."

"Really?"

"Yep."

Brandi sipped her coffee and looked at me. "Good morning, Capri."

"Morning, Brandi." I bit a piece of bacon, knowing Cappy would flip his shit if he saw all this damn pork that was on the table.

Blair and Quasim were sharing off one plate. "Ms. Blair, you can have your own plate. I made sure to tell Daddy to order enough for everyone." Peach smiled at Blair, who smiled back at her.

"Well, aren't you just the sweetest princess. I don't eat much, so I don't want to waste any of your beautiful spread, and your uncle helps me not feel bad about not wasting food."

"Okay, but if you want more just let Uncle Simmy know… he'll get you what you want, right?" she looked at her uncle.

"I'll give her anything she wants… you right, Ry." He looked at Blair as she continued eating, and then winked at his niece.

"Ryder, we need to change for our spa date… are you ready?" Brandi pushed her food away, ready to get away from the table because seeing Meer kiss me on the temple while feeding me disgusted her.

I could see if he was doing it on purpose to hurt her, but Meer literally never paid her any attention. He would have been doing the same thing if Brandi wasn't at this table. Call me petty, but I kissed my man's lips just as she turned her attention to me.

"I'm ready!" Ryder pushed her food away and ran over toward her father to hug him. "See you later for dinner, Daddy."

"See you later, Peach. What's the colors again?"

"Red!" She pinched him, and then came to hug me, and I ruffled her curly hair. "How is my baby sister, Suga?"

"Oh, you just know you're getting a sister, huh?"

She wrapped her arms around me, and I kissed her head. "Daddy says it's a boy."

"And Daddy is very much delusional, Peach." I laughed with her. "Have the best spa day with your mommy, okay?"

"Okay."

Brandi wanted one day with just her and Ryder, and Meer

arranged for them to do the spa. I loved that despite how he felt about Brandi, he was always going to do what's best for her relationship with their daughter.

After Brandi and Ryder went to get ready, we all continued to eat our breakfast while Blair settled back. "You done already?"

"That bacon is too good... I could eat so much more, but my stomach hurts," she laughed and sipped her tea. "You know you don't have to have me picking in your plate, Simmy Jimmy."

"What are the plans for today?"

Quameer was on his phone. "I'm taking you shopping today."

"Me, shopping? Why?"

"Girl, you never question when a man wanna take you shopping... go with it," Blair snickered.

"Because I want to spend some money on my fiancée... problem with that?"

"Not at all, Meer. Maybe we can pick up something for the baby, too. Some neutral colors," I suggested.

Quasim stood up and went to grab a folder that was on the buffet behind us. He took his seat and slid the folder over toward Blair. "You told me about your situation with the landlord selling the building."

Blair looked at him confused as she took the folder and flipped it open. She quickly dropped the folder back onto the table like it was hot. "Quasim, wha...what the hell?"

"I didn't like how you said he was treating you, so I went to have a talk with him." I could tell from the way he spoke that he went and beat that man's ass for the way he was treating Blair, and he had good reason.

Blair showed me the text messages on how he got crazy and rude with her. Once we were shopping, he called and told her that she needed to hurry up or he was putting her stuff out. So, he deserved to get his ass beat.

I could tell that Blair didn't know what to say or how to process what was going on. "Is that the reason he randomly texted and apologized for his behavior?"

Sim smirked while cutting into his pancakes. "Probably. I'm glad he took accountability since our chat. I bought the building from him, and with your signature, I am going to transfer it into your name. There's tenants that live above the studio, so you're their new landlord."

"Quasimmy," she merged his real name and her nickname together as she flipped through the pages, her eyes becoming wider each time she flipped a page. "No, no, I cannot take this from you... I just can't... this is a lot of money... Qua... I don't know what to say." She was spiraling and didn't know what to say or do next.

Quasim touched her hand and looked at her. "I'm a solver. You had a problem, and I solved it. I couldn't think of a better person that I could give this to. No strings attached either, Blair... this yo' shit."

Blair leaped out her chair and jumped into his arms, putting her arms around him as she sobbed. Quasim slowly wrapped his arms around her as she sobbed into his shoulder, causing me to cry right along with her.

Quameer kissed my temple and pulled me close. "I'm a solver... I'm bob the builder," Meer mocked his older brother.

"Yo, Blaze?"

"Hmm?"

"Fuck ya."

I laughed through my tears as Blair returned to her seat, her face red and wet with tears. "I don't... I don't know what to even say."

"I can finish my pancakes now?" Quasim laughed.

"Want me to make you more? Because I can make you some right now."

We all laughed as she continued to look through the papers, in disbelief that this man bought a full building in Brooklyn for her. I didn't even want to know the cost he paid for the building. Knowing Sim, he probably got a good deal after fucking up Blair's current landlord.

"I can move into one of the empty apartments now... God, I

dreamed of living in the same building as my studio but couldn't afford it."

"Now you can."

"Between Cappadonna buying classes every month and this... how could I ever thank you guys? I mean, I really can't thank you enough for this, Quasimmy."

"What happened to Simmy Jimmy?" He looked over at her, as he bit into a piece of bacon, and she blushed.

It was the way he looked at her that told me that Quasim was lost in Blair. He wouldn't care that her sexual desire was gone, or the fact that she was battling cancer. He wanted to make Blair smile, and the small things like grabbing her up in a crowded club where she was drunk to allowing her to eat off his plate so she wouldn't feel bad about wasting food told me that.

"Congratulations, Blair," Meer said. "Now, you can be our doula for free since we gifted you the studio."

"Not you trying to add yourself onto his gift," I mushed Meer as we all laughed, 'cause he was a fool.

"I was always going to be her doula, and she never had to pay. Me and Capri are locked in forever." We high-fived across the table.

"We're always gonna be locked in, but girl we are paying you."

Blair nudged Quasim playfully while he finished his food. "Thank you, for real. I'll never forget something like this." He winked at her while chewing his food.

We all continued to eat our food, while deciding on which store we were going to hit on Michigan Avenue. Me and Meer sat back watching both Quasim and Blair hold their own conversation. It was how soft he was with her as he slid the pen into her hand and showed her where to sign.

I never wanted to push either of them, but I had a feeling about them both and would continue to pray that they both got happily ever after, even if it wasn't with each other. They both deserved that much.

"Meer, Baby, we… we have to go," I breathlessly reminded him, as he was tongue deep inside of me, while I was on the edge of the sink in the bathroom.

Someone knocking on the bathroom outside pulled us from our moment. Meer kissed my second set of lips before coming from under my dress and then kissing me on the lips. "Why in the fuck would you wear that dress tonight, Suga? I had to return the favor from earlier." He winked at me.

Meer helped me down from the sink. "You need to contain yourself… we're at dinner."

I turned to fix my red lipstick which was smeared because Meer followed me to the bathroom and proceeded to make out with me, shoving his entire tongue into my mouth. Well, it wasn't all one sided because somehow my tongue landed in the back of his mouth, too.

While Meer went into the stall to pee, I checked myself out in the mirror. The V-neck silk maxi dress hugged my body like a glove, giving me a little room at the same time. My gold Tom Ford strappy heels set the outfit off with the gold clutch that I paired it with. My hair was wand curled with messy beach curls, while my makeup was simple.

Meer came out the bathroom fixing his belt and fixing himself in the mirror. My baby wasn't stepping light either with his outfit. He wore a pair of chino pants that stopped at his ankle, two toned penny loafers, and a silk short sleeve shirt that he left untucked. I had pulled his locs up into a bun, and per Peach's request, he wore his gold fangs because she said he looked cool with them.

"Give me kiss, Suga," he demanded, and I left the mirror to kiss him, tasting myself on his lips, which turned me on all over again.

When we returned back to the table, everyone was talking and eating while me and Meer slipped back into our seats like we hadn't been gone for almost twenty minutes.

"Everything all good?" Of course, Brandi was the first person to say something. Meanwhile, Quasim, Blair and Ryder were playing hangman on the back of the menu, not even bothered that we were gone.

Meer looked at her, and then licked his lips. "Tasted good, too."

I pinched his thigh as I sipped my virgin drink and started to eat. Even though I had missed Peach's birthday, I had called and spoke to her. She wanted to save her birthday dinner until I came. She had a vision of going to a fancy restaurant with everyone and being a big girl.

Meer made the reservation for her, and she was so excited that she got to have drinks out a martini glasses like the rest of us. Even though mine was just pineapple juice like hers.

While Peach and Brandi spent the day at the spa, we all went shopping and went to lunch. It was such an easy and fun day. Things had been tense and we all knew this was all the calm before the actual storm, so it was nice to just exist.

Even Quasim was feeling it because he had a few laughs with Blair, as they shopped. Every time Blair picked something up, he told the sales associate to get it. By the time we were done, he and Meer were at the front swiping their cards for us.

"Peach, can I give you the gift I have for you privately?" I asked her, as she struggled to sit her glass down and her uncle helped her.

"Like a secret?" she got excited.

I swore this girl loved a good secret like everyone else. "Not a secret, but a moment for me and you. Do you two mind?" I looked to Brandi and then Quameer.

"Do you, Sug." He kissed my cheek, and got up to pull my chair out.

Brandi took back the rest of her drink. "Sure."

I took Peach's hand, and we walked out onto the outside patio that overlooked the river. Her little kitten heels she wore cracked me up. My girl didn't half step when it came to her little pink dress and matching heels. Which was rare for Ryder because she loved sneakers and to be outside hanging out with CJ. Between the both of them, they both came back full of dirt because they were riding on the back paths of the community.

I found a table in an empty spot in the corner of the patio and sat down with Ryder sitting beside me. "I know your birthday has passed, but I want to say happy birthday to you in person. You're the smartest and sweetest girl that I have ever met. I thank your Daddy almost every day for allowing you to be part of my life." I swiped my tear.

"Thank you, Suga. I thank Daddy, too, because you make us so happy. Daddy is so much happier with you." She smiled at me.

I placed the velvet black box I had been holding and handed it to her. "Awe, I'm so much happier with you two. I wanted to give this to you because it's from me and the baby. We wanted to make sure we had our moment alone."

She quickly opened the box and pulled out the locket I had made for her. It was a solid gold heart shaped locket with *Big Sister* etched in the front of the heart. On the inside, there was a small picture of the baby's sonogram, and the other side was a picture of her and Meer.

Peach gasped as she looked at it, and tears welled in her eyes. "You got this for me?"

"Yes. Your new sibling wanted to give you something before they come. A little reminder that we can't do this without big sis'."

She tossed her arms around my neck and hugged me tightly while I rubbed her back and kissed her. "Thank you, Suga."

"You're always welcome, Peach. I want you to know that I am always here for you. You never had to question that, okay? Even when I have the baby, nothing will ever change between us… okay?"

"Do you promise?"

She held out her pinky. "I promise… ready to go inside and finish dinner? You are the star of the night."

"Can you put it on me now? I never want to take it off."

I took the locket from her and put it on her, hugging her from behind before we walked back inside. Meer was saying something to Brandi when we walked in. He stood up and pulled Peach's chair out, then held my chair out.

"I want to say a toast to my favorite niece in the whole wide world." Quasim held his cup up, and we followed and did the same thing. "It's been an honor and pleasure being able to be part of watching you grow up. It's not something that I take lightly. Ryder, you are the light in all of our lives, and I know if Harley was here, you both would have been giving me and your father hell. Since she's not here, I know she's watching over you and telling you to give us even more hell. I love you Ry-Ry, for as long as I have breath in my body, Uncle Simmy will always be here for you."

Ryder smiled as she rushed into her uncle's arms, and he put his drink down to kiss her head. "Love you, Uncle Simmy."

"Love you more, Baby."

I squeezed Meer's hand as we watched them both, our hearts both filled with so much love for this blended family. Even Brandi dabbed her eyes as she watched Quasim and Ryder together. Meer kissed me on the temple as he rubbed my stomach while looking at his first born.

We were blessed.

CHAPTER 24
CAPELLA

I WATCHED my little liar rush around the room tossing everything into her suitcase. The women were catching a jet to Chicago to pick Capri and Blair up, then they were going to Barbados for a few days alone before everyone joined them.

Aimee was frustrated because she couldn't find a pair of heels she needed, and her stylist couldn't squeeze her in, so she had to wear her natural hair, and get a silk press. She kept trying to explain to me the reason for being frustrated and I couldn't find any reason.

Her hair was down her back and she was acting like she was bald, or had a short fro like Ice Spice or something. The girl she found to do her hair had done a good job. Every time she ran across our room, her hair flew in the wind like a feather.

"Aim," I spoke, still in the chair in the corner, knowing I should have tabled this conversation for another day, not when she was pissed and trying to find something to wear.

"Yes, Capella? I don't have time to explain to you how my hair will look with the humid air on the island." She huffed, grabbing a short ass dress that she looked at once more before shoving it into her suitcase.

"Why is there fifty stacks missing out the account, Aimee?" I casually asked, watching as she froze before placing the heels she found into the suitcase.

Aimee was quiet as she was trying to put together what she would say. "I thought I was free to do whatever I wanted with the money in that account?"

"Yeah, buy a purse or catch a quick flight out the country to relax, not take fifty thousand out the account and not at least have the conversation with me about it."

She sighed and sat on the edge of the bed. "I lent the money to my grandmother. She needed the money and begged me. What else was I supposed to do?"

"Baby, I'm starting to believe the rumors of you being slow might be true... 'cause why in the entire fuck would you give my money to yo' crooked wig grandmother?"

"She has a new wig, Capella," she tried to defend.

"I bet she fucking do with fifty thousand dollars in her fucking hand." I remained calm, almost too damn calm. My blood was boiling that she went behind my back to give them money without a conversation.

Whenever I made moves, I always talked to Aimee about the shit. She couldn't even give me the same respect before snatching money out an account that wasn't only for her but was for our son too.

"Can we talk about this once we're back home? This is supposed to be about Capri, and I want us to have a good time." She looked over at me.

"Why the fuck you give her the money, Aim? She holding something over you or something? Last I remember you had to pull your gun on your cousin, and did they step in to help you?"

"They're my family." She chewed on her bottom lip as she looked at me nervously. "All I have right now."

That shit hurt. "My family has accepted you and you keep going back to the same people that called you a fucking liar when your brother raped you. The same people that treated you like less than shit at the funeral. Those the same people you handing my fucking money to."

"It's your money, Capella?"

"I see you out there getting shot and keeping your head on swivel? Yeah, that shit my money since you being stupid and mishandling the shit."

"The car is here, Aimee!" I heard Alaia call to her up the stairs, and I watched her run into the bathroom to grab her toiletries bag and toss it into the suitcase before zipping it up.

"Capella, maybe we need some space? A break or something because this is too much for me right now. I have a lot going on, and clearly you don't understand that. This will give you the time to fuck the bitches you threaten me with."

"You breaking up with me?"

Aimee had been acting weird ever since we left Rory's doctor's appointment a few days ago. She'd been distancing herself and being fucking sneaky if you asked me, but I was giving her space to process whatever she needed to process.

"I need space, so yeah. We can still be parents to our son, but as far as us together… I need space right now." She grabbed her suitcase and placed it by the door.

"If that's what you want… I'll give you that. I'll go back over to my father's crib until you figure out what the fuck you want." I stood up, grabbing her suitcase to bring it downstairs.

Alaia and Erin were dancing while Zoya stood by the sink washing something off her shirt. "Why do you look like someone died?"

"Ask your girl. Have a safe trip… love you." I kissed Alaia's head on top of her hijab, and then hugged Erin. "See you, Z," I called to Zoya before heading out.

She waved as she viciously scrubbed out whatever was on that damn shirt. Alaia headed upstairs while I closed the garage door behind me.

My pops was talking to the driver, and I could tell he made this man nervous. If I knew my father, he was giving him ground rules for transporting his wife. Since finding out that Capp was my father, all I had been trying to do was make him proud of me.

He was the kind of man that I aspired to be like because he was a good man, loving father, and a family man overall. "Yeah, I'll shoot your teeth out your mouth." He laughed while the man continued to look at him horrified.

"Pops, you mind if I move back in with you?"

"I never mind... just wanna know why that would be happening when I spent a lot of money for you to have your *own* house." He leaned on the side of the SUV, while looking at me.

"Aimee broke up with me and I'm trying to give her some space."

"Don't you two ever get tired? I know I'm fucking tired of all of the back and forth between the two of you. Why the fuck she break up with you?"

"She took money out the account and didn't even have a conversation with me."

He looked at me confused. "Alaia pulls money out the account all the time. She never has to talk to me about it because her names are on the account. The reason I work as hard as I do is so my wife can do whatever she wants with *our* money. I don't know Capone's situation, but I can bet it's the same deal in his house, too. Isn't that where you and Aimee are heading? At least, that's what you told me."

As I was about to respond, Pops leaned off the truck and grabbed Aimee's luggage and put it in the back of the SUV. "Thanks, Pops." Aimee smiled.

"Kiss Baby Doll for me and record her expression once she knows what's going on." He smiled, as his wife came and hugged him.

Cappadonna pulled Alaia behind the truck where I knew he was getting his physical goodbyes in. Capone jogged across the street, hopping into the back of the truck and kissing Erin. "See you in a few days, Gorgeous."

"Love you, Winnie."

I walked away, not bothering to say shit to Aimee because she pissed me off so bad. Guess she thought I was gonna say something to her, and when I didn't, she looked disappointed.

She could look like that all she wanted, if she wanted a fucking break, then I was going to give her one.

I was either stupid or had balls the size of damn Texas for ringing the bell that I was about to ring. When I pushed the button, I stood back some and waited for whoever to answer the door. I could hear the doorknob and lock jiggle before the door opened and Rowland stood there.

When he laid eyes on me, the nigga looked like he was about to shit bricks when he saw me. "Aye, man, I ain't seen my cousin or said shit to her."

"Good to know, Row-Row." I pushed past him and entered the house. He stood there in shock that I pushed my way into his house. "Close the fucking door before you let flies in here. Already got roaches and you trying to add flies to the mix," I scolded.

"Rowland, who was that..." Tiny's voice trailed off when she saw me standing in her dusty ass living room.

The house smelled like stale weed and moth balls, and I was trying to conduct business quick so I could leave before the smell settled into my fucking clothes. "It's me, Tiny. Your niece's baby daddy... missed me?"

"Now, what the hell do you want?"

"I'm trying to find out where my money is so I can collect it?"

Tiny looked past me at my son. "You done got into business with his ass, Row? I don't have no money to be bailing you out."

"He said you... not me."

"I don't give a fuck who has it, I know I better have it in my hand before I leave out this bitch." I looked at both of them who looked equally confused. "Aimee said she lent your mother fifty thousand dollars."

"She said what? I haven't seen Aimee since she came around here waving that damn gun around. Why the hell would she lie and say she gave us anything?" Tiny was pissed off, and sparked a cigarette, while taking a seat on the couch.

"Aimee ain't been around here, Chubs... I fell back from her ass, and decided it wasn't worth going back to prison after I saw them toss yo' ass in the back of the car."

"She didn't give you any money?" I looked at Tiny, ignoring her son.

"No money, but if she wants to, she can actually give some instead of lying about it. I told you that girl is a liar and been lying for years."

I held my hand up. "Chill the fuck out. Ace fucking raped her, and she wasn't lying about it."

"The fuck happened?" Rowland looked repulsed by the fact that I revealed some family business that he hadn't been clued into.

"None of your business, boy... get that damn dryer back working!" his mother hollered at him, and he dipped to the back, while I looked at Tiny sucking on that cancer sick like a dick. "Aimee ain't been around here and she probably won't come back around here. She has her new family now, and unless she pulling her weight over here, her ass need to stay gone. Don't need her coming around showing off what she got and not helping me out. The little heifer wore my couch out enough when she first moved here."

"You know what I heard they doing to help people struggling out?"

Tiny was all ears as she leaned forward. "What?"

"A fucking job, bum." I could tell that she didn't have any money because her attitude would have been better. Aimee's family acted more loving when she did shit for them. Just off the way Tiny was acting, I could tell Aimee didn't give her family that money.

I left the house and hopped in my truck, peeling off the block before my ass could become comfortable in the seat. If Aimee didn't give the money to her family, then who the fuck did she give that fifty thousand to?

CHAPTER 25
QUAMEER

JUST AS QUICK as Capri was here for the weekend, she was gone again to Barbados with the women. I kissed her and sent her off to have some fun with her girls. When I drove her to the private airport, and she saw Alaia, Erin, Aimee, and Zoya there, she was crying and excited. That was when Blair told her the plan, and she nearly squeezed Blair to death because she was so excited and grateful.

I watched as she kissed me before boarding the jet to enjoy her bachelorette turn up with her favorite girls. Capri deserved this, and even though she couldn't drink and show out like she usually did, I knew the women would make it fun for her, and then I would see her for the ending of the trip so I could make that word wife the real thing when it came to her.

Peach enjoyed Chicago and it was all she kept speaking about. Despite her mother being petty, she didn't see that side of her and just had a good time with her favorite people. As much as I hated spending the week in a suite with Brandi, I couldn't lie and say the smile on my baby girl's face wasn't worth it.

My pops held onto my mother's hand as the jet landed and she looked out the window. I would have never imagined getting my mother on a plane after her diagnosis. It was something that I never expected to do. The fact that she was on this jet with us and would be there to see me get married made a nigga emotional.

Gams was on her second flute of champagne as she popped a grape into her mouth, excited to be going out the country and having her daughter with her. Peach sat beside Gam on her iPad while Quasim was sleeping on the couch behind them.

"How you feeling about all of this, Blaze?" My father asked.

I smiled. "I'm ready to become her husband."

It was something that I had spent so many nights dreaming about for us. I wanted to be the man that she came to for everything, the man that she would spend the rest of her life with. Capri meant the world to me, and when I thought about her, I got emotional because I loved the shit out of her. I had never loved a woman like I loved Capri, and it showed with the actions I showed her.

"Got that little jump of nervousness in your chest, too?"

I laughed. "Hell yeah. As much as I love her and I'm ready, I'm nervous too. Don't want to fail at this, you know? She's already had one failed marriage, so the pressure is on."

"And Infernos don't what?"

"Crack when it comes to pressure," I finished the saying my father had been saying to us since I was a child.

He always gave us room to be emotional and have feelings, but after that what the fuck were you going to do? You were gonna stand up, dust yourself off, and handle business. That was all me and Quasim knew when it came to surviving.

"That's my boy. You don't need to be a perfect husband, Blaze. You just need to be a present husband. I watch the two of you and you both are going to be alright."

"Reminds me of you and Mina," Gams smiled. "Capri is going to make a wonderful wife, and member to this family. She's already stepped into what would have been Mina's role for this family. Dumplin', she the one for you, and makes you so happy."

"Thanks, Gams."

The Delgatos had landed before us, so when we exited the jet, they were already getting into their cars and having them load their luggage up. My mother held onto my father as they walked down the steps, and he put her into the car.

She snatched his sunglasses and put them onto her eyes because it was sunny. "Too sunny for you, Baby," he laughed and kissed her cheek.

Peach climbed into the back and kissed her grandmother before heading to the back. Sim climbed into the front while I got in the back with Peach, and Gams. I sat back as Peach laid her head on me and we enjoyed the view.

When Capri told me this was where she wanted to get married, I had to give her this. Her entire family had gotten married here, and she never thought she would share that tradition. I didn't care what I had to do, I wanted to give her this wedding because she was forever putting everyone before her.

Capri would have gotten married at the courthouse not to inconvenience anyone. I loved that she had a heart like that, but I wanted my baby to start demanding what she needed. Letting us know what she needed, when it came to her needs.

As her husband, I was going to remind her that nothing she asked for was ever too much for me. If she asked me for the stars, then I was gonna talk to that nigga Elon and see about going up there with a Tupperware bowl to bring her a star back.

Nothing, and I mean nothing was ever too much when it came to Capri Inferno. I wanted her to have everything her heart desired, and I was going to do my best to give that to her. I felt someone nudge me and I sat up, realizing that I had fell asleep with Peach in the back.

"We're here," my father said, as he got out the car, and helped my mother and Quasim helped Gams out.

He held his arm out, and Gams held onto him. "Thank you, Handsome... senti falta de ver aquele sorriso," she spoke to him in Portuguese, and he smiled, understanding what she said.

"What is this place, Daddy?" Peach asked as I held her and walked toward the house. Quasim stood by as Gams held onto him.

"Inferno Casa. Our vacation home for us to come to and get away. A house that we can start creating memories in. I bought this house because this island means a lot to Capri. Her entire family is here, and I wanted to surprise her with us having our own home on this island. It's also our family house."

Capone and Cappadonna helped me pull it off because their cousin was a realtor on the island. They pulled a few strings and after much back and forth, I was able to purchase this Spanish style villa, overlooking the same beach that my baby wanted to get married on. The Delgato's beach ran right into ours.

As much as Capri wanted to have her family's tradition, I wanted us to get married on our beach. The start of something new for the both of us. A place we can bring our children back and show them that their parents got married on the same beach they were making sandcastles in. Small shit like that never mattered to me before, but with my Suga, all of that mattered to me.

"Are you kidding me?"

"No… as a family, we've been through so much pain and it's time for us to create happy memories. Quasim purchased the lake house a few streets over last week. I see how happy you are at the lake, and I want you to have that whenever you want, Gams. Even Mommy is happy when she's there."

Gams was a full emotional mess as she looked between both her grandsons, hugging Quasim because he was closer, and I was holding Peach. "You boys are too much."

My father looked at me, proud as he could be. He didn't need to say any words, I could feel how proud he was of me. "There's only two things that I've done right in my life, and that was marry your mother and have you two boys. Sim, even in the midst of your pain, you have stepped up for the Infernos in ways that I probably couldn't have after experiencing the hurt you have. Blaze, the father that you are to my grandbaby, and the man that you continue to show up as, has made me proud. The two of you both have been through some shit, and you always stick together and handle business."

"Appreciate it, Pops," Sim replied.

"Thanks, Pops." I nodded.

After spending the afternoon settling down and figuring out which room was whose, I was able to spend a little time with Peach before putting her down for bed. Blair was keeping me updated on the plans since they had been there.

One of the days I scheduled a prenatal massage for my baby to relax on the beach. Blair told me they were going to a club that her cousin owned on the island, so I had Capone give me his number and we arranged for him to decorate the club like Capri's birthday party. I felt bad because her party had been ruined and she never got the chance to have fun with her family like she wanted.

The club wasn't all that big, and it gave real Passa Passa party vibes anyway, without the skates. She wasn't getting her ass on those skates again, and I didn't care if she poked her lip out. I told him about my vision without the skating rink and he did his thing.

Capri didn't know what was going on, and I wished I could see her face when she saw it. We were letting them enjoy and have fun before showing up. It was still her bachelorette party, and I didn't want to ruin that, even though her ass was texting me every day saying she missed me.

"Daddy, is this house really ours?" Peach asked while I tucked her under the blankets. The house came fully furnished since it was being used as a vacation rental for the last few months.

"Yeah. So, when you go away to college, and want to do spring break, you have your own beach house in the Caribbean to come to with your friends," I smiled, knowing that it would be here sooner than later.

My girl wasn't a baby anymore and the years were flying by. Before any of us knew it, she would be going away to college and living her own life away from me. "I'm going to turn up." She busted in a fit of giggles as I tickled her.

"Yeah, alright. Keep playing with me, Peach." I got comfortable on the side of her bed. "You know I'm marrying Capri while we're here, right?"

She smiled as she yawned. "Yes, and I can't wait. Do you think I can have my juice in a fancy glass?"

"If they don't put it in a fancy glass, then we gonna have a problem." I kissed her on the head. "You alright with that?"

"Suga takes care of us, Daddy. She loves us and I love her. I want her to be my second mommy because I know she loves you, but she also loves me... maybe even more."

I broke out into laughter. "Oh really? You think so, huh?"

"I know so." She touched the necklace that Capri had given her in Chicago. "Did you get one of these?"

"Yeah, you right... she never did give me one of those. She gave me her heart, but I can't wear it around my neck, or they may call the people on me."

Peach laughed as she hugged me. "I love you, Daddy... I have to get my beauty sleep because Gams is taking me for a walk on the beach early so we can take pictures of the sun rising."

"Damn, alright... go ahead and get some sleep then." I kissed her cheek, and left her room quietly.

Quasim was coming downstairs as I closed Peach's bedroom door. "Ready to dip? Cappadonna outside with the golf carts."

"Let me talk to you real quick."

Quasim became serious. "What up, Blaze?"

"The minute that nigga call me pissy, you bet not fucking laugh."

The smile spread on his face as he looked at me. "I got you."

Cappadonna was obnoxiously beeping the fucking golf cart horn while waiting on us. "Chill out... you just pulled through the gates."

He smiled. "This shit real nice and close... thank you for keeping my Baby Doll close, Pissy."

Quasim snickered, and then tried to act cool when I looked at his ass. "I ain't gonna be too much more Pissy. Mr. *I almost drove off the bridge because I realized my sister is a grown ass woman,*" I mocked, and he flipped his middle finger up.

"Get the fuck in the back with drunky," he pointed to Capella, who had a full ass bottle of rum and was taking it to the back.

"Fuck you meaaan? I know you didn't down this shit that fucking quick?" Goon snatched the bottle from Capella, who was in his own world.

I climbed in beside him and Cappadonna took off like this was his fucking Durango. Had me holding onto the side of the damn cart as he darted through our villa's community and out onto the street.

"The fuck good with you?"

Capella shrugged, too drunk to even form any words. "Life, bro'... life," he grumbled, and then went back to staring out at the scenery as we drove deeper into town.

"Look at her ass... she so damn fucking fine. Thick fine ass... shit." Goon bit down on his lips as he watched a picture on Zoya's story.

"How the fuck you find her page?"

"Me," Core snorted.

Goon smiled as he watched the story again. "Can't nothing keep me from Ms. Lawyer."

"Nothing except the fact that Zoya ain't 'bout to date you, Crazy."

"Fuck you meannn, we gonna be married and have chocolate babies... that's wifey right there. Yo, Core, you know if she be eating a lot of pork?"

"Goon, leave me alone," Core said and laughed while sipping from the drink he had in his hand.

"You not invited to the wedding."

We pulled up to the club and it was actually packed the fuck out. I hopped out the golf cart as Cappadonna parked it on the side of the club. Mavado "So Special" was blasting and I danced my way inside in search for my baby.

Like I knew her little Caribbean ass would be, she was on the dance floor with Aimee whining and going crazy on Aimee. She had on a white beaded dress with fluffy feather pieces that made up the skirt of the dress.

She danced with her heels on with her hair pulled up in a bun with a few pieces hanging loosely. I may have had a shot or three before tucking Peach in for the night, so I was feeling nice as I galloped my ass over toward my girl.

"Oh, fuck no, I'm no—" she was about to go off until she saw me and jumped into my arms, as I tried to cover her ass.

"Surprise, Sug."

"Full of surprises, huh?" she kissed me on the lips, apparently tasting the liquor on my lips. "You been drinking, too... lucky you."

"Guess what, Sug?"

"What?"

"You marrying me tomorrow."

She studied my face to make sure I wasn't drinking. "Seriously, Meer? Is that why I was in the spa nearly all day, and then my cousin took me back to her house for us to get dressed there?"

"Yeah, everybody is here." She looked passed me and saw Capone and Erin dancing on the floor, and she shook her head.

"How did you even pull this off? I told you we could do something small... I didn't mind, Baby."

"You wanted this, so I was going to give it to you. We had this week before you're back to work and I was determined to give it to you."

She kissed my lips. "I would be a fool not to marry your crazy self. But do you really wanna marry me?"

"Without a doubt."

"Rich Girl" started playing and she jumped down and started whining her hips, turning around and tossing it back on me as I held her waist, and watched her do her thing.

"You really a rich girl, Mrs. Inferno." I moved my hips behind her, feeling that shit like Capone apparently was.

Him and Erin were going crazy, while Zoya was dancing on

Goon. This nigga was showing all the gold in his mouth as she danced on him. When I looked at Quasim, I nearly knocked Suga over 'cause the nigga was on the dance floor as Blair danced with him.

"You gonna get yourself in trouble, Sweet Joy," I could hear Cappadonna behind me, and I could only assume Joy was out here acting up on her husband.

Aimee was still dancing over near us, and Capella came behind her, and held her around the neck. "I'll snap your fucking neck if you out there fucking somebody else and giving them my money, Bitch."

Me and Capri's dance ceased when we heard what came out his mouth, and I quickly grabbed his ass up. The music was bumping loud, but I heard that shit clear as day, as if he said the shit in my ear.

"Yo, Chubs, what the fuck... you tripping, nigga." I grabbed him and pulled him over toward the bar.

In my opinion, he needed to stay away from the damn bar. "That bitch fucking another nigga... I know. I can smell the shit on her."

"Alright Chubby the vampire slayer... how the fuck you can smell it?" I mean, I could smell my baby a mile away, but this wasn't about me.

"I'm over all this shit," he stumbled back right into his father, who looked at him with that look.

"The hips are fucking moving... ayeee, aye, aye!" We all looked toward the entrance and Jaiden came whining his hips with Elliot behind him. "My aunt getting married... aye... aye." Capri laughed as she danced to Jaiden.

Apparently, Jaiden was taking advantage of the fact that his ass could legally drink here. "My fucking brother!" Capella switched his mood when he saw Jaiden.

Jaiden stopped mid dance and was hopping his ass over to Capella, and they hugged each other. Their relationship was something that was amazing to witness. They were super close, like brothers. He had a bandage around his forearm, which meant his ass went and got another tattoo. My guy was on his way to being just as tatted as the rest of us.

Even though Jaiden had been drinking, he wasn't drunk. "Yo Capp, what up?" He hugged Capp, who kissed his head.

"How you doing, Elliot?" Capp hugged her, as she stood by the bar, looking at her boyfriend that wasn't her boyfriend pretend like he forgot she was with him.

Once I got Capella's ass straight, I went back to dance with my baby. "What was that about?"

"Not about us... let's enjoy our night, okay?"

She turned in my arms and kissed my lips. "Okay."

CHAPTER 26
CAPRI

"I SWEAR *I wish I never married you. I should have left you right in that prison because you don't deserve me,*" I talked my shit while sitting across the table from Naheim, as the passion mark on his neck stared right back at me.

He pushed his food around his plate as he looked up at me. "You say anything until I give you dick... then you back in love again, Muffin. Put the damn liquor down... you fucking drunk."

I was drunk and he was right. As I watched the passion mark move as he swallowed his food, I knew once he slid inside of me it would be temporary relief until the next problem came up. "What's her name, Naheim?"

"What are you talking about? I got hit playing basketball earlier," he lied right through his teeth as he stared at me.

"You know all I have to do is tell Capone and he'll fucking kill you. He already didn't approve of us getting married, so you know all I have to do is tell him the shit you're doing and that man will break your fucking jaw... pull it right off your stupid face," I took back the shot and slammed the glass back down onto the table. "I love you so much that I would never do that. Living with knowing that I was responsible for you drinking your meals out of straw is too much for me to bare, apparently. You missed me being sworn in as an attorney and then have the nerve to come in with a damn hickie."

Naheim leaned back in the chair and looked at me. "I give you love and then you complain. Now you wanna get me tossed up by your brother. I married you because you wanted to get married... said your mom said that you couldn't shack up with some man. I wasn't thinking about getting married, Muffin. We're married and I love you, so we gonna make this work. I didn't miss it, I was there and saw the ending of it. You wanted to ruin the day because shit didn't go your way like always."

"Fuck you, Naheim."

"Yeah. You want me to fuck you, but I got to handle business... there was eggshells in the mash potatoes, too... sober up and get back to your books... those is what you care about, right? Actually, shouldn't you be packing for Cabo with your friends? It's always someone or something before me, Muffin... I'm the villain though, right?"

"Capri, are you alright?" My mother gently shook me as I was on the couch in the backyard. I had been out here since before the sun came up, wondering why nobody was setting up for the wedding.

"Mommy, is the wedding happening today?"

She looked at me and put her hand across my forehead to check my temperature. "You're not warm... do you feel alright?"

I sat up on the couch and looked at her. "I feel fine. I've been here since the sun came up and I haven't seen anyone preparing the backyard or the beach for the wedding."

She took my hand and sat down, while smiling at me. "That is because your future husband has handled all of that. He told us to make sure that you show up, so that is my job."

My mother kissed the back of my hand. "Do you think I'm doing the right thing, Mommy?" I searched her eyes for any sign that I shouldn't be doing this.

"Why do you ask me if I think it's the right thing?"

"Everything just feels so right with Quameer. I felt the same with Naheim, and you see how that turned out. I don't know if I could trust my gut anymore, and I'm scared."

She grabbed my chin. "I know I've been hard on you for your decisions when it came to your marriage with Naheim. I was so sure that I could get you to turn around your marriage and stick it out like my mother taught me that I wasn't seeing you, Capri. I didn't see how you were hurting with me shoving it down your throat." She removed my hair from my face. "You showed us what you wanted us to see with your marriage while only showing us the good with him. I think I allowed my own feelings to get in the way with the way I babied him. He was the missing piece that I was missing when it came to my kids, and that was wrong of me."

"I loved him until I couldn't do it anymore. It was either him or me, and I had to choose me, Mommy. I had to pick me for once and allow Naheim to do his thing. It took me a while to let him go because it was hard. I couldn't think of being divorced so young because I didn't want to disappoint you."

She drew a sharp breath. "I am sorry, Capri. I am sorry for making you feel like you were never enough. You have always been enough, and I pushed you too hard. I pushed you because I was battling my own feelings about having a little girl. I felt like I had nothing to show to you, nothing for you to be proud of, so I pushed you so hard because of me, and I'm so sorry," my mother sobbed, as she held my hand.

Me and my mother's relationship had always been up and down. I've always wanted to be closer, and it seemed like the minute I got married was when we became closer. I was now a wife, and she could give me advice on how to keep my husband. Being honest, she was one of the reasons I considered staying with Naheim. Trying to give it another chance, and possibly raise NJ together. It was hard knowing NJ had been staying across the street at Capone and Erin's and not going over there.

He was part of his father, so I had to cut him out my life, too. There was no room for growth if I continued to keep my past strapped to me like a backpack. "Mommy, I'm always proud of you. You came to this country with nothing and raised three children while working around the clock. We may have not had a lot, but we had love in that house. I know giving Corleon up was hard for you, and you still beat yourself up about it, but I'm not judging you. As I carry my own baby, there's nothing I wouldn't do for my baby, including giving it a better life if I knew I couldn't provide that."

She was hysterical as I pulled her into my arms and kissed her cheek. "I love you so much, Princess. I am so sorry… I will never forgive myself for being that way to you and saying those things to you. You are my baby daughter… I should have chosen you without questions asked."

"Choose me now," I whispered. "Allow me to be happy and in love with a man that cherishes the ground that I walk on. Be here and help me prepare for my first baby, one that I prayed for. We can choose to leave the past behind and start fresh. We have more time ahead of us, Mommy."

"I would like that, Princess… I would like that so much." Me and my mother continued to hug as we looked out on the beach.

I needed this.

I needed to hear those words from her, and I needed to hear them this morning. Right before taking a step forward and shedding the Delgato name for the last time.

Meer was going to make sure that this was the last time I would change my name. The last time I ever felt alone, the last time I winced when I thought about my past marriage. Meer was going to make sure this was the last time I walked alone again.

Leave it to my cousin Telly to make sure that the dress that I wore was fitted. Capri and Alaia both said they made an executive decision when it came to me choosing my wedding dress, which meant those hoes went on my Pinterest board and put together the kind of vibe that I wanted.

My dress was completely lace with a corset top and lace off the shoulder sleeves. It hugged me like a glove, although Telly had to alter it some because it was too tight for me to move in. My veil was lace and was so long that it trailed behind me as I walked.

My hair was pulled back on one side with a hair clip holding it back, while my curls cascaded down my other shoulder. I had deep curls, and I loved how I looked as I looked in the mirror. Alaia kissed my cheek as she looked me over.

"You look so beautiful, Capri. I could cry, but I know that I need to pull it together."

Erin hugged me. "I'll cry enough for the both of us... I'm sure. We love you so much and you deserve this."

Alaia held my other hand. "You are beautiful. Meer appreciates you. Meer respects you. We know you are worthy of all good things." She removed a loose strand of hair from my face as I saw the sparkle in her eyes. "You belong to Meer in the best way. I love you, Capri Inferno... just leaving the Delgato girls, huh?"

Erin dabbed her eyes. "She's leaving Delgato for good... I couldn't be happier for you. Meer loves you so much."

The tapping on the door caused us all to look at the door. "Sug, you in there?"

Erin helped me out the seat as I held my dress up and walked over toward the closed door. "I'm here, Meer."

I could hear the smile in his voice. "Good. I wanted to tell you that I love you so much, Baby. And I wanted to make sure you didn't skate on a nigga."

"I'm not leaving you... ever. I'm here, and I will see you down that aisle," I sniffled, catching the tears, careful not to mess up my makeup.

"Alright, we needed to make sure."

"We?"

"I'm here, too, Suga," Peach said, and I smiled, losing control of my tears as I listened to my future on the other side of the door.

"Meer?"

"Yeah, Sug?"

"I'm crying and messing up my makeup."

It got quiet. "I'm sorry, Suga. You wanna know something?"

"What?"

"He's crying, too," Peach blurted.

"Damn, Peach... just tell my business." I could hear his sniffle. "Sug, remember when I said your deck just didn't get shuffled with mine yet?"

I remembered that conversation like it happened yesterday. "You told me I was missing my king in my deck, and you were missing the queen."

"Timing plays a key in all of this.... I think we got that timing thing down pretty fucking good... what you think?"

"I think the same thing, Meer."

"See you in a little bit, Baby."

I touched the door and smiled. "See you soon."

Alaia and Erin were both sobbing hysterically when I turned around. "Why did you have to have that damn conversation? I'm a mess." Alaia blew her nose and tried to fix her makeup.

The light tap at the door and the sound of it opening made me turn around. My father walked into the room with his sharp tux, and looking like a GQ model. Cappadonna, Capone, and Corleon got that the smooth demeanor from Desmond Delgato.

"Suga Cane," he choked as he took in my dress, hair, and make up. "You look stunning. My little girl... not such a little girl anymore." He kissed my forehead as I hugged him.

"We'll be out there waiting to see the most beautiful bride come down that aisle." Erin kissed me, and then hugged my father.

"Love you girls." He kissed both Alaia and Erin before they left the room, and it was just the two of us.

"Daddy, tell me how you feel... I need to hear it."

He rubbed my hands as he looked down into my eyes. "Proud. I'm proud of the woman that you have become and will become. You've done what you wanted and did it in your own way. I know life hasn't been easy for you over the past few years, but baby girl, it's going to get so good. I have no worries about giving you away to Quameer because I know he'll protect your heart the way it should have always been protected. No more tears, alright?"

I smiled through the tears as I looked up at my father. He kissed me on both my cheeks like he used to do when I was a little girl and held my hand. "I'm ready."

"I've watched both my sons get married, and now I get to witness my baby girl."

We held hands, and I paused. "Daddy, whose house is this?"

My mother had us come to this house, and I had been in this room getting ready for hours. I never questioned why we weren't doing it on our beach because she said Meer had planned it all out.

He smiled. "Your husband bought this villa because you wanted to get married on our family's beach. He's Quinton's son for sure because he did it his way. Our beach runs into this beach, so you'll be married on this beach, as Inferno... starting your own tradition, Suga Cane." He swiped away a tear as he looked down at me.

"I have to get down the aisle to him... why wouldn't he tell me this?"

"He wanted to surprise you. The right man will do whatever he can to make his woman smile, and from the smile and tears, Quameer did the right thing."

We held hands as we walked from the back of the house and took in people running around like chickens with their heads cut off. The massive pool was decorated with flowers floating along with candles as we walked toward where the wedding was.

Cappadonna, Capone, and Corleon were waiting before we made it down onto the beach. I watched as my brothers wiped the tears that fell down their face.

"Baby Doll, you look beautiful... like a real-life doll." He kissed my head and hugged me. "I love you, Capri. I couldn't have trusted a better nigga to have and hold your heart, you hear me?"

"I hear you, Cappy."

"Pri, I love you more than life. Quameer is the man you were meant to marry. I can see the love when he speaks about you, and I know he will protect you with everything inside of him. Go get your forever, Pri," he whispered, as he hugged me.

"I haven't been around long, but I could tell how much you both love each other. As one of your big brothers, I'm honored and blessed to be here to witness this." Core smiled at me and swiped the tear that fell down my cheek.

"You next, Boy," My father winked at Core.

"Yeah, if I ever find the right one... I'm chilling right now." He chuckled and my father squeezed his shoulder.

I held onto my father's arm as we slowly took the steps that were littered with volitive glass candles. When we touched the bottom, I took in everything and held on tighter to my father's arm. The floral arches with roses were coming up the aisle, that happened to be solid flooring. I had to walk up a step to get onto the aisle.

The background was the beach, and the most beautiful view. The clouds reminded me of cotton balls with how perfectly they were positioned in the sky. Everyone was seated on either side of the aisle. I looked past all of them and I saw Quameer.

My Meer Cat.

His suit was white and black, and fit him perfectly. I don't know who he got to put his locs up, but he had them put up as he held a mic, and finally looked up, seeing me at the other end. He smiled so wide, as he put both his fingers to his lips and winked at me.

I did the same back to him, as we walked forward, and the music played. Charlie Wilson's "You Are" played, and Meer put the mic to his mouth, and I stopped.

I loved to hear him sing, and he didn't do it often. You could usually catch him singing when he was cooking or doing something where he wasn't really paying attention to it, just messing around.

Soon as he started to sing, Gam stood up and recorded with her phone, holding her hand to her mouth. Meer looked me directly in my eyes as he sang the words to me with his entire soul, hitting every note.

"You are the reason I love, the reason I trust, God sent me an angel," he belted out, and I held my hand over my chest as he continued to sing directly to me.

Nobody mattered as I was nearly racing down this aisle to get to him. He was singing so hard that his bun had come unloose, and he continued to sing. We were in our own world as I listened to him sing with his entire heart.

I remember when he sang to me at karaoke, and I had chills. Something told me he was special then, and I ignored it. I was too hurt to see that God was giving me a preview of my future. We made it down the aisle, and my father reached for Meer's hand.

He handed off the microphone to someone and took his hand. My father placed my hand into Meer's hand and looked at him. "Choose each other. It's you and her against the world. Protect each other, and never give up on each other. Love like this doesn't come around often, and when it does, you honor it by protecting each other. I'm giving my baby girl to someone once again, and I trust this time I'm making the right decision."

"I got her with everything inside of me. Put that on my life, Des," Meer stared my father in the eyes, and they embraced.

Meer helped me up the steps, and we stood under the arch, and I wiped the tears that came down as I listened to him sing. "You sang for me. No Pretty Wings?"

He held my hands. "Nah. That was when you left me... you not ever leaving me again. I wanna sing to you for the rest of my life, Capri."

The pastor looked out at everyone and spoke about everything about love and marriage. I was so focused on Meer, and he was so focused on me that he we weren't paying attention until the pastor nudged Meer to say his vows.

"I don't have long vows because I don't let a day go by without telling you how I feel about you. I hated the idea of love and was good getting by how I had been. Then we crossed paths again. Cappin' ass Capri came back into my life, and I didn't know how to react, how to feel. I could tell you weren't the same girl I knew back then. You had life happen to you, so I knew I wanted to be your friend. I wanted to learn you, figure out how to be the man that you needed, because I was broken my damn self. Baby, you know how I'm coming when it comes to you." I felt a small hand slip into mine, and I looked down and it was Peach.

"You know how *we* coming when it comes to you. You accepted my family like your own... Suga, you don't know it, but you're slowly restoring the spark that we lost a long time ago. I love how you love my daughter like your own, always wanting what is best for her. I have no doubt that you're going to be the same way when you have ours. I know you have had it hard, but no more... I'm gonna make sure of that. I'm always behind you, because I'm never letting you fall again."

I should have just come out here without any makeup on because my face was a mess. I wiped my eyes with my father's tissue and looked at my baby.

"Quameer. My Meer Cat. I remember getting on my knees and praying to God. I asked him to guide me for the next year, be the man that I had always been desperately searching for. Give me the love that I was looking for in every man. I told him to remove those who don't mean any good for me, and he moved a lot of people in that year, but he never removed you. He moved you to the front, he showed me that you were my person. Every day you remind me of who I am, when I'm not feeling it. When you speak on me, I see how proud you are of me, how much pride is in your eyes that I belong to you."

I wiped the tears that fell from his face and rubbed my hand across his burn. "You make me feel safe. I know my heart is safe with you and I never have to question things because you are it, Baby. When I used to cry myself to sleep on my couch, I never thought I deserved this. You showed me that you don't have to struggle to have love. That we make our own story, and Baby, we have done that. Your family and legacy means so much to you, to me. As I stand on this beach, connected with my own family's beach, I have never been prouder to become your wife, Mr. Inferno."

"My Suga." Meer licked his lips as he looked at me.

I smiled as I kissed his hand and looked into his eyes. "Você é meu coração. Minha vida. Eu vou te amar até meu último suspiro."

Both Peach and Meer looked at me like they had saw a ghost. "Daddy, she just spoke Portuguese."

I smiled and looked at her before turning my attention to her father. "I made a personal goal while in Singapore to learn things that I want to say to you. I don't know everything, and understand everything, but I know somethings." I put my hands over Peach's ears. "Mal posso esperar para sentir Big Pa esta noite. I'm sorry, Gams," I smiled at her, and she winked at me.

"Gams, cover your ears." Meer smirked, and Gams put her hands over her ears. "Big Pa vai usar essa merda."

"Nigga, I still understand," Quasim reminded his brother, and I laughed.

I removed my hands from Peach's ears, and looked down at her. "Ryder, I promise every day I will put my best foot forward, loving you like you are my own. You are still my best friend, and I never want that to change. Like I love your father, I love you more than life."

Peach hugged me. "We locked in, Suga."

I held my pinky out and she locked hers with mine. "Locked in."

Meer wasn't paying the pastor no mind as he was taking me in with his eyes, showing me that he had fangs in. The minute he gave us the go ahead to kiss, he rushed over toward me and had his entire tongue down my throat while holding me.

"Oh, fuck no, let her ass breathe, Quameer!" Cappadonna's loud ass mouth hollered, and I held his face, pulling him back toward me, while Meer flipped his middle finger at him.

"I introduce to you Mr. and Mrs. Quameer Inferno," the pastor announced as we were still kissing.

We finally came up for air, and held hands as we walked

down the aisle, Meer stopping where Cappadonna and Capone were seated with my sisters. "You know you done fucked up, right? Should have never let me marry your sister," he fucked with them, and Cappadonna laughed.

"Nah. For the first time we did what was right for Baby Doll." Capp kissed me as we continued down the aisle.

"Pri, you married Pissy ass Meer." Capone hollered.

"Pissy ass Meer had you about to rip your ears off though," Meer smirked.

I held on tight to my husband's hand, as he looked back at me. I was someone's wife for the second and last time.

Stopping when we got to the end of the aisle, I dug in the pocket of my dress, and I placed his lighter in his hand. "I don't need this anymore, Meer Cat."

He looked down at his gold lighter and smiled when he noticed I had got it fixed, and had it engraved with Meer Cat on the side. "Yeah, you don't need that anymore, Mrs. Inferno." He kissed my forehead and held my hand tight.

I was Capri Inferno.

CHAPTER 27
QUAMEER

SUGA WANTED to prove that she could drive my new truck so bad that she insisted on driving us to our doctor's appointment for the baby. I held onto the door handle as she hit the brakes more than she needed to. I admit, the brakes were a little stiffer than my other truck, before Capone told me I had to total the shit.

That nigga went through whips like boxers, and it was no skin off his back. My truck was personal to me because I had hooked it up to my liking, and it was mine. Seeing her be towed away, knowing she would be reduced to parts in five seconds broke my damn heart more than being away from Suga for that week.

At least I knew I would see her after that week, but I wouldn't see Big Booty again, and that shit broke me. Now I had a new truck, and I had to get acquainted with her and become comfortable like I had been in Big Booty.

"Sug, you don't have to hit the brake so damn hard," I said, secretly squeezing the door handle as she whipped in and out of traffic, forgetting she needed to make sure she could clear the whole truck.

"It's so damn stiff… baby, why is it like that?" she asked, as her ass stomped on it again, and we both jerked.

A loud ass horn sounded from behind us, which caused my baby to jump in her skin. I knew she was already nervous driving this truck and then some ass face wanted to lay on their horn behind us.

I pulled my gun and turned around ready to shoot his fucking front windows out, and Capri grabbed my hand. "Suga, he not about to beeping at you like he lost his mind. I'm gonna show him a nigga who mind really lost."

"Meer, can we please get lunch and celebrate the fact that this baby is healthy?" she pleaded with me, and I settled back in the seat.

She was lucky I was still reeling from the fact that everything with Suga was perfect. I was worried she was stressing herself too much and not eating enough. According to our doctor, everything was good, and my baby's heartbeat was nice and strong.

Since being back home, life had gone right back to normal. The only difference was that I had my wife sleeping beside me every night. Since Capri had to be back to work, we were staying at our crib. I had to keep correcting her ass when she called it my house like it wasn't hers. Until the house on the compound broke ground, we would be living here.

Capri still didn't know I had wired over the money to Cappadonna, after much going back and forth. The nigga wanted to gift the land, and I couldn't have that. I was a provider, and I needed him to know that I could provide for his sister.

Once this was over, I wanted to whisk my baby away on a honeymoon and have her relax. I could tell a lot had been on her mind, and she wasn't telling me everything 'cause she knew I would shut this shit down. As her husband, I also knew that this was important to her, and she needed to see this through for her brothers.

No sooner than I had calmed my crazy and put all those niggas back inside my head, the black Camaro pulled up beside Capri, and laid on his horn again before rolling his passenger window down and nearly sticking his head out the shit.

Capri rolled her window down thinking he wanted something. "You too damn fucking fine to drive like a fucking retard, bitch!" he spat, as he pulled away from the curb.

I tasted blood with how hard I bit the inside of my cheek watching him speed up and cut us off. I memorized that plate and shot Corleon a text message with the plate number.

> Me: Y7YS7U Find me him.

> Core: it's always core find me somebody, change the light, wipe the security… damn, say hi nigga lol

I never replied because I was steaming mad. "Sug, pull over for me so I can drive."

She could hear the tone in my voice, so she didn't protest. Instead, she got over the few lanes and double parked in front of a bank and hopped out. Before allowing her to go to the passenger side, I kissed her on the lips.

"I'm sorry that he fucked this up for you."

She smiled. "It's alright, Meer."

Her voice was shaky, and I didn't like that shit. "You're not alright… you're shaking, Sug." I pulled her into me.

"This baby is making me so soft, Meer," she tried to laugh, to ease my mind and it was too late for all of that.

"Nah… being loved right by your husband got you in your soft girl era. You know your man got you, so you're able to show fear, and admit when you're uncomfortable. You always been used to sucking it up and being strong." I placed a kiss on her forehead.

She lifted her head and stared right into my eyes. "You did that."

"Damn right." I held her hand and helped her into the passenger seat before hopping into the driver's side and peeling back into traffic. I reached for her hand, and she placed it in mine, while we headed to eat.

"This the address... nice ass neighborhood, too," Corleon scoped out the neighborhood, pulling his phone out to look on Zillow. "Damn, houses go for bread in this area... I might need to come look over here for some investment properties. Menace always on my ass about buying more."

I looked at him, as we sat across the street from the rustic bungalow style house, that had modern touches. "Wanna call the fucking listing agent from the house down the block, too?"

"You the crazy ass nigga that wanted me to look this man up, because he cut your fiancée off in traffic."

Suga went to dinner at Jesse's house tonight with Blair, so I figured while she was gone, I would handle this nigga. He cut my wife off, and fucking startled her, which wasn't like her at all.

I stared straight ahead at the house. "Nah. It was the way he did that shit... I don't like shit like that, and he called her a bitch."

"He called her a bitch?" Core nearly yelled, reaching for the doorknob and I pulled him back, and he settled back in the seat.

"Who the crazy nigga now?"

"What's the fucking plan?" Core asked, settling back in his seat, and looking out the window at the house.

"He's not home, so we about to go in his house and chill while waiting for our new friend. I mean, that was my plan. Didn't count for you tagging along."

"You randomly text me for information and then don't wanna invite me along... fucking rude if you ask me," Core shrugged, as I killed the engine and got out my truck.

We both watched our surroundings, which wasn't nothing to look out for because everyone was in fucking bed, except this nigga, which worked out perfect for me. We stayed in the shadows as we made our way around the back of his house, breaking the glass, and pulling the sliding door open.

"How reckless, he don't even have a security system set."

We heard small taps on the floor and paused for a second. I followed the sound because I knew it wasn't a damn person with light ass floor taps like that. In the living room, there was a dog in a little playpen shit with shit and piss everywhere. The water and food bowl was empty, and I could tell this dog had been here all day.

Meanwhile, his ass was out there honking his horn and cursing out pregnant women while driving. I don't give a fuck if he didn't know Capri was pregnant, I knew she was, and he had fucking startled her with his aggressive ass driving.

Core finally joined me in the living room. "It smells like shit in here." He covered his nose with his shirt and looked at me. "His security cameras don't fucking work... stupid ass don't even have them connected."

"Looks like he just moved into this shit, too." I kicked a moving box, and continued to look at the dog.

It was a cute little toy yorkie, and she was a fucking mess. Been in this pen all day and was jumping up and down in her shit trying to get to me. "The fuck you doing?" Core asked when I picked her up, careful not to get shit on me.

"Helping this damn puppy," I replied as I went to the kitchen sink and turned the water on, putting a little bit of dishwasher liquid in the water and dipping its feet in the water.

Core looked at me like I had lost all my marbles while I used the dish rag to dry her off. "You bugging the fuck out? We didn't come here to play ASPCA, nigga."

The sound of the front door being unlocked caught both of our attention, and Core moved into the kitchen near me, so when homie walked in, he wouldn't see us.

"That shit was lit tonight...those bitches are def gonna call us." I heard his feet shuffle. "This fucking dog, bro'. I'm about to let that shit go out in the street because Kenyetta's ass left me with it. Talking about she don't want the shit because I fucked another bitch." He went on talking about how he was neglecting a dog because his bitch didn't want it.

I made my appearance known when I walked out the kitchen and around the corner. The nigga jumped back, almost falling back into the dog's pen. I held little Poopsie in my hand. She was so relaxed as she looked at her traitor ass owner.

"W...who the fuck are you?"

Core came out the kitchen with his gun drawn. "Get yo' stupid ass on that broken ass couch and shut the fuck up." The nigga nearly leaped over on that ratty ass chair. "Matter fact, why the fuck would you move that bum ass chair into this nice ass house?"

He shook as he looked at Core, then at me who remained quiet while petting my new puppy. "It was my fat...father's chair from college... means a lot to me," he stammered.

"Fair... I can respect that." Core went and leaned over on the fireplace while I handed him the puppy.

"I just didn't want to go to Arizona, Martin," I mocked in his tone, and he looked even more scared now that he didn't know what I was talking about. I may have been watching an episode of Martin with Peach before I came to handle his ass.

"You gotta take the dog and make it jump at his ass, too." Core was clearly amused over by the fireplace petting Poopsie.

"You make it a habit to cut pregnant women off in traffic after cursing them out? Think you said she was too fine to be a retard or some wild shit like that."

"Which is a fucked up term to use by the way," Core pointed out.

The nigga was over there thinking like he went around doing it to every damn body. "Oh, the bitch in the truck?"

I pulled my gun out and he jumped back on the couch. "My fucking wife." I turned my gun around and slammed the handle into his face and pulled my arm back repeating the action until my arm ached.

When I released him, his face was a bloody mess, and his teeth were missing. "I...I didn't know," he weakly replied.

"Now you fucking know not to drive like a dick face and yell at fucking women while they're driving. The only reason I'm letting you live instead of shoving the barrel of this gun in your mouth is because you're giving me a gift, and I like gifts."

Even through the blood and open gashes, I could see the look of confusion on his face. "G...gift?"

"The fucking puppy... I'm taking that shit. Let me be real clear, I never leave shit unsettled, but I don't see this as a reason to kill you. Don't make me regret this shit, because I can promise you like I found you tonight, I can find you again and the next time I'm not gonna fucking use this end of the gun."

Homie held his hands up and tried to scoot even further on his daddy's ugly ass chair. "You...you got it, man... shit... I thought you were one of my gambling buddies... shit."

"So, you owe niggas money, and you got the nerve to be out here driving reckless and calling my baby a retard." I kicked his ass in the knee, and he gasped, not knowing which hurt more, his face or his knee.

"Who you be betting with?" Core asked while petting Poopsie.

"Ralph Amanté."

Core laughed. "Yeah, we don't even have to do shit because you owing money to the Amanté cartel is crazy."

I didn't know what the fuck Core was speaking about, but it wasn't my business. "I'm good for it... Ralph knows," he stammered like I gave a fuck.

I made it my business not to muddy up someone else's lawn, and whatever the fuck he was in wasn't my business, other than him cursing my baby out. "I'm taking the fucking dog, Dick breath... and clean this shit up. You think a dog should be left for hours to sit in they own waste?"

"T...take em... my girl don't want it, and I don't have the time for it anyway," he stammered.

"Nigga, don't tell me what the fuck to do... clean this shit up and maybe step back from fucking gambling... stupid ass. I'm taking the fucking food, too...Poopsie gotta eat."

"S...sure thing."

We walked back to my car as I held the dog in my arms. It was a girl, so I needed to figure out a new name. "What the fuck you need a dog for?" Core asked when I shoved the dog in his arms and pulled off the block.

"My daughter been wanting one and now she got one... think her name gonna be Draco."

Core looked at the small dog and nodded his head. "It's a girl... Beretta seems fitting."

Suga's name popped up on my car's screen. "What's going on, Wifey?" I greeted her with my new greeting now that I was her husband and shit.

"Nigga too damn hype to be a husband," Core snickered.

"Meer... I need you to look at my location and come to me now. Baby, I know you have my location."

I grabbed my phone while driving and went to the app I had with her location and rerouted it to where my wife was. She wasn't going to speak over the phone, so I didn't ask any questions. "Coming."

Suga ended the call, and I sped the whole thirty minutes to where she was. "If we about to slide on niggas with Beretta, we gonna look crazy as shit," Core said, as he checked his phone.

I pulled up into the neighborhood and parked across the street, leaving the dog in the car. I prayed Beretta's ass didn't use the bathroom in my shit like she did at her old owner's crib. We crossed the street and went through some tall ass shrubs.

"You got a call, too?"

I damn near jumped out my skin at my brother's creepy ass. "You almost got fucking shot, nigga."

He ignored me. "Blair called me."

"You got her location cause I know her ass wasn't dumb enough to tell you where she at over the phone."

Quasim shrugged. "I have my ways to find where she at."

"Yo?" Corleon answered the phone, as we stood on the side of this damn house, unsure on why the fuck we were even here.

"I swear I'm not with your brother... I'm with Quameer. Zoy, I'm outside... bet."

"Zoya there, too?"

Zoya rushed out from the side door over toward us and waved for us to follow her. We entered the house, and I was impressed cause this shit was nice as fuck. The oak wooden floor, and the expensive hotel scent had me floating through the house.

"Meer, we need to tell you something." Capri dipped out of from around the corner, and I looked at my wife and knew she wasn't good.

"What the fuck is going on?"

"Brandi is fucking with Tookie!" she blurted and looked at Zoya. "Zoya saw them together when she was visiting her friend."

"What *friend* is this, Zoy?" Core asked the question like he already knew the answer to the question already. Zoya avoided eye contact with him.

Quasim walked around Capri and Zoya and went into the kitchen. I followed behind him to see what the fuck was going on. The energy was different in here, and I couldn't process what my wife had told me without knowing what is going on.

When I rounded the corner, nothing could have prepared me for what I saw. Jesse was lying face up with her eyes opened, and a knife in the middle of her head.

"Baby, if you doing shit like this, we gonna need to call a family meeting."

Zoya looked at Blair. "Blair protected us."

"Jesse's fiancée was the man that Blair was dating... babe they knew everything," Capri said as she looked toward the stairs.

"Where is her fiancé? Who the fuck is he?"

"Fuquan's boss...he's upstairs...dead." Tasha came down the stairs with blood on her hands. It was then that I noticed my wife's hand and she had blood all over her hands, and on her dress.

CHAPTER 28
AIMEE

"HI MRS. DELGATO, I wanted to set up a meeting with you and your husband to discuss Rory's autism diagnosis. I think it's very important to discuss our next steps along with therapies we need to be starting with. I'll try back again later, but I am in my office until three today. My personal number is—"

I exited out of the voicemail before she could finish leaving her personal number. I was always tickled how she called me Mrs. Delgato because that was what Capella requested. Since we had left out her office, I had been ignoring her calls. I didn't want to come to terms that something was wrong with my baby. When she spoke, Capella was taking in everything while I was zoned out. Was this my karma for the way that I lived my life?

Life was dumping on me at every angle, and I felt like I was drowning and couldn't come up for air. I was alone and didn't have anyone to talk to when it came to this, and I was scared. My life could be ruined if Khalil made good on his threats.

Hell, my life was already ruined because once Capella and Pops found out that I gave him fifty-thousand dollars, I may have to go back to fucking for money because they would be done with me. It was funny how I was so overwhelmed a few months ago with motherhood and trying to keep the house together, and now I wish I had those problems again.

Cappella refused to speak to me after he threatened to snap my neck in Barbados. I tried to go to his room after the wedding, and he wasn't even there. Since being back, he didn't want to speak to me, and when he came over to the house to get Rory and clothes, we barely shared any words.

I missed him so much.

I should have been honest and told him what was going on, but he wouldn't have understood. Capella would have found whatever reason to be upset with me and I rather him be mad because he thought I gave it to my family, and not Khalil.

The silent treatment was getting old between us, and I wanted to just talk and figure out what was next. I missed him and wanted him next to me at night. I've said some words that I couldn't take back, and now I had to eat those words and live with the fact that I broke up my family.

It was bad enough that I had the abortion behind his back, but now I was paying my ex-boyfriend money to keep his mouth shut.

"Your father is really starting to piss me off," I said to Rory, who was in the back watching his iPad.

I wasn't a big fan of him having so much screen time, but with the drive from the lake house, he needed something to entertain him while I drove. Capella was in the city, and he was supposed to get Rory from me.

Since he wasn't answering his phone, I had to bring my baby boy around with me to run errands. Imagine walking into the bank to take money out, and they tell you that your access has been blocked and your name was removed from the account. All while Rory is screaming because he wants me to pick him up while this lady was explaining to me that she couldn't give me any money out the account. I used to feel like that girl walking into the bank, and now they made me feel like I was a crook.

Now, I had no choice but to bring Rory with me to drop the little bit of money I had. Khalil was calling me every day like I hadn't just given him fifty-thousand dollars a few weeks ago. How do you blow through that much money that quick? All I had was ten thousand dollars from my own account, and the hacking jobs I did with Landon.

I tried Capella's phone again and got the voicemail this time, so I tossed my phone in the passenger seat and went to meet Khalil before his ass called my phone again. Nigga never called me this much when we were together, and now all he seemed to do was blow my phone up.

I looked in the back at Rory, and he had fell asleep sucking on his three fingers. It was something that he had done since a baby. I was grateful that my baby was verbal, and he almost always came to life when it came to his Quack-Quack. We hadn't told the family what we found out, and that was mostly because of me. Capella was ready to leave out the office and go tell his father. I needed time to process it before I could even tell anyone.

As I pulled onto Mother Gaston Blvd, I pulled in front of the corner store across the street from Plaza residences, better known to everyone as Plaza. It was only one way in, and one way out. Apparently, Khalil had been staying here. He was never in the same place for long. It was like he was running from somebody, or just didn't have anywhere to stay so he was couch surfing with whoever would allow him.

I texted him and got the money I had to take out my own account. He better had made this ten thousand dollars last, because I didn't have anything else for him. Like Swiper no Swiping, his ass slid through the gates and jogged across the street, climbing into the front seat of my truck.

"Aimee, I don't understand why the fuck I gotta throw threats around for my money." He didn't have time for any hellos or salutations. He was more interested in the money, and from the way he looked, he needed the shit.

"Look, I can't keep giving you that type of money. My man found out and he won't give me the money... I have ten thousand and I will get you more after I do this favor for a friend." I shoved the money into his hands.

He looked at it, not even bothering to count it. "Bitch, do you really think this shit a game? Fuck telling your punk ass man about the pussy you was selling, I'm gonna fucking kill you if you don't get me the rest of my damn money!" spit flew as he yelled in my face.

"I'm going to need fucking time, Khalil, who has that much money sitting around?"

"Bitch, your fucking man... that nigga probably got that shit sitting around for play money," he spoke like he knew my life with Capella.

Fifty-thousand dollars was light work when it came to the Delgatos, which pissed him off. "Well, I don't know what the fuck to tell you. I'll hit you up next week with some more."

Khalil looked at me, and then reached for the door handle while still staring at me. He knew that he had no other choice but to wait until I could give him the money. "Since you playing games, you gonna come run errands with me."

"Hell fucking no... go on with your money."

My head hit the window when he hit me in the face with his fist. I could feel the blood leaking from my nose as my head rested on the window, throbbing in the process. "I said get the fuck out the car and, in this seat, over here, Aimee. Stop acting like I'm not really about that." He went to throw a punch again and I held my hand up.

"A...Alright," I stammered as I unbuckled my seatbelt, and climbed out the truck. Kahlil walked around the truck, as I tried to blink to correct my vision, because it was now blurry.

RATA TATAT!

Guns started blazing and I jumped, and I immediately went to jump back in the car, and Khalil had already jumped in the driver seat and took off while the car behind him was shooting.

"My fucking baby!!! My baby!!" I ran as fast as I could, as I watched the hand extend and shoot into my truck with my son in the back seat.

My breath was shallow, and my head was spinning as I was running as fast as my legs would take me. Khalil drove over the sidewalk, and did a U-turn coming back my way as I ran into the street, and the nigga on a dirt bike pulled up on him, sending shots directly into the side of the car that Rory was in.

The car accelerated through the intersection of New Lots and Mother Gaston, and I dropped to my knees when I saw the B35 bus Collide and take my truck further down the block.

My knees were weak as I collapsed on a woman that was crossing the street. "I need... I need. Please... I need your fuck... fucking phone," I could barely make out my words because everything was happening so fast.

I knew the number by heart and dialed it in when she shoved her phone into my hands. "Who the fuck is this?" Cappadonna answered.

"Pops... Pops, Rory!! They shot my fucking car up with him inside! They...They got my bay.. baby," I said breathlessly as I collapsed into the lady's arms, and everything went black.

To Be Continued

DISCUSSION QUESTIONS:

Discussion Questions:
1. Do you think Jean and Des were wrong for giving Corleon up to Linda?
2. How do you think Capella will react with Aimee having an abortion? Do you think she was wrong to not to tell him?
3. With Capri having to kill Jesse, do you think she will go through with it?
4. Tasha being offered to be saved by Forty and the Delgatos, do you think she will be loyal? Or will she stab them in the back?
5. Jean repeating the mistakes of her mother with Capri, do you think that she and Capri can mend their relationship?
6. Is Quameer wrong for tossing that ring at Brandi, and telling her that Capri is pregnant at the lunch? Do you think he is too hard on her?
7. Do you think Capella was wrong to say what he said to Aimee before leaving the house? Do you think he will cheat on Aimee because of his frustrations with her?
8. How do you think Cappadonna and Capella will react when they find out what happened with Aimee and Rory?
9. Quasim is usually quiet and avoids Blair. Do you see him opening up to her, and letting her in? Do you think he would care that sex is hard for her now?

10. What do you think about Quasim buying Blair's studio?
11. What do you think happened at that dinner with Jesse?
12. The wedding. What is your thoughts on Capri and Quameer's wedding?
13. Do you think Aimee should have just told Capella or Cappadonna instead of trying to handle things on her own with Khalil?
14. Was Quameer wrong for allowing Brandi to stay in their suite during Peach's birthday trip?
15. Do you think Morgan will try to cross those lines with Capri?
16. What are your thoughts on Peach's reaction to Capri's pregnancy?

Made in the USA
Columbia, SC
18 April 2025